OUR
TIME
HAS COME

OUR TIME HAS COME

SYLVESTER STEPHENS

A

SBI
PUBLICATION

A STREBOR BOOKS INTERNATIONAL LLC PUBLICATION
DISTRIBUTED BY SIMON & SCHUSTER, INC.

Published by

SBI

Strebor Books International LLC
P.O. Box 1370
Bowie, MD 20718
http://www.streborbooks.com

ISBN 978-1-59309-026-5
LCCN 2003112287

Distributed by Simon & Schuster, Inc.
1230 Avenue of the Americas
New York, NY 10020
1-800-223-2336

Cover art: © André Harris

First Printing September 2004
Manufactured and Printed in the United States

10 9 8 7 6 5 4 3 2 1

DEDICATION

Our Time Has Come is dedicated to the greatest parents in the world....mine! Henry and Ora Bell Stephens

ACKNOWLEDGMENTS

I would like to thank my Lord and Savior.
And I would like to thank Isaiah, Simone, Sylvester Alexander,
Andrea, Annie Austin, Henry Clay, Janie, Bobbie, Henry Jr, J. Dallas,
Patsy, Paul, Glen, Mark, David, Larry, Ricky, Rita, Oramae, AnnieJean,
Howard, Terry S, Chris C, Harold Y, Reggie S, Marc B, Marc H,
Todd B, Tony T, Mike H, Que, Nic S, William C, Cordell I,
Darrick H, Melvin, Teri M, Cassandra H, Pam G,
Gloria, Kim P, Calvin B, D. Outlaw,
And a special thanks to my biggest fan, Bria!

CHAPTER ONE

SAGINAW, MICHIGAN, 2008

Every family has a story. A chronology of time, where names and people in the history of that family serve as a vessel from the past to the present. This is the story of my family. A story about the prophecy of a man named Alexander Chambers, told through the hearts and souls of his children. A story that tells of three generations to fulfill one prophecy. The first generation was given the prophecy, the second generation interpreted the prophecy, and the third generation fulfilled the prophecy. I am the fourth generation of the Chambers legacy, and though my father Solomon Chambers would fulfill the prophecy, I am blessed with revealing the prophecy to you.

My great-grandfather, Alexander Chambers, was born in a place called Derma County, Mississippi, in 1855. He was an only child, and a slave. He was college-educated, and not accepted very well by white people because of it. He met my great-grandmother Annie Mae while they were children growing up on the West Plantation in Derma County, Mississippi. After the Emancipation Proclamation, slavery was abolished, and Negro people were freed. However, my great-grandparents continued to work on the West Plantation. They eventually married and had one child, a son they would name Isaiah, my grandfather. He met and wedded my grandmother, Orabell, whom I loved with all of my heart. They, too, were blessed with only one child, Solomon, my father. We are generations of ones, for I, too, am an only child.

My great-grandfather Alexander decided his family would not be just another colored family satisfied with being free on paper, and not free in life. He wanted his family to be prideful, and understand that freedom is given to all men at birth. Great-grandfather Alexander believed that his son Isaiah had the hands of God upon him, and he was destined for greatness.

My great-grandfather created a book to chronicle our family's history. He said it would be our family Bible. He wrote the title of our family Bible: *Our Time Has Come! Our Time Has Come* originated from his inspiration that his family would one day overcome the manacles of slavery, and rise to the pinnacle of humanity. He started the Chambers Bible with the first verse. Each generation was to incorporate his, or her, new verse to pass on to the next generation to come. And these are the words of our family Bible:

> *"Our Time Has Come"*
> *Alexander and Annie Mae Chambers—1902*
> *The dawning of a new millennium, sing songs of freedom, Our Time Has*
> *Come. Our God send signs it's time for unity, this is our destiny,*
> *Our Time Has Come.*
> *Isaiah and Orabell Chambers—1939*
> *Today begins the day, thought never be, when we rise, in unity, One God,*
> *One Love. Our voices be the sound of victory, when we, stand proud*
> *and sing, Our Time Has Come!*
> *Solomon and Sunshine Chambers—????*

These are the inspirational words of my great-grandfather, and my grandfather. But here it is in the year of our Lord 2008, and my father has yet to add his generation's verse to the family's Bible. He is a sixty-eight-year-old man and his opportunity to pass the Bible to me with his verse inscribed, is rapidly decreasing.

My father does not believe in the prophecy as my grandfather, and great-grandfather. He believes in today, and making the most of it. He wants his legacy to be remembered for what he has done as a scholar and professional, and not as a martyr, or activist. He does not believe in the struggle for the advancement of Black people. He believes that every man should make his own way through the means of education; regardless of the circumstances. He believes that success is colorblind. All that he sees is determination and hard work. Any circumstance can be overcome by determination and hard work. I adamantly disagree with my father. I believe that success, first of all, is a relative word. I think that one can dream of success, but when one arrives at the reality, he has lost so much of himself that the passion for success has turned into a mere achievement.

My father has a lifetime of achievements: certificates, honorary degrees, memorials, foundations. If you can think of any outstanding award that is bestowed upon a human being, my father has one somewhere with his name on it. He is one of the most famous attorneys in the United States. His name alone is said to have settled cases without ever going into litigation. And yes, this man, is my father. A man of strong character, and resiliency, of course he has suffered as all men have suffered. But through his sufferings, he emerged a stronger and more determined man than he was before his crisis.

A "trailblazer" in the field of law for African-Americans who follow in his footsteps; a title he publicly denounces. He is called a paramount of an attorney not just for African-Americans, but for all Americans. When asked of his contributions to law, he humbly refers to Thurgood Marshall and says, "Without his contributions, there would be no place for my own." This man is my father.

At this hour, my father is doing what he has done his entire life; searching for the perfect solution to his current problem. This time the issue he faces is greater than any other he has faced in his life. For the issue is not about losing or winning a case. It is not about the prestige of his name, or his crafty courtroom tactics. It is not about awards, certificates, or foundations. It is about an issue he has eluded, and escaped for sixty-eight years. It is time for my father to relinquish his past, and embrace the present. The time has come for my father to face his ultimate nemesis: himself.

★★★

WASHINGTON, D.C., 2008

"As I stand here before you, Lord, my mind reflects upon the past sixty-eight years of my life. And I wonder why destiny has led me to this place, and this time. I am an old man, Lord. If You had given me this task twenty years ago, I would have been more than able to fulfill it. But tonight, what good am I to you?

"I have spent the last year working, and trying to do Your will but I am tired, Lord. I don't know if my old feebly body can hold on until tomorrow.

"But I do know one thing, Jesus. When I leave this courtroom tomorrow, one way or the other, I won't have to worry about ever coming back into another one again in my life. I'm going to have to rest these old bones.

"Well, Lord, I'm almost through praying. My knees hurt so bad I can hardly stand up. Wait a minute, Lord. I've changed my mind. I'm not quite through yet. I wonder how my father would feel if he knew that his only son had grown up to be in this dubious position. My guess would be very afraid. Afraid that I may die in the same manner in which he died. Could You tell him I'm sorry, Lord? Aw, don't worry about it. As old as I feel, I may be able to tell him personally in a day or two.

"Lord, my mother always said that you won't put any more on us than we can handle. How much more do You think I have left, Lord? Give me my strength for one more day, Lord; just like you did Sampson. Please, Lord, just one more day." Solomon continued to stay on his knees as he held the back of the pew in front of him for support. He said, "Amen," to conclude his prayer, and looked up to see an old man entering the rear of the courtroom.

"I'm sorry, sir, this courtroom is not open to the public. You are not supposed to be in here. This is a top security building. How did you get in here, anyway?" Solomon asked.

"That's the one good thang 'bout bein' a broke-down old man. Nobody ever pay you no 'tention. 'Course they don't pay you no 'tention when you need it, too. I walked up to that do' and walked straight through it, and ain't nobody said one word to me. When you old like this, son, you 'come invisible." The old man laughed.

"I know the feeling of being old," Solomon said.

"Why, you just a baby, Solomon." The old man laughed again.

"You know my name?" Solomon asked.

"Who don't know Solomon Chambers, the modern-day Moses," the old man whispered. "We need you, son. We need you bad."

"What can one man do against the powers that be?" Solomon asked.

"You ain't just one man. You God's man, and like the good book say, if God be fo' you, who can be against you? If God is in you, son, then you the powuh that be. Who can stand against you?" the old man said with his chest stuck out and shoulders pulled back.

"The United States government!" Solomon sighed.

The old man laid his cane to his side, and slid onto one of the benches.

"Let me tell you somethin', son. Sixty-eight years ago I was convicted of robbin' somebody. I was only sixteen years old. They stuck me in a prison with old overgrown men. I was only a boy. Sixteen years old! And they stuck me in that hole and let me rot for sixty-eight long years. I don't have no family. I don't have no friends. I don't have no nothin'!

"They only let me out so I can die, and they won't have to foot the bill. My whole life is gone. Just wasted! You know I done asked God a million times to just let me die. But He wouldn't. As a matter of fact, I ain't never been sick a day in my life until they let me out of jail. And even now, my body ailin' me, but I ain't been down sick. Who say God ain't got no sense of humor, huhn?" The old man laughed.

"Well, thank Jesus you're a free man now," Solomon said.

"Free? What make me free? I ain't got no place to live. I ain't got nobody to love, and I ain't got nobody to love me. I ain't even got nowhere to die. My freedom was taken from me when I was sixteen. I'm an eighty-four-year-old man; the only freedom I got waitin' for me is death. And I can't wait for it to come neitha! I spent my last cent, and probably my last breath comin' all the way up here to talk to you about how important this trial is, Solomon, and I thank God I did."

"I know that this is a high-profile trial. But the bottom line for me is that I see this as yet another trial that I must bring to a just and strategic conclusion."

"Is that why you was prayin' to the Lord? 'cause this is just another trial?"

"I was praying to the Lord because I need him."

"You don't have to worry about the Lord helpin' you, son! You know He gon' do that. You gotta help yo'self!"

Solomon sat up, and tried to stand. It took him a while, but he eventually completed the task. He grabbed his briefcase and thanked the old man for the words of inspiration.

"Thank you, sir, for the words of confidence. I am curious about one thing, sir," Solomon said. "How in the world did you possibly get sixty-eight years in prison for robbery?"

"Hell, I sat in prison for two years befo' they even stuck a charge on me."

"No trial, no conviction, no due process?" Solomon asked.

"Due process? In 1940? In Mississippi? I was happy fuh due life!"

"Did you come all the way up here to tell me that story?"

"No, son, that ain't the story."

"Well, why did you travel all of this way to talk to me?"

"I came to tell you about a man. But befo' I tell you 'bout anybody else, do you know who you are? I ain't talkin' 'bout you bein' no lawyer. Do you know who you is inside? If not, you need to think. Think, son! Before I go any furtha," the old man said.

★★★

DERMA COUNTY, MISSISSIPPI 1935

It was a small county where the colored people made up seventy-two percent of the population. However, the imbalanced number of white people were the beneficiaries of wealth, and power from prior generations. Most of the white people were the children of former slave owners, while most of the colored people were children of former slaves.

The white families had spacious plantation homes, with long driveways that started so far from the house, it was impossible to see the house from the road. There was a social and economic status that was commonplace for mostly all of the white people.

Derma was a rich county, and there were only a few white families who were not wealthy, or financially established. Those few lived in small houses, and worked for the wealthy whites. They also socialized with coloreds, more than whites. The coloreds still called them "Ma'am" and "Sir" and entered through the rear of their homes. They had to respect the color barrier, because the laws of Jim Crow were in full effect.

Jim Crow Laws were the laws formed by Southern states to fight the federal laws incorporated by the Emancipation Proclamation. It kept the spirit of the old South alive.

The colored people lived in large groups in small houses, only a few feet apart. Two or three generations often shared one- or two-bedroom cabins. There were some colored people who moved far into the woods where land had not been claimed to create breathing room for their families. These few families often broke the mold of the poverty-stricken coloreds and became educated and financially stable themselves.

One of those families was the Chambers family, Alexander and Annie Mae Chambers. Alexander was college-educated and worked as a teacher, which was the most prestigious profession for a colored man in Derma County, outside of the clergy. Annie Mae worked on the West Plantation as a maid. She and Alexander were raised together on the West Plantation.

Alexander left Mississippi and went to college up north in Pennsylvania. There he witnessed colored people who were respected and accepted in everyday society. He met a young minister who would later move to Mississippi and hire Annie Mae from the West Plantation. When he returned to Mississippi he could no longer accept the blatant discrimination against colored people without voicing his opinion.

Alexander and Annie were married in 1883 and had their only child, Isaiah, eighteen years later in 1901. Alexander taught Isaiah that he was the equal to any man on this planet: colored, white, rich, or poor. Alexander instilled in his son that the only way to fight discrimination was through education. He made Isaiah believe that an education may not stop some doors from closing in your face, but it can sure open a lot of doors that have always been locked. Annie Mae, on the other hand, taught Isaiah how to be an educated man in Derma County without ending up with his neck at the end of a rope.

In 1911, Alexander's inability to adapt to Mississippi's growing defiance of the advancement of colored people caused him to rally colored families together and speak out against their mistreatment from whites. He told them to save money and buy plenty of land, as he had done, and farm it to support themselves. He told them to learn to depend upon themselves for survival, and not white men.

Alexander explained that coloreds in Derma County outnumbered whites three to one, and they should be a part of the decision-making process. He was met with angry and violent resistance from the white politicians.

On Christmas Eve of that same year, Alexander went out to fetch Christmas dinner for his family, and never returned. Isaiah and one of his friends found his body two days later hanging from a tree in the woods. They dragged his body on a blanket four miles to their house. Ironically, the boy who helped him carry his father's body from the woods was a white boy named John, who lived on the next acre of land with his mother. Isaiah had nothing to give the boy to repay him for his kindness. So he made him a necklace out of the twine used to hang his father. The boy may not have realized where the material to make the necklace came from, but nevertheless, being an impoverished child himself, he was happy to receive it.

Annie Mae was devastated, and never mentally recovered from Alexander's death. Later, her land was confiscated and all that remained for her to support herself and Isaiah was her job working as a maid; a job most colored women sought for employment. But Annie Mae had become accustomed to Alexander's income from farming their land. The land was gone, and the income went with it. Her strength for living was to protect and provide for her son. Isaiah, at the age of ten, suddenly became the man of the house.

Annie Mae raised Isaiah to be a God-fearing man, to believe in God's book, and not man's book. Isaiah, although having been raised by Alexander for only ten short years, was truly his father's son, for he decided to believe in both.

Isaiah grew up to be a strong-willed, but gentle man. His father's murder left an indelible mark on his heart and soul. Like his father, he, too, went up North to attend college. He also witnessed the acceptance of colored people in society, and the conspicuous difference between Negroes in the North, and coloreds in the South.

After college, Isaiah went back to Mississippi to take care of his mother and the land his mother's bossman had purchased for her while he was away. He did not want his mother to lose her land again to the manipulating scoundrels who had stolen their land after his father's death.

He became a schoolteacher and a leader in the colored community. He was respected by coloreds and whites. He had an even temper, and was respectful to every person he met.

In 1934, Annie Mae was stricken with a severe case of pneumonia and died peacefully in her sleep. On her death bed, she revealed to Isaiah certain secrets she had kept hidden from him. The news paralyzed Isaiah's emotions and, after Annie Mae was buried, he became more involved in the church.

A year later Isaiah met a young lady by the name of Orabell Moore in church, where he taught Sunday School. Most people said he had missed his calling to be a preacher. Isaiah started to invite Orabell to church functions, and they fell in love and wanted to be married. He knew that before they discussed marriage any further he had to discuss it with her parents, whom he had never met personally. Mrs. Moore was the sweetest old lady you'd ever find, but Mr. Moore was stubborn, and settled in his ways. He was notorious for carrying a shotgun named Susie and shooting it at people. Though his reputation preceded him, no one ever found proof that he had actually shot someone.

Mr. Moore was a balding, white-haired old man with light skin and sharp, gray eyes. His eyebrows and mustache matched the white color of the hair on the top of his head. He was a small man who spoke fast with a high-pitched voice. He often stuttered, which made it difficult to understand him sometimes. He was in a hurry to get things done; even when there was nothing to do. He wore baggy pants held up by suspenders and corduroy shirts with a white undershirt even in the midst of summer. And he capped it off with a gray and black evening hat. He was a religious man, with the tongue and temper of the devil, who often spoke before he thought.

Mrs. Moore was dark-skinned with long white hair that she kept plaited in one big ball. She wore the long thick skirts that tied around the waist. Her shoes were black with buckles on top. She was the exact opposite of her husband. She was humble and courteous and often resolved issues instead of create them. Mrs. Moore had long patience and tough skin. But when her patience ran out, she could be as vicious as anyone.

The Moores lived back in the woods on land founded and owned by Mr. Moore's father. As most black men in those days, Mr. Moore's father died young, and he had to take over being the man of the house. After he and Mrs. Moore were married they lived together in the house with his mother until her death in 1889. Mr. Moore farmed the land until his body would no longer allow him.

Mr. Moore was proud of his house and his land. His house was huge with a grand porch. The driveway was long like the white folks' driveway and led to the front door of the house. The house sat back far from the road with trees in the yard that hid most of its view until you were almost directly in front of it. There were six stairs leading to the porch making the house appear to be sitting high off of the ground. The porch had two rocking chairs and a porch swing. You entered through the front door and into the living room. The walls were painted with bright colors. The floor was hardwood and shiny. The furniture was antique but in new condition. The kitchen was huge and green. It had a green floor, green cabinets, green walls, and white sink. Upstairs there were five bedrooms. The Moores occupied one, their daughter Orabell and son Stanford occupied one apiece, and the other two were for occasional visitors.

Isaiah had taken notes on all of the habits, beliefs and ideas of the Moore family, and he was going to use them to his advantage when he was courageous enough to go to the Moores and ask for their daughter's hand in marriage.

Mr. Moore refused to allow Orabell to court any man, and she was twenty years old. In that day, an old hag. Isaiah felt that he could convince Mr. Moore to change his mind. He was nervous and perspiring when he walked up the porch stairs to the Moores' home. They looked at him strangely when he stood before them but did not say a word. Finally he found the courage to speak.

"How are you doing this evening, Mr. Moore, Mrs. Moore?" Isaiah asked. "Wonderful evening, isn't it?"

Isaiah was about five feet, ten inches tall, fair-skinned, with dark black curly hair. He had very broad shoulders with light brown eyes, and spoke softly and articulately. He had finally gotten up the nerve to ask for his girlfriend's hand in marriage. A girlfriend whose parents had no idea she was dating.

"It sho' is, son. What might you be payin' us a visit fa tonight?" Mrs. Moore asked.

"Ya look too old to be runnin' around wit my boy, so ya must be comin' fa somethin' else. I hope it ain't fa my gal. Tell me dat ain't why you here, son?" Mr. Moore snapped.

"Well sir, here is the situation. I want to explain this properly so that you won't get the wrong understanding of my intention. I've been a little sweet on your daughter. Yes, sir, I'll admit that to you face to face, like a man, and get that out of the way. I know I am talking a little fast, sir, but that's because I'm nervous...not shady like I'm trying to be crooked, sir, but nervous...nervous. OK, sir, here it is! I am a schoolhouse teacher, and a Sunday School teacher. I give my tithes every Sunday. Even more than the ten percent the Bible tells us to give. I...I...I...I don't drink, I don't run around chasing after a bunch of different women...I don't have any children running around here either, sir! You can believe that straight from the horse's mouth," Isaiah rambled nervously.

"Hey, boy! You tryin' ta court me, or my daughta?" Mr. Moore asked.

"I'm sorry, sir. I want your daughter, sir," Isaiah said calmly.

"AHA! I knew that's all you wonted!" Mr. Moore screamed.

"No! No, sir! I don't want anything...well, I want Orabell, but that's it!"

"Henry, stop it! You 'bout to scare that boy halfway to death." Mrs. Moore laughed.

"You sure are, sir; you're about to scare that boy halfway to death," Isaiah cried.

"See what you done did, Henry? That boy done fuhgot who he is," Mrs. Moore whispered.

"Mr. Moore, please listen to me, sir. I plan on taking care of your daughter.

I have a big house that I built, outside of the West Plantation; I have just as much land as any white man in Derma County. If we ever needed money I could always sell my land so that Orabell would never want for anything," Isaiah said.

"You might not be shady, but you sho' sneaky. You think we don't know 'bout you creepin' round here wit' Orabell?" Mr. Moore asked. "Hadn't been fuh my wife, and me bein' a Christian, me and ol' Susie woulda came and paid you a visit, boy!"

"Mr. Moore, I stand to tell you that yes, I have been courting your daughter, Orabell, but only to church picnics, and revivals. I am not tied up, nor have I ever met anyone named Susie."

"Boy, are you sho' you from Derma County?" Henry asked. "Susie is my shotgun!" Mr. Moore said, erupting in a very loud laugh.

"Oh," Isaiah said, feeling embarrassed.

"Say what you gotta say, son. I gotta get ready fa bed," Mr. Moore mumbled.

"Well, Mr. Moore, all that I have to say is that I love your daughter, and I came over here to ask you for her hand in marriage."

"Son, if I'm right, and I figur' I am, you 'bout twice my daughta age, ain't ya?" Mr. Moore asked.

"No, sir. I am approximately fourteen years older than Orabell, but that doesn't matter."

"The hell it don't!" Mr. Moore shouted. "You done had women, grown women, and my baby ain't had no exper'ince wit' no grown man...ha' she?"

"Oh no, sir! No! No! No! No!"

Mr. Moore looked at Isaiah out of the corner of his eye, as if to let him know that he was watching him to see if he was lying or not.

"We gon' have to pray on it, son. Like my husband say, you near 'bout twice huh age. She don't know nothin' 'bout bein' wit' a man, 'cause I ain't taught huh yet." Mrs. Moore smiled.

"Ma'am, I don't mean any disrespect, but what do you think you can teach her about me, if you don't know me?"

"I don't aim to teach huh nothin' 'bout you, son. She might not even end up wit' you. I'll teach huh what she need ta look out fa in any man. You seem like a good enough fella. You just too old fa my baby. I don't think huh daddy too happy 'bout dis either."

"Hell naw, I ain't happy!"

"Stop all dat cussin', Henry!"

"Well, dis boy could be a crook, a bank robba', anythang! Hell, we don't know!" Mr. Moore said, pointing at Isaiah. "Son, I had my baby when I was almost sixty years old. She is the most preshus thang I got. I can't just let anybody walk up here and take her off."

"I understand what you're saying Mr. Moore," Isaiah said, walking backwards down the stairs. "I think it's about time for me to leave, but 'm happy to have met you and your beautiful wife, and I wish you both a lovely evening."

"Boy, you sho' know how to suck up, don't ya?" Mr. Moore laughed.

"Henry, leave dat boy alone! Thank you fuh stoppin' by, Isiaer," Mrs. Moore said.

"You're welcome," Isaiah answered, nodding his head and holding up his hat.

Isaiah walked off of the porch, and down the driveway to his car. Mr. and Mrs. Moore immediately began to discuss their opinion of his visit.

"I'm gon' tell you sumthin', Cornelia; dat is da fanciest talkin' nigga' I have evuh seen in my life. Talk like a ol' fashion woman. Ain't no man dat good, and he a fool if he think I believe one word of dat mess."

"Well, I believe him. He sound like he was tellin' da troof."

"Lissen at you, ol' woman. A young man come 'round here talkin' fancy to ya, and ya ready to just give ya daughta off to him. Don't dat beat ev'rythang?"

"Say what you wont 'bout his age, but dat's a good man, and ya know it. You just don't wanna give ya baby up."

"You dam' right I don't, and I ain't neitha!"

"You gon' have to one day, if ya wont to, or not."

"Where O'Bell at? Get out here, O'Bell!" Mr. Moore yelled.

Mrs. Moore stood up and yelled through the screen door.

"O'Bell, come see what ya daddy wont!"

Orabell took her time, but eventually she stepped through the screen door to see what her father wanted. Orabell was stunningly beautiful. Dark, smooth skin. Naturally wavy hair, that trickled down her back. An hourglass figure, which displayed every curve on her body, even in the loose-fitting dress she wore. Although she was quite petite in stature, her presence was amazingly noticeable.

"Yes, Daddy?" Orabell asked.

"Ya new beau came ovuh here askin' fuh ya hand in marriage. Nah you wanna tell me what dat's all about?"

"What you talkin' 'bout, Daddy?"

"You know what I'm talkin' 'bout, guhl. Don't talk to me stupid! I'm talkin' 'bout dis grown man comin' up to my house askin' fuh ya hand in marriage. Where you meet dis man? And what make you think I'm gon' let you run off wit' him?"

"Daddy, I ain't runnin' off with nobody. Isaiah and me, we go to church together. He taught me how to read good, and not like how they taught us in school. He's a good man, Daddy, and I love him...I just love him."

"You love him? What you know 'bout love, O'Bell? What make you think dis man gon' make a good husban'?"

"He treat me special. He always askin' how I'm doin', or what can he do to make me happy." Orabell sobbed. "Sometime, Daddy, I wonder why God even let me be born. Think about it, Daddy, what do I have to live for? All I do is take care of you, and Mama. I ain't complainin' 'bout that, but who am I goin' to live for when y'all ain't here no mo'? What's gon' happen to me when I have to live my life all by myself? You ever think about that, Daddy? I don't care how old Isaiah is, he love me for me. And I'm goin' to marry him if you say yes, or if you say no. Now I love you and Mama with all my heart, and I ain't never in my life stepped against nothin' y'all ever told me to do. But I ain't goin' to let this man get away from me," Orabell said with tears in her eyes.

"Cornelia, you ain't gon' say nothin' to dis guhl, talkin' crazy like dis?" Henry shouted.

"It ain't my place to say no mo', Henry, and yours neitha. That guhl know if she love dat man or not. She right, she gon' have to live huh own life. And if she know she love dat man, and dat man love huh, Henry...leave huh be."

"I said what I had to say 'bout it. Until I get to know dis man, ain't nobody marryin' nobody! So get dat notion out of ya head right now! Ya hear me?"

"Yes, Daddy." Orabell sighed.

Mrs. Moore wrapped her arms around Orabell and whispered, "Ev'rythang gon' be all right, baby. Go on in da house and get ya some rest."

"I know it will, Mama," Orabell whispered back. "Goodnight, Daddy."

"Goodnight, baby," Mr. Moore mumbled. "Hey! Come on ovuh here and give ma a kiss."

Orabell kissed Mr. Moore and told him she loved him.

"I love you too, baby. I hope you know I ain't tryin' to huht ya. I'm tryin' to pratect ya."

"I know, Daddy."

As Orabell started to walk back into the house Mr. Moore reached for her arm and stopped her. Orabell saw that her father was on the verge of crying, something she had never witnessed before, and she wiped his eyes.

"Baby, sometime it's hard to say goodbye to somethin' you love so much, but I guess holdin' on ain't gon' make thangs no betta. I guess it's time fa me to say goodbye and let go...goodbye, angel." Mr. Moore cried.

"Goodnight, Daddy." Orabell smiled.

At 4:00 a.m. the next morning, Orabell was awakened by cries from her mother. She quickly jumped out of bed and rushed to her mother's bedroom.

"What's wrong, Mama?"

"Yo' daddy, child, yo daddy ain't movin'! Help me wake him up!"

Orabell shook Mr. Moore, and cried along with her mother. Her younger brother, Stanford, rushed into the bedroom bewildered and hysterical. After unsuccessfully waking Mr. Moore, Orabell shouted for Stanford to run and get Dr. George West. Most colored folks in Derma County didn't have telephones, and the Moores were among the many who didn't, so when there was a medical emergency their only communication for help was primarily through word of mouth. Dr. West was the only doctor in Derma County. A lot of people believed that the West family kept other doctors from practicing in Derma County because Dr. West wanted all of the business for himself. Which meant he treated his patients less than respectable. Especially the colored patients.

Mr. Moore was still alive when Stanford left for Dr. West. He was breathing weakly, and had no control over his body, but he was alive just the same. Stanford returned from Dr. West's house at 7:00 a.m., but Dr. West did not arrive at the Moores' house until 5:30 p.m. He apologized for the delay, saying he had prior plans to visit some friends for breakfast and lunch. Unfortunately, by the time he arrived Mr. Moore was dead.

"Excuse me, doctor, how long my daddy been dead?" Stanford asked.

"I reckon he ain't been dead no more'n an hour or so," Dr. West answered.

"Are you tellin' me my daddy might still be alive if you woulda got here when you was supposed to?" Orabell cried.

"Can't say yeah, can't say no, but what I can say is that he sho' is dead now, ain't he?" Dr. West snickered

"How can you stand there wit' a man lyin' dead in front of you and laugh like that. Knowin' that you could have pro'bly saved his life?" Orabell screamed.

"I can stand here on my two feet," Dr. West snarled. "Nah, Cornelia, I know this is a sad time for you and yours, but don't let ya pretty little girl get herself in trouble talkin' back like that. Get her on outta here befo' I lose my patience and fuhget her daddy layin' up here dead."

"She just huht, Dr. West; don't pay no 'tention to huh," Mrs. Moore pleaded.

"I'm gon' pay plenty 'tention to her if she don't shut that black mouth and let me do my job," Dr. West said, then went back to discussing Henry. "Henry looks like he's in good shape for the night, but I advise you to round up some of these boys and get him outta here by tomorrow morning. It's gon' be a scorcha, and that heat will rot Henry up quicker than a lit match light to a gallon of gas. I guess my job here is done. Cornelia, do you have some of ya famous cool lemonade?"

"Yessuh, Dr. West. I'll go fetch ya some," Mrs. Moore said.

"I'll go get it, Mama; you just sit down and cool off." Orabell smiled.

Dr. West stared at Orabell and shouted as she was going into the kitchen, "I betta not see no suds floatin' round my glass. You look too eager to be fetchin' some lemonade," alluding to the possibility of Orabell spitting in his drink.

Orabell went into the kitchen and fixed Dr. West a glass of lemonade, then took it back to him. Dr. West reached into his coat pocket and took out a handkerchief. He carefully wiped the mouth of the glass before he took a drink.

Meanwhile, Isaiah was walking up the driveway and noticed Dr. West's automobile. Orabell saw him and went outside to meet him.

"I'm so happy to see you, Isaiah." Orabell sighed.

"Hey, Orabell, what's going on, who's sick?" Isaiah asked.

"Nobody sick no more. My daddy died today."

"What happened?"

"When mama woke up this morning she tried to wake my daddy up, but she couldn't. But he was still alive, Isaiah. Stanford went for Dr. West at five-thirty in the mo'ning, but he didn't get here until five o' clock this evening. He had all day to help my daddy, but he had betta things to do like go eat wit' white folks."

"Orabell, talking that way is only going to bring on worry, and worry is going to bring on pain, so stop fretting over things you can't change and go take care of your mother. I'll see to Dr. West."

Orabell went back into the bedroom with her mother and dead father, while Isaiah pulled Stanford aside and took him into the living room with him.

"Good evening, Dr. West," Isaiah said.

"How do! What's yo' name again, boy? I know you that schoolteacher. You Annie Mae's boy, ain't ya?"

"Yessir, Annie Mae was my mother. But I haven't been a boy in nearly twenty years. I'm a grown man and I'd appreciate it very kindly if you would refer to man as such. Especially in front of the boy, sir."

"Henry ain't been dead a day, and you done came in and made yo'self right at home, ain't you, boy?" Dr. West laughed.

"As I told you, sir, if you are going to address me, I'd appreciate it if you would address me as a man. Especially in front of the boy!" Isaiah said firmly.

"Looka here, you done went out and got you a little education, and yo' britches done got too big for yo' own good, boy."

"Dr. West, this family needs to be alone. I am asking you to please leave so that they can get some peace and quiet, and get on with their family business of burying their dead."

Dr. West stood up and brushed off his hat. He placed the empty glass on the end table next to where he was sitting and told Isaiah, "You know what, boy, it ain't been too long ago when I coulda had you hung for shootin' off at the mouth like that. You niggahs don't appreciate how good you got it these days. I come all the way out here to check on ol' man Henry and all I get from you ungrateful niggahs is a bunch o' smart-mouth sassin'. Tell you what, the next time one of ya get sick, don't call me, ya hear?" Dr. West screamed angrily.

Stanford slowly raised his head and muffled, "Don't you worry 'bout dat, Dr. West. It don't do no good no way. 'cause ev'rytime you come 'round here seem like somebody dead when you leave."

Dr. West was enraged by Stanford's comment and took the backside of his hand and slapped him to the floor. Isaiah immediately grabbed Dr. West and slung him out of the screen door and onto the ground. Isaiah stood on the porch and angrily pointed his finger at Dr. West, who lay flat on his back looking upward.

"Now, Dr. West, I am sorry for losing my temper, but I just can't stand here and let you slap that boy around like that. I didn't mean to hurt you. Once again, I apologize, now you just calm down and I'll make this up to you."

"There's only one way you can make this up to me, and that's for me to see a rope around your neck, niggah! And I'm here to tell ya, that befo' they can put ol' Henry in the ground, they gon' have to dig another hole for you." Dr. West screamed. Then he jumped in his automobile and sped off with wheels spinning, and dirt flying.

"You all right, boy?" Isaiah asked.

"Yessir, I'm fine," Stanford answered. "That old man can't hurt me."

"Let's go check on your mother and sister to see how they're holding up."

Later that evening Mrs. Moore, Orabell, Stanford and Isaiah were all sitting around Mr. Moore's bedside. They were exhausted from the events of the day. They sat in silence until Mrs. Moore thanked Isaiah for helping them during their crisis. "I thank you for stayin' 'round here makin' sho' ev'rythang all right, Isaier."

"It's only fitting that in times like these, we reach out to one another as one family. As common as death is, ma'am, it is still something that you can never get used to experiencing. I'm going to pray for your family that God has mercy on you all."

"We gon' need Him, and all of ya prayers. I don't know what we gon' do 'bout Henry. Lookin' back, I know I shoulda been prepared for him leavin', but I saw Henry as a young man, and I just didn't think he would be leavin' no time soon."

"Don't you worry about Mr. Moore, ma'am. I will take care of all the burial business. We can bury him on my land. I have a nice pretty spread where Mr. Moore can rest. And no thing, or no one, will disturb him. I'll be by first thing in the morning to take care of everything. We can have service for him in a day or two. Once everyone has been notified of his death, and given an opportunity to see him off. Then we can put him to rest."

"It ain't nobody to be notified," Mrs. Moore said.

"Well, that settles that. I will have Mr. Moore resting by this time tomorrow."

"You a good man, Isaier. You don't even much know us and you helpin' us like this," Mrs. Moore whispered.

"I know, Orabell, and if she is hurting, then I am hurting, ma'am. And I can only start to feel better when I know for sure that she already feels better."

"Whoo-whee! That man gotta tongue like a snake; I see why you fell fuh him." Mrs. Moore laughed.

★★★

In the days to follow Isaiah arranged for Henry to be buried on his land. Meanwhile, Dr. West had organized a lynch mob which plotted to kill Isaiah for pushing him to the ground. The colored community was well aware of Dr. West and his mob so they carefully hid Isaiah until they felt the situation had boiled over.

Isaiah became impatient with running and hiding. It was not his nature to hide from anyone, and sitting back waiting for a man to track him down did not rest well with him. He decided to confront Dr. West face to face. He figured that if he was going to be killed, he'd rather die like a proud man, than a sniveling coward. Of course Dr. West didn't care how he died; he just wanted him dead.

Isaiah picked a Sunday afternoon when coloreds and whites would be uptown in the Square enjoying ice cream and hot dogs after church. The Square was an enclosed four-block business district, except for the streets leading into and out of this business district. In the center of the four enclosed streets was a park for social activities. Most small Southern towns had a Square and the same activities went on at almost all of them.

Isaiah figured that Dr. West would be more forgiving if he was in broad daylight in front of his church friends wearing a white suit, than on a dark night with his Klan friends, wearing a white sheet.

Orabell pleaded for him to stay hidden until Dr. West had cooled off. This was considered to be a manner of paying back your disrespectful dues. When a white person had been publicly disrespected by a colored person, in order for the colored person to re-establish himself in his humbled inferiority position and return to the public without the threat of violence, they would have to not show his or her face again until an appropriate amount of time had passed. This was to re-establish the superiority status for that white person in society.

Isaiah had not served that respectable length of time because Dr. West was as mad as ever. However, it was a gorgeous Sunday afternoon, church was over, and the Square was filled with good spirits. Isaiah almost felt guilty about confronting Dr. West with all of the jubilation on the Square. But he knew it was confront him now, or be confronted later, with a shotgun and a rope.

The white people were in the park were enjoying themselves, while the colored people were standing around in the streets enjoying themselves. Dr. West and his wife, Mamie, were walking from picnic table to picnic table communing with other groups of white people and didn't notice Isaiah walking directly toward them.

Isaiah walked up to Dr. West and Ms. Mamie and stood in front of them. A few colored and white people noticed him, but it was no big deal to see Isaiah talking to white people no matter where they were. Isaiah cleared his throat and began to speak to the Wests very nicely.

"How are you doing, sir? Lovely day isn't it, Ms. Mamie?" Isaiah said.

"Boy, you must be outta yo' niggah mind to be walkin' up to me like this in broadlight!" Dr. West whispered.

"Is everything all right, Isaiah?" Mamie cried.

"I'm sorry, Ms. Mamie; I didn't come here for any trouble. I came to apologize to Dr. West about a certain matter. I want it to be done with this afternoon, one way or the other."

"I don't know what matter you're referring to, but this is hardly the time for you to be walkin' up to my husband for any kinda matter. You know you know betta than that Isaiah, now gon'." Ms. Mamie shooed with her hands.

"Ms. Mamie, I'm afraid that if I don't get this settled right now, the next time I see your husband he'll be wearing a white sheet, instead of the clean white suit he has on." Isaiah smiled

"I demand to know what Isaiah is talkin' about right now, George!"

"This nigga has completely lost his mind, darling," Dr. West said.

"Oh no, Ms. Mamie, I am in my right mind and your husband knows it. He and some of his hooded bandits are going to kill me first chance they get. It may as well be right here, and right now. Ain't that right, Dr. West?"

"You know daddy wouldn't stand fa nothin' like that, Isaiah, 'specially from George!"

"I don't know what this fool talkin' 'bout, Mamie!" Dr. West cried angrily.

"Let me tell you something; my husband is a good Christian man, and he wouldn't harm a fly. So go on over there with the otha culluds before I forget about how much yo' mama meant to me."

Isaiah leaned over to Dr. West and said, "You know what I'm talking about, don't you, Dr. West?"

Grinding his teeth, Dr. West walked up to Isaiah and said, "Get out of my face befo' I kill you right here and now, nigga!"

"It's too bad you couldn't hear what your Christian husband just said in my ear, Ms. Mamie. But then if you did, you'd only pretend you didn't hear him anyway, now wouldn't you, ma'am?"

Dr. West pulled away from his wife, grabbed Isaiah by his arms and whispered in his ear, "Consida yo'self dead, boy."

"I already have, that's why I'm here..." Isaiah whispered back, with anger in his voice, "....Boy!"

"Leave Isaiah be, before everybody start lookin', George," Mamie said.

Dr. West pulled out a cigar, and puffed the smoke in Isaiah's face.

"Come on, honey, let's go," Mamie added.

Mamie did not want to be the center of gossip, especially if it involved Isaiah and his family. Her father was Reverend Willingham, who was particularly fond of Isaiah because of his mother, Annie Mae. She was the Reverend's maid, and best friend for the last forty-two years of her life. He treated Annie Mae as if she was his family. He bought all of the land within a two-mile radius of her house, and gave it to her. He was at her side when she died, and prayed while her soul crossed over to the other side.

Reverend Willingham was born and raised in Pennsylvania. His wife, Annabelle, was born and raised in Mississippi in the old traditional ways. She died two years after they moved to Mississippi in 1892. He met her in Pennsylvania and they were married in 1868. Before she died, Annabelle often fantasized about her early childhood and how magnificent it was before the Civil War. After she was stricken with tuberculosis, the reverend decided to move his family back to Mississippi, thinking maybe they could find a miracle in her joy to return to her home. To their dismay, they did not.

Annie Mae was working at the West Plantation when Alexander convinced her to work for Reverend Willingham. The West Plantation did not want to let her go, but Reverend Willingham had a way of getting what he wanted, even from the West family. She took care of Annabelle, and made her feel comfortable up until the day she died. After that, Annie Mae helped raise Mamie until she was grown and married to Dr. West. Reverend Willingham was indebted, and shielded Annie Mae and her family from the everyday confrontations of bigotry. Even with the protection of the reverend, it was not enough to save Alexander. Annie Mae made sure that, what happened to her husband would not happen to her son. She armed him with information that would protect him from the people that could harm him most, and she befriended the only person who could destroy those people once they realized he had that information, Reverend Willingham.

Reverend Robert Willingham was the minister of the largest church in Derma County, and the son of Abolitionists from Pennsylvania. Reverend

Willingham's father aided in the escape of many slaves to freedom, using the underground methods of communication between the slaves, and the freed colored people, helping a countless number of slaves to escape from the South to the North.

Because of his upbringing, Reverend Willingham always preached and practiced equality to all men in his church. He fought discrimination and prejudices throughout the state of Mississippi. His battles ended up as defeats most of the time, yet still, he never refused a single challenge. Unfortunately, he had no inkling that his greatest foes sat on his pews every Sunday morning. He foolishly believed that his congregation believed and practiced as he taught, but even his precious daughter Mamie grimaced at the thought of a colored man living as her equal. Mamie dared not to speak a word of this to Reverend Willingham for even at his old age, he would probably take a strap to her behind.

Reverend Willingham was also one of the wealthiest men in the United States; a quarter of his assets could dwarf the entire West fortune if he chose to invoke his estate from Pennsylvania. His father was a mogul who helped build the railroad system from the East Coast to the West Coast. His father also traded in international metal trading. He had one sibling, a brother who was killed in the Civil War so he was sole heir to the Willingham Estate. Reverend Willingham, however, lived a humbled life and provided his family with only the necessities. He wanted his family not to be dependent upon money, but upon God. The Willingham Estate was to be inherited by his grandchildren. When Dr. West's two children inherited the Reverend's estate that would make the West family one of the wealthiest families in the country as well.

Reverend Willingham was nearly eighty-two years old, and his health was fading fast. Certainly, it would only be a matter of time before he passed on. The West family knew the reverend's health could not sustain much longer. So they patiently waited for him to die. But if he knew of the hypocritical manner in which they ran their business and the county, it would definitely strike a fire in him. Reverend Willingham would use every cent of his estate to bring them to their knees. The last thing they wanted was to give him a reason for staying around a few more years. They remained his most faithful members, for as far as his eyes could see them. They patronized him by standing in his church and giving testimonies on how they want all of the coloreds to one day be treated the same as white folks. Clapping their hands in celebration and telling the Reverend he had brought forth a peaceful way of living to Derma County. But all the time they were praising his name to his face, they were the decaying scab that covered the sores of Derma County.

The Wests believed that niggas should always be niggas, and white folks should always be white folks, and the two shall therefore never mix.

Privately, they were suspected as being the leaders of the Derma County chapter of the Ku Klux Klan. The Klan members of Derma County were not just redneck bigots who wanted to keep the white race pure. The Klan realized that they could benefit from utilizing the resources of the colored man. They developed businesses on colored people's land, and allowed the colored people to work at these businesses to support themselves. They had plenty of work, for minimal wages, if there were any wages at all.

The West family owned nearly sixty-eight percent of the businesses in Derma County. They came of their wealth during old slave-trading days, and in the production of agriculture.

The Wests used their money and power to manipulate the political process, and intimidate the coloreds and poor whites into not voting. That was the way the small population of whites was capable of holding every political office in Derma County. They considered this to be the necessary means of keeping white folks, white, and niggas, niggas. And assuring that the two would never mix!

★★★

Isaiah and Orabell were married in early spring, 1937. Isaiah had become a quiet activist for the equality of colored people. He didn't want to create a negative situation between the whites and coloreds, because that would only worsen the condition for coloreds. He kept his information and his approach very subtle and tried to bring awareness to the eyes of both races.

Whites, he tried to convince to assist in advancing the lives for coloreds, and coloreds he tried to convince to become unified, and self-sufficient. And to accept the belief that equality should be the manner in which all men live. Both races thought Isaiah's views were too radical and too progressive, and they rejected them with harsh criticism. Isaiah figured that if he could get them to conquer their fears, they would begin to co-exist in an equal society. First, he had to get them to understand their fears. One, the fear of losing superiority, and the other, the fear from the wrath of gaining equality. Despite the reluctance from the people of Derma County, Isaiah still tried to unite the races.

While Isaiah was crusading the causes for colored people, Orabell had become paranoid with the thought of her husband being lynched by a mob of white men. She begged Isaiah to stay home and try to start their own family. He tried to assure Orabell that there was nothing to fear, and she should stop worrying. But it is much easier said than done for a woman who loves a man the way that Orabell loved Isaiah.

"Orabell, you're too young to have such an old soul; why do you worry so much?"

"I can't help it. My whole life I've been carin' for folks, and I can't change that now."

"You don't have to change. Being kind has never been a bad thing. Just stop worrying about the things you can't change."

"What I'm s'pposed to do, Isaiah?" Orabell shouted. "You're stirrin' up mess every day wit' these white folks! I know one day you ain't gon' walk through that door; I just know it! Why can't you just be happy wit' me, and start ya own family instead of runnin' 'round tryin' to take care of every otha' colored fam'ly in Derma County?"

"See, baby, that's where we're both alike. You give of yourself to your family, because that's the way God made you. I give of myself to my fellow man because that's how God made me. Can't you understand what I'm saying?"

"But carin' for my family ain't gon' get me killed! I don't wont to be no widow. I wont a family! Children! I just...Isaiah, I just want us to have our own fam'ly, wit' our own children. And leave everybody else alone."

"Listen to me, Orabell, please! My mother and my father were both slaves.

After they were freed, life was even harder for them. My father was hung from a tree like an animal, just because he wanted what was his...and that's freedom, baby! Don't you see, just because Lincoln signed that piece of paper, it didn't make us free? The only way that we're going to be free is if we fight for our freedom!"

"My mama and my daddy was slaves, too, Isaiah! But I don't see what that got to do wit' nothin'! This is your family right here. You and me! You the head of this family, and you need to start actin' like it!" Orabell screamed.

"I've always been the head of this family. You don't want for anything, Orabell."

"I wonts for you, Isaiah! Can't you see that? I wonts for you! All this land don't mean nothin' to me if you ain't here wit' it! You ain't even here enough for us to even make no babies!" Orabell cried, bursting into tears.

Isaiah pulled her to his chest, and wiped her eyes.

"No, baby, no. We don't have any children because it's just not time for us to have any children. Why would you say something like that?"

"Because, Isaiah, everybody we know got babies, but us!"

"So what?"

"So what's wrong wit' us?

"There's nothing wrong with us. All that I can say is that if God wants us to have children, we will have them. And if he doesn't...well, I suppose we won't. Right now, I know that we have each other, and that's all we need to worry about."

"You know you got me, Isaiah, but I'm not so sure I got you. Seem like everybody in this world got you, but me."

"Nobody has me, Orabell, but you and the Lord. And I have to do what the Lord tells me to do. So please, let me be your husband, and God's servant."

"I don't wanna come between you and your God, but I love you so much, and I don't wanna lose you."

"I'm not going anywhere until God calls me. And what makes you so sure he's going to call me first?" Isaiah joked, "Ol' Gabriel may be playing his trumpet for you, before he plays my tune."

"That will be fine by me." Orabell laughed. "'cause when I'm gone, you'll just be the one crying like a baby instead of me."

"You are full of yourself today, aren't you, lady?"

"Oh, I'm full o' myself every day, baby, every day!" Orabell laughed with him.

Isaiah did not want to cause his newlywed any additional stress, so he stayed home more often and helped with the issues that only concerned colored versus colored. Orabell was happy. She finally had the marriage, and the man, she wanted.

★★★

One Saturday morning, in the fall of 1937, a young colored man by the name of William Crowell was riding the railroad passenger train back to Michigan. The young man had returned home to Derma County to attend his mother's funeral. He was only supposed to be there for a few days, and he then get back up North.

His mother was laid to rest, and so was his business with Mississippi. William missed his family and friends, but he could live the rest of his life and never return to the sweltering climate of bigotry and discrimination that hovered over Mississippi.

Although William was born and raised in Derma County, he was distinctive in his appearance, and his dialect. He had straight, sandy brown hair. His eyes were green. He had very thin lips. An extremely tall man of six feet four inches, he spoke very articulately, and his skin resembled that of a white man. It was well known that William's father was indeed a white man, but unknown was his identity. William was often mistaken for being a white man himself. As he grew older in life when that situation occurred, he learned to deal with it. If it was beneficial to him to pose as a white man, he acted accordingly. If it was not to his benefit, he simply explained himself as being colored.

After completing college William moved up North to a small Midwestern town to work. At that time, jobs were difficult to come by, due to the Great Depression that began in 1929, the year William left Mississippi. The South still had the same jobs, paying the same wages for colored people, educated or not. Adding to the pressure was the scramble for so many colored people to occupy so few jobs. The North was in the middle on the industrial revolution and jobs were a little more plentiful than in the South.

The automobile industry had just begun its assembly boom, and cities in Michigan, particularly cities near Detroit, maintained a steady work flow. When William first arrived in Detroit he was intimidated by the progressive lifestyle, having grown up in such a rural area. He decided to go further north, and settled in the town of Saginaw. He had not returned to Mississippi since he had moved to Saginaw. This was his first visit back since he had left eight years earlier.

★★★

As William sat on the train he had just one regret on his visit back to Mississippi, and it was that he didn't get the opportunity to visit his lifelong friend, Isaiah, whom he affectionately referred to as Zay. The two grew up as best friends from spanking new babies. They were born a couple of days apart, and were inseparable until they both became grown men and went their different ways. They were alike in many ways, but when it came to patience, God must have given all of William's to Isaiah, because he had very little.

Both of their mothers were strong women who raised their sons to be strong, and ambitious young men. They taught their sons to fear God, and God only. And that righteousness takes precedence over self. That standing as an upright man regardless of the circumstances, will always keep wrong from climbing all over your back.

While William sat reminiscing about his youth, two attendants from the train approached him and questioned him on his seating. William was sitting in the very first coach, which was for white persons only. He tried to defuse the situation by offering to move to another coach. The attendants were about to allow William to move to one of the coaches in the rear, but the conductor demanded that he be removed from the train and escorted to the nearest law office. William thought the conductor's request was outrageous and for that instance he forgot that he was in the great state of Mississippi.

He asked the conductor to explain himself. The conductor returned William's question with a question. He wanted to know if William was white or colored. If he was white, and he could prove that somehow, he would be allowed to catch the next train heading north. If he could not, he would have to go to court for violating the Whites Only Law. William refused to answer the conductor's question. He was forcibly removed from the train and escorted to the Derma County Courthouse, which doubled as the post office. He was placed in a cell and held for the remainder of the weekend. He would have to wait for his trial on Monday morning when the honorable Judge Woodrow West, the older brother of Dr. George West, returned from his fishing trip.

The sheriff was also out of town, transferring an escaped prisoner back to Jackson. He would have to stay in Jackson until Wednesday as a witness against the escaped prisoner. The sheriff was so well known for hunting down escaped criminals in the state of Mississippi, other counties, including Hinds, would call on him for assistance.

On Monday morning William was brought before Judge West for indictment, then immediately following, his trial. He was given a court-appointed attorney who wouldn't even look him in the face. William tried to make conversation with the attorney but he wouldn't talk back.

"Good morning, sir. I'm glad to make your acquaintance," William spoke. He held out his hand to shake his hand, but the man ignored him and walked to the judge's bench. They talked and laughed for a minute or two, then the man returned back to their desk. The attorney opened up his briefcase and pulled out a newspaper and began to read while the judge asked William to stand.

William stood before Judge West believing the judge would understand that this had been a huge misunderstanding, and he could clear everything up with an explanation and a sincere apology. William was indicted, and his trial began before he was ever allowed an opportunity to speak. The judge quickly moved forward to the trial. William never had to move his feet, or utter a word. The matter of due process was being moved right along. The judge finally spoke to William to begin the process of the trial.

"Mr. Crowell?" the judge asked.

"Yes, sir," William answered.

"Mr. Crowell, can you read, and, or write? And can you understand white man's English?"

"Yes, sir, I can read, write, and speak very well, sir."

"Well then, Mr. Crowell, you have been charged with violating the state of Miss'ippi Whites Only Law. Mr. Crowell, you are also being charged fa conspirin' to impersonate a white man to therefore violate the Whites Only Law. Is there anythang you would like to say on yo' behalf?"

"May I discuss this with my attorney first, sir?" William asked.

"Go right ahead, help ya' self." The judge smiled.

William sat down next to his attorney and asked him to advise him on what to say. "I kinda need your help here, sir. What should I say to the judge?"

"If I was you, boy, I wouldn't be sayin' nothin' to the judge; I'd be prayin' to the Lord about now." The man smiled and looked back down at his newspaper.

"But you're my lawyer; aren't you going to defend me?"

The man stood up and said, "Judge West, he said he didn't do nothing wrong, and he wonts to go home. Oh, and Judge, we rest our case"

William looked at the lawyer in disbelief, then turned to the judge. "May I say something to the court, Your Honor?"

"Help ya' self, but make it quick," Judge West said hurriedly.

"Sir, I have not intentionally violated any law. I boarded the train and I sat where the porter directed me."

"Where you from, boy? I 'clare you talk betta than me, and lookin' at ya, I can't tell if you white, cullud, or Injian!" Judge West joked.

"I am from Derma County, sir. Born and raised. I reside in Saginaw, Michigan where I work every day and abide by the law."

"What you doin' down here?"

"I came to attend my mother's funeral. All that I am trying to do now is get on a train, and get myself back to work before they let me go."

"Well it ain't that easy, boy. You done committed a serious offense here. We can't have niggas tryin' to pass as white. If I let you get away wit' it, every light-shade nigga in Derma County would be tryin' to get away with it. And we can't have that!"

The courtroom was silent as the judge thumbed through some of William's paperwork. He looked up, and asked William about his family.

"Who's your kin, boy?"

"My mother was Ruthie Lee Crowell."

"What's ya daddy's name?"

"I never knew my father's name, sir," William said reluctantly.

"You mean ya mama don't know what's done been up in her?" Judge West laughed.

William was enraged with the insensitive comments said by the judge. Once again, for an instance, he forgot that he was in the state of Mississippi. He responded with a malicious and resentful attack against his white father.

"Yes, sir, my mother knew exactly who my father was. He was a white man who raped her, and left her pregnant. A man who never accepted responsibility for his child, nor did he accept the responsibility of stripping my mother of her dignity."

"Boy, you already in hot water. That water you sittin' in now, is only stove hot. But you about to make that water *hell* hot in a minute!" Judge West pointed at William. "Let's just get straight to the point: are you white or are you a nigga?"

William stood there carefully contemplating the words he wanted to say.

"Judge, as an American citizen I choose to call upon the fifth, fourteenth and fifteenth amendments to the Constitution and not answer that question until due process of the United States justice system has been fairly served in this courtroom."

"What the hell?" Judge West looked around with confusion. "I asked you a question: are you white, or are you a nigga?"

"Judge, at this time, as an American born citizen, I choose to call upon the fifth, fourteenth, and fifteenth amendments to the Constitution, and not answer that question until due process of the United States justice system has been fairly served in this courtroom."

"Well, at this time, smart ass, I find you guilty on both counts. I'm gon' read your sentence to the court," Judge West snarled.

Judge West jotted down quick notes, then adjusted his glasses to read the sentences.

"On the first count, I find the prisoner guilty of violating the Whites Only Law of the state of Miss'ippi, and I sentence you to five years imprisonment in Parchman State Penitentiary. On the second count, I find the prisoner guilty of conspiring to impersonate a white man, to enable hisself to commit a violation of the Whites Only Law of the state of Miss'ippi. For that charge I sentence the prisoner to five years imprisonment in Parchman State Penitentiary. These sentences are to run consecutively, startin' one week from this day. At this time, Mr. Crowell, yo' due process of the United States justice systum has been fairly served. And for the recuhd, down here we call it, Miss'ippi justice! Lock the prisoner up, and this here courtroom is adjourned!" The judge loudly sounded his gavel, and limped out of the courtroom.

CHAPTER TWO

William was processed to be transferred to Parchman State Penitentiary, and then taken back to his cell. He sat on his bed in total disbelief. Shocked by the events which led to his imprisonment, he felt vulnerable and hopeless. He had returned to the place he once successfully escaped, only to become its prisoner again.

William knew that if he was taken to Parchman, odds stood that he would never be released. He pleaded with every person in the courthouse to listen to him as he proclaimed his innocence.

His cries fell upon listening ears when the cleaning woman recognized him. She was an elderly colored woman named Betty Jean White. She had grown too old to work for the West Plantation, so they moved her to housecleaning at the courthouse. The elderly woman used to worked with William's mother years earlier. She was one of the few attendees at Mrs. Ruthie Lee's funeral, and she remembered his face.

"Hey! Ain't you Ruthie Lee's boy?"

"Yes, ma'am!" William said, jumping off of the bed and pressing his face between the cell bars. "Do you remember me?"

"Why sho' I remember you. What in tarnation they got you locked up in here fo'?"

"They say I broke the law. I sat in the front coach, and that violated the Whites Only Law. The judge said that he is going to send me to Parchman Prison for ten years. I can't go to prison for ten years, ma'am. Not for sitting on a train!" William cried.

"Son, I ain't tryin' to make light o' ya situation, but some folks 'round here done been killed fa a lot less than sittin' in the front of a train," Mrs. Betty cried.

"Mrs. Betty Jean, please, please, you have to help me."

"Help you? Son, whatta ol' woman like me gon' do?"

"I need you to listen closely, Mrs. Betty Jean. I need you to contact someone, and tell him I'm in trouble. Bad trouble! Tell him I need him to help me. I need you tell him everything I just told you. Tell him that they are going to send me to the penitentiary for ten years in a couple of days, if he don't help me. All I need you to do, is get a hold of Isaiah Chambers, and tell him William Crowell is locked up in the Derma County Courthouse. Please, can you do that for me, Mrs. Betty?" William asked, folding his hands in front of his face as if he were praying.

"I can't make no promises, 'cause he and O'Bell live way up there on Church Hill, and that's a pretty good piece from my house. But I'll see if I can't get one o' my boys to run over there and tell him fo' ya."

"Thank you, Mrs. Betty, thank you," William said, sitting back down on his bed.

"You welcome, son, and I hope Isiaer can help you. Don't make no sense a good boy like you sittin' up here 'bout to go to jail fa nothin'," Mrs. Betty added. "They locked up one o' my boys ten years ago fa stealin' a pack o' bread. My otha boy was shot in the back; they killed him. Said he always kept up trouble. Used to follow Isiaer ev'rywhere he went, trying to help color folks 'round here. I nevuh understood, why they shot my boy, and nevuh did nothin' to Isiaer. He kept up way mo' mess than my boy," Mrs. Betty said, leaning on the tip of her broom handle with her chin rested on her hands.

William lay stretched out on his bunk with his fingers clasped behind his head. While he was listening to Mrs. Betty tell of her pain, he realized that she needed for him to hear what she had to say, as much as he needed her to listen to what he had to say. He watched her old, crippled fingers grip the broom handle tighter and tighter as she spoke more and more of her sons. He imagined the amount of pain the old woman must've been harboring. It made him feel stronger about his own situation. If this old woman could get up every day, and face the world with a good heart, surely he could face whatever fate awaited him. He stood up and walked back over to the cell bars to give Mrs. Betty his complete and undivided attention.

"I thank God every day fa my otha three boys. I'm proud of 'em. They take care of they mama, too. Do anythang fa me. I'm gon' make sure they get up to see Isiaer fa ya, too, son. So lay down and get you some sleep. These white folks always creepin' back in here doin' all kinda God knows what's up in here afta dark. They can get plenty mean when they get some of that devil water in 'em, too. So just lay down, and be quiet. And if you hear anythang, act like you don't. You hear me?" Mrs. Betty asked.

"Oh! Yes, ma'am! I won't say a word. Thanks for helping me, Mrs. Betty."

"Shhh! You just be quiet, and get you some sleep," Mrs. Betty said. She cut off all the lights in the building except for the single one in the hallway.

★★★

Two days passed and William had not heard, nor seen, any sign of Isaiah. He could not afford to believe that he was on his way to prison; the mere thought would shatter the little faith he had remaining. He needed to continue to have faith, and not allow the judge and deputies to know how truly afraid he was of going to prison for ten years. He smiled, and maintained his composure through all of the abuse handed to him.

On Wednesday, the sheriff returned. Sheriff John Hankins, a tall, strong mountain of a man, was known as Big John Hankins to everyone. He stood six feet seven inches tall and rock solid from head to toe. They say he was the biggest man who ever lived in Derma County. He was an ex-football standout from the University of Mississippi Rebels. Sheriff Hankins spoke with a very deep, slow Southern drawl. When he spoke, everybody listened. He was a fair man to whites and coloreds. He tolerated Judge West and his bigoted ways because despite his beliefs, his word stood as solid as concrete. There were several occasions when the sheriff sacrificed his job for the safety of poor whites, and coloreds. He abided by the Jim Crow Laws, to keep Derma County as peaceful as possible. He was adored and respected by everybody in the county, except of course, by Judge West's brother, Dr. George West. They clashed on many different occasions, mostly over the treatment of coloreds. Judge West often settled the disputes by siding with Sheriff Hankins, which brought on more resentment from Dr. West.

Sheriff Hankins walked through the courthouse and made sure everything was in its proper order. He did not recognize the old inmates from the new inmates. He checked the paperwork, and saw that a couple of men were scheduled to be transferred to Parchman State Penitentiary the following week. He passed Isaiah walking toward the courtroom, and held a short conversation with him. Isaiah and Sheriff Hankins had met when both of their mothers worked for Reverend Willingham. They talked briefly about the unusually warm autumn weather. Then the sheriff went on his way and Isaiah headed for the courthouse.

Isaiah received William's distress message the day before, but it was too late in the evening to make it to the courthouse before it closed. Mrs. Betty's oldest son, H.E., rushed over to tell Isaiah. He wanted to join him at the courthouse, but Isaiah kindly asked him not to come along. Isaiah knew that representing William as a group may cause the judge to believe that he was trying to lead the colored folks in a stand against William's arrest. That would've been chaotic for Isaiah and William, because the whites in Derma County would've loved nothing more than to have open season on niggas! H.E. understood and offered his help in any way possible.

Isaiah walked into the courthouse and asked to see William; the deputies refused to let him go into the jail. He had seen the sheriff leave, so he asked to see the judge. He sat patiently, but the judge refused to see him. After an hour or two, Isaiah left and walked around the square for a while. He returned to the courthouse later that day, and asked to see William again, and once again, the deputies refused him. He asked to see the sheriff, but the sheriff was still out on duty. When he asked to see the judge, the deputies warned him that he was in violation of the law, and threatened to lock him up if he did not cease with his public drunkenness. Everybody in Derma County was aware that Isaiah Chambers would never take a swallow of any moonshine, even the deputies, so he knew they were attempting to railroad him into jail. Isaiah apologized for his rudeness, and went home. In order to help William, he would have to fight fire with fire. He gathered some important documents to take to the courthouse the next day.

The next morning he arrived at the courthouse before it opened and quietly waited for Judge West to arrive. He carefully stayed out of sight until all of the deputies were in the building. He knew Judge West would be the last to arrive. Sheriff Hankins always arrived late, and departed late, so he would probably be of no assistance.

Judge West pulled into his reserved parking spot. In that day and age, it was not known as reserved; it simply read, "JUDGE WEST PARKING SPACE." Judge West stepped out of his car wearing his usual all-white attire. White cloth suit, white shirt, white tie, white socks, white shoes, white suspenders, and white straw hat, with an enormous red feather. His white mustache and eyebrows matched the neatly cut white hair on the top of his head. His debilitating arthritis caused him to walk with a cane, and of course, it too, was white. He took his own sweet time, but eventually, he made it out of the car.

As he walked toward the front door, Isaiah met him halfway and tried to strike up a conversation about William. The judge gripped his cane to strike him, but Isaiah protected himself the way he had for most of his life, with a few simple words.

"Now, Judge, if you hit me with that cane, you are going to have to kill me right here. And if you kill me, you don't know who's going to wind up with my Last Will and Testament in their hands. Now do you, suh?" Isaiah smiled, speaking in his old colored tongue.

"I don't know what you talkin' 'bout, boy. What in the name of God you keep comin' 'round here fa? You ain't got nothin' to say to me, and I sure as hell ain't got nothin' to say to you. Stop comin' 'round my jail befo' you wind up bein' a permanent guest. Get on away from 'round here!"

"I think it's time for us to talk, Judge," Isaiah said, holding up a stack of papers.

"What you holdin'?"

"Something I think will make you mighty happy!"

"It ain't nothin' you got gon' make me happy unlessin' you plan on high-tailin' it outta here befo' dark." Judge West laughed.

"Let's put it this way, suh, if you don't talk to me now, you'll talk to me later. I'm sure Reverend Willingham would like to know all about your brother's dark family secret."

"You ol' nigga! I'll cut you from ear to ear if you say anythang about my fam'ly!"

"That's just it, suh, you don't have to cut me, and I don't have to open my mouth. All I want is for you to let William out of jail. He has no business in there, suh, and you know it."

"What I know is that he's gettin' locked up fa ten long years fa bein' a smart ass nigga, and you 'bout to be hung fa the same thang."

"Judge, you know the truth, like I know the truth. We don't have to say any more about it. You know there is only one reason why you and your brother haven't thrown a rope around my neck. You hate me more than you hate any other colored man in Derma County, and with all the lynchings that have happened ever since I can remember, there's no reason why my life is spared. But then there is, isn't it, Judge?"

"I don't know what you talkin' 'bout. This early mornin' sun must be playin' tricks on yo' nigga mind," the judge said. "And I see you can turn that tongue o' yours to talkin' fancy any time you wont to."

A deputy noticed Isaiah talking with the judge and walked up to inquire about the situation. He pulled out his side stick and slapped it into the palm of his hand.

"Is this nigga botherin' you, Judge? You oughtta let me go 'head and get rid of him for you, once and for all."

"Get on 'way from here, you stupid fool; you know I can't stand fa that kind of nonsense!"

"All right, Judge," the deputy said. "But I'll be watchin' you, nigga, and if I see you gettin' outta line I'm gon' give yo' coon ass the whippin' of ya life, ya hear me, boy?"

"I hear you...suh."

The deputy walked off, but continued to watch Isaiah and the judge.

"Let's go into my office. I can't be standin' out here on the street talkin' to no nigga' like this."

Isaiah followed the judge into his office. He had never been farther than the clerk's desk before then. He was amazed at the size of the judge's office. It was huge, with elegant antique furniture. The walls were made of new wood, in the style of old cabins. He wanted to sit and admire the scenery for a while but the judge wanted to get down to business. He put on his robe as an intimidating method as if to convey that their conversation was being spoken under the law.

"Now tell me, boy, what is this so-called family secret you talkin' 'bout?"

"I know the truth about your brother. My mother told me, and I wrote everything she told me in the properties of my Last Will. She told me everything, Judge."

What make you think ya' mama was tellin' the truth?"

"The fact that I'm still alive. The fact that I'm sitting in your office right now talking to you, and you are sending William to jail for sitting in the wrong coach of a train."

"All I have to say is that you a lyin' nigga, and who gon' believe you over me?"

"Nobody will believe me over you. But Reverend Willingham will believe the letter my mother wrote to me, telling me all about your brother."

"Oh, I see. You have to bring him to this, huh? You know one day that old man ain't gon' be around to pratect ya. Then what you gon' do?"

"I'm going to hope and pray that you and your brother are already gone, and if not, that will be the last day I set foot in Derma County." Isaiah smiled.

The judge let out a laugh himself.

"Let's quit with the fam'ly history. What you wont from me?" Judge West asked.

"I want you to let William go, Judge. That's all I want."

"I can't do that, boy. That boy broke the law and he gotta pay fa his crime. We can't have niggas runnin' round here tryin' to pass fa white. That's the worse sin befo' God. You know that!"

"What about if I could pay you for his freedom?"

"What kinda money we talkin'?"

"I can sell a piece of my land, and give you everything I make from it."

"I'll tell you what; we can fuhget the middle man. If you hand me the deeds to all of ya land, you can come pick ol' Willie up first thang in the mornin'."

"I can't give you all my land; what about my family?"

"What about yo' fam'ly?" Judge West laughed.

Isaiah sat back in his chair and contemplated his options. There was no way he was going to let William go to jail, but then, there was no way he could sell his land.

"I have to think about it, sir. Can I at least see him?" Isaiah asked.

"Sure you can. One of the deputies will take you on back in a minute," Judge West said. "One thang though, boy. That reverend betta not find out one word of what we talked about, 'cause if he do, you don't have to worry one bit about ya' brother goin' to prison 'cause I'll puhsonally make sure he never make it!"

"I won't say a word. Can I see William now?"

The judge screamed for the deputy to escort Isaiah back to William. Isaiah walked silently down the hall with no hint of what was awaiting him.

When he got to the back of the jail he found William in a cell balled up in a fetal position. His clothes were ripped to shreds. His light-skinned complexion was purple and black from the bruises. His left eye bulged from his head, shut tight from the massive swelling. There were no shoes on his feet, and the whip marks covered him from his head to his bare feet. It looked as if someone had taken a blade, and sliced his back to the meat. Blood seeped from his wounds, and ran onto his bed.

"Oh my God! How you doing back here, man?" Isaiah whispered.

"They beat me, man! All I wanted to do is go home, and they beat me like this, man! Why?" William tearfully cried. "What did I do? Why would they beat me like I'm some kinda animal, Zay?"

"Shhh! Shhh! Don't talk, man. I'm getting you out of here. Somehow, someway, I'm getting you out of here." Isaiah cried.

Isaiah took William's shirt and wiped off as much blood from his body as he could.

Then he took the shirt he was wearing and put it on William. William was so badly injured Isaiah had to dress him as if he was a child who could not fend for himself. Isaiah hugged William, and told him not to worry. He stood up and marched back into Judge West's office.

"OK!"

"OK what?" Judge West smiled.

"The land is yours; let him out!" Isaiah cried.

"Let me make sure I'm hearin' this right. Are you agreeing to swapping yo' land, fa that nigga back there?"

"Yes...I am."

"Well, I'll be damn! I been tryin' to get that land fa all of these years, and all I had to do was lock up one them niggas you love," Judge West joked.

"Let him out, please, let him out."

"I can't let him out on yo' word; we got to get some paperwork done. Make sure everythang look legal to ol' Willingham. I'll have everythang ready fuhst thang tomorra mornin'. Bring the papers by, and you can take ol' Willie home wit' ya! How that sounds to you?"

"Sounds like justice, sir...Miss'ippi justice."

"Damn right!" Judge West said, lighting a cigar. "Guess our little business here is done, Isiaer. We'll see ya tomorra, OK!"

Isaiah stood there wanting to say more, but no words would pass his lips. Judge West paused when he noticed Isaiah wasn't moving.

"I said we'll see ya tomorra, didn't I?" Judge West repeated.

Isaiah stared another moment or two, then turned around and walked out. He had spent the majority of the day at the courthouse and did not tell Orabell where he was going. He knew she would be worried sick. He also knew that once she was over her sickness, and she knew that he was all right, she would be mad enough to kill him herself. He didn't know which one was worse: him selling the land, or staying out all day and late into the evening without telling her. On his way home he tried to come up with the best possible way to explain to Orabell that he had promised all of their land to Judge West to get William out of jail. He concluded that the best possible way to tell Orabell was to tell the truth, the whole truth, and nothing but the truth; as he recollected.

Isaiah walked up the stairs to his house, and tried to slowly open the door so that Orabell wouldn't wake up. She played 'possum the entire time, watching him sneak into bed. Isaiah turned his back and smiled figuring he would have a good night's sleep before he broke the news to Orabell in the morning. As soon as he lay down and closed his eyes, Orabell whispered, "Where you been, Isaiah?"

"Um, well baby, I had to go to the courthouse and talk to Judge West about a matter," Isaiah said, still lying with his back turned to Orabell.

"What matter?"

"I had to talk to him about some paperwork, that's all."

"What kinda paperwork take all day to talk about?"

"Orabell, I promise, I will tell you everything in the morning," Isaiah said, fluffing his pillow, then closing his eyes again for sleep.

"Naw, Isaiah, you gon' tell me tonight, or you gon' be here by yourself tomorrow," Orabell said as she snatched the blanket off of the bed and walked out of the room. Orabell went into another bedroom, and laid down.

"Oh Lord!" Isaiah said, staggering into the bedroom with Orabell. "You wanna talk? OK, let's talk."

"Talk then!" Orabell shouted from beneath the blanket.

Isaiah stood in the doorway and contemplated if he should get in the bed with Orabell, or remain where he was until he knew for sure she had calmed down.

"Well, here it is, Orabell. I went to see Judge West about William Crowell. I tried to talk him into setting him free."

"What did he say?"

"He said he would, but under one condition," Isaiah frowned, in preparation for the next question.

"And what's the condition, Isaiah?" Orabell snapped quickly.

"I give him all of our land," Isaiah said, then buried his head in his shoulders.

"WHAT?" Orabell screamed. "I know you told him no, didn't ya?"

"No, baby. I told him yes."

"You did what? I know you didn't give everythang we own in this whole wide world to that devil of a man!"

"I had to, that was the only way he would set my brother free, Orabell."

"Isaiah, all we got is that land," Orabell cried.

"I know, sweetheart, but that was all I had to give."

"Now what we gon' do? How we gon' live if we don't use that land for farmin'? Your school teachin' ain't gon' feed both of us."

"I don't know, but the Lord will provide."

"He provided us wit' that land, and now you done gave it all away!" Orabell screamed. "How could you give that land away wit' out talkin' to me."

"Hold on a second now, woman, that's my land!"

"Yo' land? I'm the one out there in them fields while you in that school-house! I'm the one that pull up them crops while you runnin' around tryin' to save everybody! I'm the one that stand over that pot stove cookin' them crops, to fill yo' belly! And I'm the one that spread my legs fa you ev'rytime you in need. Let me tell you somethin', mista, that land is just as much mine, as it is yours!" Orabell screamed loudly.

"Would you lower your voice, woman! Everybody on Church Hill is going to hear you. Now what else could I do, Orabell; would you let your brother go to prison for ten years when you know he doesn't belong there?"

"Why do you keep callin' that man yo' brother?'

"Because he's my brother, Orabell!"

"Stop sayin' that! You just got to help ev'rybody don't you, Isaiah? You willin' to ruin ya' own fam'ly tryin' to help this man, ain't you?"

"Orabell, I'm going to tell you something, and I want you to sit down and listen to what I have to say. Then maybe you'll understand why I have to do what I have to do. You've heard me speak about my mother and father. I told you that my father was murdered, and I found him hanging in the woods. Can you imagine how that made me feel? That man was everything to me. Proud! Strong! He didn't stand for being treated like some kind of animal. I can't help how I am, Orabell; I am my father's son. I love you with all my heart and soul. I know you want us to sit up here on this hill and just live happily until we die. But my father is in me, and I can't get him out. For him, I have to be more than a good nigga who minds his own business. If that's all I am, then my father truly died for nothing. Please understand what I'm trying to tell you, baby. I can't live just sitting up here on this hill, and if I have to die trying to live as a man and not an animal, then let God's will be done."

Orabell walked over to him and put her arms around him. She laid her head on his chest and closed her eyes. There was nothing more she wanted to say about land, helping others, or fighting white people. She only wanted to feel her man, and shield him from his pain. They both stood in each other's arms not wanting to move. The security of their embrace made them want to stay in that moment forever. Isaiah pulled her face away from his chest to continue his conversation.

"Orabell, you know my mother worked on the West Plantation up until Reverend Willingham moved down here, and she started working for him. I guess it's time I tell you everything.

"My father was a farmer and a schoolteacher. He married my mother when they were young. My father went to Pennsylvania to work on the railroad, and that's where he met Reverend Willingham. While my father was working on the railroad, he ran into a white woman named Ms. Annabelle, from Derma County. The two of them would talk from time to time when she rode the train, and they became friends. Reverend Willingham immediately fell in love with Ms. Annabelle, the first day he saw her on the train, but he didn't quite know how to tell her. He noticed my father talking to her, and asked my father for all of the information he had on this Southern belle. The three of them became friends. The Willinghams were so fond of my father they took him in, and he worked for them.

"Reverend Willingham's father had all kinds of money, and offered to pay for my father to go to college but only if he went to college up there. It took my father over twelve years to finish college, but he did it. When he returned to Derma County he had changed, and he could never go back to being that good nigga he was expected to be down here in Mississippi.

"My mother never left Mississippi a day in her life. This life was all she ever knew. When my father returned with his new ideas of how the colored man should be treated, my mother reacted the same way you're acting now. But like my father, Orabell, I know a man is not supposed to live like this. I know this, Orabell! I have lived up North, and colored folks can walk with their heads up, and look at white folks in their eyes without worrying about being beaten."

Isaiah walked over to the window and stared into the dark, dark, night.

"Orabell, you wanna know why these white folks haven't put a rope around my neck yet? Do you?" Isaiah asked, turning towards her. "Well, I'll tell you. Back at the turn of the century, my mother, my sweet mother, bless her soul; My Mother was working for the Reverend, and I believe Reverend Willingham's daughter Mamie was just starting to court Dr. West. At that time he was just troublemaking George West.

"Anyway, my mother was working for Reverend Willingham at the time. But as a favor to the West Plantation, she worked there for one day helping out with some big celebration. Dr. West showed up, and asked my mother to go make his bed. My mother kindly told him that she was not there to do house chores, and if she did not complete her business for the celebration she would be in some serious trouble. Dr. West yelled at her, and made her go upstairs and straighten up the covers on his bed. After my mother finished making his bed, he had her stand there until he finished inspecting her work. He snatched the covers from the bed and screamed for her to do it correctly. After she did it the second time, he inspected it, and snatched the covers from the bed again. When she reached to make the bed for the third time, he slapped her, and threw her on the bed. He had his way with her. My mother had only been with one man in her life, my father. And that bastard did that to her. Nine months later...I was born."

"Are you tellin' me that Dr. West is your daddy?"

"Yes. That's what I'm telling you."

"Aw naw, baby! I'm so sorry! I'm so sorry!"

"That's OK, sweetheart. That means nothing to me. My father was, and always will be, Alexander Chambers. Like you and I, my mother and father didn't have children in their youth. And my father never suspected that I may never be his child, even though I didn't have any of his features. He never knew anything about my mother and Dr. West. If he had found out, he would have killed Dr. West just as sure as I'm standing here talking to you. He wasn't afraid of these white people, and he wasn't afraid to die. I was his son, Orabell, and he loved me as much as any man could love his child. And he loved my mother as much as any man could love his wife. He was our rock, and when they killed him, my mother refused to step back one inch to anybody. She became my rock, and I leaned on that woman up until the day she died. Now, Orabell, it's my turn. It's my turn to be the rock for my family.

"Listen to me, baby. That day Dr. West took my mother, Ms. Ruthie Lee was working at the West Plantation, too. He had his way with her just as he had his way with my mother. William was born two days after I was born. Ms. Ruthie was a lot younger than my mother, and she wasn't married. Dr. West threatened to kill them both if they ever told the truth what happened that day. I think Ms. Ruthie told everybody some rich, white man filled her up, and he was coming back to get her and William some day. As you may figure, he never came back, and Ms. Ruthie never took up with another man. At least nobody we knew about.

"My mother heard Dr. West as he was having his way with Ms. Ruthie, and she kept pressuring Ms. Ruthie to tell her the truth. Eventually they confessed to each other after William and I were both grown. Ms. Ruthie never told William, but my mother explained everything to me. She even gave me a letter to give to Reverend Willingham explaining everything that happened on that day, if the West family ever try to harm me or my family. That's the whole story! That secret is what's keeping me alive."

"Well, why don't you tell Judge West that if he don't let Mr. Crowell out, you will tell ev'rybody about what Dr. West did to yo' mama?"

"If I threaten West by telling him I'll reveal that secret, he will feel like he has nothing to lose in killing me and William. And he probably not stop there."

"I don't understand."

"I know you don't, but think of it this way; I'm alive right now because he's more afraid of the secret than the threat of me telling the secret. And maybe he would let William out if I threaten him with telling his secret, but that's a chance I'm not willing to take. I have to give him the land. I have to save my brother's life. If it was Stanford, wouldn't you expect for me to do the same for him?" Isaiah asked. "Because I would."

Orabell held Isaiah's face in her hands and looked him directly in the eyes and said, "I would expect for you to do exactly what you doin' right now. You go on and do, what you got to do. Whoo! One day, Isaiah. One day our time gon' come. Life ain't gon' be so hard. One day Lord, one day!"

CHAPTER THREE

saiah got an early start the next morning, not knowing what to expect. He arrived at the courthouse early again, to prevent running into any of the deputies. To his surprise, Judge West was already there waiting on him. He walked in the courtroom and went into Judge West's quarters. He knocked on the door, and Judge West gladly told him to come in.

They discussed the terms of their agreement. Isaiah would sign over the deeds to his land, and Judge West would set William free, with no strings attached. The judge could not ethically release William for land, so there were two different sets of paperwork drafted. The first set read that Judge West had bought and paid for the land he received from Isaiah. The second set read that after confidential evidence had been presented, he had reversed the verdict of finding William guilty, and he would be released from the custody of the Derma County Courthouse, effective immediately. They signed the papers, and the deal was done.

Isaiah stepped into William's cell, and he was still lying in the same position he had left him the evening before. He brought William fresh clothes, and shoes. He didn't know if the clothes would fit, but he didn't think William would complain. He turned him on his side, and carefully pulled off the torn clothes he was wearing. It took a few stops and starts to get him fully dressed, but he did. Isaiah reached down, and picked William up in his arms. William was not a small man, much bigger than Isaiah, but Isaiah carried his brother in his arms, as if he was his child—all the way to the automobile. He laid him in the back seat, then rolled him over on his side to allow him to breathe easier.

As he opened the car door to get in, he noticed a shadow behind him. He turned around and it was Dr. West, holding a fishing rod and a small pail of minnows.

"What's goin' on here?" Dr. West asked.

"I'm taking this man home," Isaiah said. "Judge West set him free."

"Oh he did, did he? Well, let me go in here and see. We can't have no escaped convicts runnin' 'round here loose."

"I understand, sir; can I take him home now? He's awfully sick."

"Where you goin'?"

"I'm going up to Mrs. Moore's to meet my wife."

"Get on outta here, but don't go too far. Let me go see what my dear brotha done got himself into now. Run along now," Dr. West said.

Dr. West went into the courthouse, and Isaiah drove to Mrs. Moore's house where he was supposed to meet Orabell. Mrs. Moore's health was failing so Orabell spent a lot of time at her house taking care of her. She refused to leave her home and go live with Orabell and Isaiah. Orabell's brother, Stanford, was little help because he was hardly home. He worked by day, and hung out with older men breaking the law at night. Sheriff Hankins and his deputies had chased Stanford around Derma County many times. Orabell constantly argued with Stanford about his behavior. She knew that he would surely be killed if he did not stop running around getting into so much trouble stealing, and drinking. The white folks of Derma County had little, if any, tolerance for a trouble-making nigga. Stanford was no exception.

When Isaiah pulled up into Mrs. Moore's front yard, every window in her house was opened to suck in a breeze from the unusually hot autumn weather. Stanford was in the kitchen cooking breakfast. The house, from front to back, was filled with smoke and the smell of burnt sausages. Isaiah blew the horn several times, but no one came to the door. He walked around to the back porch and saw Stanford standing over the stove trying to put out a small fire with a rag. Isaiah ran in the house and quickly put the fire out.

"Man, what are you trying to do, burn Mrs. Moore's house down?"

"I was fixing me and Mama some breakfast. Here, you want some?" Stanford said holding up a plate of burnt sausages and eggs.

"No, that's OK. I'd rather eat some of that grass out there."

"What's wrong with my cookin'?"

"That's not cooking, that's poison. What are you trying to do, kill your mother?" Isaiah laughed.

"Mama eat my cookin' ev'ry day, and she don't never complain."

"If she eats this cooking every day, I see why she's sick." Isaiah laughed.

"Come on, try it, Isaiah."

"That's OK. Where's your sister?"

"She ain't here yet. She went to go check on Mama up at A'nt Coreen house, see if she was ready to come back home," Stanford said.

"OK. I need you to come out here and help get my brother out of the car. Come on, let's go."

"Yo' brotha'? You ain't got no brotha."

"Yes, I do, and I need you to help me bring him in the house. He's hurt."

"That's a white man!" Stanford said, looking out of the kitchen window into Isaiah's car.

"Would you shut up! He's not white, and he doesn't know he's my brother yet, so try to just act normal until I can explain it to him. Got it?"

"Yo' secret safe wit' me, but do O'Bell know?"

"Yes, she knows. Now would you be quiet and help me get him out of the car?"

"OK! OK! Let's go!"

They went out to the car, and picked William up by the legs and the arms. Isaiah grabbed the arms, and Stanford grabbed the legs. Stanford asked questions from the moment they grabbed William until they laid him down on Mrs. Moore's couch. Isaiah answered every question the same way: "Mind your own business."

Isaiah cooked Mrs. Moore, William, and Stanford a good breakfast. William was still asleep from his ordeal at the jail, but Isaiah wanted a nice meal waiting for him when he woke up.

It wasn't long before William started to toss and turn. The pain from the bruises he had suffered was beginning to take effect. He started to moan loudly, and Isaiah went to see how badly he was actually feeling.

"How you doing, young man?" Isaiah asked.

"Not too good; I feel like I've been run over by a mule, but I whooped his ass."

"You look like you've been run over by a mule, too." Isaiah laughed.

"Well, we know why I look this way; what's your excuse?"

"We are going to get you better, and get you back up North. You don't know how to handle these white folks down here anymore. You're going to end up dead somewhere."

"You ain't lying; get me out of here as soon as possible."

"Hungry?" Isaiah asked.

"Hungry as that mule that ran me over. What you got?"

"Doesn't matter. You gotta eat whatever I got, so don't worry about it."

"Boy, if I hadn't just whooped that mule's ass, I'd put something on you right about now with all your smart talking. You must have forgotten who I am."

"Oh, I remember exactly who you are. You've always been the biggest, and I've always been the toughest," Isaiah said, passing William's plate of food to him.

"Tough! Man, you too red to be tough!"

"I know you're not calling me red, when you're about two shades brighter than daylight." Isaiah laughed.

Stanford was in the next room listening to the two men joke around. He had never heard, nor seen, Isaiah behave so childishly. As a matter of fact, he had never heard Isaiah laugh out loud since he knew of him. The laughter was cut short when William felt periods of sharp pain to his abdomen.

"Hey, man! You OK?" Isaiah asked.

"I'm fine." William grunted.

"Maybe I should just let you get some rest."

"I'm fine! I'm fine! It's probably just my stomach breaking wind because of those stale eggs you made me eat," William said.

"Give me my eggs back," Isaiah said, snatching the plate out of William's hand.

"Boy, you better pass those eggs back over here, before I have to get up off this couch."

Orabell walked through the front door with a scarf around her hair, an apron around her waist, and a basket full of corn. She stopped in her tracks when she saw William lying on the couch, covered with severe bruises. Isaiah told her that William had been beaten, but she had no idea that he was in such condition. She tried to overlook his injuries and pretend that she didn't notice them.

"Good morning, Mr. Crowell, good to see ya," Orabell said.

"Call me William, Orabell. You're a grown woman now."

William had been Orabell's schoolteacher before he moved away. She was a teenager at the time, and she had to respectfully call her elders Mister, Miss, or Mrs., especially her schoolteacher. She was so used to calling William, Mr. Crowell, her first reaction when she saw him was to address him in the same manner.

"How are you feeling then, William?" Orabell mumbled.

"I'm fine," William said. "Let me stop lying; you can look at me and tell that I'm not fine. I'm doing as well as to be expected. How you doing?"

"I'll do. I guess," Orabell said. "I'll get on outta here and let you and Isaiah catch up on old times."

"I'll see ya." William waved.

"Isaiah, can I speak to you for a minute in the kitchen?" Orabell said.

"Sure," Isaiah said, walking into the kitchen.

"Oh-Oh! Somebody in trouble!" William joked.

"Shut-up!" Isaiah said out of the corner of his mouth.

Isaiah followed Orabell into the kitchen to hear what she had to say.

"Where's your mother?" Isaiah whispered.

"She still up at Aunt Coreen house. My cousin Sarah spoil her every time she go up there." Orabell smiled, then frowned. "Don't change the subject. Now I know you gon' tell that man about his mama and Dr. West, ain't you?"

"I hadn't planned on telling him today, no," Isaiah whispered.

"He know we in here talking 'bout him, and he pro'bly thinkin' we sayin' somethin' bad. When you go back out there, Isaiah, you have to tell that man the truth."

"I'm going to tell him the truth before he leaves. Right now he needs to get a little stronger."

"You always tryin' to protect somebody. You know what? I'll tell him myself!" Orabell said, then walked out of the kitchen.

"Orabell, don't you go in there running your mouth," Isaiah whispered, following behind her. "Dangit, woman, I swear!"

"William, I don't know what you and my husban' have been talkin' 'bout, but he needs to tell you somethin', and needs to tell you somethin' now!" Orabell said, folding her arms.

William looked at Isaiah and said, "What is it?"

"Man, this woman is crazy. I don't know what she's talking about. When she gets like this, it's best to just let her talk her way through it. If you interrupt her, it will only cause more problems."

"William, I'm gon' let Isaiah tell you what he needs to tell you after I'm finished. Hold on one second," Orabell said.

Orabell yelled for Stanford to come listen to their conversation. He walked in and sat on the floor.

"Now you all are the men of this family. And what you see, is what you get...and that's us. Mama too old to be the woman of this family so I'm the only woman, and I'm all you got. Now we got to do betta than what we doin'. Isaiah, if anybody on this earth know you a saint, it's me. I know you will give the shirt off yo' back, and the shoes off yo' feet to anybody who need 'em: colored or white, that don't matter to you. A heart like that can only be from God. But God also gave you a fam'ly to head, and sometime you gotta use that head on yo' shoulders, instead of ya heart. It's just as bad for you to neglect ya fam'ly, as it is to neglect a stranger. Yo' family should always come first.

"Stanford, now you just plain cuttin' up! Mama and Daddy didn't raise you like this. You gon' end up dead if you don't start actin' like you got some sense. The first thang you gon' do is go back to school. A colored man with no education ain't gotta chance," Orabell said.

"I don't need to go back to no school, O'Bell," Stanford said.

"Well, you goin' anyway!" Orabell said.

Isaiah leaned over to Stanford and whispered, "Now Stanford, you know you're not going to win this man. Best thing to do is just let her talk her way through it; now you know that."

"Won't say anotha word; the soona she let us outta here, the betta," Stanford whispered back.

"Thank ya, little brother, I have a feeling it will be later than sooner. Listen and smile man, listen and smile."

"AMEN!" Stanford laughed.

"What y'all two over there whisperin' about?" Orabell snapped.

"Nothing," Isaiah answered.

"Nothin'," Stanford agreed. "We ain't talkin' 'bout nothin'."

"Well, that's all I gotta say anyway. William, I'm gon' let Isaiah tell you what he need to tell you," Orabell said, sitting down and folding her arms.

"Orabell, maybe we need to wait until William is feeling a little better before he hears this."

"No, Isaiah! What is Orabell talking about?" William asked.

William positioned his aching body in an upright position to prepare for the news he was about to hear.

"OK, here it is. You know that your mother was raped by a white man, and that's how she became pregnant with you, right?

"Of course, yeah! Yeah! Why?"

Isaiah took a deep breath and sighed.

"Well, my mother was raped by that same white man, and she too became pregnant, with me! I guess that explains why we're so fair-skinned. But you, you're just a shade away from being white," Isaiah joked.

Their usual way of ignoring their emotions with laughs and jokes did not work this time. This time William didn't laugh. Instead he looked at Isaiah and Orabell and said nothing.

"Whoa! That's a lot to soak in; where did you get this from?" William asked.

"My mother told me shortly before she died. It killed me inside to know a man put his nasty claws all over my beautiful mother. And to find out the man I love and respected all of my life was not my natural born father. I asked her why she waited so long to tell me the truth, and then I asked why she chose to tell me in the first place."

"What did she say?" William asked.

"She said that if she had all of those answers I would be praying to her at night, and not God. She said things like that can only be explained with time, and not words. I left it at that."

"Too bad we don't know who that disgraceful bastard is," William said.

"How come we don't?"

"You know who it is?" William asked.

"Do you remember Judge West's brother, George?"

"Who don't remember that fool." William laughed.

William suddenly realized that Isaiah was telling him that their father was Dr. George West.

"No! No, man! Don't tell me...no, no, no, no, no, no, no, no! Tell me it's not him."

"Yup. It's him."

"That son of a bitch!" William shouted.

"Hey! Hey! Calm down," Isaiah said.

"I can't believe! I can't believe I have that bastard's blood in me, Zay!" William gasped for air, and he began to lose his breath.

"William, calm down, man. We can talk about it when you're a little stronger."

"No! I want to talk about it now!" William's pain turned unbearable, and he grimaced in severe pain.

"You're only causing yourself more pain, William! Now lay your mule-headed butt down and get some rest!"

William turned away from them and stared out of the window. He quickly fell asleep and Orabell tended to his wounds. After he had a short nap he woke calm and ready to talk. He positioned himself toward Isaiah and began to speak.

"Well, what do we do now, brother?" William asked.

"I guess we act like a family, and start taking better care of each other."

"You ever thought about moving up North?"

"Up North, for what?" Isaiah asked.

"To live, Isaiah. Why don't you move up North to live? Things are a lot of different jobs for an educated colored man up there. You can do good for yourself."

"I don't think so. I'm a Mississippi boy, and Mississippi is where I belong."

"I'm a Mississippi boy, too. I love Mississippi, Zay. But Mississippi don't love me back. And it don't love you either," William said.

"Up North can only change so much. My skin will still be colored. I lived up North, and I know that life is considerably better for a colored man, but a colored man is still a colored no matter where he goes."

"You're right. Your skin will still be colored, but your life don't have to be. When I get home from work, Zay, there are no crosses burnin' in my yard. My name is William, and not nigga. I'm not persecuted for having an education. God didn't mean for man to live like that."

"This is home. This is where I was born. This is where I live..." Isaiah said.

"And this is where you will die," William interrupted. "Because if you stay down here, they are surely going to kill you dead. You have all that land. Sell it! Get the money and move up to Michigan with me. With all that money you can live like a king. Hell, man, we'll call you king of the niggas."

"I'm OK being a plain ol' country boy."

"He couldn't do it if he wonted to, William," Orabell said sarcastically, referring to Isaiah having sold his land to get William out of jail.

"Why not?" William asked.

"Do you ever shut your mouth, woman?" Isaiah asked.

"Remember, Isaiah, no more secrets. Tell the man," Orabell said

"Tell me what? Oh Lord, don't tell me you have another secret?" William asked.

"Just one more, William. Tell him, Zay," Orabell said to Isaiah, mocking the way William referred to him.

"I don't own that land anymore. I had to use the deeds to keep you from going to prison," Isaiah said.

"What? You did what?" William asked.

"That was the only way Judge West would let you out of jail, so I did what I had to do."

"Damn! That's everything you have. Zay!" William shouted.

Stanford stood up and said, "This sound like grown folks' stuff to me. I'm 'bout to finish eatin'."

"Go 'head," Orabell said.

Orabell looked at William and she could see the anguish on his face.

"Don't you let this get to you. You are family, and we know you woulda done the same thang for Isaiah."

She patted him on the back, and took Isaiah by the hand. They walked out on the porch to give William some time to himself.

"You know what, Isaiah? You was right about one thang. I am too young to have such an old soul. I'm only twenty-two years old, and I feel like I'm fifty. You fourteen years older than me, and I act like your mother. I feel like I'm too old to even have babies."

"You were just born with a nurturing heart. You want to take care of everybody, and I want to take care of every problem. It's impossible for either one of us to do what we want, so let's just do what we can. And how many times do I have to tell you that there's nothing wrong with you, there's nothing wrong with me, and there's nothing wrong with us. One day we're going to have so many kids you're going to want to give a couple of 'em back," Isaiah said.

"This been a long day. You got William out of jail, and he's holding up pretty good. You told him y'all were brothers. I think this turnin' out to be a pretty good day after all." Orabell smiled.

"Oh Lord, here y'all go. Can y'all go home if y'all gon be doin' all that?" Stanford asked, squeezing between them.

"Be quiet, boy!" Orabell said.

CHAPTER FOUR

"Who's that comin' up the road?" Stanford asked, putting his hands above his eyes to shield the sun.

"I don't know...looks like the sheriff," Isaiah mumbled.

They watched the car as it turned into Mrs. Moore's yard. It came down the driveway and pulled up to the stairs leading to the house, and stopped.

Out stepped Sheriff John Hankins. Everybody called him Big John. He stood at the side of the car and spoke from there.

"How do, Isaiah?" John said.

"How's it going there, John?" Isaiah replied.

"I got a little problum but I think you might be able to help."

"Well, I'll do what I can; what seems to be the problem?"

"This morning a convict escaped from jail, and word is, you know where he is."

"No, I can't help you, John. I don't know anything about an escaped convict."

"Well, do you have company here?" John asked bluntly.

"Yes, I do."

The sheriff went into his holster and pulled out his gun.

"Isaiah, I think you need to send him out here so I can take him in."

"What are you talking about, John? Why are you pulling out that gun?"

"You know I ain't got no problem wit' you, Isaiah. I just need to take ya brotha in befo' my deputies try to come out here wit' ol West and get ya whole fam'ly."

"There must be some kind of misunderstanding. I made an agreement with Judge West this morning, and he set William free."

"That's between you and the Judge, Isaiah. You and Judge West can get that straightened out later on. Right now, I gotta take him in. Now, how you wanna do this? You gon' send him out, or am I gon' have to go in there and get him. I tell you now, if I have to go in there and get him, I reckon I'm gon' be a little pissed off."

"OK, let's go down to the courthouse. We can get Judge West to straighten this out for us."

"Not today we can't. He gon' fishin'. He'll back in about a week or so. Isaiah, I been knowin' you pretty much all of my life. Don't make me do this. I just want whoever you got in the house to come out, and we can get this straightened out when Judge West get back."

"All right, when will the judge be back?" Isaiah asked.

"Next Tuesday."

"He's scheduled to go to Parchman on Monday. I'm sorry, John, but if you want my brother, you have to go through me."

"Yo' brotha?" John said surprised. "I didn't even know you had a brother."

"If you want my brother, John, you have to go through me first."

"Isaiah you know I'm not gon' do nothing' to you," John said. "O'bell, do somethin' with yo' stubbun husban' befo' he go and get himself hurt. I 'clare some time, Isaiah, you got the hardest head in the world."

"You know how stubbun that man is when he think he right, Mr. John," Orabell said.

William heard the men arguing, and stumbled his way to the door. He wanted to give himself up before Isaiah got himself hurt. "Now ain't that sweet; are you two gentlemen arguing over me?" William asked, leaning on the side of the house.

"Get back in the house, William!" Isaiah shouted.

"Wait a minute. What in the world is goin' on? Ain't that William Crowell?" John asked, putting his pistol back into his holster.

"Yeah, John, it's me! Don't tell me you the sheriff?"

"I been sheriffin' for near 'bout six years now," John said. "Don't tell me you my escaped convict."

"In the flesh." William laughed.

"Speaking of flesh, what happened to you? What kind of mean raccoon you run up on?"

"These are welcome home bruises, courtesy of the Derma County Sheriff Department."

"Who did that to you?"

"Your deputies," Isaiah said.

"I just got back from Jackson, and I don't know a hoot 'bout all this. Now do one of y'all wanna tell me what this is all about?" John asked.

"Isaiah, talk to him. I'm about to prop myself up against this wall until it's time for me to go back to jail," William joked.

"William was arrested for riding in the front coach of the train. Because he has that white skin, and those green eyes, the conductor thought he was trying to pass for a white man. Judge West tried and sentenced him to ten years in Parchman.

"This morning I swapped my land for William's freedom. We have everything signed legally. I have William's release papers in my automobile. I can't understand what this is all about."

"I'm gon' tell you somethin'. Me and Judge West done had our scraps, but there's one thang I can say about the man. If he gave his word, he meant it. If he plan on gettin' ya, he gon' get ya straight to ya face so you know it's him," John said.

"I'm a witness to that, John!" William said.

"Well, if that's the truth, and Judge West is a man of his word, why are you here?" Isaiah asked.

"The clerk gave me a warrant to pick up an escaped convict, William Crowell. Hell, I didn't know it was *William!* It's somethin' to this, and I'm gon' get to the bottom of it. The judge may be a lot of the things, but he ain't no Welsh. Sorry, but I'm still gon' have to take you in, William, until I find out what's goin' on. Isaiah, fetch me them papers the judge gave you."

Isaiah reached in his auto and pulled out the paperwork the judge had given him earlier in the day. John took the papers and read them.

"Yup, you right. Says here William was set loose this morning by Judge West. I betta get this taken care of, so the clerk won't be issuin' no more

warrants out for ya. One thang though, what's the big idea of you two claimin'
to be brothas?" John asked.

"It's a long story, John," Isaiah said

"I woulda known who William was if y'all hadna' said y'all was brothas.
Pro'bly wouldn't be goin' through all this now. And fa you, William, you ain't
up North no more! You betta be careful down here; ain't nothin' changed."

"You dam' right about that!" William said, limping down the stairs to the
police automobile.

Suddenly another automobile came zooming down the road. It made a
sharp turn into Mrs. Moore's yard, almost hitting a tree, then came to a
screeching halt. Dr. West pounced from his automobile ranting to John. "I
see you caught our escaped nigga, sheriff. And once again the great nigga,
Isaiah Chambers, is in the middle of a big ol' mess. Now you harborin'
fugitives, huh, nigga?"

"With all due respect, Dr. West, everythang is unda' control. Crowell done
gave hisself up, and I'm 'bout to take him back to the courthouse," John said.

"What about that nigga right there? What you gon' do wit' him?" Dr.
West said, pointing to Isaiah.

"Nothin'. He ain't broke no laws, no laws I know of anyhow," John said.

"You betta lock that nigga up wit' that otha nigga!" Dr. West screamed.

"What I betta do, is my job. And I'm havin' a hard time doin' it with you
hoopin' and hollerin' like that."

"If you won't do yo' job, then I'll do it fa ya!"

Dr. West rushed over to the sheriff and grabbed him in his collar

"You betta take both of these niggas, and lock 'em up! You hear me?" Dr.
West yelled.

"If you don't get yo' hands off me, I'm gon' hit you upside yo' head so
hard, yo' gon' fuhget yo' own mama's name!" John shouted.

"If you gentlemen are going to be presenting such entertainment, can I
get a good seat in the car and rest?" William joked.

John knocked Dr. West's arms down from his shirt. Dr. West then picked
up a stick laying on the ground, and hit William with all the power he
possessed. William slumped over and fell to the ground.

Isaiah ran to his automobile and pulled a small handgun from under the seat. He rushed towards Dr. West. John quickly snatched his pistol from his holster and yelled for him to stop.

"Now Isaiah, don't make me pull this trigger. You cool down. This is gettin' way outta control. Dr. West, I'm takin' William in, and that's it. Now let's get on outta here and leave these people be," John said.

William rolled over, and sat up—dazed, but coherent and bleeding profusely from the side of the head.

Orabell ran in the house to find a clean washrag for William's head. She ran past Dr. West on her way to William, and he snatched her by the arms.

"Leave that nigga be, heffa! Let him suffer!" Dr. West yelled

"Get yo' hands off me!" Orabell cried.

When Isaiah saw Dr. West grab his wife, it reminded him that this was the man who raped his mother. He exploded with all of the anger and frustration he had been resisting since his mother first told him.

"Mista! If you don't take your paws off of my wife, I'll kill you with my bare hands!" Isaiah yelled.

None of them had ever heard Isaiah raise his voice. Every one of them, even Dr. West, looked in amazement.

"Hey, Zay, who woulda thought our daddy still had a little punch left in him after all these years. Didn't think he had any more bullets left after us. After all, we were the only two colored babies he had. Two bullets, two bastards!" William murmured.

"What you say? What you say, nigga?" Dr. West shouted.

Dr. West pulled out a small revolver handgun from his pants pocket and shouted, "I'll blow yo' dam' brains out, nigga!"

"You wouldn't shoot ya own son nah, would you, pappy?" William said sarcastically.

Dr. West was about to fire at William, but the sheriff aimed his pistol at him and yelled for him to drop his gun.

"Somebody betta tell me what the hell is goin' on, and ya betta tell me right now!" John said, aiming his gun back and forth between Dr. West and Isaiah.

There was a quiet standoff for a second or two. John's gun was pointed at Isaiah, Isaiah's gun was pointed at Dr. West, and Dr. West's gun was pointed at William.

"I'm about to get some law and order around here or else I'm kickin' some ass. And I don't care what color ass it is, white or colored. Now put them guns down now!" John shouted.

John walked up to Isaiah and snatched the gun out of his hand. Dr. West withdrew his gun and put it back in his pocket. John walked over to help William into the car, and Dr. West went for his gun again. He pulled it out, and pointed at William. He asked John to step away

"Now Dr. West, take it easy. We know you plenty mad 'bout what these boys here done said. But don't go gettin' ya'self in no trouble," John said, reaching for Dr. West's gun.

Dr. West fired the gun, shooting John in the hand. John let out a scream and grabbed his hand tightly to try to stop the bleeding, and the pain.

"You crazy son of a bitch, you shot me!" John yelled.

"I tried to tell you to take both of these niggas in. This is the last day I ever have to worry 'bout these half-breed niggas!" Dr. West said.

Isaiah jumped between Dr. West and William.

"If you want to shoot somebody, Dr. West, shoot me. You've already raped my mother, killed my father, now kill me, too! Leave the rest of my family out of this."

"Why you piece of shit!" John screamed at Dr. West.

"Isaiah, please! Run, baby, run! Please! Baby, run!" Orabell screamed.

"Why don't you tell John why you hate us so much, George? Huh? Why don't you tell the sheriff how you raped our mothers, George!" Isaiah said, walking towards Dr. West.

"Isaiah, back up! That ol' fool will shoot!" John shouted.

"Zay, you don't have to do this, man, you have a family! Run, man, run!" William shouted.

Isaiah continued to walk towards Dr. West, yelling louder with every step.

"Tell him, George. Tell him how you hung my father from a tree. Tell him you're a low-down, belly-crawling snake in the grass!" Isaiah screamed.

"Isaiah! Isaiah!" Orabell screamed at the top of her lungs.

"Zay! Zay! Stop fool!" William yelled.

"For God sake, Isaiah, stop!" John yelled.

Dr. West smiled and pointed his gun in the center of Isaiah's chest. "I shoulda killed yo' black ass, yo' very first day on this earth. Tell the devil I said betta late than never."

POW!!!

No one moved as his body seemed to fall to the ground in slow motion.

"Oh God! What have you done?" Orabell screamed hysterically.

"Lord Jesus!" John sighed.

"Oh God! Oh God!" William cried.

They all stared at the porch as Stanford lay on his back with a smoking shotgun in his hands. His eyelids did not blink, and his body did not move, as he lay in shock. Orabell walked over and pulled the shotgun from his hands and threw it to the side. She held Stanford in her arms and rocked back and forth. He lay there in a catatonic state not responding to Orabell.

There he was, lying face down on the ground. John tore off the tail of his shirt, and wrapped it around his wounded hand. He turned the body over, and checked to see if it was indeed dead. It was still alive.

"Is everybody else OK?" John hollered.

"We're fine," Isaiah whispered.

"What we gon' do, Mr. John?" Orabell shouted.

"Calm down, I'll think of somethin'. Dr. West is in bad shape," John said.

"We have to get him some help!" Isaiah said.

"From where? He the doctor!" Orabell cried.

"We have to try to get this man some help!" Isaiah cried.

"We in a world of trouble... Ain't we, sheriff?" Orabell shouted.

"Orabell, please, calm down. Let me think!" John snapped.

"We ain't mean to hurt nobody. That man tried to kill us! You seen it! That man tried to kill us!" Orabell shouted.

"Orabell, stop all that yellin'. I can't think with you screamin' at me like that!" John screamed back.

Stanford stood up and held on to Orabell's dress. He kept asking if he had shot Dr. West, and Orabell consoled him by saying everything would be all right.

"Looka here, Isaiah, if I take that boy in, they gon' kill him just as sure as we standin' here. And they gon' kill y'all, too. The only way outta this is to take Dr. West somewhere and bury him where he can never be found, and y'all get outta Derma County today! Best thang to do is drop him off somewhere between here and Memphis," John said.

"But John, he ain't dead!" Isaiah shouted.

The sheriff drew his pistol and pointed at the top of Dr. West's head, and pulled the trigger. *POW!* The gun sounded loudly.

"He dead now. And if you want to keep yo' family alive, you betta hightail it on outta here befo' somebody find out what happened," John said.

"How can you shoot him like that, John?" Isaiah asked.

"I got my reasons. Would you rather we try to get him some help, and you end up with yo' whole fam'ly dead?" John asked

"Good shot!" Isaiah answered.

"That's what I figured you'd say."

"Y'all think somebody heard anythang?" Orabell cried.

"O'Bell, you out here in the middle of nowhere; ain't nobody within miles of here," John said. "I'm sure nobody heard."

"William, are you OK to move?" Isaiah asked.

"You don't think I'm going to stay here and let these white folks lynch me, do you?" William mumbled through the side of his mouth

"Now if I get y'all outta here safe, I betta not ever see y'all faces 'round here again, you hear me?" John asked.

"You won't, Mr. John!" Orabell cried.

"Orabell, go home and pack as little clothes as possible. We can get some more once we get to Michigan," Isaiah said. "Looks like you're about to have some company, brother."

"Just like you colored folks. I find out you family one day, and you movin' in the next," William said.

"What we gon' do 'bout Mama, Isaiah?" Orabell asked.

"On our way to Memphis we'll stop in at your Aunt Coreen's and tell your mother what happened," Isaiah said. "Do you think your cousin Sarah would be willing to come stay with your mother until we can come back and get her?"

"Sarah love Mama; she'll be more than happy to come stay wit' her," Orabell said.

"I have to find away to get my auto up there," Isaiah said.

"Don't worry about that auto. I always wonted a fancy car like that; it's mine now. I'll send ya payment for it." John smiled. "Isaiah, you and the boy take West somewhere and bury him where he can't ever be found. Drive his automobile up to Memphis, and leave it near the train station. Don't worry about what's gon' happen to it. I spent some time in Memphis and if you leave anythang near that train station for more than five minutes it won't be there when you get back. I'll give you directions from Derma County into Memphis.

"Orabell, you and William meet me at the train station at seven-thirty. The train get there between eight and eight-thirty every evenin' comin' from New Orle'ns. It's a late train that mostly colored folks ride, so you should be just fine. Those clothes William wearin' got blood all on 'em. You might need to get him some clothes that won't draw no attention to him.

"Isaiah, that same train pass through Memphis at about midnight, so be at the station. Orabell will have ya tickets beginnin' in Memphis and it will take y'all all the way to Detroit."

"How much are four tickets?" Isaiah asked. "I am going to have to leave Sarah some money so that she and Mrs. Moore can make their way for a while, too."

"Don't worry 'bout no money for no tickets; I can take care of that. You just drop that auto off, and be at that station to jump on the train wit' ya wife." John smiled.

"I got some spots out in them woods where I used to hide from the law." Stanford glanced at John, forgetting that John was the law he used to hide from. "I'm sorry, Mr. John. Anyway I got some spots; ain't nobody gon' find him."

"We burnin' daylight standin' 'round here talkin'; y'all get movin'," John said.

Orabell and Stanford helped William into Isaiah's automobile. Isaiah touched John on his shoulder to catch his attention. He did not want the others to hear what he had to say

"One more thing. John. I've been knowing you just about all of my life, and we've been good friends. Not the usual way whites are friends with coloreds. We've just been friends. But you are still white, and we are still colored, and even though we've been friends, I can't understand why you would put your own life in jeopardy to save ours?"

"When West pulled that trigga he didn't care if I was white when he shot me, and he didn't care if you was colored when he was about to shoot you. But even after the man wonted to kill you, ya still wonted to help him. That ain't got nothin' to do with color; that's right and wrong. I gotta to do what's right. There was some terrible thangs that went on up at that West Plantation. I just realized how much the law let them get away with doin' all them thangs to those women when you and William was talkin'.

"That boy did the world a favor. And I ain't gon' miss a drop of sleep over that waste of satan sperm. We talkin' too much. Get on outta here," John said.

"God bless you, John," Isaiah said.

"God bless you, too, nah get!" John said, shooing Isaiah off.

★★★

Isaiah and Stanford took off and drove the body deep into the woods and buried it. Isaiah looked at all the tall thin trees, and remembered the last time he was in those woods. He and John were cutting his father's body down from a tree. As they covered the fresh grave with leaves, Isaiah mumbled words under his breath so that Stanford couldn't hear.

"It's funny how God take care of his bad business, ain't it, Dr. West?" Isaiah said, implying that Dr. West had his father lynched in those woods because of hatred, and now that same hatred had caused him to forever rest in those same woods, in an unmarked grave.

"Take your hat off, Stanford. Let's pay our respects to the dead," Isaiah said.

"That no account man don't deserve no respect!"

"Shut up, and bow your head."

"Can we hurry it up; it's gettin' dark out here. As evil as ol' West was the devil might come get him right in front o' us!" Stanford cried, inching closer to Isaiah.

"Would you get off of my foot, Stanford? You have to be the scariest crook I have ever seen in my life."

"Well, can you please hurry it up?" Stanford whispered.

"Didn't you used to hide from the law in these woods?"

"Yeah!" Stanford whispered. "But it hadn't no dead bodies around neither!"

"Bow your head," Isaiah said, clearing his throat. "Rest in peace, Dr. West, and may God have mercy on your soul."

The leaves started to rustle around Dr. West's grave from the crisp autumn breeze. The movement of the leaves startled Stanford, and made him very nervous.

"Do you hear that, Isaiah?" Stanford asked.

"I don't hear anything. Grab your spade, and let's go."

"I think it's something out here with us!" Stanford whispered.

"It's nothing out here but a big chicken; now grab your spade and let's go," Isaiah said, pointing to the spade.

When Stanford reached for the spade, he stepped on a dry stack of leaves which made a crinkling sound, as if someone had walked up behind him.

"OH LORD, Isaiah!" Stanford screamed. "HERE THEY COME!"

He dropped the spade, and ran wildly toward the automobile.

"Get back here, boy!" Isaiah yelled. "Get back here!"

"I ain't comin' back over there!" Stanford yelled back without slowing down, or turning around.

Isaiah picked up both of the spades, and headed for the automobile. While he was walking he heard an owl hoot, and stopped in his tracks.

"Anybody there?" Isaiah whispered.

He turned his head from side to side and saw nothing.

"I've let that boy get to me," Isaiah said, shaking his head.

He took another step and landed on a stack of dried leaves, and he, too, thought someone had crept up behind him.

"Now I'm not going to run from you; I'm going to get on out of your woods, and you have a good night," Isaiah said, walking slowly.

At that moment, an owl let out a loud shriek that echoed over Isaiah's head. It caught him off guard and spooked him.

"I guess I'm not moving fast enough for you, so I'll pick up the pace a little," Isaiah said, running at full speed.

He threw the spades in the backseat, and tried to crank the auto. He had never driven the type of auto Dr. West owned, so he had difficulty. It finally cranked and the two of them sped away. Stanford covered his face with his hat until they were far away from the woods. They disassembled the gun and left bits and pieces along the dark roads.

The drive to Memphis went with no problems. They stopped in Calhoun City and told Sarah what had happened. Isaiah asked her not to mention that Dr. West had been killed by Stanford. He didn't want to cause Mrs. Moore any more grief. Sarah told Mrs. Moore that there were white people chasing Isaiah and he had to leave for Michigan immediately to save his life. Mrs. Moore was heartbroken she didn't get the opportunity to tell her children good-bye, but she figured that it was better for them to be alive and escape, than to risk a suitable farewell.

When Isaiah and Stanford finally arrived in Memphis, they parked the auto a couple of blocks away from the train station as John instructed, then waited for Orabell and William to arrive.

★★★

Orabell scurried to pack a suitcase of clothes, then she and William drove to the train station. John was at the ticket window waiting for them. He handed Orabell four tickets: two originating in Grenada, and two originating in Memphis. All four tickets were bound for Detroit.

Orabell had never ridden the train before, and William was still recovering from his beating. Orabell was nervous that she may get them lost or they would miss their layover in Memphis. John quickly explained to Orabell the cities where they would be making their stops and changes. They would not have to switch trains because the train was from New Orleans to Detroit. The route read from Grenada, Miss. to Memphis, Tenn.; Memphis to Nashville, Tenn.; Nashville to Cincinnati, Ohio; and Cincinnati to Detroit.

Orabell was wary about handling the tickets. She could read and write basic words, but she was not very literate. She asked what if she couldn't read the names of the cities on the tickets. John told her the solution to that problem was to never get off. William heard them talking, and he joked that he was sore, not blind.

Before they boarded, John gave Orabell an envelope with Isaiah's name on it. Inside, it contained several unknown items, and Orabell didn't bother to look. She slipped it into her pocketbook and forgot all about it. John hugged her good-bye, and shook William's hand. Orabell could not believe that a white man was hugging her, and hugging her because he truly cared for her.

She kissed John on his cheek and said, "God made you special, Mr. John."

"Get on that train, young lady, and don't look back."

They waved their goodbyes for the last time, and the train pulled out of the station.

★★★

The train arrived in Memphis ahead of schedule. When they pulled up to the station, Orabell was frightened by all of the people and the bright lights. She knew she had to get off the train to find Isaiah and Stanford, but she was quite hesitant. She had their tickets and somehow she had to muster the courage to look for them. William volunteered to find them but he was in no condition to walk.

As soon as she stepped off the train, there they were, sitting on a Colored-Only bench. Orabell ran to them and hugged them tightly. She gave them their tickets and they boarded the train safely. The train was filled with only colored folks, from front to rear. The conductor allowed some coloreds to sit in the whites-only coach until they arrived in Nashville. William told them that no matter what the conductor said, they all were going to sit in a rear coach until they passed the Mason-Dixon Line.

At William's request, they all took their seats in the very last rear coach. Before long, they all fell asleep—afraid, yet comforted that maybe their nightmare may soon end.

When they arrived in Nashville, the coloreds who were seated in the whites-only coaches had to get up and give their seats to the white boarders. Some coloreds had to give up their seats even though it was a colored-only coach, in order to make room for the white passengers. Some colored passengers had to get off, and wait for the next available train to arrive. They went coach by coach, selecting single colored men and women to exit the train. Fortunately for Orabell and her men, they never made it to the last coach. Sometimes, riding in the rear had its advantages.

CHAPTER FIVE

DETROIT, MICHIGAN 1937

It took them two days to get to Detroit, and when they arrived, they were exhausted and hungry. William had arranged for someone to meet them at the train depot to pick them up.

When they stepped off the train there was a beautiful woman standing with her car door wide open. One leg was in the car, and the other planted firmly on the ground. The way her legs were spread so far apart, caused her tight-fitting dress to rise, and it revealed plenty of skin. She stood there, and smiled as if she didn't care who was watching. She wore a waistlong coat, with fur around the neck and wrists. She had on a hat with a pink flower in the band. Her lipstick was red and thick, and it traced along the outer edges of her lips. She had on shoes with heels two or three inches high. Her fingernails had polish that matched the color of her lipstick. She had a long thin stick in her hand with a cigarette at the end. She was high yellow, just like William. Her body was thin, but very shapely. Her face was delicately sculptured, beautiful to say the least. But her beauty did not reflect her youth. She closed her car door and ran toward William. She jumped in his arms and dangled her legs back and forth, as William picked her up by the waist.

"Hey, baby! I'm so glad you're back," the lady shouted.

"Whoa! You are going to kill me. I had an accident while I was down there and I'm still a little sore," William said.

"What happened to your head, baby? Where did that scar come from?" the lady asked.

"I'll explain later. Right now I want you to meet my family."

"You never told me about anybody but your mother." The lady smiled. "How you all doing?"

They all returned the lady's courtesy and waited to be formally introduced.

"Well, this is my brother Isaiah. And this is his wife, Orabell, and that's her brother Stanford." William pointed. "And this here is my girl, Red."

"Orabell. What kind of name is that? Did your mother name you that?" Red asked.

"Yes, she did. But if you don't mind me askin', did your mother name you Red?" Orabell answered looking at Red from head to toe. She had never seen a colored woman dressed so elegantly. Then she looked at herself wearing the clothes her mother had passed down to her. An old dress, made of different fabrics that resembled a quilt, with ruffles around the neck. Hard black shoes, with stained white socks. And an old sweater that was too big. Her hair was braided in plaits, which made her look much younger than her twenty-two years.

"No, honey, my mother named me Claudette, but the men named me Red; ain't that right, Suga'?" Red laughed at William.

"I guess so," William answered with embarrassment.

"Have you ever been up North before, honey?" Red asked Orabell.

"This here is my first time," Orabell said.

"Well, that explains it. The first thing we need to do is get you out of those old clothes, and get you into some clothes that were made in the 1900s." Red smiled.

Red took Orabell by the arm, and led her back to the car.

"Let the men folk get the bags; that's how we do it up here," Red said.

Orabell looked back at Isaiah and William as if she was asking them to save her. Isaiah hunched his shoulders and held his hands in the air, signaling that it was out of his control. Then he nudged William in the side. They both laughed as Orabell balled up her fist and waved it at them.

Stanford's eyes followed Red until she and Orabell were sitting in the car. Isaiah caught him looking and gently slapped him in the back of his head.

"Put your eyes back in your head, boy." Isaiah laughed.

"I ain't never seen nothin' like that befo' in my life. That's the prettiest thang I've ever laid eyes on," Stanford said.

"You see this boy slobbering over your woman, William?" Isaiah asked.

"You're slobbering, too, so don't get on him," William joked.

"I have two eyes, and they can only see one woman, and that's that pretty chocolate thang sitting in that back seat."

"You won't ever try to step out on Orabell because if you ever get caught she'll kill you, but you look. Your eyes almost jumped out of your head when you saw that dress," William said.

"Don't say that, man; you know I wasn't looking at that woman."

"What do you think, Stanford; think he was looking?" William asked.

"Well, if he whudn't lookin', he eitha half blind, or half crazy!" Stanford said. "I ain't never seen nothin' like that befo'."

"Well, I must be half crazy, 'cause I wasn't looking."

"I don't know how my sista got that rope 'round yo' neck like that, but it's real tight. And it must be plenty long 'cause she ain't got to be 'round to yank on it." Stanford laughed.

"OK, that's enough of that," Isaiah said seriously.

William and Stanford noticed that Isaiah did not find their jokes funny and they backed off, and changed the subject.

"Red is going to drive us over to her place to get a little rest and a bite to eat. We'll be leaving for Saginaw once we're well rested," William said.

"How far is Saginaw from here?" Isaiah asked.

"It's about a hundred miles or so."

"How long does it take in an auto?" Isaiah asked.

"About four to five hours."

"Let's get these bags in the auto before your woman turn Orabell into some kind of blues singer," Isaiah said.

"Up here they don't call them autos, Zay; up here they call them cars," William said. "You're talking about getting your woman away from my woman. I better get my woman away from Orabell before she have Red somewhere trying to show her how to pick cotton."

"If your body heals as fast as your mouth, you'll be fine in no time," Isaiah snapped.

"Mr. William, forgive me but I got to say this; if all the women up here look like Ms. Red, I ain't never goin' back to Mississippi!" Stanford shouted.

"Be quiet, and get the bags, ol' mannish boy!" Isaiah said.

They loaded the bags into the car and drove to Red's place. Red lived in an old, large three-story house, a gift from one of her former customers. She had it painted and remodeled so well, most thought the house was an antique classic. The interior matched the outside with its elegance and unique decor.

As glamorous and materialistic as Red appeared, she was kind by nature. She had a heart of gold, and the great thing about it was that she believed it was normal. She believed that everybody gave from their hearts, and tried to preserve instead of destroy. A big city girl, with a small-town heart. Red was born and raised in Detroit. She had never been south of Cincinnati, and to her, looking at Orabell was like looking at a picture in a history book. Orabell would be a difficult project for her to transform into a Northern colored girl, but one that she welcomed with open arms.

Red had a pitiful childhood. Her parents were killed in a furious blizzard, leaving her an orphan at the age of eight. She lived in and out of orphanages for seven years until she started working in a brothel at the age of fifteen. There she found a family. She found companionship, and she felt loved. Red felt the offering of her body for money was a small price to pay for the acceptance of love. In Red's eyes, affection for money was better than no affection at all.

She had met William as a client when he first moved to Detroit, and he fell in love instantly. He convinced her that love did not require a sacrifice such as her body. It should be received and given freely from desire. William would visit her at the brothel as a paying customer, but only for the benefit of an opportunity to speak with her. He refused to touch her, unless it was a mild kiss, or a hug. He tried desperately to get her to leave the brothel, and as much as she wanted to leave, that was the only life she knew. Red eluded his pursuit for as long as she could, and when she fell, she fell for him as if she had a ton of bricks on her back. She had never met a man who just loved her, for her. And if he could love her so strongly, knowing what she did for a living, she knew she had to take a chance and love this man back. She was hurt when she found out that William was moving to Saginaw; she thought that would be the end of their relationship. They managed to keep their relationship together by visiting one another as often as possible.

One of her former sisters from the brothel had quit the business and became a midwife. She took Red under her wing, and taught her everything she needed to know about the business. Red built her own respectable reputation of being a midwife, and never looked back at her old profession.

Red was thirty years old, only eight years older than Orabell, but her life's hard knocks had added years to her beautiful face. She had no friends outside of the people associated with her old life. So she was happy to have a descent, respectable person to call a friend. She also thought that if William could see what is was like to have a wife, he would finally ask her to marry him.

Red took Orabell to her closet and showed her all of her clothes. She told her to take whatever she wanted at no charge. Orabell thought the offer was generous, but she felt as if she was an imposition.

"Look, suga', take whatever you want. It's my pleasure. William told me that you needed some clothes. We have to look out for one another. With you around it'll be like the sister I never had. You're going to be my good luck charm."

"I don't mean no harm, Ms. Red, but these clothes look a little too fancy fa my taste."

"Take that old dress off and let's have a look at your figure."

"I don't feel right takin' my clothes off in front of ya, so if you don't mind I'd much rather keep 'em on for right now."

"Don't be ridiculous, honey. Take them old rags off and get into some clothes that show off what you got."

"That's just it; I ain't got nothin' I want to show to nobody but Isaiah, and he done seen everythang I got."

"Stop being so shy, suga'. You up North now; you don't have to dress like a slave," Red said, loosening the string off of Orabell's dress, which fell to the floor. She quickly picked it up to cover herself.

"Are you sure you married? I have never in my life seen anything so timid. Drop that dress, and try this on," Red said, handing her a nice long skirt from the closet.

Orabell slowly dropped her dress, and took the skirt.

She tried it on and Red pulled a full-length mirror in front of her so that she could see herself. Orabell looked in the mirror and turned different angles to see how the skirt fit. She liked it, but she didn't want Red to know how much.

"Now hold on; I have a shirt to match the skirt." Red ran to the closet and pulled out the shirt. She held it out for Orabell to try it on. She hesitated for a second, then snatched it out of Red's hands and gave a big smile.

"Put it on, let's see how you look."

Orabell put on the shirt, and stared in the mirror again.

"You like it?" Red asked.

"It's nice."

"It's yours if you want it."

"I can't take your stuff like this, Ms. Red," Orabell cried, taking off the clothes.

"I don't want them back now. Not after you've had your cotton-pickin' body all up in 'em." Red laughed. "Take 'em or I'll throw 'em away."

Orabell held the clothes in her hand, rubbing them up and down.

"I guess I'll take 'em if you sure it's OK."

"Come here, honey. Let me show you something," Red said, walking to another closet. "You see all these clothes; I don't have enough time to live to wear all these clothes. If you don't take some of them off my hands, I'll see it as an insult."

"Are you sure, Ms. Red?"

"Suga', if you don't stop callin' me Miss, I am going to scream up in here. I ain't that much older than you."

Orabell tried on several different outfits, and thanked Red for her generosity.

"You don't have to thank me, honey. It was worth it just seeing your face."

"I don't know why you being so kind to me, but I thank you again."

"You happen to be the sister-in-law of the man I love. Once he told me he needed me that was all I needed to hear 'cause believe me, no matter where we are, if I need him he's comin' to me, come hell or high water. It feels good to have a man tells you he need you, and he ain't talking about in the Biblical sense. I'm sure that if Isaiah came to you and he needed you to help William out, you'd do the exact same thing."

"I understand what you're saying. I guess if everybody try to help everybody when they need help, in time it will all work itself out," Orabell said.

"Can you cook?" Red asked.

"Can I cook? You can't be from Mississippi and not know how to cook!" Orabell smiled.

"Let's go down here and throw somethin' together for our men."

"I woulda never thought a fancy woman like you would know her way around a kitchen."

"Don't let the fanciness fool you, honey. I have to know my way around every room in the house. I live all by myself, and if a man give me some help, he's going to want something in return, and I ain't givin' up nothin' to nobody but William. I cook, I clean, I fix whatever's broken. I ain't married that man yet, and until I do, the bedroom ain't the only place I need to know my way around."

"I hope my husban' don't have no heart attack after seeing me in these clothes. I don't want him to think I'm tryin' to show myself off." Orabell laughed.

"He might just have a heart attack as good as you look, honey, but I bet he's not going to want you to take that skirt off," Red said, placing her arms around Orabell's shoulder as they walked down the stairs.

★★★

Isaiah, Stanford and William were sitting in the parlor room of the house talking about their women. Stanford was bored with the grown-up talk and wanted to get away from it.

"Isaiah, would it be all right if I go upstairs and lie down till it's time to eat?" Stanford asked.

"Yes, but don't go snooping in Ms. Red's stuff."

"Hey, Stanford, you ever played a phonograph before?" William asked.

"Naw, sir."

"Red has one up there in that room you're staying in. Come on, let me show you how to play it."

"Oh yeah! Let's go!"

William took Stanford upstairs and showed him how to play records on the phonograph. He returned to the parlor with Isaiah and they continued the grown-up talk.

"Do you think Orabell will like her?" William asked.

"Who cares?" Isaiah asked.

"I do! We are brothers now. And that means Orabell is my sister. I want her to get along with my woman."

"All you need to worry about is how much you care about your woman."

"I'm scared, man!" William whispered.

"Scared of what?"

"I love this woman, and I want to marry her, but when I think about coming home to the same woman every day for the rest of my life, I get scared to death."

"I have only one piece of advice to tell you, brother."

"It better be good, and not any of your preacher stuff."

"Oh, it's good. And here it is: grow up!" Isaiah said. "Grow up and start acting like a man. If you love this woman, and you want to marry her, be a man and ask her. If you're too worried about having to come home to the same woman every night, then don't ask her. But when another man comes and asks her to spend the rest of her life with him and she accepts, don't try to run up behind her then. Just put your tail between your legs and crawl back into your doghouse, OK?"

"Damn!" William said. "That was good, Zay!"

"It was good because it was the truth. It's that simple, William; if you love that woman, go get her."

"You know, Zay, that's exactly what I'm going to do. Right now!" William said, standing up and pulling his pants high above his waist.

William heard Red and Orabell on the stairs and sat back down.

"Why'd you sit back down, William?" Isaiah asked.

"I just thought of something that hadn't crossed my mind before."

"What's that?"

"What if when I get up the nerves to ask, she tells me no?"

"Man, go ask the woman to marry you, and stop these excuses."

"It's not right!" William said nervously.

"What's not right?"

"This! This moment; it's not right, man."

Red stepped around the corner leading into the parlor and she gathered the men's attention to introduce the new Orabell. While she was talking, Isaiah interrupted and asked her a question

"Now fellas, feast your eyes on this," Red said, gesturing for Orabell to enter the room.

At the same time, Isaiah asked Red, "Would you say no if William was to ask you to marry him?"

Red heard what Isaiah asked during her introduction, and it shocked her so badly, she stumbled against the table and knocked the table to the floor.

William turned his back to Orabell and Red and screamed to Isaiah, "Man, have you lost your damn mind?!"

Orabell stepped around the corner very slowly not aware that Isaiah had asked Red to marry William, and whispered, "Ta-Da!"

"What did you say?" Red said to Isaiah.

"Lord, have mercy!" Isaiah said, as his mouth hung opened from seeing Orabell.

"You don't like it, Isaiah?" Orabell said.

"Lord, have mercy!" Isaiah repeated.

"Did you ask me what I would say if William asked me to marry me?!" Red screamed.

"Isaiah, you have started some stuff in here; now say something!" William mumbled under his breath.

"Lord, have mercy!" Isaiah said one more time.

"Well baby, you wont me to take it off," Orabell asked.

"Yes, yes, Lord," Isaiah said with embarrassment, "but not right here."

"To answer your question, Isaiah, yes! Yes, I'll marry William!" Red shouted.

"You happy now?" William asked Isaiah, turning towards Red and Orabell.

When William saw Orabell in the tight skirt, he raised his eyebrows and said, "Damn, Orabell!"

Red jumped in William's lap and screamed, "I'll marry you! I'll marry you anytime, and anywhere, sweetie!"

Red kissed William all over his face. "Smack! Smack! Smack! Smack!"

"Do you like the skirt, Isaiah? If you don't I can give it back. I know you don't like tight-fittin' clothes."

"If you like that skirt, then you keep it! It doesn't matter what you wear; it's how you act. And you always act like a lady. If you find anymore up there that you like, I will tell you now, I like them, too. Lord, have mercy! My, my, my!" Isaiah sighed.

"Come on, honey. Let's go in here and start plannin' my wedding. I told you, you were going to be my good luck charm!" Red shouted, pulling Orabell into the kitchen.

William sat with his hands up in the air and asked, "What happened? What the hell just happened in here?"

"You proposed to your fiancée, brother." Isaiah chuckled.

"Zay, I asked one question. I mean one measly question: how in God's name did that one question get me engaged?"

"You popped the big question, brother." Isaiah smiled patting him on the back.

"But I popped the question to you, not her," William cried.

"Well, we both said yes. Now let's go see if we can help out in the kitchen."

William reached into the collar of Isaiah's shirt and looked around.

"What are you doing?" Isaiah asked.

"I believe that boy was right; Orabell got a rope around your neck so tight she don't have to be in the room to pull on it."

"Don't laugh too loud; Red threw her rope around your neck tonight."

"Never! Never! Never!" William laughed louder.

"OK, brother, we'll see."

The family ate dinner and went to bed. Early the next morning they headed for Saginaw.

CHAPTER SIX

SAGINAW, MICHIGAN 1937

A month after they settled into the house with William, the newest Saginaw residents were enjoying their surroundings. They were finding their way around on their own. Isaiah was hired at an automobile plant paying more money than he had ever made in his life. They rented a house near William's, and quickly moved in. Isaiah enrolled Stanford in high school, and he actually enjoyed it.

William was a member of the Prince Hall Free & Accepted Masons Fraternity, the eldest of all the fraternal organizations. He wanted Isaiah to join the Masons to meet and mingle with some of the distinguished colored men in town. He thought Isaiah could make friends, and become comfortable living up North.

Isaiah applied, and after receiving his third degree, he became a Mason. His Masonic brothers embraced him, and made life accommodating in Saginaw. Eventually, Isaiah drifted away from their hand-holding and started to meet people on his own.

He saw a lot of promise with the progressive thinking of the colored people up North. He thought they would be much more accepting to his way of thinking than the colored people in Mississippi.

Isaiah felt he could educate the colored people in his neighborhood on how they should learn about economics and politics to better their environment. He could do it with passion and devotion, without the threat of being lynched. He immediately went to work, going from door to door.

The houses were so close together he felt that he could walk the entire city without becoming exhausted. He passed out paraphernalia on the evolution of the civilized colored man. His first meeting was in William's house, and it was standing room only. He moved the next meeting to a church that was offered by one of the ministers in attendance. The more he spoke, the more people wanted to hear.

Isaiah formed an organization called Working Negro Men to help assist families who were poverty-stricken. They would donate portions of their check into a savings, and distribute the funds to pay rent, utilities, food, and other necessities for the families who most needed their help. In return, the out-of-work people would use their skills within the community for free. For example, for a carpenter's family that received assistance, if there was carpentry work to be done, he would work on a person's house for free. Isaiah taught that having a good job didn't always mean having good cash. He said, "Sometime you have to work hard to put food on your plate, and clothes on your back. And when you're colored, just to stay alive is a job in itself. So as long as you're living, and you're living right, no one in America has a better job than you."

The crime rate all but disappeared after the WNM was formed. The neighborhood took on the character of the group and neighbors looked out for neighbors, instead of minding their own business. Their optimism for colored people's success elevated their confidence to achieve that success.

★★★

As autumn turned to winter, the meetings slowed down, and so did the enthusiasm of the community. Isaiah tried to rally the WNM to rekindle the zeal of the movement, but the support was minimal. Isaiah took complete control of all the activities of the group, which included collecting and dispersing the funds, setting all the meeting dates, keeping the minutes of the meetings, and placing unemployed workers with work to qualify for their assistance funds. There were not enough hours in a day to maintain the WNM, and work his full-time job. He asked Orabell to help, and she did. She inevitably became the bookkeeper, secretary, and honorary member.

She was assisted by Red, who showed her how to keep the books, and how to schedule the meetings so that all the members could attend. Red suggested that Orabell read books to improve her vocabulary. She told Orabell that books can take her on journeys to different places all around the world. Orabell accepted Red's advice and put it to use. She began to read different books about different people and places. Her knowledge was reflected in her awareness to identify with situations and conversations that formerly held no interest to her.

Red, now known as Mrs. Red Crowell, was a natural, and she quickly organized a structure for the WNM, and they started to slowly pick up momentum. As Red faded out, Orabell began to run the WNM alone. She knew that if she encountered any problems, Red was living in Saginaw with her new husband, only a few blocks away.

Orabell took the responsibility of heading the WNM very seriously. She was involved with something other than cooking and cleaning, and she felt important. She discussed with the members of WNM the possibility of including women. After all, if it was a community group, then all of the members of the community should have an opportunity to participate in its activity. The members agreed, and women were invited to become members, with the agreement that the name should remain the same. The name remained the Working Negro Men, but the women of the group quickly outnumbered the men, slightly changing the complexion of their purpose. The WNM placed parameters on what they considered to be their immediate community. They set the parameters for Washington Street to the west, Johnson Street to the south, curve around Washington Street to the north, and 23rd Street to the east. The majority of colored people lived in that area. If they didn't live in that area, they probably didn't need the WNM anyway.

★★★

Orabell appeared to be content with living up North. However the more it snowed, the more apparent it became that she was not content, but miserable. Outside of the WNM, she had nothing to do but mope around at the disappointment of not having a child. She tried to maintain a positive image for Isaiah, but for as hard as she tried, she could not.

Her depression caused her to have emotional outbursts where she would bawl uncontrollably nearly every day. She would rip Isaiah's work uniforms, out of resentment for him bringing her to Michigan. He noticed the rips of his uniforms, and he would ask Orabell to mend them for him. She would smile, and sew the uniforms back together. More and more his shirts became ripped, and more and more Orabell would smile and sew them back. Until the day she had had enough, and it was time to make a change.

One evening, Isaiah came in from working at the foundry. Orabell was sitting on the couch with her coat and gloves on. She stood, and picked up her suitcase. She was not crying at that time, but the dried tear trails were evident enough that it hadn't been too long since she her last tear had fallen. Isaiah stood in the doorway with the door ajar. He couldn't believe what his eyes were seeing

"Isaiah, I packed my bags and I'm going home."

"What?"

"I packed my bags. I can't take livin' here anymore. I feel like I'm losing my mind. And if I stay here too much longer, I will."

"Hold it, sweetheart, listen to me. Tell me what's wrong. If I knew what you were going through, baby, I could fix it. But if you don't tell me, what can I do?"

"That's just it. There's nothing more for you to do. I can not live here in this God-forsaken ice place. It's freezing cold up here. I have never seen a drop of snow in my life; I wasn't made for this weather. I got to go home. Now, are you going to take me to the bus station or do I have to walk?"

"What about me? What about our babies?"

"Shut up! Just shut up!" Orabell screamed. "You been saying that ever since we been married, and we don't have one baby! Why can't you make no babies?"

"Orabell, calm down before you say something you'll regret later."

"I ain't gon' regret nothin'."

"Just calm down, OK?"

"You calm down!" Orabell screamed. "What's wrong with you; why can't you put no baby in me?"

"There's nothing in the world wrong with me."

"So what you sayin'?" Orabell sobbed. "You sayin' somethin' wrong with me? You sayin' I can't have no babies? Is that what you think?"

"I don't think there's anything wrong with you either. It's just not meant for us to have a child."

"I bet I can go grab any man off the streets and he can put a baby in me the first time. Too bad you can't do it!"

"Is that what you think, Orabell?"

"That's what I said, ain't it?"

"You know what, if you feel like you can find any man on the street to be the father of your child, then you go find him."

Orabell looked in disbelief, waiting for Isaiah to come to his senses and realize his error and apologize for bringing her to Michigan. When he didn't, it only made her angrier, and she attacked.

"I guess your mama and Dr. West gon' be the last ones to make a baby in your fam'ly!"

Orabell had had moments when she needed to get things off of her chest, and Isaiah normally listened until she finished and then he would make his point known. He never took her fits personally, or to heart. Even though he knew Orabell was reacting mostly due to depression, this time he couldn't excuse her cruel and insensitive behavior.

"For as long as you live and you are black, you better not ever say anything against my mother."

Orabell ignored Isaiah and picked up her suitcase.

"Do you hear me talking to you?" Isaiah said, grabbing Orabell by the arm.

"Let go of my arm!"

"Get out! Get your stuff and get out!" Isaiah said.

Orabell, with her suitcase in hand, walked out of the house and slammed the door behind her.

Isaiah flopped himself on the couch and covered his face with his hands. He could not believe he had spoken to Orabell that way. On the other hand, he couldn't believe that Orabell had talked to him that way either. He wanted to run after her, but he knew that as angry as she was when she left, she would only resist his attempt for reconciliation. Angry or not, he couldn't sit on a couch while his wife was outside in the cold, after dark. He knew that she could only be going to one place, but he had to be certain. He put on his coat and followed her for a few blocks and she ended up knocking on William's door. Once he saw that she was in the house safely, he turned around and went back home.

Isaiah fell asleep, and about an hour or two later, he was awakened by constant pounding on his door. He jumped from the couch startled.

"Who is it?"

"It's the police!"

"Oh Lord! I can't believe Orabell called the police on me, man!" Isaiah said to himself.

"Open up. It's the police!"

"Be there in a second, sir. I'm just slipping on some pants!"

Isaiah unlocked, and opened the door, and William laughed all the way to the couch where he collapsed.

"Boy! I didn't know a pair of eyes could get that big."

"I'm not laughing, man," Isaiah said, pushing William off of his couch so he could lie back down.

"Man, what the hell happened up in here tonight?"

"Are you talking about Orabell?"

"Yeah, man, what happened in paradise?"

"She had her bags packed when I got home from work. We discussed the reason her bags were packed and everything went out of control. We had a huge argument, and we started to say things we shouldn't have said. To make a long story short, I told her to get out."

"Man, you have just made a big mess."

"I know, man, but I'll fix it."

"Why did you let that woman walk down the street after dark like that; have you lost your mind?"

"I followed her all the way to your house to make sure she made it safely."

"Zay, until Dr. West lit a fuse in you I had never seen you lose your temper in all of the years I've known you. Now in a matter of months you are ready to start World War Two."

"I promise you this, brother, you will never see me lose it again. If I can get my wife to come back home, no matter what she says from this point on, I won't allow myself to behave the way I did."

"Zay, what did she say to set you off?"

"It's kinda personal."

"Oh, I understand! When a man says that his woman made him mad enough to put her out the house...in the middle of winter...at night...with no gloves, it can only mean one thing."

"You have no idea what it was."

"If I guess right, will you tell me if it's true or not?"

"Sure, William, sure."

"She said you had a small ding-dong, didn't she?"

"Go home, man."

"I'm serious, man, is that what she said?"

"Get out of my house!"

"Look, Zay, you don't have to be ashamed in front of me. Remember, me, you and Big John used to swim in the same river. And I have seen yours and Big John's ding-dongs, and I know why they call him Big John, but for a colored man, Zay, I'm going to have to tell you the truth; you weren't very impressive."

"Did you practice that joke on the way over here?"

"That's called improvisation, big brother."

"Well anyway, that's not it."

"All right, enough with the jokes; let's get serious. Whatever Orabell said, it couldn't have been anything bad enough to kick her out."

"You're right, I shoudn't have lost my temper."

"A sweet girl like Orabell, she's not capable of saying anything that malicious. You are going to have to apologize, wash dishes, clean clothes, and have sex with yourself for a looooong time."

"As long as I get her back home, I'll do anything."

"She must have really made you mad. What did that sweet girl say to you?"

"She thinks there's something wrong with us because we don't have children."

"I know that kills her. She talks about it all the time to Red. Poor girl, I knew it had something to do with your little ding-dong somehow."

"With all the women you've been with in your life, you don't have any children either. So what's your problem?"

"I'm fixed."

"Yeah, you fixed to tell a lie."

"No, I'm just careful, and very lucky. I can imagine how Orabell feels; Red drives me crazy over that nonsense, Zay. Let's have a baby! Let's have a baby!" William mimicked. "The doctors say that her insides are messed up, and she may not ever be able to have children. And if she did become pregnant, she could possibly die. But if she may not, it means there's a chance that it just may happen. That *may* is all she needs to keep her faith. I don't want any babies anyway. As much as Stanford is over to my house I feel like he's my son; that's enough for me right there. By the way, Stanford told me to give you a message. He told me to tell you that he was going to whoop yo' ass for kicking his sister out."

"Don't get that boy hurt."

"All this excitement has me in the mood to put on some blues, and lie to Red and tell her I want to make a baby. So that means you have to come get your family. Put your coat on, and let's go."

"Brother, I know Orabell is still madder than a wet hen. I might need to wait until tomorrow, after she's cooled off."

"Zay, she's not the only one that's hot. Bring your little ding-a-ling butt on, and come stand up to your wife. That little thang is never going to grow if you don't use those two thangs hanging at the bottom of it."

"Let's go. I'm tired of hearing your mouth," Isaiah said, putting on his coat.

Isaiah locked the door to his house and the two of them walked back to William's house.

★★★

Earlier that evening when Orabell knocked on William's door frantically without Isaiah, Red sensed that there was either something wrong with Isaiah, or something wrong with their marriage. In this case it was both.

Orabell explained to Red that she needed a place to stay for a couple of days because Isaiah had put her out. After she let Orabell vent for a while, Red sent William to talk to Isaiah. She and Orabell went into the kitchen to talk themselves. Stanford hadn't seen the suitcase when Orabell arrived, so he wasn't aware of what was going on. And Orabell wanted it to stay that way.

Red sat Orabell at the table and asked her what had happened. Orabell explained that she was tired of living in the cold weather, and she missed her mother badly. She explained that she packed her bags and she was waiting for Isaiah to come home to give him a choice to leave with her, or stay in Michigan. Red listened to Orabell tell her story, then asked if she could give her a little advice. Orabell said that she wouldn't mind the advice, and Red gave her objective opinion.

"Well, honey, let me tell you straight out; you were wrong!" Red said.

"If you were homesick, you should have told Isaiah. Instead, you let all of your frustration build up and you exploded."

"Well, he shoulda knowed I wasn't happy up here."

"Now Isaiah may be a saint, but he's not God, suga'. I'm a witness; don't ever expect for a man to understand how you feel. You gotta tell him what you want, and how you want it. Men can be so simple-minded sometime, and so you have to talk to them like they're simple-minded and explain everything clearly."

"Maybe I shoulda told him, but I can't go back there after that man done kick me out. I'm too shamed!"

"Isaiah didn't kick you out anymore than there is a man on the moon. You packed your bags because you wanted him to ask you not to go. And I'm quite sure he would have, but you went about it the wrong way, sweetie," Red said, "You should have just given him some time to assess the situation. He probably thought you were half crazy when he walked in that house and saw your bags packed. When I saw you standing out there on that porch, I know I did."

"Do you think I should apologize to him, then?"

"Only if you mean it, suga'. You have to ask yourself if you love your husband more than you hate Michigan. Because no matter how much you want to go back to Mississippi, your husband can't go back. If he does they'll kill him."

"I know that, Red, but I feel like I just can't breathe up here. I thought that if we moved up here, get away from all of those white folks, we'd be able to have some babies."

"What does white folks killin' your husband have to do with you having babies?"

"I thought that maybe they were putting so much pressure on him he couldn't make a baby right."

"Don't they teach you country folks where babies come from?"

"I know where they come from, Red; I'm just trying to figure out why mine haven't came."

"How can you be so selfish, Orabell?"

"What you talkin' 'bout, Red?"

"I am eight years older than you, and my man is the same age as yours. Did you ever think that maybe I want a baby, just as much as you? Did it ever occur to you that maybe your husband want a baby just as much as you? Did you ever think that your complaining about not having a baby can hurt other people?"

"You never said nothin' about havin' a baby to me, Red. I'm so sorry."

"That's the point, Orabell, I shouldn't have to. That's my, and my husband's business. You married a grown man, you're in a grown marriage, and now you have to start acting like a grown woman. Keep your personal business to yourself. Don't go running around telling folks because you want a little pity, 'cause they'll use it against you later."

"It hurts so bad, to wont something so bad, and can't have it. You live a fancy life, and you can just about have anything you want, Red. You don't know how it feel to be hurt."

Red poured them both a cup of coffee and sat back down at the table.

"What do you think I did for a living before I became a midwife?" Red asked.

"I don't know, you probably had some fancy office down there in Detroit."

"You wanna know what I did for a living?"

"Yeah, what did you do?" Orabell asked, sipping slowly on the steaming hot cup of coffee.

"Grab a hold of your chair. I don't want you to fall off," Red said. "I was a prostitute."

Orabell stopped in mid sip, and held her mouth wide open as the steam of the coffee drifted into her eyes.

"You was what?"

"I was a prostitute. I was raised in a whorehouse. My mother and father were killed in an awful winter storm and I went from orphanage to orphanage until I just got tired of it, and lived on my own. I wanted a family so bad, I accepted anybody who wanted me.

"I used to think that I was something special when men paid to have me. I thought that was what I needed to feel whole, to feel loved. It took me a while to understand that those men could care less about me. All they wanted was my body! Even after I realized they didn't care two cents about me, I felt that after how I had lived my life, I deserved to be treated that way. Like a spoiled piece of meat.

"I met your brother-in-law one day, and he started coming around to the house just to see me. He didn't want to do anything but talk to me, girl. He'd pay his money and told me I'd better not touch him. I almost went crazy over that man. I knew then I was going to marry him; I just wanted to be sure. And I wanted him to be sure. I made him chase me for a while, and then he moved up here to Saginaw.

"You see, I made the man wait too long. I was trying to be sure for me, but it took so long it made him unsure. After he moved up here, I started to chase him then. I chased him, too, and as you can see, I caught him!

"He gave me a choice. He said that it was either the business or him. Of course at first I chose the business because I knew the business wasn't going anywhere. But after I started to miss him, I left the house and I never went back.

"I hope you understand what I'm trying to tell you, suga'. Ever since I met you and Isaiah, he's been chasing you. Making sure you're happy, and you're not upset. Tonight, he got tired of chasing you, so it's your turn to chase him a little. Don't be worried about your pride; if there is any man on this earth worth fighting for, it's Isaiah, and you know that, don't you?"

"I guess you're right, Red."

"If you want to stay here, you're welcome to stay here as long as you want. But if you really love your husband, I wouldn't get too comfortable, and I wouldn't stay too long."

"I will talk to Isaiah first thing in the mornin' before he leave for work. He was fightin' mad when I left, though. I ain't never seen him like that before."

"Aw, honey, he'll be just fine. He probably miss you just as much as you miss him. Just get you some rest, and worry about everything in the morning."

Orabell took Red by the hands and rubbed them gently.

"Red, I had no idea you had such a rough life. You seem so happy, like you have had the best life in the world. And I'm sittin' up here complainin' about cold weather. You a good friend, and I love you."

Red began to cry listening to Orabell.

"Honey, we're not friends," Red said, wiping her eyes. "We're family. It seems as if I've needed to hear those words my whole life. Not coming from a man, but from somebody who truly loves me, for me. Not Red, the glamorous-clothes wearing lady, but me, Claudette.

"Honey, everything you walked away from tonight, is everything I ever wanted. You think that because I walk around with a smile on my face, I have no pain in my heart? Well, I do. I got so much pain, that I can't help but smile to keep from crying. I love you, Orabell, like you were my flesh and blood sister, and the last thing I'll do is give you some advice to make me feel better.

"Listen, suga, Isaiah loves you in a way that I have never seen a man love a woman. He is happy just to be around you. Everything he says and does somehow come back to you. You better do whatever you can to fix your marriage. You have a man worth fighting for, and if you don't want to lose him you better put up your dukes and start swinging."

"Thank you, Red, and I feel like you my flesh and blood, too."

"Have you been reading those books I told you to pick up from the library?"

"Yea, they're at home."

"Are you sure?" Red asked. "Seems like you slipping back into that Mississippi tongue you came here with."

"Please, I'm talking much better than I did when I first got here."

"If you say so. You better save some of that sweet talk for your husband."

They heard the door open and close, then heard Isaiah's and William's voices coming closer to the kitchen.

"Oh Lord, William done went down there and got Isaiah. I ain't ready to talk yet," Orabell said.

"Well, you better get ready, and you better get ready quick, 'cause he'll be back here in a minute."

"OK! OK! Don't leave, I don't wanna be alone with him right now. I don't know what to say."

"OK, suga', I'll stand by you through thick and thin," Red whispered.

Isaiah and William entered the kitchen, and the four of them stood silently in the kitchen.

"OK, me and William, we're going to go out to the living room while you all stay back here and talk," Red said.

"Red, I thought we had a deal," Orabell mumbled.

"We did. I said I'll stand by your side through thick and thin, and I'm still by your side. I'm just going to be standing in the living room. Take your time, and Isaiah, there's a piece of chocolate cake in the refrigerator. Orabell, you let..." Red said, before William interrupted.

"Red! Would you let these folks handle their own business? Come on!" William said, pulling Red by the arm.

"Orabell, remember what I told you: put your dukes up, child, put your dukes up!" Red yelled as William pulled her playfully through the kitchen door.

Isaiah walked over to Orabell and kissed her on the forehead.

"Sit down, baby, and let me talk to you," he said.

"Shhh! Don't say a word; let me talk first," Orabell said.

"OK, you talk first," Isaiah said, repeatedly kissing Orabell's hands.

"You know I'm not good at talkin' with big words, or with all that fancy talk like the rest of y'all, so I'm going to say this the best way I know how."

"Baby, no matter what you say, you always sound like an angel to me."

"Thank you, sweetheart," Orabell said. "I am so, so, so sorry for not talking to you, and explaining to you how I felt about living up here. I'm sorry for saying those mean, mean things to you. You are everything I want and need in a man, and I thank God every day for sending you to me. I hope you can find it in your heart to forgive me. I want to forget tonight, and start over living in Michigan. I want to be your wife, and stand by your side in what ver you want to do."

"Listen, baby, I owe you an apology, too. I should never lose my temper, especially if it means I'm going to lose control of my house. I am the head our household, and I asked you to leave your home. As the head of the household, I am supposed to make sure the house stays intact, not divide it. I will never lose my head like that again. You are my wife, and I love you more than life itself. I can't live without you, baby. Please, please, come back home with me."

"Red is listening from this side of the door!" William shouted. "She's smiling, so I guess you two are doing all right in there!"

Isaiah took Orabell by the hand and led her out of the kitchen. They pushed the door into Red as she was still standing against it.

"Girl, would you get your nosy butt away from that door," William said.

Red straightened out her dress and walked towards the kitchen. "Excuse me, I was just going to get a glass of water."

"Sure you were," Isaiah said.

Red never went into the kitchen. She stood beside Orabell and Isaiah and stared; waiting for one of them to say something.

"We're sorry for bringing you two into this, but we're glad you did. You talked some sense into us both. Orabell is going to come back home with me, and we'll finish our conversation there," Isaiah said, holding Orabell's hand.

"There is a God," William said.

"Oooh! I'm so glad; go home and do some making up." Red giggled.

"Better hurry up and get home; you don't want that good feeling to wear off now," William said, pushing them toward the door.

"Man, will you calm down. You act like a high school boy who has never had any!" Isaiah said.

"OK, maybe I am acting like a high school boy, but you just grab Orabell's suitcase, and get on out of here so I can learn my lesson, little bit," William said, opening the door.

"Who are you calling 'little bit,' William?" Red asked.

"Oh, little bit knows who he is; it's our little secret, to keep to our little selves." William laughed.

"Red, you are married to a fool. I hope you know that," Isaiah said.

"A hot fool right now!" William smiled.

"Let's go, Orabell, and leave this dog in heat," Isaiah said.

"Don't forget to get your other luggage before you leave," William said.

"What other luggage?" Isaiah asked.

"STANFORD!" William called.

"Uh-huhn," Stanford answered.

"Isaiah said it's time for you all to go home; he's waiting on you," William said.

Stanford ran downstairs and put on his coat. Isaiah, Orabell, and Stanford walked the few blocks back to their house. Stanford noticed Orabell's suitcase and asked why Isaiah was carrying it.

Isaiah answered as always, "Be quiet, and stop asking questions."

They made it home and Orabell and Isaiah finished their conversation. Orabell opened up to Isaiah and told him how she felt about moving to Michigan. He tried to console her by telling her that their lives were much better up North, than in Mississippi. After their discussion, they both felt content with their lives and their marriage.

CHAPTER SEVEN

SAGINAW, MICHIGAN 1938

The following year, when the winter snow started to melt, Orabell experienced the beauty of Michigan's springtime. And as depressing and menacing as the winter weather had been, spring was equally, or even more refreshing and liberating. Trees started to grow beautiful green leaves. Flowers bloomed in a variety of colors, and the landscape changed from solid white to the colorful spectrum of a rainbow. The frozen Saginaw River thawed, and as it flowed once again, it seemed to indicate to the rest of the city that it was time for life to resume. The birds began to chirp, and children played. But the most amazing transformation was seeing the last of the snow melt, and the green of grass take its place.

Orabell was warned in advance that the first winter is always the worst winter. But in contrast, the jubilation of the first spring could never be duplicated as well. As the days grew longer, everyone came out of hibernation.

In late spring on Saturday evenings, families would pull their phonographs outside and play music. The block parties were a community event; everyone was invited. They would block off a certain area with their cars, and people would gather within the area to eat and dance. They would load pails with Faygo soda pop, and tables of potato chips for the children. Faygo red pop was a classic for the occasion. The adults' favorites were fried chicken and potato salad. Orabell's blue ribbon chicken was routinely the first to disappear.

The children would dance until it was dark, then the adults would take over. Everyone wanted to get at least one dance with Red. William didn't mind; he enjoyed the attention she received from all of the men, and a few of the women who seemed interested.

Orabell never danced. She sat back and watched Isaiah as he went from lady to lady. It was so much fun, as she cheered Isaiah on by clapping her hands every time he danced. Isaiah sometime pulled Orabell near the area where everyone danced to convince her to join, but she always pulled away and sat back down.

Orabell never imagined that colored folks up North danced, and socialized in such a manner. She thought to herself that no matter where they are, colored folks were colored folks. Saginaw was beginning to feel more and more like home. It was no substitute for her mother, but it was not such a bad place to call home.

On Sundays, everyone attended the different colored churches. Afterwards, they would open the windows to their homes and play gospel music. The sweet sound of gospel, mixed with the sweet smell of dinner, brought a sweet sense of contentment to the people of Saginaw. Poverty was not a state of being, but a state of mind. For most believed that to have a family housed, and a family fed, is to have a family loved, so what other need is there to have?

★★★

As the temperature heated up, Isaiah pushed the WNM group to become more active. He started to give speeches in Flint, Pontiac, and Detroit, trying to get those cities to start their own WNM groups.

Isaiah didn't have a car, so William volunteered to drive him to his speaking engagements. That would include traveling to different cities. It gave William an opportunity to get out of the house without Red harassing him.

On one occasion, Isaiah spoke in Detroit at a Prince Hall Free & Accepted Masons regional conference. It was the largest crowd that had ever asked him to speak. He was slightly nervous, but he himself was a Prince Hall Mason. Being in the company of his fraternity brothers alleviated, but not eliminated, the nervousness. Being the last speaker added to his nervousness because the last one had to be most emphatic and effective.

A group of members from the WNM, who were also Prince Hall Masons, made the journey to Detroit with him to hear his speech. They knew it would be quite different for Isaiah because he was not going to be surrounded by people he saw on a daily basis. These people would be strangers—prestigious colored men from all over the country.

The Masons had the largest organization in the United States for colored people at the time. The majority of the leaders from their lodges would be in attendance. Isaiah was intimidated, but his purpose far exceeded his fear.

The room was huge—filled with colored men wearing black suits, black shoes, black bow ties, black derbies, white gloves, white shirts, and a white apron wrapped around their waists. All of the derbies were removed to respect the opening of the lodge. As crowded as it was, strangely enough, no one sat in the south side of the room.

Isaiah approached the podium, and cleared his throat. He had never spoken into a microphone before, and he didn't want to look or sound foolish. He tapped it a couple of times, and he heard the echo throughout the room. He assumed that everything was in working order and began his speech.

"Good evening, Worshipful Masters, Senior Wardens, Junior Wardens, and brethren. I would like to speak to you about the trials and tribulations of the present-day colored man. As we have now been out of bondage for nearly three-quarters of a century, it is time for us to reflect back upon our triumphs and our failures, with our so-called New Freedom.

"Like most of your mothers and fathers, my mother and my father were slaves. They were born at the end of slavery on the West Plantation in Derma County, Mississippi. They taught me self-pride, and self-preservation. They also taught me how to live within the fears of the white man.

"By the grace of God I was fortunate enough to know a good white man who helped me get to Pennsylvania and go to college. When I returned to Mississippi, I had problems adjusting to my life back at home, because things had changed. Things had not changed in Mississippi, things had changed in me. I was no longer satisfied with the bigoted and discriminatory rules of Mississippi.

"I wasn't satisfied with looking at the ground when a white person passed me on the street! I wasn't satisfied with talking like an ignorant fool, when

I knew I could speak proper grammar. Probably better than every last one of those to which I had to alter my way of speaking! I wasn't satisfied with having my mother work as a servant up until the day I had to bury her in the ground! I wasn't satisfied with my wife being afraid to learn too much, in fear that she would have to die in return for her knowledge! I tell you, I wasn't satisfied! And if you are, and I hate to use this kind of language, but I must. If you are satisfied with these things, then you're a damn fool!

"My brothers, God has made us a strong people for a reason, and he has a will for us to fulfill as His witness that though we were once the child least born, we will someday rise above the sun to shine as the brightest one. It is incumbent upon us to see that His will be done, and done right.

"As we sit here in this elegant building tonight, we may look upon ourselves as being privileged! Or all right! Or just fine! But we are not! You may be able to leave this room, and go back from whence you came, and life may be wonderful to you. But what about the colored man who is somewhere scared to read a book? Scared to speak proper grammar? Scared to look another man in his eyes? What about that man, brothers?

"Until we can answer that question brothers, are we truly free? Because just as sure as I am standing here before you, that man is not free. And neither are you and I. Because some way, somehow...one day, you and I will be that man."

Isaiah paused to take drink of water, then resumed his speech.

"I remember as a child, growing up on a farm on the red dirt of Mississippi. I recall how my father used to grow hogs. He treated those hogs like they were his children. When I acted up, he even treated them better than me."

The crowd of Masons burst in laughter.

"As a full-grown colored man living in America, sometimes I feel like I am one of those old hogs my daddy used to have. Let me explain that to you. When it came close to the time for the hog to be slaughtered my father fattened him up, let him walk around anywhere he wanted to go on that farm. All the other hogs had to still stay in the pen, but not the hog soon to be slaughtered. I'd watch him as he strutted around everywhere not knowing that he would be breakfast in a day or two. I always wondered why my daddy thought he was doing those hogs a favor by fattening them up, and letting then have liberty to the farm. It's too late to ask Daddy now, but I can only assume that he felt compassion for the hog.

"My brothers, living in today's America, we're just like those hogs my daddy used to slaughter. We think that because white folks let us walk around the country saying we're free, that everything is all right. You just don't realize that they are fattening us up, and giving us liberty to walk over their farm. But as soon as they are ready, they send us straight to the slaughterhouse. What they don't realize is that they are not dealing with a hog; they are dealing with a man. And they have no right to suggest, or even think, that I am indebted to them to walk God's earth. When I pass a white man on the street, and he stands in front of me to block my path, I owe him nothing but the words, get the hell out of my way!"

Isaiah stepped away from the podium to take another drink of water. The men in the room stood to their feet and clapped. He cleared his throat and continued with his speech.

"It is 1938 and everything we own, or think we own as colored people, has been given to us by white people. We have to stop thinking that the only way we can learn is to be taught by white people. And that the only way we can make money is to work for white people. It has to stop, and it has to stop today!

"The only way for us to deprogram ourselves from this slave mentality is to reprogram ourselves to think like masters.

"We have to believe that what is ours, is ours. Sure, colored man to colored man, we'll stand like a tree for our own, but when it comes to the white man, we tend to become timid. I will go as far as to say that it could be broad daylight outside, and if a colored man tell you it's night, you'd call him a madman. But if a white man comes right behind him and tell you it's night you'd question yourself and tell him he's right. If you think I'm lying, ask my brother way in the back. The way he put his head down so fast you would have thought that happened to him this morning."

Isaiah laughed, and apologized to the man for joking with him. The room burst into laughter again. The man smiled and waved to Isaiah as if to say he understood that it was only a joke. A few men who were sitting around him at his table patted him on the back and laughed with him. Isaiah let the room finish their laugh, and then he resumed his speech.

"My brothers, in order for us to let America know where we stand as colored people we have to have our own leaders to say the words we want to say! We have to have our own money to buy the things we need to buy! We have to have our own schools to teach our children what we want them to know! Until we do, we're not free!

"All that we have is the freedom to strut across the white man's farm until he is ready to send us to the slaughterhouse!"

The crowd members stood to their feet again and clapped for a few minutes. Isaiah stepped away from the podium again, and waited patiently for them to be seated

"Some of you may not agree with what I am about to say, but it needs to be said, and it needs to be said today. My brothers, we have to start including our women in the development of our neighborhoods. I'm talking politically, economically, and socially. We can not uplift ourselves without the backbone of our existence.

"Furthermore, there is strength in numbers. By including our women, our wives, our mothers, our daughters, our sisters and so forth, in our struggle to make a better way *for* our colored people, we strengthen the foundation *of* our colored people. They serve themselves, nor us, any purpose by standing in the background watching us, when we are millions of voices short already. If you all know colored women like I do, for everyone of their voices, it sounds like two of ours," Isaiah joked.

The men in the room laughed along. Then Isaiah continued.

"It's time for us to wake up and realize that freedom is not anything to be delegated to us. Because when delegated, it can be revoked. We have to stand up, as one people, under one God, and fight for our freedom. Not with fists, or guns. But with education and finances. Brothers, please heed my call, until all colored men are free, then none of us are free!

"The time has come for this nation to stand before God, and justify herself for what she has done to people of color. When will that day arrive when America will see, a time when all are equal, a time when all are free... gentlemen, our time has come!" Isaiah said, completing his speech.

He gathered his speech papers and sat down to a standing ovation. The congregation stood for minutes whistling and clapping their hands. The host speaker of the event waited for Isaiah to receive all of his accolades, then closed the meeting. William walked on the stage and hugged Isaiah as the group stood and dispersed.

"Who woulda thought quiet ol' Zay could preach to a crowd like that. I wish Orabell and Red were here to hear you, Zay; I'm proud of you, big brother," William said.

"Are you crying, man?" Isaiah asked.

"No, man, that's from the extra onions on those scalloped potatoes."

"No, it's not! I know the difference between onion tears, and baby tears. You're crying like a baby because you're proud of your brother. Don't be ashamed, William; every man has to cry sometime."

"Zay, if you ever breathe a word of this to anybody I'm going to have to make you disappear," William said, putting his arm around Isaiah's shoulder and leading him off of the stage. "I feel good. Now I know how all you crying fellas feel; it's a big relief. I feel kind of...kind of womanly. To make up for all of the times I should have cried, I think I am going to go home and cry to Red just for the hell of it."

Isaiah looked at William, and William looked at Isaiah, as a group gestured for Isaiah to come and sit with them. They were the Grandmasters, who were the governors of all the lodges in their respective states.

"What do you think they want with me?" Isaiah asked. "You think I went too far in my speech?"

"I don't know, but let's go find out, Marcus Garvey."

The two brothers walked over to the table of the distinguished elderly men and formally introduced themselves.

"Young man, that was the best speech I ever heard. Are you a preacher?"

"No, sir, I am just a passionate speaker about our rights to live freely in our country," Isaiah replied.

"Me and the brothers would like to invite you to our conferences in our home states to speak. You are inspirational, and some of our people need to hear what you have to say. If you don't mind, would you like to hear some advice from an old man?"

"Why, of course, sir, absolutely."

"We need you to do exactly what you are doing, just the way that you are doing it. But I want to tell you, your heart is ahead of its time."

"I don't quite understand, sir."

"Your heart is in the right place; it's just ahead of its time. This country is not ready for a black man to talk the way you are talking, black or white. I'm not telling you to stop preachin' or stop speechin'; we need to hear that. All that I'm sayin' is that colored folks were slaves for three hundred years. That means you have generation after generation of folks thinking like a slave, depending on white folks for everything—when to sleep, when to work, when to eat, even when to be with your own wife.

"Black folks have only been free for seventy-five years; that's only a quarter of the time we spent as slaves. As much as we may want to act free, we can't! Because we still hear the sounds of screams from our women being raped, and the visions of our black men being hung. That fear is not easy to forget."

Isaiah was all too familiar with the plight of the colored man. He drifted back to his childhood, frozen with the image of his strong, courageous father hanging from a tree. He heard the voice of the old man through his thoughts, and maintained his focus on their conversation. The old man was still talking, unaware that Isaiah had been lost in thought.

"I don't want you to be discouraged, I am simply warning you of the day when you run across one of us black folks who may not have forgotten those first three hundred years. They won't be too supportive of the way you're thinking. You just remember that you are not here to be their enemy. Don't be offended, and don't offend them."

"With all due respect, sir, why do you refer to colored folks as black?"

"Look at yourself, son. To refer to yourself as colored, is to disclaim any foundation of ethnicity. To be called colored calls you everything and nothing. It is to say that you are, but it does not say who you are.

"Every man on this earth is of color. And we have to specify who we are from birth, to death. It may not seem so important today. But as you get older you are going to want to pass to your offspring the tree of your family. You are going to want to tell them about the pride of their culture, their heritage. But how can you when you do not know from whence you came, my son?

"Our families, our heritage, our roots; they have been lost to time because of slavery. Now we allow ourselves to roam as people without a tribe. We ridiculously call ourselves colored! Don't your skin have color?"

"Yes, sir. But it's brown, sir."

"It's black, son! Black as the night's impregnable darkness. Black to define the infinite will of your people that has lasted four hundred years. Black to conceal the bruises of whips, rapes, and ropes. Black to be proud, and defy the definition of being dirty, sad, evil, sullen, dismal and wicked. Look at you, son; you wear a black suit, black shoes, black tie and black hat, and you look cleaner than you'll ever look in your life. You're a black man, and you should wear your skin with the same pride that you wear that suit."

"Thank you for your bit of information, sir. It certainly gives me something to think about," Isaiah said, shaking the man's hand.

The other men at the table gave their agreeing head nods. Isaiah told the men how honored he was that they took the time to give him their advice. He walked around the table, and individually shook their hands.

As he was leaving, his Masonic brothers took the opportunity to invite him to speak at several different engagements not associated with Freemasonry. Isaiah accepted every invitation. Hopefully this would provide an opportunity for him to spread his message.

Isaiah and William mingled for a while, then went back to their hotel room. They left for Saginaw early the next morning.

CHAPTER EIGHT

saiah traveled from city to city throughout the Midwest of America speaking at a variety of engagements. William accompanied him whenever he had to travel overnight. He was rapidly becoming a household name for colored people in Ohio, Michigan, Indiana and Illinois.

Orabell missed Isaiah when he had his overnight trips. But to see him fulfill his dream of educating colored people of their right to equality made the loneliness less painful. When Isaiah and William were out of town, Orabell would stay with Red, or Red would stay with her. They spent most of their nights discussing their husbands—confessing to one another how proud they were of them.

Isaiah asked their wives never to emphasize, or boast about their roles as public leaders to their friends and neighborhoods. As difficult as it was, the women kept their lips tight, and would only boast to themselves.

Red was ecstatic with the maturity of William after he involved himself with Isaiah's trek to emancipate the minds of the Negro. His sarcasm was ever present, but his appreciation for his family became first and foremost. His yen to leave behind a legacy to his offspring surfaced with enthusiasm and declaration.

When making love, Isaiah exhibited passion of which Orabell had never experienced. After every trip, the lovemaking would intensify, and the post-coital tenderness would have a lingering effect. These were the conversations the women shared, and enjoyed before bedtime. During the day, they went shopping for clothes, or to the market for food. They were always together, truly thinking of each other as sisters. Red had become the second big sister to Stanford. She disciplined, and rewarded him as if they were blood brother and sister who had known each other forever.

On occasion, Stanford would ask to go to the market with his sisters to meet girls his age. Most of the time they would make him stay at home, but when they knew they would be bringing back a lot of bags from shopping, they would let him follow along

In May of 1938, while Isaiah and William were away on a trip, Stanford tagged along with Orabell and Red to the supermarket. Orabell and Red split up to get their individual items. Stanford went with Red. He felt he had a better chance of persuading her, than Orabell, into buying him the foods he liked.

Orabell gathered her items and headed for the cash register. Shortly thereafter, Stanford and Red pushed their cart behind her. Orabell noticed some of the items in Red's basket were Stanford's favorite.

"Why do you let that boy trick you into buying all that mess, Red?"

"You know that boy can't trick me; it's not going to kill him to let him have a little young folks' food. Instead of eating greens and peas all the time."

"He know better than to come up to me begging for that mess!"

"That's a mean woman right there," Stanford said, pointing at Orabell.

"You ain't seen mean. You keep clownin' in this market, and you will," Orabell said. "Go stand over there by the door until we sack this food."

Stanford walked towards the door and a package of cigarettes fell out of his jacket. The store clerk, a middle-aged white gentleman, noticed the cigarettes and picked them up.

"Where'd you get these cigarettes from, boy?" the clerk asked.

"I had 'em in my jacket pocket, and they fell out."

Orabell and Red hurried to push their baskets through the line to see what was the matter.

"Stanford, what are you doing with those cigarettes?" Red asked.

"Those better not be your cigarettes!" Orabell shouted.

"Somebody gave them to me!"

"You got those cigarettes from off that shelf, didn't you?" the clerk said, pointing to a shelf stacked with cigarettes.

"Naw! I told you somebody gave them to me!"

"You stole them cigarettes, now admit it!"

"I ain't admittin' nothin', 'cause I ain't stole nothin'!"

"I'm callin' the law! You folks are not coming in here liftin' our products without payin' for it, one way or the other."

"Liftin' your products?" Orabell said. "Mister, it ain't nothin' in here we need to lift!"

"I know my ears must have heard wrong. Because I know this man didn't just stand here and call us thieves, did he?" Red asked.

"I think he did, Red," Orabell said, putting her hands on her hips.

"Mister, let me tell you something. My friend and I don't have to steal nothing from this store. If we need something, we'll buy it. But if you want to insult us by calling us thieves, it may be best if we never come back in this store at all," Red said.

"I don't give a rat's ass what you do, but this boy here is going to pay for these cigarettes," the clerk said.

"I ain't payin' for somethin' that already belong to me."

The clerk grabbed Stanford by the arm and pulled him to the rear of the store, creating a spectacle for everyone in the store to see. Orabell and Red rushed behind them. The clerk was accompanied by another clerk, who assisted in dragging Stanford to the office in the back.

After they dragged him into the office, his shirt and jacket were ripped, and one of his shoes had fallen off. Stanford fought the clerks off, and jumped to his feet. Orabell and Red pushed their way into the office and stood between Stanford and the clerks to try to get the situation under control.

"Stop it! Stop it! Before somebody get hurt!" Red said to the clerks.

"Somebody is going to get hurt, and it's going to be that nigger!"

"You put yo' hands on me again, and I'll kill yo' cracka ass!"

"Shut up, boy! Now you just stand there and keep yo' mouth shut! Do you hear me talking to you?" Orabell screamed.

"Yeah, I hear you," Stanford mumbled.

Red stood behind Stanford, wrapped her arms around his waist, and pulled him out of the office. Red put Sanford behind her, and she held him back with her body. Orabell stood in the doorway where the two clerks were, and tried to reason with them. The two men warned her to move out of the way, or they were going to knock her out of the way. Orabell accepted their challenge and told them what they had to do.

Most of the customers in the store were colored people, and it goes without saying that they knew Orabell and Red. A woman named Janie saw the clerk grab Stanford by the arm and left the store immediately. Janie's husband was a member of the WNM group, and she was proud of the contribution Orabell and Red had given on behalf of the colored women in their neighborhood. She was not going to stand by and watch these proud women be treated with such indignation. She ran to get some of the men from the WNM to help resolve the altercation.

Janie had no idea that Isaiah and William had returned from their overnight trip. When she saw them taking their suitcases into the house, she quickly told them what was happening at the store.

"Isaiah, y'all gotta come help Orabell and Red. They in trouble at the store," Janie said, completely out of breath.

"They're in trouble," Isaiah asked. "What's the matter?"

"Two white men at Crawford's Store jumped on Orabell's brother, and I don't know what they're going to do next."

"Don't worry about it. Everything will be all right, Janie," William said.

"Let's get down there, man!" Isaiah said, throwing his suitcase in the house, and ripping back outside.

Isaiah and William sprinted the six blocks to the grocery store. Their adrenaline prevented them from being short of breath when they arrived at the store. There was a crowd of people standing outside of the store, which forced them to have to push and squeeze their way to the front. The crowd let them through and they forced their way inside.

"I know our wives didn't cause all of this," William said.

"Your wife may not have caused all of this, but mine is quite capable!" Isaiah shouted, yelling over the crowd.

After they were inside of the store, they were greeted by two white men, who tried to stop them from going any further.

"You all can't come in here right now, come back later when the owner reopens the store," one man said, holding a broom in his hand.

"You don't understand; my wife is in this store, and I need to make sure she's all right," Isaiah said, stepping in front of William.

"Naw, I think you don't understand. The store is closed and nobody is coming in, or going out, until the owner takes care of this problem. Now turn on around, and go on back outside."

The crowd outside started to chant the words, "Let him in! Let him in! Let him in!" But the men were not fazed. William heard Red's cries asking someone in the back to let her go, and it was too much for him to handle.

"Look here, we don't want any trouble, we just want to make sure our wives are OK. Now I am going back there whether you want me to, or not. I'd rather we do this peacefully, but if you insist on violence, you're gonna need a lot more than that broom to stop me from taking my wife out of here," William said.

"Aren't you Isaiah Chambers?" the man asked. "You better talk some sense into this boy before he gets all of you niggers hurt."

"To tell you the truth, Mister, I feel like we've said too much already," Isaiah said, snatching the broom out of the man's hand, and striking him to the floor.

William smiled as he watched Isaiah send the man to the floor.

"Oh shit!" William said. "I guess that little ding-dong has grown up. Let's kick some ass."

Isaiah and William fought the two men all the way to the back of the store where their wives were being held. When they got to the office, Red was standing in front of Stanford, holding him back. Orabell was standing in the office door trying to reason with the two managers.

One of the managers pushed her violently out of the way, knocking her against the wall. The other was reaching for Red when William leaped in front of her.

"I see you like to push around women and children," William said. "Here I am; let's see how you fare with a grown man."

As William reached for the manager, the second manager attacked him. Isaiah grabbed Orabell to see if she was injured, but Orabell was made from a tough fabric and a little push was nothing more than an irritating mosquito bite to her.

Isaiah saw William battling the two managers, and quickly went to his aid. The physical confrontation didn't last long. The police arrived and got the situation under control very quickly. The police questioned everyone involved, and in the end, the store employees, Red, and Orabell were released, and Isaiah, William, and Stanford were arrested and taken to jail for disorderly conduct. They would only have to spend one night in jail, and then be released on their own recognizance the next morning.

They were placed in a cell that housed fifteen men. It was the first time Isaiah had ever been behind bars. William was jailed once, for violating a White's Only Law in Mississippi. Stanford on the other hand, was a former frequent guest of the Derma County Courthouse. Jail was like a second home. However, in Michigan, he had not sought trouble, and trouble had not found him.

While locked up, Isaiah and William interrogated Stanford to find out what had led him, and their wives, into that situation.

"They say you stole some cigarettes, Stanford. I want you to tell me what happened, and I want you to tell me the truth," Isaiah said.

"All right, Isaiah," Stanford said, "but you got to promise me you won't tell Orabell. She'll kill me."

"You run around like a gangster, staying in trouble. But you're afraid to tell your sister you stole some cigarettes," Isaiah said.

"You're scared of her, too!" Stanford said. "You know how she is when she get mad. She was about to fight both of those crackas in that sto'."

"You better forget your sister and worry about me. You don't have any-where to run up in here. Now tell me what happened."

"I forgot that I had a pack of smokes in my jacket, and when I pulled my hands out of my pockets they fell on the floor in the store. That ol' cracka thought I stole 'em from the store, and he tried to drag me to the back of the sto'."

"Why didn't you just go to the back and tell him you didn't steal them, instead of trying to fight them?" Isaiah asked.

"He never gave me a chance; he just grabbed me by my arm, and started pulling on me. Orabell and Red got mad when he did that, and they made him let me go."

"OK, Stanford, I believe you, but you better be telling the truth," Isaiah said.

"I ain't lying; ask Orabell. She'll tell you, those crackas started everything," Stanford said, sitting against the wall in a corner.

"What were you doing with cigarettes anyway?" William asked.

"Nothin'."

"You were going to do something with them, or else you wouldn't have had them in your jacket," Isaiah said.

"I'm not your daddy. I can't tell you what you can, or can not do. But until you are grown, and taking care of yourself, I better not ever see you with another cigarette. That's for grown folks," William said.

"They ain't gon' hurt me; why can't I smoke?" Stanford said.

"Because smoking is for grown people, and you're not grown, Stanford. I'm not your father either, and I'm not trying to be. But we're telling you right. Wait until you're grown," Isaiah said.

"All right, I'll leave 'em alone. But you have to promise me you won't tell Orabell."

"Stanford, by now, she already knows. Go home and take your medicine like a man." Isaiah laughed.

"Hey, Zay, I could not believe my eyes when I saw you snatch that broom out of that man's hand and knock him down. I asked myself, is this the Zay I know?" William said.

"It take a lot to get you mad, Isaiah, but when you get mad, you will fight like everybody else," Stanford said.

"I wasn't that mad. A person doesn't always fight because he's mad; a fool does that. Sometimes a man fights because he has to. I wasn't mad at those men today. But they had my wife in the back, and they weren't listening to reason. I did what I had to do to get to my wife. I can stand before my God with no shame," Isaiah said.

"Zay, I swear, you one hell of a man. You're the only man I know, who can kick somebody's ass, then turn around, and preach about it," William said.

"This is 1938, Uncle William; niggas can do that nowadays!" Stanford said.

"Why do you refer to your own people as niggas?" Isaiah asked.

"'cause that's what we are. We niggas! And they crackas!" Stanford said.

"No, my little ignorant brother. We are Negroes, not niggas. They are white, and not crackas. And all of us are people. How are we to convince white people that we are not niggas, if we still believe that we are niggas?" Isaiah asked.

"Isaiah, ain't nothin' gon' ever change between us and them. I want to believe what you sayin', 'cause I know you a man who ain't never lied to me. But just because I'm young don't mean I don't know what I'm talkin' 'bout," Stanford continued.

"You can go preach all over the world, and get people excited 'bout colored folks and white folks gettin' along. But look at you; as soon as you get back home, back to your real world, you have to fight to save your wife, and go to jail for protectin' your family."

"If we all just people, how come it ain't no white folks in here with us?" Stanford asked.

"You see, it's that way of thinking, Stanford. That way of thinking is what I'm trying to change. White people can't make you a nigga, by mistreating you.

"Colored folks were slaves for three hundred years. It's going to take time for the former masters, and the former slaves to identify their roles as just being man and man. Our battle has just begun, and we've got so far to go, I doubt if I will ever witness any significant change. But perhaps you will, or maybe our children. Maybe even our children's children. But one day, son, we will thank God and say, our time has come!"

William had been present at the majority of Isaiah's speeches, and he thought of them as great. But Isaiah was still Zay from Derma County, Mississippi. However, listening to him talk to Stanford made William realize that he was in the presence of an extraordinary man. For after all the attention Isaiah had received, all of the praises, and the glory, he was still a humbled man—humbled by the passion to fulfill his prophecy.

Isaiah spoke to Stanford with the same passion, the same enthusiasm and desperation with which he spoke to a congregation of thousands. He didn't care who listened, or who turned away. William found himself, for the first time, eager to hear the message and not just the messenger.

Isaiah walked over to Stanford and wrapped his arm around his shoulder.

"Hey, man, you have come up here, and turned your life around. Don't let anybody make you think you deserve anything other than first-class respect. You understand?" Isaiah said, looking up to Stanford who had grown to be an inch or two taller than he was. "Did you grow while I was gone?"

"If he did, he got every last inch from out of my refrigerator," William said.

The three of them laughed and joked until an officer allowed them to make one call each. Stanford refused his call. He didn't want to hear Orabell until he had no choice. William talked to Red, and she told him her version, and then Isaiah spoke with Orabell and she told him her version. Both versions were the same: Stanford dropped a pack of cigarettes, a clerk grabbed him and took him to the back—which led to a squabble. Then Isaiah and William arrived and things got out of control.

Isaiah convinced Orabell not to come down so hard on Stanford. He also told Orabell that Stanford needed an ally more than an enemy when he was released, to reinforce his positive attitude. She agreed that that would be best.

The night went quick, and after appearing in court for disorderly conduct, they were released. They were met by a crowd of cheering spectators. The newspaper showed up later in the day to write a story on the incident, to get the colored folks' side.

The incident gave Isaiah instant notoriety, then fact gave way to myth as the word spread, and the truth changed. Isaiah was no longer recognized solely in the colored neighborhoods, but also in the white ones. His reputation preceded him everywhere he traveled. He was in such demand, he was offered money for his speaking engagements to help him with his travels. The extra income enabled Isaiah to provide for his family in ways he had only imagined. He bought a brand-new car, along with new furniture for the house. Money, or the lack thereof, was never an issue in his household again.

As his popularity increased, so did the risks for danger. He received numerous death threats from anonymous people. One of his hotel rooms was set on fire, in an attempt to prevent him from speaking. On another occasion, William's exhaust pipe was plugged, causing minor damage to the car. Although the threats were being carried out, they did not hinder the progression of Isaiah's prophecy.

CHAPTER NINE

SAGINAW, MICHIGAN 1938

In June, Stanford graduated from high school. Isaiah saved the money from his speeches to pay for his tuition for his freshman year. He also helped him register for college.

Isaiah tried desperately to get Stanford enrolled at Howard University in Washington, D.C., and eventually he was successful. William attended graduate studies at Howard and had friends who still lived in the capital city. He asked them if they would look after Stanford and help him adjust to being in college, in a big town.

Stanford was excited about going to college and leaving his family to become his own man. He knew he would encounter some difficult times, and maybe even occasional homesickness, but to be on his own was worth it all.

Before he left for college, he had a great obstacle to overcome. That was to make it through the summer. The weekend after he graduated, Isaiah had to speak to a group of students at a college in Wilberforce, Ohio. It was supposed to be an overnight trip, but he was anxious to get back to his family so he drove back the same day.

When he arrived home it was late. He thought Orabell and Stanford would be asleep, but he found Orabell sitting on the couch staring out of the window. He was deeply concerned that maybe she was becoming depressed again.

"Hey, baby, what are you doing up?"

"I'm worried about Stanford. He left this afternoon, and he ain't been back."

"He's probably over to William's house."

"I already walked down there. He ain't there."

"Don't worry about it. He'll turn up."

"You're right. Go get some sleep. I know you're tired from all that driving," Orabell said.

"I sure am." Isaiah yawned.

Orabell separated the curtains, and continued to look out of the window from side to side. Isaiah undressed and lay in the bed. He tried to sleep, but couldn't, too worried about Stanford. He growled forcing himself to get back out of the bed, and put on some clothes. He walked passed Orabell sleeping on the couch, with her hands still holding the curtains back. Orabell heard his footsteps and woke up.

"Where you going, baby?"

"To get your brother."

"You know where he is?"

"I think so."

Isaiah drove over to Potter Street, and parked. Potter Street was the social area where you could find nightclubs and bars. If there was anything you needed, and it wasn't on Potter Street, it wasn't in Saginaw.

Isaiah walked up and down Potter Street, but found no signs of Stanford. He decided to stand around the clubs in the middle of the strip, because sooner or later, he would have to pass his way. Much sooner than later he saw Stanford and two other boys walking down the street holding brown paper bags.

"Out pretty late tonight aren't you, Mr. Moore?"

"What you doing down here, Isaiah?" Stanford asked. "Never thought I'd see you on Potter Street."

"What am I doing down here? The question is what are you doing down here?" Isaiah said. "And drinking!"

"I'm just hanging with my buddies," Stanford said.

"You know you should have been home a long time ago. Your sister is worried to death. It's against the law to have alcohol; now put that bottle down and get home."

"You ain't my daddy; my daddy dead."

"I'm not your daddy, huhn? You live under my roof! You eat my food! I put clothes on your back! So I am your daddy, and your mama, too!"

"I don't have to live with you. I can live with Uncle William until I go to college."

Isaiah slapped the bottle out of Stanford's hand, pointed in the direction of their house and shouted, "Get yourself home....NOW! And I better not hear another word come out of your mouth, Stanford."

Stanford walked toward the car angrily, but quietly. Isaiah turned to Stanford's two friends and looked them up and down, trying to figure out if he recognized them.

"You boys ever heard of Prohibition?"

"Pro-what?" one of the boys asked.

"Prohibition, it's a federal law. You can go to jail for being in the possession of an alcoholic substance."

"I ain't never heard of that before," the boy said.

"You're Janie's son, aren't you?" Isaiah asked.

"Yessir."

"Pour that poison out and get in the car and let me take you home, son."

The two boys turned their bottles upside-down until all of the alcohol was poured out. Then they jumped in the car where Stanford was already waiting. Isaiah walked both boys to their doors, and explained to their parents that they had been drinking.

Orabell was waiting at the door for Isaiah. As soon as she saw that Stanford was not harmed in any way, she let him have it.

"Where in the world have you been, boy?"

"I was outside down the street."

"You weren't down no street. You almost gave me a heart attack. You always sittin' around here talkin' about how much of a man you are, you need start acting like a man."

"I do act like a man."

Isaiah covered his ears, walked into the bedroom and closed the door behind him.

"If you was actin' like a man, Isaiah wouldn't have to go lookin' for you."

"Isaiah didn't have to come lookin' for me. He came lookin' for me because you probably bugged him to death. I can take care of myself."

"You can take care of yourself, huhn? Boy, you don't have a hole to piss in, nor a shovel to cover it up. How can you take care of yourself?"

"I'm tired of you yellin' at me all the time, O'Bell. Leave me alone!"

Stanford stomped to his room and slammed the door. Isaiah tried to ignore their sister/brother argument, but once he heard Stanford yell, then slam his door, he knew Orabell was going to do something drastic to him. Isaiah threw on some clothes and walked into Stanford's bedroom before Orabell erupted.

"I know you not slammin' my do', in my house!"

"I'm tired of you, O'Bell. Why won't you get away from me, and leave me alone?"

"Leave you alone, you wont me to leave you alon,e nigga? OK, I'll leave you alone. Stay right here. I'll be right back, and then I'll leave you alone!"

Isaiah was standing in Stanford's doorway, as Orabell barged passed him and rushed into their bedroom.

"Boy, what have you done now?" Isaiah asked.

"Man, just tell her to stay away from me, and leave me alone!" Stanford yelled.

"I bet you better take some of that bass out of your voice, when you to talk to me!"

"Y'all make me sick!"

"I ain't made you sick yet, but I'm about to," Orabell said, flapping a belt in her hands.

"Orabell, that boy is too old for you to try to whoop."

"Watch and see!" Orabell said, swinging the belt at Stanford's legs.

Stanford jumped from the bed and tried to snatch the belt out of Orabell's hand. Isaiah snatched him by the arm and tossed him back on the bed.

"Don't be no fool, boy. It's better you take that belt, than me," Isaiah said.

"Let him be a fool, Isaiah. I wish he would!" Orabell shouted.

Isaiah walked out of the room, and let Orabell give her brother something he should have received a long time ago. Isaiah smiled as he heard the continuous sound of the belt, and the cries that immediately followed.

Within a minute or two, Isaiah had fallen into a deep contented sleep.

The next day Stanford surprisingly apologized to his sister and Isaiah for his behavior. He joked with Orabell about taking a belt to his hide at his age. But inside he knew that it was love behind his whipping.

★★★

In the weeks that followed, Stanford concentrated on preparing to live in another city, far from the security of his family. He researched the history of Washington, D.C., and even more specifically, Howard University.

Isaiah decided to take Stanford on the road to a few of his conferences, to expose him to different people from different parts of the country. Stanford traveled with him and William to Washington, D.C. This would be their longest trip, and largest conference. There would be professors from Howard University, and other colleges participating in a review on the progression of the colored man since the Emancipation Proclamation. By meeting some of the professors from Howard University, this conference would allow Stanford to get a head start on his collegiate career.

They arrived at their hotel to check in, and Isaiah went to register them in one room as usual, but William decided to rent a room of his own. He wanted to give Isaiah and Stanford space. Isaiah thought it was a generous gesture and thanked him. They settled into their rooms and prepared for the conference.

Isaiah started off the meeting with an opening speech that motivated the crowd. By this time he was well known, and people looked forward to his unique speeches. Isaiah used parables, and experiences from his past to get his audience to relate to his speeches.

This conference was the first time Stanford had ever heard Isaiah speak. He sat in amazement listening to this normally quiet man, lift his voice, and speak like a bass-voiced angel. He watched the audience as they responded with laughter, and tears. He never imagined that this was what Isaiah was doing when he was away from home. He started to view upon Isaiah with reverence. *Pride* was much too shallow a word for the way he was feeling.

"Good evening, all of you Black men." Isaiah saw that there were numerous women in the audience as well as men and he quickly apologized.

"Excuse me, ladies, I sincerely apologize for being so disrespectful. I am so used to only speaking to my brothers that I almost made a grave mistake. Well, I guess I did make a mistake, but I caught myself. Let me shut up before I put my foot deeper in my mouth than I already have. I'm sorry, sisters, and as beautiful as you all are looking tonight that should have been the first thing that came out of my mouth. I hope we can have more conferences where more of our sisters come out and join us. I tell the brothers all the time, once we get our sisters on the boat, we won't have to worry anymore about how the ship will sail, because everything will be smooth sailing.

"Ladies and gentlemen, as I speak tonight, you will hear me refer to Negroes as Black people. Some of you may have heard of the term, others may not. A wise old man explained to me the definition of the term and I will pass it on to you.

"He told me that Black is symbolic of the night's impregnable darkness. Black to define the infinite will of your people that has lasted four hundred years. Black to conceal the bruises of whips, rapes, and ropes. Black to be proud, and defy the definition of being dirty, sad, evil, sullen, dismal and wicked. Just as we have defied the dirt, the sadness, the evil, the sullen, the dismal, and the wickedness that has been brought upon our people.

"We have gathered here this evening to discuss the progression of the black man since the Emancipation Proclamation was instated. We know one thing for sure: if it wasn't instated we wouldn't be united here to night like this. Let's all clap our hands for the Emancipation Proclamation."

The crowd gave a round of applause.

"Notice, my brothers and sisters, that I didn't say let's give a round of applause to our sixteenth president, Mr. Abraham Lincoln. I can not stand here and take away the enormity of his liberal thinking on behalf of slavery. Nor can I stand here and praise his name for the deliverance of God's people. Lincoln did what he had to do to keep America united. If it meant freeing the slaves, then that is what had to be done. If it meant not freeing the slaves, then that is what had to be done. Lincoln did what was best for his political agenda, and that agenda was freeing the slaves. If the pressure would have come down the other side of the pole, we would still have to carry papers on us ever where we go. Some of them would say *free*, and some of them would say *slave*. Don't get me wrong. I thank Mister Lincoln just as much as the next man. But before I jump up and down, and start singing hallelujah to Jesus, I need to know one thing. And that is, what would happen if President Roosevelt was to face the same crisis. If our nation was divided upon reinstating slavery, I wonder what would President Roosevelt do? What if the South decided to stage a war against the North again to deny the freedom of Black people, what would our president do? Huhn? Does anybody here think they know? Shoot! I know I don't."

The crowd mumbled slowly, responding to the rhetorical questions Isaiah had asked.

"As we migrate up North looking to make a better way for ourselves, we tend to forget that as we migrate, so do the same bigoted white folks we left in the South. Pretty soon, they will inhabit just as much of the new land as we Black folks. So you are not going to outrun discrimination; you can just run from it for a while. And by the way the white people up North are not that much different from the white people down South anyway. They feel as if they are not as ignorant as the ones in the South, so they try to cover up their uncivilized behavior. Their discriminatory tactics are not as blatant, but they're apparent.

"I don't care if you're in Derma County, Mississippi, or Saginaw, Michigan. New Orleans, Louisiana or New York, New York. Northern or Southern Carolina, or Northern or Southern California.

"Don't think you can talk to a white man like you can talk to a black man and get away with it. If you're willing to talk that way to a white man, you better be willing to die!

"Don't think that you can go to a bank and get a loan, just like a white man can!

"Don't think you can sit next to a white woman on the front of a train or a bus, just because you see an open seat!

"Don't think that when you're sick and dying, a white doctor is going to care for you just because he has no other patient to see after!

"Don't think that my light skin is any different from your dark skin when it comes to a noose!

"Don't think that your woman is safe from master, just because he sneaks through the back door now, and not the front door to have his way with her!

"Don't think you can be President of the United States of America just because Abraham Lincoln signed a piece of paper saying you are free!

"If you want to know what I think about your Emancipation Proclamation, I will tell you, brothers and sisters. Until the words on that piece of paper become actions on this earth, I don't think about it one bit!" Isaiah screamed.

The crowd members jumped to their feet, and cheered loudly.

"I say this time and time again. We give too much credit to white men, and not enough to the Lord. We congratulate Abraham Lincoln, for freeing us and treating us like people, instead of getting on our knees and praying to the Lord to give us the will to free ourselves. We have him on our side, and we can stand against discrimination, bigotry, prejudice…whatever. We have the strength, and the power to walk behind God into freedom. And I mean into true freedom. Not the freedom where another man tells you where to live, and where to die. But into freedom where you can make your decisions to live and die wherever you choose."

The audience gave Isaiah a short applause.

"Some white people may think that I am the bigot, and they are the victims. They say that I'm starting trouble by dredging up the past. But I say unto you, my brothers and sister, if I have been victimized for centuries, should I not finally stand up, look my perpetrator in the eye, and tell him, you did this to me?

"Should I not say that I was a slave?

"Should I not say that my wife, my sister, my daughter, my mother and my grandmother were raped?

"Should I not say that my brother, my son, my father, and my grandfather were murdered?

"Should I not tell the truth?

"Why of course I do. I would not be a man, if I didn't.

"I should stand before the judge, and my perpetrator and I tell him the truth just as it happened and let my perpetrator deal with my testimony however he wishes. And that is what I am doing here today. I am standing before the highest judge of them all, and that is the Almighty God. I am confessing to him what has happened to me. I will let him lay down the verdict, and the sentencing. For vengeance is mine, sayeth the Lord."

Isaiah picked up his glass and drank a swallow of water to clear his throat.

"Before I go, I would like to have my brother and my brother-in-law stand up," Isaiah said, gesturing for William and Stanford to rise, which they did reluctantly.

"The old man, he's my brother William. He travels with me everywhere I go. No matter the conditions, he's always right there with me. That handsome young man right there is Stanford, and he's my brother-in-law. I am extremely proud of him. He will be the first one in his family to ever go to college. I've been raising him for so long I don't even think of him as my brother-in-law anymore; he's more like the son I always wanted.

"Outside of God, and my beautiful wife, they are the strength that keep me going. At this time, I will let Brother Hill come get the podium. God bless you all, and have a good evening."

The crowd gave Isaiah a lasting ovation, and Brother Hill, the host, waited for the applause to subside, then thanked Isaiah for his motivating speech.

"I have heard that brother speak on many occasions and I swear he gets my blood going every time. God bless you, brother," Brother Hill said, pointing to Isaiah.

When Isaiah introduced Stanford as the son he always wanted, it was nothing Stanford could do to stop himself from crying. He sat down and wiped his eyes with both hands, then Isaiah winked his eye to let him know that everything was all right.

After the conference meeting was over, Isaiah and William took Stanford around the room and introduced him to several prominent professors. Stanford was in awe of the men and their distinguishable manners.

The evening lasted for hours after the meeting and finally Isaiah suggested to Stanford that they retire for the evening. They looked for William to tell him that they were leaving for their rooms. William had made his way around the room, and there was no telling where he was at that time. They decided to walk back to their rooms without him. Stanford excitedly told Isaiah that he couldn't believe how he stood in front of that crowd and spoke the way he did.

"Isaiah, I ain't never heard a colored man speak like that before in my life. You sound like one of those smart white college boys."

"You need to understand that black people are just as intelligent as any other people. Although we are generations behind other races here in America as far as education is concerned we still have the capacity to learn as any other race on this earth.

"Almost ninety percent of our Black families have never had anyone in their family ever to attend college. Most of our families never even make it pass the eighth grade. It's hard to keep up with the changes in the outside world, if your inside world never changes."

"But you and Uncle William went to college."

"Who else do you know from Derma County went to college?"

"Nobody. I guess that's why y'all so much smarter than the rest of us."

"Intelligence is a relative word, Stanford. Where we come from, most people work on farms and they tend to animals. They can tell you everything about chickens, cows, hogs, all kinds of animals. How to raise them, how to take care of them when they're giving birth to new animals. What to do if they're sick. How to grow a good crop. All of these things are forms of intelligence. A man's intelligence in the White House means nothing if he had to go to Mississippi and tend to a farm. Unless of course he was raised on a farm.

"In order for us to compete with the other races, we have to learn what they know, and not just live with what we know. We have to learn how to speak articulately. That means to talk properly," Isaiah said.

"So you say if I learn how to talk, I can be smart?"

"Not exactly. What I am saying is that you need to learn how to speak articulately so that no matter where you are, you will be understood clearly."

"So I gotta learn a lot of big words to be a doctor?"

"You don't necessarily need to know a lot of big words, but you do need to always improve your vocabulary. Big words are not nearly as important as correct words. It is best to say the words you know for sure, than to try to say big words you may not say, or use properly."

"Man, how do you know all of this stuff, Isaiah?"

"Listening. Just like you're doing now."

"I wish I knew as much stuff as you do."

"You will as you get older, son."

They started their way down the hall to their room and Isaiah changed the subject.

"When was the last time you wrote your mother a letter, Stanford?" Isaiah asked.

"I don't remember."

"If you can't remember, that means it's been too long. You have nothing to do when you get in this room. I can't think of a better way for you to spend your time than to write Mrs. Moore."

"OK, Isaiah, I'll get started as soon as we get in the room."

They passed William's room first. Isaiah noticed that he had accidentally left his key in the door. Thinking that William was asleep, he knocked on the door, then immediately walked in.

"Man, what are you doing in here?" Isaiah shouted angrily. "Stanford, stay outside; better yet go on to the room and wait for me there."

"Hey, man, what are you doing?" William said. "Give me a second to get ready."

"Don't ask me what I'm doing; what are you doing?"

William reached for his pants, while a young woman covered herself with a blanket.

"Who is that?" she yelled.

"That's my brother," William said.

"I'll talk to you later, William, when you're more suitable for conversation," Isaiah said. "Excuse me, young lady, I didn't mean to startle you."

"Zay, wait! Zay! Wait a minute, man, let me explain!"

"Don't explain anything to me, man; explain it to your wife."

"Your wife?" the woman shouted.

"Shhh!"

"I didn't hear you tell me you had no wife!"

"I didn't hear you ask either. Get up and put your clothes on. I have to get you out of here."

"I ain't going nowhere. You said we were stayin' in a hotel all night, and I'm stayin' all night!"

"You know what, you can have the room. I'll get my stuff, and you can have the room," William said, gathering his clothes.

"Too bad, 'cause I was just getting started with your pretty red ass."

William paused holding his clothes. He looked at the door, and looked at the pretty young woman lying in the bed. Going back and forth from one to the other.

"Damn! I bet you were, baby," William said, kissing her one last time, then then dashing out of the door.

William ran a couple of doors down, and knocked on Isaiah's door. Isaiah opened it and stepped into the hallway to keep Stanford from hearing their conversation.

"Well, well, well, my brother the adulterer."

"I didn't do anything, Zay. I'm not going to lie; if you hadn't knocked on that door I'd probably be knee deep in it right now."

"That's just it, William. What if I hadn't knocked on your door, man?"

"I would have cheated."

"You have a beautiful woman that most men would kill for, and you step out on her. The woman worships the ground you walk on, and you do her like this. What's wrong with you, man?" Isaiah said, reaching up to smack William in the back of his head.

"Did you not see that girl, Zay?" William said, pointing at his room.

"So what! You have a beautiful wife at home who loves you to death."

"But that young girl made me feel young. I felt like I had my youth back."

"William, you are talking as if you have completely lost your mind. The fact is, that you're a thirty-seven-year-old man, with a wife. A young girl can't change that. You know it surprises me how someone so intelligent can be so stupid."

"Zay, she said she was going to put something on me, man, and I believe she was going to, too."

"You're still thinking about her, William. If you don't act like you have some kind of respect for your marriage I'm going to tell Red myself."

"You wouldn't dare."

"I was the one who asked her to marry you; you think I won't tell her to divorce you if you get out here acting a fool."

"You would, wouldn't you?"

"In a heartbeat, with no loyalty to you."

"Damn, Zay, I'm your brother."

"So!"

"Look, Zay, I didn't cheat, and I'm not going to cheat. Let's forget this ever happened and go to bed."

"You may not have gone all the way with that young lady but you did cheat," Isaiah said. "Get that girl out of your room and get some sleep."

"How about if I get rid of her, and I let Stanford have the room so you and I can talk?"

"That's fine, maybe I can keep an eye on you that way."

William went back to his room, and talked to the girl. Then he went back to Isaiah's room for the night.

"Stanford, the room is all yours. Let me walk you down here to let you in. The key is kinda tricky."

He and Stanford walked out of Isaiah's room, and into the hall.

"Let me ask you something, Stanford. Have you ever had a woman?" William whispered.

"I messed around some."

"Tell me the truth, son. Have you ever been with a woman before?"

"No sir, Uncle William."

"Well, tonight's your lucky night! There's a pretty little thang waiting for you in that room. Go get her."

"A girl in your room?"

"You're wasting time out here talking to me. Get on in there and do me proud."

"What if she don't like me, Uncle William?"

"She already likes you. Now are you going to go in there, or are you going to stay out here like a chicken?"

"How she look?"

"How much have you had, son?"

"I ain't had none yet."

"Well, she look better than anything you ever had before. Now go in there and do your business," William said, pushing Stanford towards the door.

"I'm going, Uncle William, don't push me!" Stanford said nervously.

William grabbed Stanford by the back of his pants and whispered, "Orabell and Isaiah better not ever hear about this, you hear me?" illiam said. "This is your graduation present."

"I won't tell nobody."

"Go get her, champ," William said, winking his eye at Stanford.

He watched until Stanford closed the door behind him. He stood in the hall for a minute to make sure he didn't run back out. The lights went out beneath the door, and William went back into Isaiah's room. Isaiah had cut the lights off, so William thought that it would be a great opportunity to slide under a blanket and go to sleep without hearing a sermon. He took his time covering up, careful not to disturb Isaiah. As soon as he was comfortable, and he thought he made it without a speech, he heard that old familiar voice of reasoning echoing through the room.

"You know, you just beat it all."

"What are you talking about, Zay. Go to sleep, man," William said.

"How could you have that woman in your room like that, William; you're a married man?"

"It was a moment of weakness!"

"You left a while ago. That was no moment of weakness; that was deliberate lust!"

"Now wait a minute before you start your preaching, if there is anyone in here who is without sin, let him cast ye, the first stone."

"You want me to cast a stone, William. Here's your stone!" Isaiah said, throwing a shoe at William.

"You almost hit me in the head with that shoe, man! You are acting more upset than Red would."

"We are supposed to be upstanding men and husbands. How can we honestly present ourselves in that light if we are acting like whoremongers, William?"

"Whoremongers! Damn, Zay! You sound just like a preacher. I didn't do anything, so stop preaching and go to sleep. Damn, man, calm down!"

"All that I know is that it better not happen again. If it does, I'm going to have to disassociate myself from you."

"Zay, you don't have to wait until it happens again. You can disassociate yourself right now! Tonight!" William shouted. "Please let me get some sleep, man, OK?"

"Take your sorry self to sleep, William. I'll finish my speech in the morning."

"Amen!" William shouted.

Isaiah left William alone and they both fell asleep. They were awakened the next morning bright and early with the sound of Stanford pounding on the door. He burst into the room excited about the trip. He admitted that without a doubt, this trip was the best time he had ever had in life. Isaiah was happy the trip made such a positive impression on him. William was resolved to know the truth—that it wasn't so much the trip, as it was the visitor he had been with the night before.

They packed their bags and headed back to Saginaw. On the way home, no one mentioned the visitor in William's hotel room and all of the secrets were kept intact. In the months to follow, Isaiah had so many speaking engagements he eventually quit his job at the automobile plant. The pay from speaking doubled his salary. Unfortunately, William could no longer attend all of the engagements because he still worked at the plant. But when Isaiah was in the state of Michigan, William was right by his side.

CHAPTER TEN

SAGINAW, MICHIGAN- 1939

By the fall of 1939, Red had opened a nurse's office out of her home. Stanford was comfortably settled in Howard University, and Orabell was comfortably settled as a Saginaw resident. However, Orabell was concerned with her health. She had become increasingly tired, and it made her recall the decline of her mother's ability to do daily functions for herself. She was very afraid, but she did not want to alarm Isaiah if it was only a seasonal ailment.

She asked Red if she could make an appointment without anyone else knowing. Red agreed to her request, and Orabell snuck over to Red's house for a physical examination.

"Good afternoon, Red. How ya doing today?"

"I'm fine, how about you?"

"I could be better. I'm not doing too well."

"What's wrong ?" Red asked. "Hold on, Orabell, I'll be right back."

Red went into her office and returned with a thermometer.

"Here, put this in your mouth."

Talking with the thermometer in her mouth, Orabell explained her symptoms. Red then snatched out the thermometer.

"Now talk. I can't understand a word you're saying with this thing in your mouth." Red laughed.

"I said sometimes I feel dizzy, and it's hard for me to stand up. I feel like I'm about to throw up or something. One time, I was so weak, I had to grab the zink just to keep myself up. I think I got what my mama got."

"Judging by your symptoms, Orabell, I think you may have what your mama had, too. Let me ask you a question. When was the last time you had your menstrual cycle?"

"My what cycle?" Orabell asked confusingly.

"Your period, girl!"

"I was supposed to been on my period three weeks ago. It's almost time for it to come back around again. I think it ain't came because of whatever this is that's making me sick. And if that's the case, I must be mighty sick."

"I declare, sometimes ignorance is almost funny, child."

"Am I sick? Is that why I can't have my period?"

"Well, you halfway right. The sickness you have is preventing you from having your period, and it is the reason for all of your ailments. But it's not a bad sickness, it's a good sickness. Sweetie, you are about to yourself have a baby!" Red shouted.

"Did I hear you right, Red?" Orabell whispered.

"Yes, you did, Darling. You are about to have yourself a baby!"

"Thank you, Jesus! Thank you, Jesus!" Orabell cried, "Are you sure Red?"

"By all accounts and reasons. I'm positive."

"I'm gon' be a mother? I'm gon' finally be a mother! What am I gon' do?" Orabell screamed.

"Run on home and tell your husband. I'm quite sure he wants to know."

Orabell went home and cooked Isaiah a meal with all of the fixings. When Isaiah walked in, he stopped dead in his tracks and looked around. He did not speak. He walked into each room and glanced over them very carefully.

"OK, it's a weeknight, and we have a Sunday dinner. Something is either very right, or very wrong. I just want to know that if it is something very wrong, am I the one that's in trouble?"

"Honey, what can I give you that nobody else can give you?" Orabell smiled.

"A headache in less than one second."

He walked into the kitchen and lifted the lid off of each pot to sniff its aroma.

"Stop foolin' around, Isaiah. I'm serious! What can I give you that no one else can give you?"

"I have no idea, sweetheart. As long as I have your love I don't need anything else."

Orabell stood at the stove and slowly placed the food from the pot onto Isaiah's plate. Isaiah pulled out a chair and prepared to sit down.

Orabell smiled, and stared into the pot that she was reaching into, and whispered, "I can give you a baby."

Isaiah missed the chair, and fell flat on the floor.

"Huh?" Isaiah mumbled as he looked from the ground upwards into Orabell's face.

"You gon' be a daddy, Isaiah!"

"Me, I'm pregnant? I mean you're pregnant?"

"Yes! Yes, baby! I'm pregnant! We pregnant!"

"I can't believe it. I'm going to be a father, and you're going to be a mother! I told you that when the Lord wanted us to have a baby, we would be blessed!

"You sure did, baby! We finally have a baby on the way!"

Isaiah stood up, and hugged Orabell. As they held each other in their kitchen, Isaiah looked up and mumbled the words, "Thank you, Jesus," then closed his eyes.

★★★

SAGINAW, MICHIGAN 1940

The winter was slow and long, but Orabell was unusually excited amidst the snow and freezing temperatures. And as the spring of 1940 began to thaw out the ice from the winter of 1939, she became even more excited.

However, her excitement was halted by a letter from her cousin Sarah, informing her that Mrs. Moore's illness had taken its toll. Orabell was devastated and grew sick from anxiety. She was never satisfied with the way that they had left her mother without saying a proper goodbye. Although she had exchanged letters with her mother, she had not spoken or seen her since they had left Mississippi.

Orabell's constant worrying began to make her blood pressure rise. In order to keep her pressure down, Isaiah told her that if Mrs. Moore was strong enough to travel, he would catch the train to pick her up, and bring her back to Saginaw.

Orabell pretended that she was feeling better, to keep Isaiah from going back to Mississippi. But Isaiah knew that she was still concerned about her mother's welfare, and it was causing her to have difficulty with her pregnancy. Isaiah also knew that he had to do something to reduce her anxiety

He tried desperately to contact Sheriff John Hankins to ask if he could help him with getting his mother-in-law out of town. But it was to no avail. He found no way of contacting him. Orabell suddenly realized that Sheriff Hankins had given her an envelope to give to Isaiah when they left Mississippi. She went into her closet and searched for the old pocketbook. To her surprise, she found it, and the envelope safe and sound. Orabell appreciated that Isaiah was willing to go get Mrs. Moore, but she did not want him to risk his life doing it.

Isaiah decided that he would take the train on his own to get his mother-in-law. Orabell realized that she was not going to talk him out of going, so she gave him the envelope. Inside the envelope was indeed Sheriff John's address and telephone number.

There was also a note explaining to Isaiah that Dr. West had also raped his mother while she worked on the West Plantation as well. Consequently, he, too, was the illegitimate son of the late Dr. West.

Isaiah stared at Orabell for what seemed like an eternity.

"What the letter say, Isaiah?"

"It says here that John is one of ol' West boys, too. I guess that makes the three of us brothers," he said, referring to William as the third brother.

"And there's no telling how many more he got runnin' around."

"I guess I need to get to a telephone and call John to see if he can help me get Mrs. Moore out of Derma County without people noticing."

"Isaiah, I love my mama, but I don't wont you goin' down there. Mama is in good hands. Sarah's not going to let anything other than God take Mama away from here."

"Orabell, you're worried sick about your mother, and it's causing you to have trouble with the baby. I'll go down there, get her and we'll be back within a week. Now don't go worrying about me. I'm in good hands, too, baby, God's hands."

Isaiah walked to William's house to use his telephone to call John. Isaiah wanted to discuss his leaving with William, but he was not at home. Red told him it was all right to use the telephone, and dialed John's telephone number for him. After John picked up the phone, there was a warm and unbelievable silence between both men when they heard each other's voice. Isaiah told John his situation, and John advised him to stay up North, and leave Mrs. Moore to the Lord. Isaiah pleaded with him, and told him that he didn't think Orabell, or perhaps the child, would survive the pregnancy if she continued to stress herself over her mother's illness. John finally agreed, and they worked out a plan to get him in and out of Derma County without being noticed. Red overheard the conversation and suggested that Isaiah waited until William returned home and discussed it with him before he left. She felt that William may want to take some time off of work and travel with him. He smiled and told her that one of them had to stay there and make sure the women folk were all right. She laughed at his sarcasm, knowing how often they left the women alone. He told Red he loved her, and she told him that she loved him, too. His words brought serious concern to her heart.

On Isaiah's way out of the door, he noticed a brand-new dictionary sticking out of Red's bookcase. He asked Red how much she wanted for the book, however, she refused any money and handed it to him.

Isaiah went back home and took a nap. When he woke up, he grabbed his suitcase and headed for the door.

"Tell my son that he may not have been born with wealth or white skin, but he was born with something much more valuable. And that's the hand of God. For the child least born will rise above the sun, to shine as the brightest one," Isaiah said softly.

"What make you think you are going to have a son, and why are you talking like you're not coming back to us, Isaiah?" Orabell said, hugging him tightly.

"I know that I am going to have a son because God has told me. And don't worry about me." Isaiah smiled.

"Please, please, be careful, Isaiah."

"I'm in God's hands now."

He held up a Bible and a dictionary and handed them to Orabell.

"Make sure my son knows the differences of these two books, Orabell." Holding up a dictionary, he said, "This one is to learn man's words, to live my by man's laws." Then he lifted the Bible. "And this one is to learn God's words, and live by God's laws."

"Isaiah, stop talkin' like that! Please, you makin' me scared. I don't want you to go down there!" Orabell cried.

"I have to go, it's my destiny. One way or the other, I have to go back and face my destiny. I'm in God's hand now, so don't save your tears for me. I love you with all of my heart and soul. And don't you let a day pass that you don't think about that. Goodbye, baby!" Isaiah kissed Orabell on her forehead, picked up his suitcase, and walked out of the door.

"Lord, please, please watch over my husband. He's all I got," Orabell cried.

A short while later, William burst through the door, yelling for Isaiah.

"Zay! Zay!" William shouted.

"He left already, William."

"That's not what I wanted to hear, Orabell."

"He's on his way to the bus station to catch the bus to Detroit."

"I swear that is the most stubborn, mule-headed man I have ever met in my life!"

"I gave him John's house telephone number, and he called him to meet him in Derma County."

"Orabell, why'd you let him go?" William said, slumped in the chair.

"How could I stop him?"

"Orabell, besides my wife, he's all that I have in this world as family. I can't lose him. I just can't lose him."

"He'll be fine."

William leaped from the chair and ran to the door. "I know what I'm going to do. I'm going to grab that mule-headed jackass, and pull him back by the tail."

He rushed out of the door, and sped down to the bus station. He drove up and left the car parked in the street. He ran into the station and asked for the bus destined for Detroit. He was told that the bus had just pulled off ten minutes earlier.

William jumped back into his car, and headed for the bus station in Detroit. As William sped off for Detroit, Isaiah walked out of the bathroom. Knowing he had missed his bus, he asked the bus clerk what time the next bus departed for Detroit. She told him it would be another three hours. Isaiah felt that since he had already broken Orabell's heart the first time he had left, it would serve him no purpose to duplicate her sadness by going home and leaving again. He grabbed a newspaper, and waited for the next bus to Detroit.

Meanwhile, four hours later William was sitting at the bus station. When the bus arrived from Saginaw, he was disappointed and confused to find that Isaiah was not on it. He asked the driver if had noticed a thin, light-skinned colored man who spoke properly. The bus driver said he'd had no one on his bus who fit that description. William climbed back into his car, and headed back to Saginaw

At that same time, Isaiah was boarding the bus, bound for Detroit. He found himself a seat with no one beside him, and quietly fell asleep.

Isaiah woke up as the bus was pulling into the Detroit station. He stepped off and grabbed his bag. He flagged down a taxi with two other colored people and they rode to the train station. He was too late to catch his train to Cincinnati so he spent the rest of the night sleeping on a bench. The next morning he finally settled on his train, and prepared for his long ride to Mississippi.

He sat next to the window and looked out at the remaining snow piled against the side of the road. He thought to himself: this is home. He eventually drifted back to sleep, and dreamt of his unborn child. In his dreams, the child was neither lightskinned, nor darkskinned. It had no eyes nor arms nor legs. The child didn't whimper or whine nor fret or moan. All that he heard was the soft, innocent sound of a child's laughter. In his dreams, there were two angels. Beautiful angels drenched in white. White that was unblemished. White that was much purer than the snow he had just witnessed in his reality. In his dreams, the angels sang songs unlike any song he had ever heard on earth. As the angels came closer to him, their faces materialized and he recognized the angel on his left to be his mother, and the angel on the right to be his wife. They spread their wings and the gentle breeze kissed him on his face. His mother stood behind him, and wrapped her wings around his body. As he opened his mouth to speak to her, he was awakened by the loud sound of the train's horn as it pulled into Cincinnati.

He quickly switched trains and headed on to Nashville, Tennessee. He switched trains in Nashville, heading for Memphis. When he boarded the train in Memphis, he was asked to move to a rear coach so that a white woman could have his seat. He moved to one of the rear coaches where there were only colored people. He gazed out of the window and noticed the sun seemed unusually orange. Blending in with the red dirt that sat as its feet. A far cry from the white snow of Michigan. He thought, *this too, is home.*

He arrived in Grenada, Mississippi tired and hungry from his two days of riding on trains. His suitcase was lost on of the transfers so he had no change of clothing. He walked the four miles to his relatives' community. They had a stretch of land with nearly twenty houses filled with nothing but Chambers.

As word spread that Isaiah was back, people came for miles to come and wish him well. In their eyes, Isaiah was nothing short of a hero. He was the first colored man that had ever stood up to white people and lived to see another day.

He shook the hands of men, hugged the women, and held the children. It was a celebration for their great colored hero, until the law pulled up and demanded to see Isaiah. One of Isaiah's relatives ran through the back door to warn him.

"Isaiah, you gotta get outta here! Quick! The law done pulled up outside, and he comin' to get you! Come this way!" the man said as he gestured for Isaiah to follow him.

"Where is he?"

"He right outside; now we best be gettin' on!"

Isaiah went to the window and peeked through the curtain. He smiled when he saw Sheriff John Hankins sitting on the hood of his squad car smoking a cigarette.

"He's OK. He's here to pick me up and take me to Mrs. Moore's house. I'll be staying with him until I go back up North." Isaiah laughed.

"Wait a minute, you tellin' me that afta all that ruckus you caused over there in Derma County, you gon' stay wit' a white man? And the sheriff at that! You hell, boy!" The relative laughed.

"Tell everybody I said goodbye, and it was good to see them again."

He walked outside and stood in front of John, they smiled and shook hands.

"It's been a long time, and I see that you're still a pipsqueak, Isaiah," John joked.

"And you're still a giant." Isaiah laughed back.

"How you been, friend?"

"I've been doing quite well…" Isaiah paused, then continued, "…brother."

★★★

When they pulled into John's yard, he told Isaiah that his wife did not know anything about Dr. West or his mother being raped. Nor did she know anything about him being Isaiah's half-brother. He also warned Isaiah that his wife grew up in an old traditional Mississippi household and she had that old traditional Mississippi mentality.

They walked into John's living room, as his wife, Rebecca, walked out of the kitchen drinking a glass of tea. Becky had long, red fluffy hair. Her complexion was quite pale for a Southern belle. She had a thin body which was not so fashionable in 1940. When she saw Isaiah standing there, she dropped the glass, and it shattered as it slammed against the floor.

"Hey, ba', we got company. This here is Isaiah Chambers, the colored man I was telling you about. He gon' spend the night with us tonight, and I'm gon' take him on over to Mrs. Moore's first thang in the mornin'. He won't be no trouble."

"That niggah ain't sleepin' in my house; you can just forget it!" John's wife snapped, then stormed back into the kitchen.

"Sorry 'bout that, Isaiah. Becky's kinda high-strung. Let me go talk to her," John said, walking into the kitchen behind her.

Isaiah stood against the wall as he heard the shouting from behind the thin kitchen walls.

"What the hell is wrong wit' you, woman?" John shouted.

"You get that niggah outta my house, right now!"

"He ain't goin' nowhere! He's our guest, and he's stayin' right here!"

"I'll tell you what, Abraham Lincoln. If you wanna act like one of them damn Yankees, you'll do it without me. I'm leavin' and I ain't comin' back!"

John's voice became lower as he dropped his tone to reason with her. After a few minutes, John came back into the living room.

"Isaiah, why don't you come with me."

Isaiah followed John out to the barn where he led him to the hayloft.

"This will be your sleeping quarters for the evening, young man."

"Well, if it was good enough for Jesus, it's certainly good enough for me." Isaiah smiled.

"You never let anything get to you, do you?"

"Of course things get to me. Your wife got to me. But before I react stupidly, God always steps in and gets to me, too!" Isaiah said, pulling the blanket over his body. "Now get on back in there to your wife before she gets even more upset with you."

"You know what, this is my house, and I'm going to go in my house, and tell my wife to mind her business and keep her mouth shut!"

"John, don't do anything you'll regret later on my account. I am fine out here."

"No! I am going to tell this woman who the man of the house is, right this minute!" John shouted as he shut the barn door behind him and rushed back to his house.

Moments later, John returned to Isaiah in a huff.

"Let's go back to the house. It's my damn house, and if I want somebody in it, they're comin' in it, and that's all it is to it!"

John opened the door, and Isaiah followed him in. He pointed at the floor, and told Isaiah to find him a comfortable spot. Isaiah did as instructed.

"Like I said, this is my damn house!" John snapped out loud for Becky to hear him.

Isaiah saw John fumbling around with a blanket on the couch, and wondered what he was doing.

"What are you doing up there?" Isaiah asked.

"What does it look like; I'm goin' to sleep."

"Why aren't you sleeping in there with your wife, John?"

"Hell, Isaiah, I said this is my damn house, but it's her damn bedroom."

They both laughed so loudly that it woke Becky.

She yelled down to them from upstairs. "What's going on down there?"

John yelled back up to her, "Not a damn thang; now go to bed!"

Isaiah covered his mouth and laughed. "Thanks, John."

"No problem..." John paused, and then said "...brother."

The next morning John drove Isaiah to Mrs. Moore's house. He told Isaiah that he would return that evening before dark to take him back to the train station. Before he could pull off, Sarah walked out of the front door to greet them. She was crying, and pulling the tail of her long dress. John stepped out of his car to find out the matter.

"Are you all right, ma'am?" John asked.

"Yessuh," Sarah said to John, and then turned to Isaiah. "You too late, Isaiah; she gone. She died two days ago. She laid down for a nap, and never woke back up."

"Where is she?"

"She in the backyard. I got some boys to bury her early this morning. How O'bell doin'?"

"She's a little sick from the pregnancy, but she and the baby will be fine."

Isaiah sat on the stairs and rubbed his head.

"You say she's in the backyard, Sarah?" Isaiah asked.

"Yeah, right below her bedroom window."

"That's not a good resting place. It's too shallow; dogs dig there. I'm going to have to get her out of there."

"Isaiah, you can't go diggin' Mrs. Moore up!" John said.

Shaking his head Isaiah, said, "I can't walk away and leave her back there like that, John. She'll never get any rest. She deserves better."

"Isaiah, we have to get you out of here. If people see you back here diggin' around, and the word get out to the coloreds, believe me, it will only take an hour or two before it get to the white folks, too. And there's still plenty of people who would love to see you dead."

"I understand. I'll get started, and I'll be finished before nightfall."

"Still stubborn as ever. All right then. You watch your back, and if you hear any cars comin' up the road, you hightail it out here."

"I will," Isaiah said. "John, can you do me one last favor?"

"Sure, what you need?"

"Call William in Saginaw, and tell him to go tell Orabell that her mother has died, and I'll be catching the next train back to Saginaw alone. I don't want her getting worked up over seeing her mother, and I arrive to tell her she's dead. It may be too much for her. Can you do that for me?"

"Consider it done."

Isaiah reached into his pocket and pulled out a piece of paper with William's telephone number on it, and handed it to John.

John climbed back into his car and pulled off. As soon as he got to his sheriff's office he called William and told him that Mrs. Moore had died. William was sad to hear the news, but relieved to know that Isaiah was all right.

They talked extensively, and caught up with what the other was doing in their lives. They never once mentioned the shooting death of Dr. West. They also never mentioned any word of them being brothers.

William conveyed the message to Orabell and she was painfully saddened, but she, too, was relieved to know that Isaiah was fine, and returning on the next train back to Saginaw.

In Derma County, the day was nearing its end, and the sun was beginning to go down. The cool springtime night was forging its way through. The temperature was slowly dropping and Isaiah was completely exhausted. It took him all day, but at last he was finished. He walked into the kitchen and fixed a pitcher of lemonade. He took the pitcher on the back porch along with a glass and stared at Mrs. Moore's newly dug grave. He drank the pitcher of lemonade one glass at a time until it was gone, then went and fixed another. Sarah had returned by then, and so she volunteered to fix it for him.

"Hey, Isaiah."

"Hey, Sarah."

"That seem like a much betta spot than before," Sarah said, pointing at the grave.

"Yeah, she should get plenty of rest there, with no disturbance from man or animal."

"You got to be tired, Isaiah. You need me to fetch you some covers?"

"No, I think I'll sit out here and just rest for a while. Feels good to be back home."

"Feels good to see you back home."

"We certainly appreciate all of your help taking care of Mrs. Moore, Sarah."

"What help?" Sarah laughed. "That lady was like my mama."

Sarah wrapped a sweater around her shoulders, and hugged Isaiah good-bye.

"I betta be gettin' on over to my mother-in-law's house befo' it get dark. I'm stayin' there 'til my husband get back from Jackson. You know I believe in lettin' the dead rest in peace when they first pass on to the other side. I'll give Mrs. Moore a few days alone, and when my husband get back, I'll come back. You take care of my cousin, and my new cousin when it gets here, you hear?"

"Of course I will, and you take care of yourself, OK?"

"OK, I will. Bye!" Sarah waved.

"Bye."

Sarah walked around to the front of the house, and within a few minutes Isaiah heard the sound of a car drive up, a car door open and shut, then the sound of a car pulling off.

Isaiah filled a glass of lemonade and looked into the sky.

"Lord God. All that I ever wanted to do was Your will. Lord, I don't want to complain, but I'm getting tired. I don't know if I have the strength to keep running this race. But if it is Your will for me to keep running, then that's what I'll do. I'll go whereever, and whenever you want. I just need a little strength, Lord. Not in my faith, but in my legs and arms.

"I thank You for Your blessings, Lord. I thank You for my wife, and child. My brothers, and friends. I thank You for allowing me to be your humbled servant. I look into your night, Lord, and I feel happy and satisfied with my life. I am prepared for my destiny, Father. Whatever it may be, I am prepared."

Isaiah stopped talking to fill another glass of lemonade.

"Lord, all that I am saying is that Heaven must be a beautiful place to call home. And if it is Your will for me to call Heaven my home, sooner than later, then let Your will be done. All that I ask my Father is that You bring an understanding of peace to my family to alleviate their pain. For Thine is the kingdom, and the power, and the glory, forever and ever. Amen!"

As he concluded his prayer, John pulled up honking his horn. Isaiah walked up front and got in the car. John smiled, and patted him on the shoulder.

"You 'bout ready?" John asked.

"Yup! Let's go."

"I brought you a shirt to wear back home, thought you'd need it. It's a plaid farming shirt, probably not your taste."

"If it's clean, it's my taste. That's very thoughtful, man, thanks."

The ride to the station was quiet at first, then Isaiah looked at John and spoke.

"You're a good man, John. It's strange how one circumstance can cause two men to behave entirely different. Because of my ties to Dr. West, his heart wanted to see me dead. And because of my ties to you, your heart wants to see me live. Funny, isn't it?" Isaiah said rhetorically.

"It may be a lot of thangs, but funny it ain't," John answered.

"When did you find out ol' West was your father?"

"It didn't take me too long. He was always around the house, and for no reason. My mama told me when I was young that my father was dead, but as I grew up, she kept mentioning that she glad I don't know who he is.

Now Isaiah, I ain't the smartest man in Mississippi, but I ain't the dumbest neither! Something wasn't right. One day I heard him cussin' at my mama, threatenin' her about if she ever told anybody that he was my daddy, he'd kill her. That was the main reason why I wanted to become the law, 'cause if that bastard woulda ever put his hands on my mama, I was going to hang him myself."

"I understand how you feel," Isaiah said. "Despite the fact that we share the same biological father, it still amazes me how you are willing to help me. The reality is that you're still white, and I'm black."

"No, Isaiah, the reality is that you're a man, and I'm a man. And white or colored, we brothers. Nothing can change that. Ol' West has done damage to a lot of people. There's no tellin' how many of his children I see every day who are my brothers and sisters and don't know it, colored and white."

John pulled into the station and the passengers were already boarding. He rushed to get Isaiah on the train. They shook hands, and Isaiah found him a comfortable seat in the colored coach. John received a disturbing-the- peace call over his radio way out on Highway 8. Two drunken men were fighting in the road. John drove out to the location, but there was not one single soul around. John was irritated and called back to the dispatcher for clarification, but received no answer. He stepped out of his car, and put on his flashlight. It was obvious that he was the only person out there that night.

"What the hell is goin' on?" John said to himself. "Oh shit!"

John jumped back in his car, turned on his siren, and spit dirt and rocks all the way back to the train station.

Isaiah had turned sideways in his compartment seat, and was approaching sleep when he was awakened by two white men.

"What's your name, boy?" the tall, slender young man asked.

"Who wants to know?"

"Me!" the second man replied. He was an older man with balding hair.

Isaiah sat up straight and said, "My name is Isaiah. Is there a problem, gentlemen?"

"You bet your nigger ass, there's a problem! Get up and come with us!" the old man said.

"I'm afraid I can't do that," Isaiah said.

The two men grabbed Isaiah and dragged him off of the train. A few colored porters, on the orders of the conductor, tried to stop the men, but other local men joined in and overwhelmed them. They threw a big potato sack over Isaiah's head, then tied his arms and legs together and pulled him to the back of the depot.

The two men hit him with a stick and a baseball bat. Others kicked him wherever they could, without being hit with the bat and stick themselves. Isaiah twisted and turned to get the ropes from around his hands and arms, but only managed to get the sack from over his face. He looked up at his assailants and prayed out loud for their souls. The pain had left him by then, his body was numb, and all that he could feel was the pressure of being forcibly pushed around. The mob watching the men beat him, yelled and screamed as if they were at a football game cheering their team on to victory.

Within his horror, Isaiah saw a young teenaged black boy lying on the ground peeking through the trees behind the mob. Had the boy been standing, the crowd would have noticed him easily. But he was at ground level, and only Isaiah could see him. Isaiah made direct contact with the boy's eyes, and he could see the tears filling up. Isaiah forced himself to smile, and he gestured for the boy to get out of harm's way.

"What you smilin' for, nigger?" one of the men yelled.

The man stood over Isaiah, and shoved a knife deep into his back several times. The boy crawled as far as he could until he thought the mob would not notice him, then stood up ran as fast as he could. He stopped when he heard Isaiah let out a loud gasp, then he ran again.

"We don't hear your smart nigger mouth no more, do we?" another shouted.

Isaiah clenched his fists, and gasped for air. He did not know if he was dying, or if his body was simply reacting to so much pain.

One of the men who pulled him from the train shouted, "Let's have us a barbecue, y'all!"

They reached in the back of a pickup truck and snatched a container filled with gasoline. They poured it all over Isaiah's body and started dancing.

"Heat up some of that tar, and throw it on 'em. We gon' show 'em what a scared nigger chicken look like."

"Hey, let's have a ho-down tonight!" A man laughed.

"We ain't had a time like this in a spell!" another shouted.

"Light the dam' match. I'm ready to hear this nigger squeal!"

They lit matches and threw them on top of Isaiah's gasoline-drenched body. His body shook violently, and then they tossed the hot tar on top of him.

"Who got the dam' feathers?" A man laughed.

"Hurry, befo' the fire go out!" another man said quickly.

They threw a box of chicken feathers on top of Isaiah and stepped back. His body rolled around on the ground convulsively, until the flames subsided. It was difficult to tell the burned skin which fell from his body from the burned feathers that clung to it. Still, he lied there whimpering and waiting for death.

"Lord, please, please, take me home. I have had enough. I am ready to come home, Lord," Isaiah whispered, as smoke drifted from his body into the air.

Isaiah straightened out his body, took a deep breath, and died

"This nigger is as stubborn about dying as a deer."

"Get me some rope; we'll hang his ass on that pole."

"Where's the head? I can't tell."

They pulled his body to the front of the depot by a rope. They threw the rope over a telegraph pole and hung Isaiah's body with a sign that read: "WARNING FOR ALL NIGGERS TO SEE THE LIGHT."

The sound of John's police car filled the air before his car came into view. The mob scattered quickly, but John paid careful attention to the people passing him in a hurry. He parked in front of the depot, and ran inside.

He asked the ticket taker at the depot if everyone who boarded the train, left with the train.

The ticket taker smiled and said, "Every last one of 'em. Exceptin' that one, of course."

He pointed outside. John turned around and saw a body dangling from a telegraph pole. He turned around and started to slowly walk toward the burned body. He could not distinguish if the body was human or animal. As he got closer to the body he could see a few fragments of clothing. He held the cloth in his hand and examined it, and though the cloth in his hand was badly burned, he could tell that some of the cloth strips were from the shirt he had just given to Isaiah to wear home. He put his hands behind his head and locked his fingers. He took deep breaths, and wondered what his next move should be. He continued to look to see who was around—partly due to his police instincts, and partly looking for some form of explanation for this insanity

Finally, he grabbed a ladder and cut Isaiah's body down, wrapped him in a blanket, and placed him in the back seat of his patrol car. He drove his body to a colored mortician, and demanded he take care of the body. The mortician was full of questions, but John answered only what needed to be answered. He told the man that it was his brother, and he wanted him buried anonymously. The mortician asked John why a white sheriff would bring his white brother to him, when there are white morticians who would be happy to take care of the body for him. John told him that it was none of his business and if ever breathed a word of this to anyone other than God, he would be in need of a mortician himself.

John prayed over Isaiah's body, then headed for home. He found a bunch of feathers in his back seat, and he kept them to remind him of this tragedy. He walked in his house, and slumped down in his chair. His wife asked him if he was OK; he told her no. He told her that the colored man who had slept in their house the night before, had been burned and hanged at the train depot. Becky, who had insisted Isaiah sleep in the barn with the rest of the animals that night before, kneeled between her husband's legs, and cried with him. And it wasn't until John saw Becky cry, that he released his own sadness. He reached for her, and pulled her into his lap. She rubbed his face as he slowly released his tears.

"I know that he was colored, and I am white, and that suppose to mean we ain't suppose to love one another, but Becky, I loved that man," John said.

"I feel sorry for his poor soul, but honey he still a nigger; it ain't like he got a real soul or nothing," Becky cried.

John stood up, and Becky slid from his lap and fell to the floor.

"If you feel that way, then what are those tears for, Becky?" John demanded.

"I'm crying because colored or not, it had to hurt him somethin' awful to be burned like that. I would cry if that would happen to our neighbor's dog. Nobody or no thing should die in such a painful way."

"So it doesn't matter to you that the man was a human being?"

"Well, he ain't no human being; he's colored."

"You know what, Becky, I've been hearing this bullshit all of my life. Colored people bleed, they laugh, they cry, they love, they hurt, they feel, just like us. The only thing that's different is that we say we are better than them 'cause we're white. If we so different, somebody need to tell my heart that, 'cause it's hurtin' mighty bad!" John said, then walked into the kitchen.

Becky had never seen John so emotional in the twenty years they had been together. She wanted to console him, but she truly didn't know how.

"Johnny, why are you so bent out of shape over that nigger?"

"He wasn't no nigger! He was my brother, dammit!" John shouted.

"Have you lost your mind?"

"Becky, I never told you, but my daddy was Dr. West, and he was Isaiah's daddy, too. I have another colored half-brother in Michigan named William. It's a long story, and one day I'll sit you down and tell you everything about it. But for today I'm asking you, please, please don't ever use that word around me again."

Becky wiped the tears out of the corners of his eyes, and promised him she wouldn't.

"If it bothers you that much, honey, I'll try not to use the word. But it's nothing but a word."

"Oh yeah, just by thinking like that, a man was killed, and left behind a wife, and a child on the way. And tomorrow I am going to have to call her and tell her that her husband has been murdered. It may only be a word to you, but try explaining that to his wife." John took off his holster and hung it on the back of his kitchen chair.

He sat up all night thinking of Isaiah, and how he could have prevented his death. He eventually decided that there was nothing he could have done to avoid it, but there was certainly something he could do to bring the men who did it to justice.

The next morning John left his house early and visited one of the men he saw running from the train depot, Ray McClendon. He knocked on the door, but Ray did not answer. He went to the back of his house, and saw his pickup truck. He felt the hood and it was cool from sitting all night, so he knew Ray was still inside. He walked back to the front of the house and banged on the door again. Finally, Ray answered the door rubbing his eyes and yawning. He talked to the sheriff from behind the screen door.

"What you want this early in the mornin', sheriff?" Ray asked.

"What happened, Ray?"

"What happened to what?"

"What happened to Isaiah Chambers, Ray?"

"I don't know what you talkin' 'bout, Sheriff. Now can I go back to sleep?"

John turned away as if he was leaving, then turned back around with brute force and kicked the screen door off of the hinges. The impact knocked Ray to the floor. John put his knee in Ray's chest, then pulled out his pistol and stuck it in Ray's mouth.

"Now I'm gon' ask you this one mo' time, Ray, and if you don't give me some answers, I'm gon' slap the piss out of you," John snarled.

"I already told you I don't know nothin'!"

John took the handle of his gun and smacked Ray across his forehead. Ray grabbed the spot where John hit him, but refused to give him any information.

"OK, that's how you want it?" John said.

He grabbed Ray by the collar, and pulled him from the ground. He beat on, or about his head, until he decided to confess.

"OK! OK! You dang fool! I'll tell ya! It was Harold Staples, and Cordell Burt. Everybody else just joined in. But it was those two that started everything. I didn't do nothin' though, sheriff! I just watched is all!" Ray screamed.

"I'm goin' to pay them a visit, and if I find out you lyin', I'm comin' back, and I'm kickin' in more'n this door, ya hear me?" John shouted.

"Yessuh, yessuh, sheriff!" Ray cried.

"You betta be telling' me the truth!" John dropped Ray to the floor, and walked over him. He pulled off in a hurry, on his way to talk to Harold Staples and Cordell Burt. But first, he had to stop at home and make the call to Michigan to inform William and Orabell that Isaiah was dead. He sat down and dialed the number. It was still kind of early, so William was still asleep. He answered the phone drowsy, but once he heard John's voice he immediately woke up.

"John, how are you? Is everything OK?" William asked.

John cleared his throat and said, "That's why I'm calling, William."

"What's the matter?" William said softly.

John's end of the line was very silent. He tried to say the words quickly, but somehow he felt that if he prolonged telling William, even if for an instance, it would spare Orabell and William the pain of losing Isaiah.

"John, what's the matter?" William asked again.

Red heard the concern in William's voice, and she sat up and put her head close to the telephone.

"What's the matter, baby?" Red cried.

John closed his eyes and said, "They got him, William. I tried to protect him. I put him on the train, but I didn't watch him leave, and they got him."

"What are you saying, John?"

"Isaiah's dead. They killed him! They got him!"

William pulled the phone from his ear, and laid it to the side. Red could hear John calling William's name, so she picked up the phone and started to talk.

"Hello, this is William's wife, and Isaiah's sister-in-law. Is everything OK?"

"He's dead, ma'am."

"Who's dead?"

"Isaiah, ma'am. He's dead," John said with a hoarse voice.

"No, no, Isaiah is on his way back to us. He can't be dead!" Red insisted.

William snatched the phone out of Red's hand, and said, "What we gon' do, John? I'm comin' down there, and I'm killin' those son of a bitches!"

"Don't be stupid, William. You take care of business up there. I'll take care of it down here. I'll get 'em. One by one, I'm gon' get 'em," John said.

"Where is he, John?" William sighed.

"He's at a funeral home, but nobody knows who he is."

"We got to get him back up here."

"That's not a good idea. I've seen the body, and it's not fit for seein', William. You gotta talk Orabell into buryin' the body down here some kinda way."

"Orabell will never go for that. She'll want Isaiah up here with her."

"I can't have Isaiah remembered lookin' the way he lookin' now, William. They tarred and feathered his body. There is nothin' on that body to remind you of Isaiah, and nobody need to see that, and I won't allow it. So do what you got to do, but nobody is seein' him in that condition," John said firmly.

"I agree with you. I'll try to convince Orabell of it somehow, but first I have to tell her that her husband is dead," William said. "John, you have to bring those men to justice!"

"One way or the other, justice will be served. By my hands on earth, and by God's in heaven. I have to go see a few people. Take care up there and keep in touch now, ya hear?" John said.

"I'll be in touch soon."

"Bye," John said.

"Bye."

They hung up, and William turned around to talk to Red but she had already gotten dressed, and on her way to see Orabell. William told her that it would be better if she did not go with him. Red refused to stay home, and William refused to leave with her. He told Red that she could comfort Orabell all she wanted as long as she let him break the news to her alone. She eventually decided to let him tell her alone, but that she would go to her as soon as he returned.

William knocked on Orabell's door, and as soon as he saw her face, he knew that she knew his purpose for being there.

Orabell opened the door, and without acknowledging his presence, turned around and walked away. William followed her in, and asked her to sit down.

"Orabell, please sit down. I'm afraid there's something I have to tell you." William sighed.

"He's gone, ain't he?"

"Yes, Orabell, he's gone."

Sniffing through her tears she asked, "How'd they kill him?"

"Orabell, that doesn't matter, what matters is that..." William said.

"Don't you stand there and tell me what matters," Orabell interrupted. "You tell me how they killed him!" Orabell shouted.

William dropped his head. "They shot him; they shot him one time, and it killed him."

"Where is he now?"

"He's with John."

"I got to get to him. He could be cold, or anything. Where my coat at?" Orabell cried, frantically walking outside without her shoes. "I got to make sure he ain't cold, William!"

"Orabell, get back in here and put your shoes on before you catch pneumonia!" William shouted.

Red had ignored her promise to William and came to be with Orabell anyway. She saw her walking outside with no shoes and led her back into the house, and sat her on the couch.

"They killed my husband, Red." Orabell cried, "He ain't never hurt nobody; what they want to kill him for?"

"He's in a better place now, and they can't hurt him, Orabell. No matter how they try, they can't hurt him now," Red said, crying along with Orabell.

William knelt on the floor in front of the two women and put his arms around them both. He laid his head on theirs, and cried along with them. Orabell rubbed his face over and over, because she knew he was the closest she would ever get to touching Isaiah again. Hours passed, without a word being spoken, then Red got up to fix Orabell some food.

"There's no use in you goin' in that kitchen tryin' to fix me somethin' to eat; there's no way I can eat right now," Orabell said.

"You sure?"

"I don't feel like eatin' nothin'. I got to call Stanford. And I gotta cancel all of Isaiah speakin' engagements. I gotta get one of his suits ironed."

"No you don't!" Red said. "William and I can handle all that."

"I'll call Stanford, and tell him," William said.

"And I'll call the WNM and everybody else, and let them know," Red said.

"Would y'all be offended if I ask you to let me have some time to myself?" Orabell asked.

"Of course not," Red replied.

"I'm grateful to God to have y'all as my family," Orabell said.

William and Red left Orabell to grieve alone and in private. But every day, one of them would spend time with her.

Stanford took the news of Isaiah's death very badly and immediately went home to be with Orabell. He had just heard the day before that his mother had died. He went through Isaiah's belongings, with Orabell's permission, and discovered all of his speeches. He took them back to school with him, and read each one over and over again. He was amazed by Isaiah's foresight on human issues. What amazed him even more was Isaiah's commitment to live his life by the words he preached. It changed his perception of being a Black man. Isaiah's pride was truly a self-pride, dignified and justified by the way he lived his life. And not by the perception of others who may have believed differently. This was the man Stanford wanted to be, and a metamorphosis began to occur in his character from that semester forward. He returned Isaiah's speeches to Orabell, placing them in a plastic bag and putting them in a box.

The news of Isaiah's death spread quickly, and reached far, both in the South and the North. No one knew for sure what had happened, but all were certain that he was dead. Orabell received gifts from people she had never met, both Black and white. She didn't realize that when Isaiah traveled, he was touching so many people's lives.

His suitcase was finally found, and returned. She took her time going through his clothes, smelling his socks, and shirts—his smell still clinging as much to his clothes, as they were to her memory. She laid a different pair of Isaiah's pants, a starched white shirt that she would iron, a tie, underwear, and socks, at the foot of her bed every morning, and rub them throughout the day. And as she had done for so many years in the evening, she would put them neatly away

A surprise came in the mail one day, when she received an envelope containing the original deeds to the property Isaiah had once sold to Judge

West, courtesy of Sheriff John Hankins. There was also an old necklace made out of rope with an attached note that explained its origin; and beautifully preserved feathers placed nicely in a glass case.

Her biggest gift came three months to the day that her husband died, when she gave birth to her son, Solomon.

CHAPTER ELEVEN

SPRING, SAGINAW, MICHIGAN, 1957

Solomon grew to be an exceptionally bright student, academically and athletically. He was so intellectually advanced, he graduated a year early. He became the first student at Saginaw Vista High School, black or otherwise, to win state honors in any sport but when he excelled in three sports, he became a legend. Saginaw Vista had traditionally been known for its academic prowess, but Solomon brought its athletic programs to a state competitive level as well. He was six feet ten inches tall, with incredibly broad shoulders, dark brown skin like his mother, and muscular from head to toe. A colossal man in comparison to his peers. But as masculine a specimen as he was, he spoke with a soft voice like his father's.

His entrance into the school allowed for other black children with exceptional grade-point averages to follow him.

Along with being the first black student permitted in the school, he became the first black class president, first black homecoming king, and unfortunately, the first black to be expelled.

In the winter of Solomon's senior year of high school, he met a girl named Susan Johanssen, a white girl he would eventually date. And although he may have been a hometown hero, he was still black. Interracial dating was not accepted, nor tolerated publicly. Solomon would meet Susan at the library, or on the playground, but he was not allowed in her home.

In school, they would meet at each other's locker, but they did not display open signs of affection. One morning just before Susan kissed Solomon as he was leaving her locker, a group of white boys saw and took offense. The boys walked past Solomon and bumped into him. Solomon, used to that type of behavior from past experiences, apologized and kept walking. The boys turned around and followed Solomon down the hall.

Solomon's best friend, Donovan O' Shaughnessy, a white boy, stepped in between the group of boys and Solomon when he noticed them preparing to strike Solomon from behind.

"What are you doing?" Donovan asked.

"Move, nigger lover!"

"No!" Donovan replied.

"What's going on?" Solomon asked, not aware of the situation.

The group of boys went back and forth, and it escalated into a huge shouting match that caught the attention of a lot of other students. One of the boys took a swing at Solomon, and he retaliated. A group of black boys were also watching the argument and joined in the brawl to help Donovan and Solomon. The melee lasted for only a few minutes, but when it was over, one of the white students lay on the floor unable to move.

An ambulance was called to the school to rush him to the hospital. While the school was awaiting the injured student's diagnosis, the disciplinary actions were swift and harsh. Donovan and the white students received warnings and were sent to class; the Black students involved received a five-day suspension; while Solomon was expelled from school for the remainder of the school year. He would be allowed to repeat his senior year in the fall of the next academic season. He was also told that he would also be facing criminal charges for assault.

Because he was no longer a student, Solomon had to leave the school premises immediately. On top of that, Mother Nature had just delivered Saginaw a blizzard, and he had to walk all the way home in freezing temperatures, and rising snow.

Saginaw was divided by a river, straight down the middle of the city. The whites, and privileged, lived on the west side, while the Blacks, and underprivileged, lived on the east. There was no way to get from one side of the city to the other without crossing a bridge. Saginaw Vista was located on the west side; Solomon lived on the east. It was a long, cold, walk home, but

Solomon knew that once he got home and told his mother he had been expelled, the winter weather was nothing compared to what he was going to receive from her.

When he walked in the house, Orabell stopped him dead in his tracks. He told her what happened and she asked him to tell her the truth about his involvement in the fight. He told her that he was trying to stop the fight, and he never hit anyone. She listened to him explain what happened, then she got up and stormed into her bedroom and started to put on a set of warm clothing. She wrapped her head up tight, and told him to get up and they marched right back up to the school.

Solomon, towering like a giant over his mother, followed her tracks in the snow all the way to the school—over the bridge that hung across the Saginaw River, and down Michigan Avenue and onto the school. Though the temperature was freezing, Orabell arrived at the school just as hot as she was when she left her house.

She walked through and made her way to the principal's office, leaving a trail of slush and ice along the way. Solomon followed behind her, not saying a word to her, or his friends he passed in the hallway.

Orabell told the secretary that was she was there to see the principal. The secretary told her that he would be with her shortly. Shortly turned into an hour. Orabell kept seeing people venture in and out of the principal's office, and she became frustrated when she wasn't called in. She made Solomon hold her purse, which he did reluctantly, and marched into the principal's office unannounced

"May I help you, ma'am?" the principal asked.

"I need to know what went on up here today, and why my boy was kicked out of school!"

"Are you Mrs. Chambers?"

"Yes I am!"

"Well, Mrs. Chambers, we had an altercation this morning involving your son, and a boy was severely injured."

"Did you send all of the boys home?"

"No, we only sent the students who initiated the brawl home."

"Let me put this another way: did you only send the colored boys home?"

"I don't know if they were all colored, but I do know that all of the boys sent home were involved in the melee."

"Hold it one second." Orabell stepped out of the office and told Solomon to come in with her.

Solomon walked in, and sat down, with his eyes to the floor. Orabell told him to stand up like a man, and get his eyes off of the ground. Knowing the tone of his mother's voice, he did so with quickness. Orabell pulled the straps of her purse over her shoulders and asked Solomon the same questions she had just asked the principal.

"Solomon, did your principal send home all of you boys involved in that fight this morning'?"

"No, ma'am," Solomon said, looking away.

"Boy, if you telling the truth you betta look at me in my face and act like it!"

Solomon looked Orabell straight in her eyes. "I'm telling you the truth Mama."

"Did only you colored boys get sent home, Solomon?"

"Yes, ma'am," Solomon said, keeping direct eye contact.

"Now one of y'all lyin', and I don't think it's my son, Mister."

"I have no need to lie to you, Mrs. Chambers. We dismissed the boys who initiated the brawl, and instead of marching yourself into my office with your outburst, you should be thanking me that Solomon is not behind bars as we speak."

"Behind bars for what?" Orabell shouted.

"For assaulting a fellow student," the principal replied, rocking in his chair.

"My boy ain't never hurt nobody in his life, and I don't believe he would just hurt somebody for no reason. You ain't gon' convince me of that," Orabell said, shaking her head.

"I don't have to, and neither do the parents who filed the charges," the principal said. "Now, Mrs. Chambers, please leave my office before you get your son into even more trouble."

Orabell stared at the principal, and then she told Solomon to put his coat on. She continued to stare at the principal as she wrapped her scarf around her face, and pulled the hood over head, and they started their march back home.

When Orabell stepped in the door, she called her brother Stanford, who was now a physician who had his own practice in Saginaw. She told him what had happened at the school, and he drove right over. He drilled Solomon on the incident, and he was convinced that Solomon was telling the truth. Stanford promised Orabell that he would get Solomon back in school. He hired a white lawyer to pressure the Board of Education into reinstating Solomon, but nothing materialized from the attorney's efforts. They never even got as close as to receiving a hearing from the Board.

He fired the attorney, then called William, and asked his advice on the subject. William had moved back to Detroit after Red and their child died during delivery.

In 1950, at the age of forty-nine, William and Red had all but given up on their miracle for a child, then the miracle happened. Red became pregnant and they knew that at her age, and her difficulties with getting pregnant, it would be not be an easy pregnancy. Everything went well while she was carrying the baby, but during the midst of her delivery she suffered a seizure. Red never regained consciousness and the child died before they were able to retrieve her.

William lost his sarcastic sense of humor after the tragedy and indulged himself in his legal career. He finally completed law school after a twenty-five-year hiatus.

He often felt strange in the company of much younger white men as he began his career. After a while he became his own man, with his own small law office. He mostly defended colored people in criminal cases, developing quite a reputation. Although he was the age of a retiring attorney, he didn't feel that he had the experience to actually be of assistance to Solomon.

William told Stanford he may not be able to help Solomon, but he knew an attorney who was more than qualified. After a day had passed, Orabell received a phone call from William. He told her that he had scheduled a meeting with the Board of Education to reinstate Solomon.

Orabell was estatic, and thanked him endlessly. He told her that she would have to let him and the attorney have the run of her home for one night to complete their strategy. Orabell gratiously agreed, and continued to thank him until he hung up the telephone.

William asked Stanford to meet him at Orabell's house, so that he could be introduced to their new attorney. Stanford cleared his schedule and they prepared to meet at Orabell's house. Everything was set, and they were now waiting for this big-time lawyer to come and save the day. Stanford would pay any amount to get his nephew back in school, but his hand shook when he imagined how much the check would be.

When William and the attorney pulled up, Stanford was already sitting in the kitchen. He wanted this big-time attorney to know there would be no slacking around while he was on the clock. William knocked on the door, and Orabell opened it up and laughed. "Oh my Lord."

Stanford looked up to see what had caused Orabell to laugh, and to his astonishment, there standing in living color, was Sheriff Big John Hankins!

"How do, Orabell?" John smiled. "It's so blessed cold out here my tail's a-shakin' like a wet dog."

Orabell wrapped her arms around John's neck and kissed him on his cheek. "Mr. John, what are you doin' way up here?"

"I came up here to get your boy back in school," John said, taking his hat off of his head, and unwrapping the scarf from around his neck

Stanford stood up, and although he was a full-grown man, he couldn't help but resort to his youthful respect for Sheriff John Hankins.

"How are you, Big John?"

"How ya doin', young man?"

"What are you doin' up here, Big John?" Stanford said.

"I'm here to get your nephew back in school."

"But you're a sheriff; what can you do?"

"Sheriff?" John laughed. "I ain't been a sheriff in over fifteen years."

"Wait a minute. Are you the lawyer Uncle William's been talking about?"

"Yup! Been a lawyer for fifteen years. I moved to Jackson and started my practice. Most of the work I do is for civil rights cases."

"How's it going?" Stanford asked.

"I suppose I could be doing better. But then try tellin' that to those po' folks who need my help."

"Do you think we have a case?"

"If all my cases were this easy, I'd have to hire a whole 'nother staff." John smiled.

"Well, why don't you meet the criminal you're defending," Stanford said. "Solomon, get in here. It's somebody I want you to meet."

Solomon walked in the room and reached out his hand to John. John stood up and shook his hand. Solomon was one of the people he'd ever met that he had to look up to greet. He stared in his eyes, as if he were looking to find a glimmer of Isaiah.

"How you doin' there, son?" John asked. "I declare you're the first man I've had to look up to in years."

"I'm doing fine, sir. How are you?" Solomon answered.

"You sound just like ya paw, son. He was one helluva man."

"That's what I hear."

"You wanna tell me what happened?" John asked, taking a notepad from his briefcase.

"I didn't hit him, sir. One of the white boys, I'm sorry, sir," Solomon apologized. "One of the boys swung at me, and I had to defend myself. I grabbed him, and we wrestled to the floor. I just held him down until he was too tired to hit me. By that time the other colored boys had jumped in, and started helping me. The next thing I know, everybody was fighting everybody. I don't know who hit who, but I know that I didn't touch that boy."

"Tell him the truth, boy!" Stanford snapped.

"Uncle Stanford, I really don't know who hit him."

"Tell him the truth, Solomon!" Orabell said.

"Solomon, if there's something you're holding back, it's best you tell John now, before it comes back to harm you later," William said.

"Boy, I'm not going to tell you again, tell the man the truth, and tell him the truth right now!" Stanford shouted.

"OK, Uncle Stanford, OK."

"Son, if you want me to get you out this mess, you got to tell me everything," John said.

"OK, well, that boy that was hurt," Solomon whispered. "My friend, my friend Donovan pushed him. But he wasn't trying to hurt him; he was only trying to stop him from hitting me. But when the boy fell, he fell flat on his back and I think that's how he was hurt."

"I see," John said. "Is that everything, son?"

"Yes, sir, that's what happened," Solomon assured.

"OK, folks. Looks like we've got a little work to do," John said.

"I contacted all of the witnesses like you suggested, Uncle William," Stanford said.

"Are they going to be at the hearing tomorrow?" William asked.

"All of the coloreds will be there. I'm pickin' 'em all up myself." Stanford smiled.

"What about that Donovan kid?" John asked. "We get him, and Solomon will be back in school by Monday morning."

"I don't think that's going to happen, John," Stanford said.

"How long have you known this boy, Solomon?" John asked.

"Just about all of my life. He's my best friend."

"Have you asked him if he would testify at your hearing?" John asked.

"I didn't have to ask, he volunteered. But his father won't let him."

"Do they have a telephone number?" John asked.

"Yes, sir," Solomon replied.

"Give it to me, and go get you some sleep, son. You gotta big day ahead of you tomorrow."

Solomon wrote down Donovan's telephone number and gave it to John. Then he went into his bedroom and closed the door halfway.

"Close that door all the way, boy!" Stanford shouted, then turned to John and said, "John, things are a lot different up here than they are down South. Well, I guess things aren't that different. But no white woman is going to sacrifice her son's education for a colored boy. I tried talking to her. She don't want any part of it."

"Well maybe she'll feel a little different when she finds out we have a white boy who will testify that he believes her son is responsible for that boy's accident," John said.

"We don't have a white boy who's going to testify that Solomon's friend is responsible. That's unethical, John!" William responded.

"Unethical? How?"

"Perjury!"

"William, this is a school board hearing, not a court of law. But we do have a white boy who will testify that he believes Donovan is responsible," John said, lighting a cigarette.

"Who?" Stanford asked.

"Me." John smiled. "I never said that I had a witness who saw what happened, did I?"

William and Stanford looked at each other and smiled.

"Well, I'll be damned." Stanford laughed.

"Watch your mouth now!" William said.

"I'm thirty-seven years old, Uncle William. I'm a grown-ass man." Stanford laughed.

"And I'll whoop yo' grown ass up in here!" William laughed.

"Big John, you think you can bluff them into believin' you really have a witness?" Stanford asked.

"It ain't no bluff, son. If none of these boys are willing to tell the truth, I'll use myself as a character witness for the boy," John said.

"That's cause for a drink, Big John," Stanford said, pulling out a bottle of liquor.

"What you got there, son; you still moonshinin'?" John joked.

"This is store-bought, and it's about to be house dranked!" Stanford joked back.

William sat at the table with John and Stanford, as Stanford passed the bottle to him. William turned the bottle up, then made a horrible face as the liquor burned his throat going down. After he finished his swig, he passed the bottle to John.

"Oh, you probably want a glass, huh, Big John?" Stanford said, standing up and reaching into the cupboard for a glass.

"I'm insulted! Is it that you don't want to drink behind me because I'm white, or do you think I don't want to drink behind you, 'cause you colored?"

Stanford stopped dead in his tracks and looked at John. Then he turned and looked at William. William shrugged his shoulders as if to say he had a point.

"Well, hell, Big John, drink up!" Stanford said, sitting back down at the table.

"You betta tell this boy a thing or two, William. We been drankin' behind one another since we was old enough to piss without having to use our hands." John laughed, putting his arms around William.

William smirked. "I remember me, you, and Isaiah sneaking in Mr. Wilson's moonshine shack trying to steal some of that nasty-tasting wine."

"Yeah, Isaiah would sneak in, but he never drank nothin'." John laughed loudly.

His laughter suddenly stopped and the three men sat there in silence, thinking about Isaiah in their own personal ways until John started talking again by changing the subject from Isaiah.

"This is my first time ever crossing the Mason-Dixon Line. And I'm gon' tell you, it's colder than a well-digger's ass up here," John said.

"Shhhh! You better keep that cursin' to a whisper, Big John. Orabell hear you, she's liable to come in here with a broom handle and whoop all three of our asses," Stanford whispered.

"She can't hear me way back there, can she?" John whispered.

"Bullshit!" Stanford whispered back.

"Stanford, cool it with the swearing!" William said.

"Uncle Will, we both cuss. Hell, you're the one who taught me how to cuss. I believe you get on me, because you know I get on Solomon," Stanford said.

"Payback is something else, ain't it?" William laughed.

"Sometimes!" Stanford answered, lifting the liquor bottle to his mouth.

"Aaah!" Stanford growled, swallowing a gulp of liquor. "Big John, since we're here, why don't you tell us what happened down there after we left?"

"You talkin' 'bout with West?" John asked.

"Yeah, you know I think about that day, every day God send around. You would think that after twenty years, I would have learned to live with it, but I haven't. But to take a man's life, and never, and I mean never, be able to give that life back, is a tormenting feeling I wouldn't wish on my worse enemy. It's like turning a knife upon yourself, and digging it into your own heart. It hurts, man. I mean it hurts!" Stanford said.

"You did the world a huge favor, son," John said. "Ever since I was a child

I knew that gutless bastard raped my mama. And there was nothin' I could do about it. That ol' bastard probably raped every woman workin' on that plantation. White and colored! You don't have nothin' to feel sorry for. As a matter of fact, I kinda envied you. You had the courage to do what I wanted to do my whole life."

"It wasn't about courage, Big John. I was scared. Scared to death. I didn't even realize that I had pulled the trigger. I just couldn't stand there and let that man shoot Isaiah down. Twenty years, and it's still fresh in my mind," Stanford said, taking two large swallows.

"I'm curious, too. What did happen after we left, John?" William asked.

"You can believe West or that car never resurfaced. West had this devilish plot against his brother, Judge West. Y'all remember him, don't ya?" John asked.

"Not right off," Stanford said.

"I do. He almost sent me to prison for ten years," William said.

"Well, anyway, Dr. West had a plot against his brother Judge West to take his land, his money, and everything else he had. That day he was out to Mrs. Moore's house, he was trying to kill two birds with one stone. He was supposed to be on his way back to meet Judge West for their fishing trip. The only thing about it, was that Judge West was supposed to end up at the bottom of the river with the fish. However, Stanford, my boy, you kinda threw a wrench in his plan.

"Judge West left that Tuesday night or early Wednesday morning for their fishing trip; I can't say today if he drowned, or if West killed him. I'm guessin' West probably killed him befo' he showed up at Mrs. Moore's, but he had to get rid of Isaiah because he still knew the truth," John said, burping quietly and rubbing his belly. "One thang I know for sure is that we ain't seen Judge West, or Dr. West since that day."

"Well, what makes you think Dr. West was plotting to kill him?" William asked. "I found all kinda forged documents. Judge West had already left on the day these papers were signed and stamped. Knowin' that whoever did it had to work in my office, I tore that sucker apart, brick by brick, and man by man, until I got to the bottom of it. Dr. West had one of my clerks forge

Judge West's signature on all of those papers. A life insurance plan was made out that day. A big one! And then the obvious, the man hated Isaiah's guts for years. I could not understand what had him so itchy fingered that day to save my life. But it all came together. Dr. West found out that Judge West had got his hands on the deeds to Isaiah's land, and he wonted that, too."

William smirked. "That's ironic; the man's lust for money made him take his brother's life, and cost him his own."

"Yup, you reap what you sow," John said.

"Too bad Isaiah didn't reap what he sowed!" Stanford snapped.

"Yeah, you gotta point. That was a feisty little fella, wasn't it?" John asked. "But he was as good as they come."

"Wasn't afraid of anything, or anyone," William added.

"Helluva man!" Stanford added.

"Let me tell ya somethin' 'bout the little fella." John burped again. "He saved my life one evening. I'm not just talkin' bullshit; he saved my life. I was out down there in them woods, breaking up a gamblin' ring in this barn. It was a bunch of colored boys, and they didn't give a hoot 'bout nothin' but their money. Isaiah told me not to go in there all by myself, to appoint me some deputies, 'cause these was some bad boys.

"I bust up in that barn, and hell, they started comin' out the woodwork. Didn't even have time to get my pistol out my holster before they had me to the ground. One of 'em said, they got to kill me, 'cause if they let me go, I was surely goin' to hang 'em. I was layin' on my back, and the boy stuck that gun 'bout this close to my head," John said, touching his forehead with his finger.

"And outta nowhere that little bastard leaped into him, and knocked the shotgun outta his hand, and they all went to runnin' every whicha way. I was kinda outta of my head, so Isaiah drug me out the barn and put me in my car. And you know I'm almost twice his size. That little fella drove me home, and dropped me off. Then he walked home himself. And that was a pretty good piece." John laughed. "Never wanted to hear a thank you, or nothin' in return."

"Sorry 'bout that, John." Stanford laughed.

"You ain't have nothin' to do with that did you, son?" John shouted.

"Just pullin' your leg. I may have did some runnin' for some people, but I didn't do anything like that. But I know who it was." Stanford laughed.

"I bet you do." William laughed.

"Yeah, but that's the kinda fella Isaiah was," John said.

"I guess they never found his murderers, huh, John?" William asked.

"Oh, I wouldn't say that, William. We found the bodies of the two men who pulled him from the train. They were both found dead with one gunshot wound to the middle of their heads. They also had a burned chicken feather, sticking out of the side of their mouths," John whispered.

William was in the midst of taking a swallow, but he stopped halfway, and pulled the bottle back down. He stared at John, and lifted the bottle back up to his mouth. He pulled the bottle down again, and stared at John again.

"What?" Stanford asked in response to William's stare.

"You never told him, did you?" John asked.

"Not one word," William answered.

"Do you know how they killed Isaiah?" John asked.

"Yeah, they shot him in the head." Stanford paused, and thought to himself for a second. "Just like those two men were killed."

"That's not what happened, Stanford. They beat Isaiah. They beat him, burned him, and hung him. We told everyone he was shot in the head to alleviate some of the pain of losing him. He was a dignified man, and John and I wanted him to have a dignified death," William said.

"I understand. There's still something you're not telling me. Why were you lookin' at John like that?" Stanford asked.

"After they burned him, they tarred and feathered him. When I carried his body to be buried, there were some feathers left in the back seat of my car. I kept those feathers," John said.

Stanford patted John on the back, and took a long swig from the bottle. He was about to open up another bottle when John excused himself.

"Naw, I think that's it for me," John said, pushing himself away from the table. "You know, Stanford, you were saying how painful it feels to take a man's life and not ever be able to give it back. That depends entirely upon the life you took. I'm about to go in here and sleep like a baby. And if I was to ever see those two sorry son of a bitches, I'd kill 'em again without thinkin' about it twice!"

John walked into the bedroom Orabell had prepared for him, and went to sleep. Stanford and William sat at the table for a while and continued to talk. William explained to him the actual events in which Isaiah was killed. Stanford relived the horror all over again. He was even more determined to get Solomon back in school.

The next morning Stanford paid a visit to the O'Shaughnessys' home. He pleaded with Mrs. Carrie O'Shaughnessy, Donovan's mother, to let Donovan speak at Solomon's hearing. She explained that Donovan wanted to tell the truth, but her husband refused for them to be involved. Mr. Bailey O'Shaughnessy entered the room and asked Stanford to leave. Stanford reminded him of Isaiah, and how he helped him get a job in the foundry when they first moved to Michigan from Minnesota. He told Stanford that he was grateful to Isaiah, but he wasn't going to lose his son because of it. They exchanged heated, but respectful words, then Stanford left.

He met up with John and William outside of the Board of Education building. Orabell and Solomon were already seated inside. The three men walked in and sat at a table facing the board. They wore sharp crisp suits, polished shoes, and matching hats. When the meeting began, John stood and introduced himself as a civil rights attorney from Jackson, Mississippi. He hoped to intimidate the board into thinking that he was there to bring a suit for violating Solomon's civil rights. He knew that his introduction would have impact on the trial in one of two ways. They would recognize that he was an expert in trying civil rights cases, concede their loss, and immediately allow Solomon to return to school. Or they would be offended that a Southerner would be so arrogant as to bring the laws of bigoted Mississippi to the peaceful state of Michigan. John played his card and now he was waiting for their next move. They reacted in the former, and quickly expressed that this was a school board hearing, and not a civil rights trial. He knew at that point, Solomon would be back in school in a matter of days, and the hearing was a mere formality.

They were allowed witnesses, and all of the black boys appeared in Solomon's defense. They were only allowed to bring one parent, the mother, so that they wouldn't fill the board room. Each boy was accompanied by his mother, and they all sat directly behind Orabell. The fathers were not permitted inside, in order to eliminate the risk of a conflict. On the other side of the aisle were the families of the white group of boys. They, on the other hand, were allowed to bring both of their parents.

The board consisted of eight white men, a couple who were relatives of the victims. They began the hearing by separating the boys by their groups—not by their race, but by victims, and perpetrators. The result, however, was the same. The white group of boys were the victims, while the black boys were the perpetrators. The board allowed the victims to give their accounts of what happened, and then the perpetrators were allowed to give theirs.

As the hearing was coming to a close, Mrs. O'Shaughnessy entered the board room with Donovan. When Stanford noticed her sitting in the back, he whispered to John that she had arrived. He pointed her out, but John asked him to hold off on calling her for a minute until he could read her reaction. She sat on the white side of the court room, and she may not have been present to declare Solomon's innocence, but to maintain Donovan's.

John asked Orabell to acknowledge Mrs. O'Shaughnessy, and she did. Mrs. O'Shaughnessy smiled and moved closer to their table. John asked Stanford to sit her next to Orabell, because he wanted to shake the board. Stanford took Mrs. O'Shaughnessy by the arm, and led her to a seat beside Orabell. John asked her privately if Donovan would be willing to speak. She told him that he was too nervous, and she would speak for him. John continued with the hearing, because he wanted the board to believe that Mrs. O'Shaughnessy was not going to speak.

Finally, after all of the witnesses had given their statements, and John knew what he was facing, he asked the board to allow Mrs. O'Shaughnessy to speak. At first they denied, but after minutes of prodding, they granted his request. She stood, and stated that she was very nervous. But through her nervousness, sincerity was ever present.

"Good afternoon, everybody. My name is Carrie O'Shaughnessy, and I am Donovan's mother. I brought my son here today to give his side of what happened, but when we got here, he was too nervous to talk. I'm a little nervous, too, but the good Lord won't let me sit back and let this boy's education be thrown down the drain. Solomon and Donovan have been friends for as long as I can remember. I see Solomon so much, sometimes I forget he's not my son.

"I remember the first time Donovan brought him home, and I saw that little colored face. I was shocked. I had heard so much about this Solomon, I just assumed that he was a white boy.

"You see, my son had a speech impediment when he was younger, and the kids always picked on him. So when he finally found a best friend, I was so happy for him I didn't know what to do. As you can see, Solomon is a pretty big boy, and he always has been, even when they were youngsters. Solomon protected my son from those children who picked on him. He didn't care if Donovan had a speech impediment or not, he didn't care if Donovan was white or not, he was his friend, and that was all that mattered. And to this day, they are still the best of friends. And to this day, they still try to protect one another.

"I guess what I'm trying to say is, like you all, I wanted to keep my son out of this mess to protect him. But that is wrong; it is dead wrong because it's not the truth. He was involved. He was the one who pushed that boy down. Now I can't say what did, or did not happen after that because I was not there. But I don't believe that my son intentionally hurt anybody. I believe my son when he said that they were attacking Solomon, and he was only protecting his friend. Just as his friend had protected him for so many years. I am sorry for the young man who was injured, but I believe it was just an accident.

"My husband asked me not to come here today, but I asked him if it was our son who was losing such a promising future would he want Orabell to keep Solomon from telling the truth. He couldn't answer me, and that was all he had to say. And I think that's all I have to say at this point."

Mrs. O'Shaughnessy tucked her purse underneath her arms and walked up to where Solomon and Orabell were sitting. She kissed Solomon on the cheek and wished him good luck.

Orabell stood up and said, "Thank you so much, ma'am."

"I did nothing more for your son than you would have done for mine, Orabell." Mrs. O'Shaughnessy folded her coat beneath her, then sat back in her seat beside Orabell. She turned to Donovan and told him to go sit beside Solomon in his hour of need. There was not room enough at the table for him, so Stanford gladly gave him his seat, moved to the row behind them and sat next to Mrs. O'Shaughnessy.

The board looked up and down at each other and concluded with the witness segment of the hearing. John saw blood and pulled out his ace card. The group of boys had been referred to as victims, and perpetrators, and John knew that it was time to call a spade a spade, so to speak. He concluded his hearing by saying that the colored boys were judged and convicted, solely because they were colored. He told them that though he had imagined it being different in the North, the truth is that no matter where you are, discrimination and prejudice exist.

The board announced that it would recess for one hour, and return with a decision. John assured Solomon and his family that he was confident the board would allow Solomon back in school.

When they returned, they reached a decision that Solomon could return to school, effective immediately. They warned that he would be on probation, and if he was to be involved in any other incident at the school his expulsion would be carried out to its full term.

John also asked if they would have leniency on Donovan for his involvement. He apologized to the families involved, black and white. Then he thanked the board, and walked out of the room. Solomon watched closely, and admired John's subtle, but deliberate way of presenting the truth to the board and challenging them to deny it. It was at that moment that Solomon decided he would someday be an attorney.

In the summer of 1957, Solomon graduated from high school. A year early as scheduled, and he did so as the 1957 class valedictorian of Saginaw Vista High. He was offered athletic scholarships from major universities, but he declined them all to attend a local university on an academic scholarship. He spent his summer hanging around the house until Stanford invited him to come with him for the weekend.

Stanford told Orabell that he was taking Solomon on a trip to Detroit to see a revue of black singers from a new black record company called Motown. But instead, he was actually driving him to Memphis, Tennessee to give him a taste of manhood. Solomon asked Stanford if he could bring Donovan along. Naturally, Stanford did not want Donovan to go on the trip, but he changed his mind and brought him along.

Stanford checked the boys' gear, and realized that he would have to help Donovan with his wardrobe. He gave him a starched, straightlegged gray suit, with a pair of black, shiny shoes. Donovan's clothes were too bland, and more importantly, too white.

Once they met Stanford's wardrobe criteria, they were headed down the highway. Stanford had the top back and they were enjoying the sun. When they reached the town of Effingham, Illinois, they were pulled over by a police car. The police officer asked Stanford for identification, and proof of ownership. Stanford reached into his glove compartment, and gave the man his information. The police officer asked him and Solomon to step out of the car, while they interrogated Donovan. They put handcuffs on them and pushed them into the back seat of the patrol car. After Donovan corroborated Stanford's story, they were released and sent on their way. He also added that Stanford and Solomon worked for his father and they were driving him to Tennessee.

Stanford was outraged when they climbed back into the car. He pounded on the steering wheel in frustration.

"What's wrong, Uncle Stanford?" Solomon asked.

"I'm tired of this, son. We can't even ride down the road without them messin' with us! I hate crackas!" Stanford yelled.

Solomon glanced in the rear-view mirror to see Donovan's reaction to Stanford's outburst. He sat there with a blank on his face with no reaction at all.

"He didn't mean that, Donovan," Solomon apologized.

"Don't tell me what I mean! I'm tired of this shit!" Stanford shouted.

"Uncle Stanford, if it wasn't for Donovan, who is white, we would probably be in jail, or dead, or something right now," Solomon said.

"That's the point, son. Donovan shouldn't have to protect us! And if you'd open up your eyes, son, you would see!" Stanford said.

"Mama taught me to love all people, not just colored people. Even those who do not want to love me back," Solomon said.

"Some of those people will cut your throat quicker than a jack rabbit's minute and not give a second thought about it," Stanford said, calming down. "I wasn't talking about you, Donovan, and I wasn't calling you a cracka."

"No need to apologize, Mr. Stanford. I never thought you were referring to me, because I can't see myself being a cracker," Donovan said, slumping down in the seat, and covering his face.

They continued on their way down the road until they arrived in Memphis. The boys were asleep, so Stanford went to a hotel he used to patronize on his many visits, during his college years. After he rented the room, he banged on the windows of the car, and woke the boys.

"You girls get up and get this stuff out of the car. I'm goin' across the street and get something to eat. Here is the key, room 704," Stanford said.

"This is nice, Mr. Stanford," Donovan said, looking up at the tall hotel.

"How'd you find this place, Uncle Stanford?" Solomon asked.

"None of your business!" Stanford snapped. "Now go get those suitcases put up."

Solomon and Donovan took their suitcases to their rooms. Donovan looked out of the window at the café across the street where Stanford was ordering their breakfast and noticed the sign on the window: "WE SERVE COLOREDS."

"Hey, Solomon, look at that sign over there," Donovan said, pointing. "Let's go have a look."

They ran downstairs and across the street to the café. They walked inside, and the bathrooms and water fountains read, "COLOREDS ONLY," and "WHITES ONLY" signs on them.

"Let's get out of here," Solomon said.

"What are you waiting for?" Donovan said, running back across the street.

Stanford returned with their food and they ate breakfast. Later, Stanford took them down to the colored section of Beale Street. They hung out there all day until it was dark, and Stanford took them to the "LIVE" section. In those days, black people used to have live entertainment of comedy, dance, and music called the Chittlin' Circuit. Stanford was proud to show the boys the Negro culture of the South. They hopped from club to club, and stayed out until it was almost day

They slept most of the day away, and when they woke up, they did the same thing all over again. Club hopping, and girl chasing. Because Solomon was so big, no one ever questioned his age. No one ever questioned him about anything.

Solomon was used to dating white girls, because the black girls in his neighborhood were too abrasive for his taste. But when he saw the black Southern women in the clubs, he eyes almost popped out of his head. He never knew black women could dress so nice, and so elegantly.

The clubs were smoky and hot. All of the men wore suits, and Solomon realized why Stanford made them bring their finest clothes. The women wore slinky dress that fit tightly at the hips. Some had splits along the side, which revealed a little skin. Solomon was in black heaven and didn't want to leave.

Solomon and Donovan were concerned about being underaged. Especially with Donovan drawing extra attention to them by being white. Stanford assured them that the South had a different set of rules for minors than the North. If you're eighteen in the South, you're grown and that's it. You're legal, you can drink, go to nightclubs, and that's all it is to it.

The boys ended up in a joint where they met two women who were interested in being their dates for the remainder of the night. The women convinced the boys to take them back to their hotel rooms. Stanford drove them back, and stayed in the car while the boys were upstairs with the women. He fell asleep, and was awakened by voices yelling from the balcony of the hotel. He peeked out of the window, and the people were standing on the balcony of their rooms. Stanford jumped out of the car and ran up the seven flights of stairs. The ladies were screaming for their money. Solomon and Donovan were scared and asked the women to calm down. Stanford laughed, and explained to the women that it was all a big misunderstanding. He paid the women their money for their services, and sent them on their way.

"Didn't you two idiots think that these women were interested in more than your pretty little faces?" Stanford asked.

"No, sir, I thought they just wanted a good time," Solomon said.

"Your good time just cost me fifty bucks!" Stanford returned.

"Sorry, Uncle Stanford, can we go home now?" Solomon asked.

"Well, did you get you some, boy?" Stanford asked.

"Yes, sir, but it wasn't what I thought it would be," Solomon said.

"What did you think it would be like?" Stanford asked.

"I don't know. But it felt kinda mushy," Solomon said.

"Boy, one day, you won't be able to sleep, eat, or drink trying to get that mushy feeling."

"I enjoyed myself tremendously." Donovan smiled.

"Yeah, you would," Stanford mumbled, turning away from Donovan

They packed their suitcases in the car and headed back to Michigan. Stanford made the boys promise they would never tell their parents they went to Memphis. The boys never forgot that trip to Memphis. They left behind some good memories, and their virginity.

Chapter Twelve

SPRING, SAGINAW, MICHIGAN, 1959

Solomon continued his academic brilliance in his freshman year at a local college. In his sophomore year, in the spring of 1959, Solomon met a young woman named Sunshine Murray. She was a junior, socially and politically minded, and extremely strong-willed. She had a perfectly trimmed bouffant hairstyle. Her skin was yellow, and without blemish. She wore no makeup of any kind. She was the most naturally beautiful woman Solomon had ever laid eyes on. Her shoulders were square, and her arms were slim. Her curvaceous hips poked out of the sides of her long plaid skirt. And her shapely legs peeked from the bottom of her skirt, and the top of her white socks. Solomon stood high above the top of her head, but she was the one who stood as the intimidator.

Sunshine was strictly about her studies. Romance was an unwanted nuisance that could only distract her from her career. Solomon was an academic scholar, and a lady's man. Sunshine was a woman who put her academics before anything else. He had never dated a black woman in his life, and he assumed that because he finally desired a black woman, the feelings would be reciprocated.

One afternoon he saw Sunshine sitting on a bench reading a book. Solomon felt that there was no better time than the present to begin his assault.

"How are you today, Miss?" Solomon asked.

Sunshine looked up at him, then looked back down at her book without acknowledging him.

"Excuse me, Miss, how are you today?" Solomon asked again.

Sunshine looked up at him again and spoke, "I was doing quite well until a minute ago."

"My name is Solomon Chambers. What's yours?" he asked, reaching out his hand for Sunshine to shake.

Sunshine looked at his hand, and dropped her eyes back down.

"Miss, I'm not trying to take up a lot of your time. I just wanna talk to you for three hundred seconds."

Sunshine laid her book to the side. "Why didn't you just say five minutes?"

"Because three hundred seconds sound like a lot more time than five minutes, doesn't it?" Solomon laughed.

Sunshine picked up her book and started reading it, ignoring Solomon again.

"Seriously," Solomon said, clearing his throat from embarrassment. "I have seen you around campus, and I wasn't going to say anything but I'm here. I turned to walk away, but I couldn't. I swear it felt like I was having a stroke. I couldn't breathe; I felt slightly dizzy. I had to say something to you or I would have passed out from anxiety."

"That's a pretty good line; is it an original?"

"Miss, before I go any further, can you please tell me your name?"

"That's OK; Miss is fine."

"I guess we're experiencing a little Indian summer, because it's extremely hot out here today. Especially on this bench."

"Believe me, it can get hotter, so go find yourself a nice cool spot somewhere else. Bye-bye!"

"Why are you so cold to me, and you don't even know me?"

"I know you, and I know your game."

Sunshine started to walk away, but Solomon grabbed her by the arm and stopped her.

"Wait a minute, please. What game do you think I'm playing?"

"Take your hands off me!"

"OK, OK. I just want to talk to you. That's all."

"If you just wanted to talk to me, why didn't you just walk up to me like a man, and talk to me, like a man should?"

"It's that I find you extremely attractive, and..."

"And man, please!" Sunshine interrupted. "You find every woman on campus extremely attractive. Especially the white ones. Anyway, I've wasted enough of my time on you this afternoon. Go chase the next skirt 'cause this one ain't givin' you the chance to put another notch under your belt."

"What are you talking about?"

"I must admit that you have a nice line. But it's just not good enough to catch this fish though, buddy." Sunshine smiled as she picked up her book and walked away.

Solomon stared with his mouth wide open as Sunshine twisted her hips from side to side.

"I got to get that. I just got to!" Solomon smiled.

The culture of the majority white university had taken its toll on Sunshine. Her only reason for attending college in Michigan were due to her relatives. Her mother died young, and she was raised by her grandparents. Her aunt moved to Flint, Michigan in 1953, and Sunshine visited every summer. She wanted to escape from Mississippi badly so she applied for admission and was accepted at Saginaw State College.

In the fall semester of 1959, she transferred to Fisk University in Nashville, Tennessee. She knew no one, and had no contacts, but she didn't care about that at all. All that she cared about was being around other black students her age.

She quickly adjusted to the predominantly black student body. She joined different groups and organizations, and became a leader on campus.

Her Southern small town upbringing made it easy for her to relate to the different Southerners making up the student body at Fisk University.

Sunshine was born and raised in a small town near Greenwood, Mississippi. Growing up in the midst of America's worst racially divided state made her socially and politically conscious. She was excited to witness her fellow students getting involved in the Civil Rights Movement. They were actively holding rallies and meetings to fight the discrimination and prejudice black people were facing. Sunshine felt that it was meant for her to go to Fisk during her last year of college. There was so much work for her to do, and people understood why she was doing it.

Sunshine held a rally in front of the student union. She had little help passing out flyers, so she expected a small crowd. She asked a couple of her recently found male friends to set up the podium in preparation for her rally. Within an hour the stage was set, and ready to go.

As she began her speech, a small crowd gathered. They were impressed by the tiny woman, with such a strong, loud voice. She was five feet two inches tall, and one hundred pounds soaking wet. She had a charismatic smile that spoke volumes without saying a word.

"Good afternoon, everyone. We are all aware of what's going on in America at this time. Most of you are from the South like myself, and we have seen our family members killed, or abused, in every disgusting manner imaginable. There comes a time when we have to say enough is enough. Slavery ended almost a hundred years ago, and they are still calling us *niggahs!* We still are not free, because we still are not equal!

"Let me give you an example of what I'm talking about. I witnessed something four years ago that I thought could never happen. This event affected me, and changed me for the rest of my life. In 1955, a fourteen-year-old boy by the name of Emmett Till was visiting Money, Mississippi. He had traveled from Chicago, Illinois to visit his relatives. He went into a store in my hometown of Greenwood, Mississippi, and on a dare, he called a white woman, 'baby.' About a week later they pulled that boy from the Tallahatchie River, with a cotton gin fan and barbed wire wrapped around his neck.

"They tried to bury him as soon as possible to get rid of any evidence, but somehow his mother in Chicago was able to get enough support to prevent that from happening. Two men—Roy Bryant, the husband of the woman in the store; and his half-brother, J.W. Milam—were arrested and charged with the murders. The trial began on September 19th, 1955 in Sumner, Mississippi. This case had national media coverage. But even with the eyes of the nation upon us, Mississippi's racism stood bold and callous in its approach to his murder. The white media people were allowed to stay whereever there were vacancies, while the black media were forced to stay in hotels, and people's homes in Mound Bayou. And for those of you who don't know, Mound Bayou is a predominantly black town located about twelve miles from Sumner.

"It was reported that the fan around Emmett Till's neck could be matched against the cotton gin if it was ever discovered. In J.W. Milan's barn, they found that the propeller and fan belt were missing from his cotton gin. J. Edgar Hoover was contacted about the new evidence, but he sent word back to contact an FBI agent, a specific one he had handpicked. An agent from our local area. That of course would be of no assistance, because that bastard was just as racist as the rest of the state.

"To tell you just how concerned the state of Mississippi felt about the eyes of the nation upon her, during the trial, the jurors were drinking beer in the jury box.

"The sheriff deputized every white man willing to hold a .45 or .38 pistol. They filled the courtroom when Moses Wright testified against Bryant and Milam. They expected trouble, and they were prepared to handle it the old Mississippi way.

"Moses Wright was Emmett Till's elderly uncle. It was also his home where these men kidnapped Emmett Till. Everybody wanted to see how this old, gray-haired man would respond to being in front of these angry white people. When that prosecutor asked Uncle Moses if the man who took Emmett Till from his house was in that courtroom, he looked over and pointed at J.W. Milam. And in our old Negro spiritual tongue, he spoke, 'Dar he!' Now I can't say if it was the judge's gavel, or Uncle Moses' courage, but the room remained intact. Tension was thick enough to cut with a knife, but neither side, black nor white, dared the other. The trial lasted five days. The all-white jury only deliberated for an hour, and returned with a 'not guilty' verdict. They said it wouldn't have taken that long but they had to order out for food.

"Uncle Moses and a couple of others had to move up North to Chicago for their own safety. One was Willie Reed, who testified he had seen Emmett on the back of Milam's truck, and heard the sounds of someone being beaten in Milam's barn. The other was Reed's aunt, who had heard Emmett scream, 'Mama, Lord have mercy! Lord have mercy!'

"My brothers and sisters, the reason I used Emmett Till's death is because I was in front of that store that day. I saw him alive, a nice, handsome young man. Then to see his body after they had done all of those hideous things to him, affected me for the rest of my life. He was three years younger than I am. He was right, when cried out, 'Lord have mercy!' Because the Lord needs to have mercy on us all.

"'Cause if we can be murdered at such a young age, then we better learn how to defend ourselves at such a young age. And it starts right here! And right now!

"I remember what my grandparents used to tell me about picking cotton. They said picking cotton was the easy part. Separating the seeds from the lint was the hard part. And that's what we're faced with today. Being free is the easy part. Separating equality from inequality is the hard part."

Sunshine stepped down from the podium, and she was greeted with handshakes and hand claps. And once again, she knew, this place was the place where she was supposed to be.

★★★

In the spring of 1960, students from four universities gathered—Fisk, Tennessee State, the American Baptist Theological Seminary and Meharry Medical College—and decided to address the issue of black people's treatment at segregated theaters, libraries, hotels, and restaurants. They formed classes on non-violent sit-ins. Sunshine was in the middle of the movement.

She went to the first sit-in on March 15, 1960 in Atlanta, Georgia. One month later, in Raleigh, North Carolina, Sunshine, along with one hundred-twenty other student leaders, met at Shaw University. By May 10, six Nashville lunch counters that had been targets opened their counters to blacks.

Over one hundred cities in the South were involved in sit-ins. They adopted the chant of, "Jail, no bail!" as their cry of freedom. Sunshine spoke at many of the rallies, and her speeches drew positive and unfortunately, negative reactions. At a rally at Vanderbilt University, when in this case, Sunshine was a spectator, two black students were involved in an altercation. Sunshine stood as a peacemaker, but she was somehow misconstrued as the initiator. Police harassed her until she was forced to leave the school, and the city. She dropped out of her last semester of undergraduate studies, and returned to Michigan.

In the fall of 1960, Sunshine returned to Saginaw State College. She was extremely disappointed by having to return to the predominantly white school, and transferring schools had caused her to lose credits, pushing her graduation back one semester. She was determined to get her degree even if she had to return to Saginaw State.

While registering, she happened to stand in the same line as Solomon. She was a few people behind him, and she recognized his large figure immediately. She pretended she didn't see him, and she hoped that he didn't see her as well.

Eventually, he noticed her lingering in the line and he let the people behind him take his place one by one until she was standing directly behind him. She saw him staring at her, but she refused to acknowledge his presence.

"We meet again, Ms. Sunshine. I thought you had transferred to another school, trying to escape my wicked evil clasp." Solomon laughed.

"Please, I'm not in the mood for you right now."

"I'm just being friendly," Solomon said, erasing the smile from his face.

"I am going to say this once, and once only. Please leave me alone."

"I'm just trying to get to know you, Sunshine. Why..." Solomon tried to complete his statement, but Sunshine rudely interrupted him.

"I don't want to get to know you! Keep your friendship, and give it to one of your blue-eyed, blonde-haired, white girls," Sunshine said, turning her back.

"Let me tell you something, Harriet Tubman, all that I ever asked from you was a little of your time. I have tried to wait for the perfect moment because I thought you were as close as I'll ever get to the perfect woman. But to tell you the truth, there is no such thing as the perfect time, and you've just proven that there is no such thing as a perfect woman!"

"You're right! From your perspective perfection is a reflection of blue eyes. There's perfection walking right now; why don't you go chase her?" Sunshine shouted, pointing to a white woman.

"You're impossible; you know that?"

Sunshine smiled sarcastically. "As a matter of fact, I do know that!"

"And furthermore, it's none of your business who I date. And who are you to pass judgment on me?"

"Who am I?" Sunshine asked, resting her hands on her hips. "Let me tell you who I am. I am the black woman who bears your children. I am your mother, your sister, your grandmother, and her grandmother. That's who I am! So don't you dare stand before me, in front of these white people and act as if you don't know who I am. I faced my death to give you breath. I am your soul mate, and not your bed mate. So respect me as if yo' ass was born from me!"

"What is your problem?" Solomon asked quietly, gesturing for Sunshine to lower her voice.

"My problem is that you walk around here as if you're black women's gift from God. And then you crawl on your knees just to get one of these white girls to smile at you!" Sunshine shouted.

She tried to gather herself, and let the moment pass, but she was so frustrated the words kept flowing from her mouth. "Please get the hell out of my face!"

Solomon was embarrassed by Sunshine's outburst, especially after he noticed other people staring. But he had no choice other than to stand there and try to reason with her. He felt that if she walked away angry, he would never get another opportunity to speak with her again.

"I'm not going anywhere! I want to talk to with you. And without the hostility," Solomon pleaded.

"Fine! Stand here like a fool," Sunshine snapped.

Solomon turned around and noticed the line had moved forward, leaving a huge gap between him and the next person. He caught up with the line and turned back to face Sunshine.

"You know you talk a lot, but you never want to listen. You accuse me of such absurdities. I can't help that I wasn't born in the South. And I'm not going to feel guilty about not experiencing what you have. But before you judge me by the way I speak, or the way I carry myself, get to know me first." Solomon growled. "On second thought, don't worry about it. Just forgive me for believing that you were the most beautiful woman I had ever laid my eyes upon. I thought it went all the way through to your soul, but I guess that beauty was one dimensional."

"Guess so!"

Solomon turned his back to Sunshine, and mumbled under his breath, "Bitch!"

When classes began, to Solomon's and Sunshine's chagrin, they were scheduled for a required class that both needed to graduate. They both tried to change the course, but it was not offered in the spring, so they had to remain in the class—together. They sat on opposite sides of the class. Ironically, they were the only two black students enrolled, making it obvious that one was no fan of the other. The first month passed, and they managed to get through it without incident.

In late September, the presidential election for Richard M. Nixon and Senator John F. Kennedy was nearing, and Sunshine started a voter registration drive. She inquired if she could ask the class to volunteer to help with the Kennedy campaign. The professor thought that her progressive thinking could be very constructive for the class, and he agreed.

Sunshine stood before the class, and asked for Kennedy campaign volunteers. No one raised their hand, nor inquired about her campaign ideas. Sunshine bounced the clipboard against her legs, and after no one said a word, she thanked the professor and sat back down in her seat. The professor told the class that they should admire Sunshine for having the courage to try to make a difference, then he resumed his teaching. Halfway through the class, Solomon raised his hand, and asked if he could interrupt the class for only a minute. He walked over to Sunshine's desk, and signed his name on her volunteer sheet. Solomon looked at a few of his friends, and gestured for them to do it as well. They eventually walked over, and reluctantly signed her sheet. The professor smiled, and he felt compelled to sign his name to the list along with the rest of the volunteers. Before long, over half of the class had their names attached to the Kennedy campaign.

After class Sunshine caught up to Solomon and thanked him for coming to her rescue. He didn't say a word. He simply smiled, and walked away.

That evening, Solomon made it home late for dinner. One of Orabell's biggest pet peeves was a hot dinner sitting and turning cold. Solomon knew what time she expected him, and he knew she wasn't going to be happy that he wasn't there at that time. He tried to sneak past her, and go into the kitchen but she threw a shoe at him in mid stride.

"Hey, Ma, what's for dinner?" Solomon laughed.

"What you cook?"

"Come on, Ma, what you cook for your big ol' baby?"

"It's on the stove, boy. What I tell you about comin' in here all times of the night expectin' to eat?" Orabell said, buttoning her housecoat.

"I was at the library, Ma."

"You wahdn't at no library! You was wit' one of them girls. I'm not goin' to keep fixin' dinner for you, if you ain't gon' be here to eat it."

"I'm here now, Mama."

"Boy, you know what I'm talkin' about. From now on, if you can't be here by dinnertime, you're on your own. This is my last time fixin' yo' food!" Orabell said, reaching for a plate to warm up Solomon's dinner.

"Mama, you don't have to fix my plate. I am a grown man, you know," Solomon said, taking his mother by the arm and sitting her in a chair. "Mama, I'm going to law school next year. Are you going to be all right here all by yourself?"

"Of course, boy."

"You've been taking care of me for so long, what are you going to do when you only have to take care of yourself?" Solomon asked. "Am I going to have to send you back a pair of my dirty underwear for you to wash every now and then?"

"You bet' not send me no draw'rs back here. If you do I'll send 'em right back to you with a note sayin' clean your own dirty draw'rs," Orabell said, punching Solomon on the arm.

"You sure?" Solomon asked, trying to cover his concern with laughter.

"I'll be OK, son. It's time for you to leave the nest. The world is waitin' on you. You may not know what I'm talkin' about right now, son, but you will later on. I ain't been shelterin' you from the world. I've been keepin' you from you. I done my job. I just hope that I did a good enough job. I'll be just fine when you're gone, son," Orabell assured him.

"I sure hope so, Mama." Solomon sighed. "Mama, can I ask you for a little advice?"

"What girl is it this time, boy?" Orabell chuckled.

"Ma, I'm serious this time."

"You always serious about the girl of the day. Lord, I hope it ain't that girl that hang up in my face every time I pick up the phone. That girl need help!"

"No, Ma, it's not her. It's a girl named Sunshine. Mama, she's not like any girl I've ever met before in my life."

"She ain't white, is she?" Orabell said, looking out of the corner of her eye.

"No, ma'am. She's a colored girl. She can't stand my guts, and Ma, the weird thing is that the more she rejects me, the more I want her."

"You crazy, boy!"

"Somehow, I have to get this woman. Now Ma, if you were a younger woman, let's say..." Solomon paused. "...about a hundred years younger."

"Watch ya mouth, boy!" Orabell said, punching Solomon in the arm again.

"Ow!" Solomon shouted. "Well, let's say you were still on the market. A young market though. What would a man have to do to get you to fall madly in love with him?"

"He would have to be hisself no matter what. Whatever that is, be it. And be it proud. I know that God didn't make no man perfect, so I wouldn't be lookin' for no perfect man. Of course, if I was younger, I probably wouldn't know that. Anyway, to get back to your point. I'd be lookin' for a provider. He wouldn't have to be rich, well off either. Just so that he made sure his family was taken care of. A man with a good heart. A man that stood for something other than hisself. A man who feared God. Who feared the consequences of doin' somebody else wrong, 'cause God ain't gon' let you get away with it. That's the man I wont right there."

"I guess you mean a man like my father. Too bad all I know about the man is a bunch of tales I've heard from other people. He was a great martyr. A great civil rights activist," Solomon said sarcastically, mocking the people who spoke of his father.

"Back in those days it wahdn't called civil rights; it was called survival. All you need to know about yo' daddy is that he was a man you should be proud of. He was a good man. A strong man. A man of characta!" Orabell said with pride.

"Ma, that's all you ever say is that he was a good man. I'm sure he was. But I also heard that he was so caught up with being a colored Moses that it eventually cost him his life. Did the man ever stop to think about his wife, or his unborn child?" Solomon asked. "I even heard that I may have some illegitimate brothers and sisters running around here."

Orabell stood up, and wiped her hands on her apron. She slowly walked over to Solomon and stood in front of him. He sat there looking at Orabell eye to eye, even though she was standing, and he was sitting. She took her hand and slapped the side of his face.

"I bet' not ever hear you say anything like that against yo' daddy. If you turn out to be half the man yo' daddy was, you'll be twice the man you are right now! You done growed up, got all educated, and now you think you can judge yo' daddy? Let me tell you somethin', a man who think he know everythang don't know nothin'! You think because you done been to college you know more than yo' daddy did?" Orabell shouted, "You ain't nothin' but an educated fool!"

Solomon instantly regretted hurting his mother by criticizing his father. He realized just how much he had hurt her. He tried to apologize but she wouldn't let him.

"Ma, I'm sorry, I didn't mean to..."

"You didn't mean to what?" Orabell interrupted. "You didn't mean to soil yo' own daddy's memory! Son, I know you got your life all planned out. You gon' be a big-time lawyer! But when you die, is that all you wont to be said about you? God got other plans for you, and you need to open your ears and listen to what He gotta say. I ain't just no mama talkin' to her son. On the day you was born I knew you was gon' be somethin' special, and I ain't talkin' about bein' no lawyer. God got somethin' special for you down the road, but you gotta open ya mind and heart to prepare for it. You may think in that educated head of yours that I'm gettin' sanctified on you, but son, this is destiny. Yo' destiny," Orabell said softly.

"I don't know what my destiny is going to be, Ma, but whatever it is, I'll be ready. If God has something in store for me, He knows my number, tell Him to give me a call," Solomon joked, winking his eye at her.

"You betta stop playin' with the Lord before He call ya number sooner than you wont Him to."

"Ma, was that slap supposed to be my passage from boy to manhood?" Solomon asked, rubbing his face. "If that's the case, you could have given me a spear and sent me out to kill a lion or something."

Solomon kissed Orabell, on her cheek, and she kissed him back.

"You got what you deserve." Orabell smiled. "When you gon' bring that little girl home to meet ya family; you not shamed of me are you?"

"Mama, if I'm not proud of anything else in my life, I'm proud of you," Solomon said. "But before I can bring her home, I have to get a date with her."

"Oh, you'll get her." Orabell smiled.

Solomon became more involved with the campaign to get closer to Sunshine, and although he workd he closely by her side, she did not exhibit any signs of romance. But by working so closely with Sunshine, her political ideas did rub off on him. He started to actually believe in the campaign, and the candidate he was representing.

Like most of the black people across America who were raised as a Baptist or Methodist, supporting a Catholic president was highly unlikely. As a matter of fact, for blacks, Senator Kennedy began as the least popular of candidates, but by the fall, he and Nixon were neck and neck. The turning point for the black community in the 1960 election in Senator Kennedy's favor was his conscientious decision to call Coretta Scott King and offer his condolences for her jailed husband, the civil rights leader, Dr. Martin Luther King, Jr. He spoke against the extremely stiff sentence King received for participating in a sit-in.

King had attended a sit-in at Rich's Department Store in Atlanta, Georgia. He was arrested and sentenced to four months on a hard labor chain gang. The judge defended the harsh sentence by saying King had a prior arrest for driving without a state driver's license. The arrest, and then the sentence, received national attention. Senator Kennedy stepped in, assisted in the release of King, and gained the support of the black vote. Not only in the South, but all across the country.

King's jailing also unified the students on Saginaw State's campus. Sunshine became the political leader for both the black and white students. The movement was rapidly becoming a young contemporary perspective versus tradition, uniting a variety of cultures and races.

Sunshine started her Kennedy rallies on campus, and across the city. She often traveled to nearby Flint and Lansing, sometimes as far as Detroit, campaigning for Senator Kennedy. Solomon helped her pass out flyers, and set up the area for her rallies.

One evening Sunshine invited Solomon over to watch the live debate between Nixon and Kennedy. It was the first time ever that such an event was being televised for the public to witness. Sunshine watched the debate with unbridled enthusiasm, and Solomon watched Sunshine, exacting those feelings.

They sat until the debate was over and Sunshine couldn't stop talking about how Kennedy had won the election that night. Solomon tried to match her enthusiasm, but it was to no avail. He watched her smile, and he wanted to kiss her lips. He watched her hands, and he wanted to hold them. He could care less about Kennedy or Nixon at that point. He wanted Sunshine, and he couldn't hold it in any longer. He looked into her eyes and he knew this would be the night that he made his move. He waited for a break in the conversation, but Sunshine was relentless in her verbal assault. Solomon looked at the clock over and over again. The dorm was nearing closing time for visitors. He had to make his move, and he had to be quick!

"Sunshine, I need to talk to you," Solomon said nervously.

"Go 'head, shoot!" Sunshine said, leaning back on her bed, and showing the full shape of her small frame.

"I don't know where to start," Solomon said.

"You better start quick because the clock on the wall says it's almost time for you to go." Sunshine laughed.

"Hey, put your coat on. Let's go for a walk."

"Boy, are you crazy? It's freezing out there."

"Sunshine, I'm nervous enough. Just put your coat on and go for a walk with me. We can stop by the pool hall and get some hot cocoa."

"I'm not goin' to no pool hall!" Sunshine said, lying back down on her bed.

"Girl, look, stop acting so high and mighty. I need to talk to you, and I need to talk to you tonight. Now put your coat on and let's go."

"Ooh, I like it when you get aggressive." Sunshine laughed.

"Stop playing and put your coat on so we can go."

Sunshine put on her coat, and walked to the pool hall with Solomon. She walked closely beside him to shield herself from the crisp autumn breeze. They walked in the hall, and it was almost completely empty, which worked in Solomon's favor. They grabbed a booth, and ordered some hot cocoa. As they sat there, Sunshine brought up the debate again, but this time Solomon interrupted her. He reached over the table and placed her delicate small hands in his large mitts, and pled his case.

"Please, Sunshine, can you be quiet about that damn debate for five minutes so that I can talk to you about how I feel?" Solomon said, releasing her hands.

"Ooh, there you go with that aggression again."

"I'm serious. Let's talk."

"Stop beggin', black man, and talk."

"OK, are you ready?" Solomon asked nervously.

"Ready as I'll ever be," Sunshine said, holding her cocoa with both of her hands.

"I need your advice about a woman," Solomon said, taking her hands in his again.

Sunshine sat back, surprised and somewhat disappointed that Solomon was asking her opinion about another woman. She removed her hands from his, and rolled her eyes.

"Go ahead, shoot!" Sunshine said, with her arms folded.

"If you knew that God had put a man on this earth for you, and you only, what would you do?"

"What kind of question is that?" Sunshine asked back. "I don't know."

"Come on, Sunshine, you're never short of words. What would you do?"

"I suppose that I would do everything within my power to get that man. And since God made him especially for me, I have the luxury of divine intervention covering any mistakes I may make."

"You know as well as I do, that there is something between us. Something we can't explain, but its' here, and it's strong."

"I'm confused. What are you trying to say?"

"I'm saying that I think I'm in love with you."

"Excuse me?"

"I said I think I'm in love with you."

"I don't know what to say, Solomon," Sunshine responded, totally surprised. "We've grown so close as friends. I see you more like a brother."

"Like a brother, huh?"

"Yes, Solomon, like a brother. I'm sorry," she said, rubbing Solomon's hands.

"I don't believe that. I think that you feel the same way I feel. You're just too stubborn to give in to your feelings."

"There's no telling how many girls you've told that line to, Solomon. Not to mention that every girl that I've seen you with has been a cracka."

"Cracker?" Solomon said sternly. "Don't call people bigoted names like that, Sunshine."

"If they're crackas, they're crackas! And you seem to love 'em."

"I love everybody, colored, white, brown, doesn't matter."

"But it should matter."

Solomon slid out of his side of the booth, and sat on the other side with Sunshine.

"You've been involved so much with political affairs, you've forgotten how to involve yourself with personal affairs. There is enough time in your life for love and politics," Solomon whispered, kissing her on both of her hands.

"Aagh!" Sunshine shouted, moving her hands from Solomon's lips. "Every time I imagine you with your hands on one of those white girls, it makes my skin boil. It's hard for me to get that image out of my head."

"Don't think about that nonsense," Solomon pleaded.

"I can't help it!" Sunshine growled. "I never considered you to be an interest of romance. I thought you weren't attracted to women like me."

"What do you mean, women like you?"

"Negro women," Sunshine said, staring Solomon straight in the eyes.

"Why do you think I'm not attracted to colored women?"

"I've never seen you with one. You've always chased white women."

"I don't chase anybody. Chasin' white women." Solomon teased, "Is that all that you have to say in your defense of loving me back?"

"Pretty much."

"Listen, growing up, I went to all-white schools, which had all white girls. I'm just accustomed to dating them. In my own neighborhood, I pretty much kept to myself. I stayed around my mother most of the time."

"So that's it, you're a mama's boy?" Sunshine laughed.

"Not anymore; now I'm a mama's man now." Solomon laughed, along with her.

"Tell me the truth," Sunshine said, turning the conversation back to a serious tone, "are you interested in me because I create a challenge for your ego?"

"No, Sunshine, no." Solomon explained, "I'm am telling you the God's honest truth when I say this. I don't want any other woman on this campus but you. I am usually good with lines when it comes to women. That's because I usually don't care about the consequences of what I am saying. But with you I want every word to be perfect, and every line to be sincere. I even listen to Nat King Cole, and Sam Cooke records for inspiration. I don't know what else to say to convince you that I want you. At this point, I don't care how you want me in your life. Politically, academically, romantically, I don't care. I just want to spend as much time with you as you can allow me."

"Love, that's a pretty strong word for you, isn't it, Solomon?"

"Love is a pretty strong word for everybody, isn't it?"

"It should be. But we both know that it isn't." Sunshine smiled. "I bet that if I gave in to you, you would not have the same persistency to get to know my thoughts, or my feelings. Probably after the first time I had sex with you, you would pay me no attention at all."

"Look, I am hands down the best athlete on this campus, and if I have to, I will chase you, and chase you until I catch you. So save both of us some and energy, and stop running right now," Solomon joked.

"Boy, you betta get in the best shape of your life if you plan on catchin' this." Solomon moved back over to his side of the booth, and reach beneath the table and placed Sunshine's feet in his lap.

"Sunshine, I may be just another man to any other woman on this earth, but to you, I am like no other. God made me just for you. My hands, my lips, my arms, all of them were made for you. It's like God told the angels to make Him a Solomon. He asked the angels, hey, we got some arms? Give 'em to me, and pass me someof those hands, and throw a couple of these lips on him; now put some Sunshine in his heart!" Solomon laughed. "If God can do all this for us, how dare you sit over there and tell me we shouldn't be together."

"I had no idea that you were so nuts!"

"You're right; I am nuts. And you're beautiful beyond belief."

"You're putting it on a little thick now; thin it up some."

"I can't. I look at your face and everything I need in this world is right in front of me. You don't ever need to put a drop of makeup on that beautiful face. You're a natural beauty. You need no makeup! No cover-up! All you have to do is just wake up! And you're ready for the day. I wish I could have it so easy."

"I also didn't know you were some kind of poet."

"I'm no poet; I'm just a desperate man, with a desperate plan."

"Can we go now? I'm getting sleepy." Sunshine yawned.

"Let's go; my work here is done."

They walked back to the dorm. But this time, Sunshine walked with her head in Solomon's jacket, and Solomon, with his arm around Sunshine's shoulder. He dropped her off at the dorm's entrance, and they kissed for the first time. It was a quick kiss, but Solomon was quite satisfied with whatever he could get.

Solomon and Sunshine eventually dated steadily and exclusively in the following weeks to come. When Election Day came, they were together, still campaigning for Senator Kennedy. The next morning they woke to find that Senator Kennedy defeated Richard Nixon by the slightest of margin in presidential history. After the election, Sunshine had plenty of free time, and Solomon took full advantage.

He finally introduced Sunshine to his best friend, Donovan, when he came home for Christmas break. Donovan was attending college in Ohio. Sunshine found Donovan to be intriguing. He was a young white man, with racial views more radical than hers. He was informed, and committed to the Civil Rights Movement. The three of them became inseparable whenever he visited from college.

Donovan had become an activist for civil rights. He and Sunshine spent many evenings discussing their personal solutions to the problems of race relations in America. They were ecstatic about the new 1961 Affirmative Action Act, and they felt comfortable with their decision to support the progressive thinking of the new presidential administration. Affirmative Action referred to policies aimed at increasing the number of people from certain social groups in employment, education, business, government, and other areas. It would serve as a way to balance the scale of democracy.

Sunshine was accepted into medical school in Washington, D.C. Solomon followed her lead, and decided to attend law school in the city. The summer of 1961 was hot and active. There was a lot going on in Saginaw, and across the country. Solomon did his best to avoid the increasing hostility developing between blacks and whites. He wanted to remain neutral and not get caught in the middle of a race riot.

Sunshine moved to Washington in the early part of the summer, leaving Solomon alone with Donovan. Donovan was just an extension of Sunshine when it came to politics and social issues. There was only a slim difference between their pro-black perspectives. Donovan tried to discuss the current social issues with Solomon, but he would quickly change the subject. Solomon felt that he had to entertain Sunshine with her save-the-world conversations because he loved her, but there was no way he was going to sit through a lecture from Donovan.

The summer came and went without any major outbreak, and then Donovan returned to school. Solomon sat around packing and preparing to move. He spoke to Sunshine almost every day, and it seemed the more they talked, the more he missed her. She had found two apartments for them in the same building. All that Solomon had to do was show up, and pay for his first month's rent. Sunshine had moved frequently, and done so, on her own. The move to D.C. was no big challenge for her, but for Solomon it was monumental. She understood that, and tried her best to make his move as simple as possible. All of the wheels were set in motion, and only the move stood in between Solomon and Sunshine.

A couple of days before Solomon was scheduled to leave, Stanford stopped by to visit Orabell, and to his surprise Solomon had not left. He thought that Solomon was afraid of leaving the nest, and had changed his mind. He began his usual antagonistic harassment. Solomon had become accustomed to his uncle's pestering, and he mostly ignored him whenever he came to visit.

Solomon saw Stanford walking up the stairs to the door. He grabbed the newspaper and lay on the couch, resting in his normal position of ignoring Stanford. His body was so long, his feet hung over the arms of the couch.

Stanford banged on the door as loud as he could, which was another annoying habit that bothered Solomon. As Stanford banged on the door, Solomon lay on the couch as if he didn't hear a sound. Orabell walked from her bedroom and slapped Solomon on the feet for not opening the door. Solomon laughed, and told her that he didn't hear the knocking.

"Hey, Stanford," Orabell said, standing to the side and letting Stanford pass. "How's business?"

"You win a few, you lose a few, and you send the rest home."

Solomon pulled the newspaper closer to his face to try to avoid any contact with Stanford.

"You still here, thought you were supposed to be going to law school?" Stanford asked. "You still plan on going, don't you?"

"Yup!" Solomon said, not removing the newspaper.

"Well, you gotta plan things like that. A black man has to take full advantage of every opportunity he has. Most importantly, you have to remember where you came from. That's the most important thing right there." Stanford sighed.

"Is that why your office is on the west side of the river?" Solomon laughed.

"Don't you go mouthin' off to your uncle like that," Orabell said.

"That's OK, Orabell. The boy's gotta point. It's a useless ignorant point, but it's a point just the same."

Solomon turned the page of his newspaper, but never lowered it to talk to Stanford.

"My job and my office is my life, and in order for me to survive, they have to survive. And they can't survive on this side of the river. My patients on that side of town, who can actually afford to pay their bills, are not going to travel on this side of the river to an office, when there are plenty of doctors right around the corner."

"So I guess your patients on this side of the river are on their own as far as traveling, huh, Unc?" Solomon laughed, with the newspaper still covering his face.

"Once you become a lawyer you will look back on this night and see how foolish you look. If you ever become a lawyer you will understand that just because you think you know the answer, it shouldn't stop you from confirming the truth. Ask questions, boy! Then let your questions try to provide the answers for you, without putting yourself in the position of looking like a fool because you don't know what the hell you're talking about. If you still can't understand what I'm trying to say, to put it simply, know your facts, Jack!" Stanford yelled.

Orabell laughed, as Stanford put Solomon in his place.

"You still didn't answer my question," Solomon said, turning another page.

"Maybe this will answer your question, son. It's business!" Stanford said, holding his hat in his hand with his arms spread far apart.

"That's what I thought. Another successful colored man catering to society. But you're always preaching to the younger generation about the struggles of the fifties."

"Solomon, befo' you put your foot deeper in your mouth, your uncle is only messin' with you, boy. Don't no po' folks travel 'cross no town to get to his office. Stanford, take two days out the week, and close that office over there down, to make house calls over here. And while you runnin' off at the mouth, I don't see no other doctor comin' 'round here," Orabell said, raising her eyebrows.

"Is that very logical for your business, Uncle Stanford?" Solomon asked. "Or is that your way of giving back to the po' colored community?"

"Shut up all that smart talk, Solomon," Orabell said sternly.

"If it was me, I would stay where I was, solicit more of the local patients, and drop the poor house calls. But then you're from my father's era; you have to be more than a successful man. You have to be a martyr, too. The only difference between you and my father is that it's your business you're sacrificing, and not your life."

Stanford snatched Solomon's newspaper, ripping it down the middle—leaving only the two ends Solomon held between his fingers.

"What the Sam Hell is wrong with you?" Stanford yelled. "Boy, have you lost your mind? You betta show yo' daddy more respect than that! I could care less if you sit over there on your arrogant, false educated ass and try to criticize me. But I'll be damned if I let you slander Isaiah's name! If you think you're that big of a man, we can take this outside, and you can put your ass where your mouth is."

"Uncle Stanford, please," Solomon said, waving Stanford off.

"Y'all cut it out," Orabell said.

"Naw, Orabell! Look at you sittin' up there so anxious to go be a lawyer. You think the world is a playground waitin' for you, but it ain't! That's what wrong with you young folks. Your eyes are so big looking at the future like it's promised to you, that you can't see the small things that are right in front of you. The things that make you human."

Stanford put his hat on his head and turned to walk out of the door.

"Let me get out of here before this boy make me lose my religion," Stanford said.

Stanford walked out the door, slamming it behind him.

"You sure are disappointing me on this day," Orabell said.

"Ma, Uncle Stanford will be fine. He loves this kind of stuff. I believe that's the main reason why he comes over here."

"That don't matter! That man put shoes on your feet, and clothes on your back. And you should be grateful that he did. He gave you them things from his heart, even though you and him might not get along like a uncle and nephew should. He ain't never throwed that up in yo' face. He care about you, and other folks, too. That's somethin' you ain't gon' find in those books up there at your school."

"Ma, you sent me to school to get an education, and when I do, you criticize me for doing so."

"I don't know a lot of fancy words, but I'm gon' try to say this the best way I know how. I do want you to get all the education you can. But I think yo' love for education done passed yo' love for people. I'm gon' be honest with you, son. If I had my choice, I'd rather see you with a good-lovin' heart and po', than to be rich and not care nothin' for nobody but yourself."

"Mama, we live in America, and America is a capitalistic society where we are allowed to make as much money as we possibly can. Unfortunately Mama, in order for some to have more money, some will have to have less. All that we can do, is try to become one of those who have more."

"Well, I guess I'm goin' to die one of those who has less. But that's on this earth, 'cause God got a place for me when I die. With many mansions, and roads paved in gold. And then I'll be one of the ones who have more, and my riches will last for all eternity. Like your father used to say, the child least born will rise above the sun to shine the brightest one." Orabell said, "By the way, I got the Chambers Bible ready for you to take with you to Washington, D.C."

"That's OK, Mama. That's for you old folks. I'll pass."

"This was yo' daddy's, and yo' daddy's daddy's."

"Yeah, but it's not mine."

"I'll just have to pray for you and your soul."

"Don't worry about me, Ma. Me and my soul will be all right. But just in case I'm dead in the morning, say a little prayer to God for me and apologize for my sinnin' ways." Solomon smiled.

Solomon stretched his long, winding body, and walked into his bedroom.

"Go to bed, boy! And I done told you 'bout playin' with the Lord like that!" Orabell yelled.

Solomon left his mother's home and moved to Washington, D.C. two days later. He was culturally shocked by the big city. But Sunshine carefully, and slowly, showed him the ropes. After a while, Solomon became used to the city, and started to make his own footprints in the sand. He found a job in a law office, working as an administrator—a job he was proud to have. However, the salary from the job could not cover the expenses of renting an apartment, and he eventually moved in with Sunshine. He hid the news from Orabell for as long as he could. But in the latter part of 1963, he found out some information to rush his decision to tell Orabell about him and Sunshine.

Chapter Thirteen

SAGINAW, MICHIGAN, 1963

On November 21, 1963, two years after Solomon and Sunshine started dating, he brought her home for the first time to meet his family. Orabell planned a special dinner, and invited William from Detroit. William was sixty-two years old, and traveling had become difficult, so he couldn't make it. Since William couldn't come to Saginaw, Solomon decided to stop in Detroit and visit his Uncle William, who had lived near the corner of Rutherford and Finkle for twelve years. He had adored and admired William growing up, and he didn't know how many more opportunities he would have to spend time with him.

William was so ecstatic to see Solomon, Sunshine suggested that they spend the night with him. She knew that would reduce a night for them in Saginaw, but William was an old man who lived alone, and the pain of loneliness seeped throughout his voice and his home. Sunshine was overwhelmed with pity for William, and thought that maybe they could spread a little joy throughout his house, if for only one night. Solomon tried to convince her that his uncle was not an old man who needed pity. Sunshine finally understood what Solomon meant when a thirty-year-old woman knocked on his door. William turned her away, and told her he had to spend time with his family. Solomon smiled at Sunshine, as if to tell her, *I told you so*. William enjoyed every second Solomon and Sunshine spent with him. When the time came for them to leave, he cried, and clutched Solomon's hand tightly, as if he did not want to let it go. It wasn't easy for Solomon to say goodbye to William either. They managed to tear themselves from one another, and Solomon drove off.

Solomon continued his trip back to Saginaw; his first time back in two years. As he entered into Saginaw County, and all of the familiar landmarks started to appear, he became increasingly excited to see his mother. He was even excited to see his Uncle Stanford. He made a right onto Remington Street, and drove the two miles to Fenton Street, where his family had lived for nearly twenty-seven years. Everything seemed old and new at the same time, but in a smaller version. Everything seemed to be smaller, or closed in.

They pulled in front of his mother's house, and Sunshine stretched as she stood on the lawn. Solomon snatched the suitcases from the trunk, and carried them up the stairs to the porch. He was fumbling for his key, when Orabell opened the door and smiled.

Solomon thought to himself that his mother didn't look a day older. As a matter of fact, he realized his mother was only twenty-five years older than him. He had always thought of her as an old woman, because she had such a huge responsibility of raising him by herself. But looking into her face, he saw that his mother was actually a young-looking forty-eight-year-old woman.

"Mama."

"My baby is back home."

Solomon left the bags at the door, and hugged Orabell. He lifted her from her feet, and she wrapped her arms around his neck as her legs dangled in the air. Sunshine turned away, feeling that she was about to enter into a conflict bigger than the Cuban Missile Crisis. She watched Solomon and thought this giant man was nothing more than a little mama's boy at heart. Sunshine prepared herself for the worst. She was beginning to plan excuses to cut their trip short to avoid the rivalry between her and Orabell.

"Put me down, boy, and show some manners."

Orabell took Sunshine by the hand and led her into the house. All of the aggression Sunshine was feeling melted away as Orabell opened her heart, and welcomed her into her home. She sat Sunshine on the couch, and told her not to move. She went into her bedroom and brought out a book filled with old black-and-white photographs. She pointed to each one, and told

Sunshine who each person was in the picture. She told her about her parents, Red, William, Stanford, and of course, Isaiah.

Sunshine listened to Orabell marvel over her husband. It was in total contrast to the way Solomon criticized the man. Obviously, there was miscommunication somewhere. Solomon described his father as a self-serving martyr who cared about his legacy more than his family. However, Orabell described him as an unselfish hero who died helping others. Sunshine knew that Isaiah was killed before Solomon was born, so he had to arrive at his perception of his father from some other source than his mother. Sunshine looked at Orabell as a woman madly in love with a dead man, who did no wrong.

An hour after Solomon and Sunshine's arrival, Stanford drove up in his annual big Cadillac. He walked in, loud, and talking nonstop as if he had known Sunshine from birth. He didn't wait for a formal introduction; he introduced himself. Sunshine found him charming, and felt drawn to his gift for gab. Stanford grabbed Solomon by the shirt and pulled him to his chest. He hugged him wildly, rocking him back and forth. Solomon was totally shocked, as he held his arms above his shoulders watching his uncle cling to him like a child.

"I didn't think I would miss you, boy, but I did somethin' terrible," Stanford said.

"I missed you, too, Unc," Solomon returned, still surprised.

"If you need anything down there, let me know. I went to medical school down there, and I have still have contacts. So if you're ever in a bind, boy, don't hesitate to give me a call. We're family, and I know how it is going to school, and paying bills at the same time."

"Sure, Uncle Stanford, if I need anything, I'll let you know."

Stanford patted him on the back, and hugged him around his shoulder.

"Well, how long are you two going to be in town?" Stanford asked.

"For a couple of days," Solomon said.

"That ain't no time; stay a week!" Stanford shouted.

"I wish we could, but we can't. Actually, we came to talk to you two about a very important issue," Solomon said, sitting next to Sunshine and holding her hand.

"Don't tell me y'all gettin' married?" Orabell asked with excitement.

"Well, Ma," Solomon answered nervously, "we're kind of already married. But that's only half of the news. The other half of the news is that Sunshine is pregnant."

"What?" Orabell asked in disbelief.

"Yes, ma'am. We're married, and Sunshine's pregnant," Solomon repeated.

"I don't suppose while you was sittin' up makin' a baby, between all of yo' fun, you coulda called ya mama and told me that you were married," Orabell said angrily.

"I wanted to do just that, Mama. But everything happened so fast. And believe me it was no fun making this baby," Solomon said.

He looked at Sunshine and saw the frown on her face, and realized what he had said. He then apologized to her.

"Sunshine, I didn't mean it like that. I had plenty of fun. I was only telling Mama that it's not fun being pregnant."

"Are you saying that you're not happy with me being pregnant?" Sunshine asked.

Solomon looked at Stanford, and he motioned for him to stop talking and be silent, by covering his lips.

"Hold on, young lady," Orabell said. "When you get him alone, you can fuss and fight all you wont, but this is my house and my son, and right now it's my turn!"

Sunshine sat back and folded her arms. She knew that Orabell, though sweet, could also be a force to reckon with, a force she may not want to provoke. And she was correct in her assumption. Orabell scolded Solomon with a finger pointed in his face, while Stanford sat back and laughed. Solomon looked over Orabell's shoulder at Stanford. Stanford motioned for him to just listen until Orabell talked herself out. He put his finger to his lips, and shook his head from side to side. Solomon rested back on the couch against Sunshine, and they both listened to Orabell until she was tired of fussing.

"Now, what are y'all going to do?" Orabell asked.

"We don't know. I guess I'm going to drop out of law school for a while, and get a job paying more money."

"Oh no the hell you ain't!" Stanford said, sitting up.

"Uncle Stanford, I need money. And this little job I have barely pays our bills."

"You can't drop out of law school, Solomon. Now think of something else," Stanford said.

"There's nothing else to think of. It will only be temporary. Once the child is a little older, I can go back to law school, and Sunshine can complete medical school."

"You're going to be a doctor?" Stanford shouted. "I'm a doctor!"

"Yessir," Sunshine answered.

"Look, you two, you're not dropping out of school, and that's that!" Stanford said.

"We don't have a choice," Solomon said.

"How come you don't?" Stanford asked. "We are a family, and family stick together. Whatever we have to do, we'll do it, but you ain't droppin' outta school."

Orabell sat between Solomon and Sunshine on the couch and held their hands.

"Look, Sunshine, why don't you let me help you and my son with my grandchild."

"Of course, but I don't know what you can do, Mrs. Chambers."

"How about I come down to Washington befo' the baby is born."

Orabell smiled. "I can help you, and make sure that baby is OK."

"That would be too much for us to ask Mrs. Chambers," Sunshine said.

"No it ain't!" Stanford shouted.

"What do you think, honey?" Sunshine asked Solomon.

"Ma, are you sure?"

"Yeah, I'm sure. I can stand to get away from here for a while."

"That is very nice of you, Mrs. Chambers."

"You don't have to call me Mrs. Chambers, baby. I'm yo' mama just like I'm Solomon's mama now, so that's what you should call me."

Sunshine smiled. "OK, Ma."

"Solomon, you don't have to worry about your rent, or hospital bills. Me and your Uncle William can take care of that until you get finished with law school. Now of course, we want our money back when you get a real job." Stanford laughed.

"Uncle Stanford, you and Uncle William can't pay my bills for me. That's my responsibility!"

"Can you pay 'em?" Stanford asked, bucking his eyes.

"By the time the baby comes I'll have a better job, and I'll be able to afford them then."

"That's being a little optimistic, don't you think?"

"No sir. I plan on having things in order, and..." Solomon said.

"You mean, like you planned on havin' this baby?" Orabell interrupted.

"No, ma'am," Solomon said, snapping his head in Orabell's direction.

"Son, we have a lot invested in you. Now we don't expect anything out of our investment for us, but for the future of our family. Our family has had a hard time surviving in this country, but we have. And a lot is resting on your shoulders to make sure that everything we've suffered through will be rewarded to our family."

"He right, Solomon. You ain't just goin' to school for you. You goin' for me, your daddy, and the baby Sunshine carryin' in her stomach. And that baby's baby, too," Orabell said.

"What do you think, honey?" Solomon asked to Sunshine.

"That's enough of that 'what do you think honey' mess!" Stanford said. "We don't care what you two think. If it wasn't for your thinking we wouldn't be in this mess!"

Solomon looked at Stanford, and gave him a half-grin. Stanford winked his eye at Sunshine, and she laughed. Stanford asked Solomon to ride with him around the corner so that they could talk. As soon as they were out of the house, Orabell and Sunshine had their own conversation. They went into the kitchen, and Orabell washed dishes. Sunshine offered to help several times, but Orabell refused help from her guest. Sunshine sat at the table, and they talked.

"Do you know how far along you are?" Orabell asked.

"My doctor said that I am probably around two months."

"Babies are a blessing. I thought the Lord would never bless me with a child, and just when me and my husband had given up, I found out I was pregnit with Solomon."

"How old were you when you had him?" Sunshine asked.

"I was twenty-five years old."

"I'm almost twenty-five myself, but I don't feel as if I'm old. As a matter of fact, I feel that I am too young to be having a baby."

"Times have changed, child. Twenty-five was a old hag when I was growin' up."

"Old hag?" Sunshine asked. "You're still beautiful, Mrs. Chambers. I hope I age as well as you have."

"When you've been through what I've been through, baby, you may or may not change on the outside. But if you could cut me open, all you would see is scars and bruises. Wrinkled, and tore up from a lifetime of pain and sorrow," Orabell said, clutching the dish rag.

"I'm sorry to hear that."

"I don't mean to put my sorrow on you, baby."

"I've dumped mine on you; it's only natural that you share some of yours with me."

"How does your mother feel about your situation?"

"My mother?" Sunshine asked. "My mother died when I was seven, and my father died when I was ten. My grandmother and grandfather raised me, but they're too old for me to worry them with my problems."

"I understand. But as far as I'm concerned, you have a mother now. And I have a daughter." Orabell smiled, removing her apron from her waist.

"Thank you. I really appreciate you helping us."

"Don't you worry about your delicate condition; the Lord will make a way."

They walked back into the living room, and watched television until Solomon and Stanford returned. They sat around and talked for a while, then Sunshine and Orabell went to bed. Stanford and Solomon stayed up and continued to talk.

"You've changed since I've been gone, Uncle Stanford," Solomon said, drinking a cup of hot cocoa. "What happened?"

"I haven't changed one bit."

"You're treating me differently. You're nicer."

"I'm treating like you're a man, because you're acting like a man."

"Uncle Stanford, you were always on my back when I was growing up."

"That's because I had to, son."

"There were times when I thought that you didn't even like me. I know there were times when I didn't care too much for you." Solomon laughed.

"Boy, what are you talking about?" Stanford asked. "I stayed on you, because all you ever cared about was books. I want you to get the best possible education, but I also want you to care for other things, too. This child is forcing you to step out of your perfectly managed world, and you are going to need help. Emotionally, and financially. And I will do all that I can to make sure you get plenty of both. I haven't changed, son, you have."

"Maybe so." Solomon smiled back. "One more thing, Unc, you've never told me how you feel about Sunshine?"

"Oh, Sunshine. If I was about twenty years younger, you'd be in St. Mary's or Saginaw General or somebody's hospital."

Solomon laughed, expecting his uncle to say something outrageous.

"Why?"

"Because of that big ol' knife I would have stabbed in your back," Stanford joked.

"Unc, you would have stabbed your nephew in the back?"

"Woulda?" Stanford said. "Hell, I'd stab you right now if I thought Sunshine would go for it."

"You're a brutal man, Unc."

"That's enough of the chit-chat; I'm getting kinda tired. I'd better be gettin' on home." Stanford yawned.

"Yeah, go get you some rest, old man."

Stanford put on his hat and made his way home. Solomon sat up thinking of all the memories from his childhood in that old house. He fell asleep on the couch, until Orabell woke him, and made him get in the bed. Some things change, and some things stay the same.

The next morning, Orabell had breakfast waiting for Solomon and

Sunshine when they emerged from their bedroom. After breakfast, they reminisced on stories of Solomon growing up. Orabell brought out the book of pictures again, to corroborate her stories. They laughed into the late afternoon until Stanford charged into the house with startling news.

"Have y'all heard what happened?"

"Naw, what happened?" Orabell shouted back.

"Somebody shot President Kennedy in Texas!" Stanford said. "Cut the television on. It's all over the news."

"Is he all right?" Sunshine asked.

"They said he was only wounded," Stanford said.

Solomon turned the television on as the newscaster announced the sad news that President John Fitzgerald Kennedy was shot and killed in Dallas, Texas while riding in a caravan with the governor. Lyndon Baines Johnson was later sworn in as president on the plane carrying the president's body back to Washington, D.C.

The nation was saddened, and no one more than Sunshine. She looked at Solomon with a blank look on her face, and burst into tears. Orabell sat next to Sunshine, and patted her hand.

"What is wrong with these people?" Stanford said.

"That's the world we live in," Solomon said.

"They need to hang the son of a bitch who did this by his nuts," Stanford said angrily.

"Stanford!" Orabell said.

"I'm sorry for my language." Stanford put his hat on his head and turned to go out of the door. "I got to get the hell out of here."

They watched the ongoing news coverage of the president's assassination for the rest of the evening and late into the night. The next morning, Sunshine and Solomon left early returning to Washington. They wanted to get back before the city was engulfed with mourners and well-wishers.

For Orabell, saying goodbye to Solomon hurt more the second time than it did the first time he had left. She wanted to keep him with her to protect him. As he drove off, her heart sank into her chest, and she held her breath to keep from crying.

The following six months came, and went quickly. In May of 1964, Orabell caught the bus to Washington to help with the arrival of the new baby.

Sunshine and Solomon lived in a tiny apartment with one bedroom. Sunshine and Orabell shared the bedroom while Solomon slept on the couch. Orabell cared for Sunshine as if she was her child from birth. She cooked, cleaned, washed; everything Sunshine needed was prepared and given to her at a moment's notice.

On June 27, 1964, Sunshine gave birth to a bright-eyed baby girl. Solomon was not there for the birth. By the time he received news that Sunshine was in labor, it was too late for him to get to the hospital before his child was born.

Miraculously, Stanford was already at the hospital, with cigars and wine. As soon as he heard that Sunshine felt her first labor pain, he drove to the airport and caught the next plane headed in the direction of Washington.

Sunshine was asleep when Solomon walked into the room. Orabell was combing her hair and rubbing her face. She handed Solomon a box of Cuban cigars that Donovan had sent to him. Donovan had received a box of Cuban cigars earlier that year from Solomon when he had his first child, also a girl.

Solomon did not want to wake Sunshine, so he whispered and asked the nurse if he could see the baby. At that time, Stanford was holding her in the nursery. The nurse led Solomon to the nursery where Stanford was sitting with the newborn child in his hands—cautiously, as if she were grains of sand slipping through his fingers. When he saw Solomon, he couldn't even speak. He could only smile. He held her up, and showed Solomon his child.

"Look at her. She's beautiful," Stanford said.

"Can I hold her?" Solomon asked.

"Of course, boy, she's your baby."

Solomon held the tiny baby in his huge hands and slowly pulled her against his chest. He looked into her face, and couldn't believe that he had created the beautiful creature he was holding. He sat in a chair, and placed her in his lap. Stanford sat beside him, and the two men caressed the child with one of their hands, and made sure she would not slip from Solomon's lap with their other hand. When Sunshine woke up, Orabell told Solomon to take the baby to its mother. She walked on one side of him, while Stanford walked on the other side, and together the three of them made it safely to Sunshine's room.

Solomon kissed Sunshine, and handed her their baby. She told Solomon that she wanted to name the child Michelle. Solomon told her that her name didn't matter; he just wanted a healthy child. Sunshine remained in the hospital for three days after Michelle's birth, then they released her to go home.

Eventually the time came for Sunshine to return to medical school, or lose her grant funds. After a month, the responsibility of having a newborn baby, and maintaining a full academic schedule was taking its toll. Orabell was actually the caretaker of the child. But it was time for her to return to Michigan. Orabell was concerned that after she was gone, the young family may have a difficult time struggling with their baby, and going to school. After considering the welfare of the child, she came up with the solution that would cure everyone's problem for the present time. After lengthy discussions and many cups of hot cocoa, they all agreed on the best possible solution. Orabell packed her bags, and Solomon and Sunshine drove her back to Saginaw. It was a quiet thirteen-hour trip, but the silence was understood between the three of them.

They arrived in Saginaw shortly after midnight. Sunshine and Solomon rested until morning. They woke early, and started on their way back. Sunshine held her baby's blanket in her hands and rubbed it along her face. Solomon watched her, but did not say anything. He felt that it was best to let her have a moment to herself.

Stanford knocked on Orabell's door bright and early the next morning. He wanted to catch Solomon and Sunshine before they left. He was too late; he had missed them by a couple of minutes. Orabell answered the door, patting little Michelle on the back. She was feeding her a bottle. Stanford took his hat off, and asked if he could hold the child. Orabell told him to be careful, and made him sit down. She handed him the baby, and the bottle, and watched as Stanford instantly fell in love.

Sunshine cried every mile of the trip back to Washington, D.C. There was nothing Solomon could say to comfort her, so he didn't. After all, what was there to say to a mother who had just left her child?

In August of 1965, Solomon and Sunshine made a trip to Saginaw to pick up their child for a few weeks. Michelle was fourteen months old, and just learning how to walk. They had visited the baby three times since Orabell had taken her to Michigan. Each time the child had developed more, and they missed every step. At first it was teething, then crawling, then standing; now she was walking. Sunshine had a tremendous sense of guilt for letting another woman raise her child, but she tried to keep her purpose in its proper perspective. Still, she felt that her child's young life was passing her by.

Orabell help soothe her conscience by telling her that what she doing was very unselfish. First of all, she was allowing a lonely grandmother to fill her life with love of a grandchild. She told her that if her heart felt no pain by what she was doing, then she was not a good mother. But if she cried, or felt guilt, that's the sign of a mother's love. She also told Sunshine that whenever her studies were completed she would have a lifetime to provide Michelle with everything she would ever need.

Michelle never had a problem recognizing her parents. She would cling to them every time they were around. On this trip, they took her to the park, to church, and wherever they were, she was comfortable with them. She loved Ojibway Island Park. It was a small island located in the middle of the city. They had a picnic, and it seemed as if they were never apart. They invited Orabell to go with them, but she declined and told them to spend some time with the child alone. She needed to get used to being alone with them. This would be the first time they would take her away from her home.

Later that evening, they sat at the dinner table and engaged in catch-up conversation. Orabell was excited for Solomon and Sunshine and she couldn't help talking about them taking Michelle home with them for the first time. Sunshine was even more excited, and she matched Orabell word for word. Solomon and Stanford tried to change the subject several times, but the women were much too much for them to handle. The subject would always drift back to Michelle, and her first visit to Washington.

Solomon had an ace in the hole to break the monotony, and he wasn't afraid to use it.

"Hey, Uncle Stanford, what do you think about all of those lynchings going on down there in the South?" Solomon asked.

Like a moth to a flame, Sunshine cued in on the topic.

"I've been hearin' about all that commotion goin' on. Whoo! I'm glad I'm up here. When we was down there, colored folks kept to colored folks, and white folks kept to white folks. Now all those colored folks down there tryin' vote, and those white folks killin' left and right. I wish the government would step in and do something," Orabell said.

"President Johnson signed an act to give Negroes the right to vote all over America. He said, 'this would strike away the last major shackle of the Negro ancient bond,' but we'll have to wait and see," Sunshine said.

"He signed an act?" Orabell said. "Colored folks should already have the right vote. I thought we did."

"No, ma'am. By the Constitution laws we do, but by Jim Crow laws we do not," Sunshine said, taking a bite of food.

"Baby, I don't know what you're talking about, but it sure sounds smart." Orabell laughed.

"Calm down, Ma," Solomon joked.

"I ain't calmed up!" Orabell said.

"When did they sign this act?" Stanford asked.

"A few days ago. August sixth, nineteen-hundred and sixty-five. Remember that day, it will live on in infamy," Sunshine said, mimicking former President Roosevelt.

"The sixth. Oh, I'll never forget the sixth. That was the day Orabell gave me those expired laxatives, because I was constipated," Stanford said.

"Stop it, Stanford; we eatin'!" Orabell said, pointing to Sunshine.

"Hell, I was. Sunshine family now," Stanford said.

"What makes that day so infamous?" Solomon asked.

"The fact that Negroes now have the support of the president is a big deal," Sunshine said.

"We've had the support of the president before. Those Kennedy boys were some good boys. I always said ol' Bobby need to run for president in '68, and make Martin Luther King his vice president. White folks all over the country will start moving to England." Stanford laughed.

"What makes it monumental is this time, he signed his name to agree to uphold the negroes' right to vote," Sunshine said.

"He needs to hold up some of them shotguns those white folks usin' to kill all them black folks down there," Stanford said.

"Look at us. We're always talking about people calling us names, and here we are defining ourselves as negroes, coloreds, and blacks," Solomon said.

"Y'all gettin' too deep for me," Orabell said.

"I don't see myself as black, colored, or a negro. I just see myself as a man."

"What the hell is wrong this boy?" Stanford asked.

"Stanford, cut out all that cussin'!" Orabell said.

"Sunshine, baby, I'm sorry. I don't normally use profanity like this. I'm a deacon, and I should know better. But what the hell is wrong this boy?" Stanford asked again.

"You do know better; you just act like you don't," Orabell said.

"That's OK, Mr. Stanford. You're trying. You're trying." Sunshine laughed.

"Thank you, baby." Stanford smiled.

Sunshine directed the conversation back to Solomon.

"Solomon, you say you don't see yourself as a black man; you just see yourself as a man. How can you make a distinction between the two?" Sunshine asked.

"I am not going to restrict myself by labeling myself as a black man. Do you label yourself as a black woman?" Solomon asked.

"Label, no, but I do privilege myself."

"Why?" Solomon asked. "What does your skin matter?"

"You are so naïve. Do you think those Negroes in the South are being murdered because they smoke, or drink?" Sunshine asked. "Or because they are Christians or Catholics? It's because they are Negroes!"

"Answer something for me: what is it that makes you black?" Solomon asked.

"Her skin, fool!" Stanford shouted.

"Is it the inside, or outside of your skin, that makes you black?"

"There is no outside, or inside of my skin. My skin is defined by my character. My skin, my character, there is no distinction between the two. I am the determining factor of who I am, and I can not understand how you could separate your character from your skin. It is you that makes your skin a hindrance. Your skin is as much a part of you as your hair, your lips, and everything that makes you, you."

"Tell him baby, tell him." Stanford laughed. "When you were born, you were born with skin, and a di...," Stanford said.

"Don't you say it!" Orabell shouted.

Stanford stopped talking, and looked at Orabell. He rolled his eyes at her and continued with what he was saying.

"As I was saying before I was rudely interrupted. You were born with two important factors to make you who you are. You were born with your skin, which made you black, and your penis which you made you male. And it would serve you better to embrace them both, than to deny either one of them," Stanford said, lighting a cigar.

"I am not ashamed to be black. I just don't want to get caught up in all of this racial mumbo jumbo."

"Unfortunately, you were born into it. When there are people being killed because of the color of their skin, and you are wearing that skin on your body, you are in just as much danger as anyone else. Ignorance is no protection from bigotry," Sunshine exclaimed.

"I didn't want to get this deep into conversation. I was only trying to get Mama and Sunshine to change the subject. So let's just agree to disagree. I do not share your philosophy of hating a race of people for the actions of a few. Malcolm X was killed earlier this year for those same tenets. When will we learn that it is not the way; you can't fight hate, with hate."

"No one is saying anything about hate. This is 1965, and Negro people are being slaughtered for wanting to elect their own representatives. You grew up here in Michigan, I grew up in Mississippi: two entirely different environments. I have seen Negro men hung from trees, and Negro women raising white children during the day, and their own at night. And I'm not going to let you, or anyone else, convince me that if we as Negro people pride ourselves, in ourselves, it concludes us as being hating any other ethnicity. And furthermore, I do not believe Malcolm X's death was the result of his hate for anyone, but others' hatred of him," Sunshine said.

"I can't believe that you are defending Malcolm X!" Solomon said.

"No, I am defending a man gunned down in front of his family. I don't know enough about him to defend, or condemn him. But murder in any case, is wrong."

"I'll defend him!" Stanford said. "Every man has a right to believe as he wants, even if his belief is in a Cadillac. If his belief is not harming his neighbor, hell, leave him alone, and let him worship his damn Cadillac. They had no right killin' that man."

"I love Martin Luther King. Nothin' like that will ever happen to him," Orabell said.

"I don't know, Ma; if they can kill the president of the United States, and get away with it, no Negro's life is out of danger," Sunshine said.

"Maybe you right, baby. I'm about to take these dishes in the kitchen. Y'all through?" Orabell asked, picking up the dishes.

Sunshine helped her clear the table. She has learned that as long as she asks Orabell to help with the dishes, she will always be told no. Now when it is time to clear the table she jumps right and helps without asking. The two women went into the kitchen leaving Solomon and Stanford alone at the table.

"Uncle Stanford, there's something I need to discuss with you," Solomon said.

"Well, if it's goin' to be just you and me, do you have to talk so proper, son?" Stanford asked.

"Excuse me?" Solomon asked.

"Could you, uh, break some verbs? Double up on some negatives, or somethin' like that. Talkin' proper like that make me feel nervous, like I'm being audited by the Internal Revenue Service, son," Stanford said.

"I'll try," Solomon said. "I really appreciate you and Uncle William helping me out with my financial situation. And I intend on paying you back every cent."

"What the hell are you talking about?" Stanford said.

"You know what I'm talking about, old man," Solomon said, extending his hand to his uncle.

Stanford reached out and shook his hand. Then he pulled him closer, and hugged him. They sat back down and Stanford pulled out another cigar and lit it up.

"You know, boy, I have to get you straight on some things. You don't owe me nothing. I am doing no more for you, than your father did for me. Your daddy treated me like a brother. No, like a son. He did whatever he had to do to make sure I went to college. I used to always try to be a smart-mouth, and tell him that I was a man. And I would pay him back all of the money he spent taking care of me. He would laugh because he knew I was just a young fool talkin' trash. Just like yourself," Stanford said. "I am going to give you the same advice your father gave me. Don't waste your time paying back lost time, unless it can benefit the future."

"That's what my father said, huh?" Solomon said.

"Yeah, if there was ever a man that I would call a hero, it would be yo' daddy. The Kennedys, Martin Luther King, they ain't got nothin' on that man," Stanford said, puffing his cigar. "Let's go make that run to the juice sto' before they close," he added, slapping Solomon on the leg.

"Man, every time I come to town, you make me ride to that liquor store with you. Why are you trying to hide the fact that you drink?"

"Because I'm a deacon in the church," Stanford whispered.

"But you make me look like I'm a lush. Every time I go in there, I get you enough of that stuff to last forever. Makes me look like I have a drinking problem," Solomon said.

"Don't nobody know you around here no more. Let's just get a little stash. We got to hurry up before it close nah, come on."

Solomon yelled to Sunshine that he was stepping out for a while, then he and Stanford made their way to the liquor store.

A couple of days later, Sunshine and Solomon took Michelle home for the first time. Sunshine was on a school break, so she stayed home with the baby. Their vacation went better than expected, until it was time for

Sunshine to go back to school, and Michelle to return to her grandmother in Michigan.

Solomon graduated from law school in the spring of 1966. He tested and passed the bar on his first attempt, a feat that some never conquer. To pass on the first attempt is exceptional. But it was just another accomplishment for Solomon Chambers. He started off working in a large law firm where he did most of the work, and received the least of the credit. He was the only black person in the firm, a position he has been in for most of his life. He bought a large, multi-acre home in the suburbs of Alexandria, Virginia.

After helping build the firm into one of the largest firms in the Washington, D.C. metropolitan area, and not offered partnership, Solomon began to move in a different direction. He developed an endless list of clientele, and decided to start his own firm.

His law firm wished him well, and gave him a going-away party. He discussed with the senior partners the possibility of taking some of his clients along with him to his new firm. They respectfully denied him the right to carry any existing clients.

Having to create an entire list of clientele on his own proved to be more challenging than Solomon expected. The disappointment affected him financially and confidently. He started to question himself on leaving the stability of the firm and branching out on his own.

Sunshine tried to reinforce Solomon's confidence by telling him he was just starting off, and things would eventually get better. Things were certainly better for Sunshine.

Although she had not yet completed medical school, she had managed to open a free clinic with a government grant. Doctors volunteered one day a week at her clinic. Since Sunshine was not yet certified, she could only practice as an intern. And though she couldn't practice as a doctor, she operated the facility.

Solomon tried desperately to solicit clients. He placed ads outside of the metropolitan D.C. area, but he was given no opportunity to try a case on his own. One afternoon Sunshine received a call from a relative in Mississippi, asking if Solomon could defend her cousin. Solomon agreed to do it, and volunteered to do it for free. He bought tickets for Orabell and Stanford to meet him and Sunshine in Mississippi. He wanted his family present at the first trial he tried with his own firm.

They met at the Leflore County Courthouse. Orabell and Stanford were staying at a hotel on the outskirts of town. Since Leflore County was not that far from Derma County, and they could possibly run into someone they knew, they kept a low profile. They didn't want word to get out that Stanford was back in town. They didn't know if there were any old ghosts living in the delta, and they didn't want to find out.

Michelle was nearly four years old, and she knew that she was in an unfamiliar place, so she held her grandmother's hand every step of the way. Sunshine had dressed Michelle in a colorful floral dress with a white collar. Her hair was braided in long ponytails—straightened by hand, from her grandmother's straightening comb.

Solomon defended Sunshine's cousin Sonny Junior Parker for breaking and entering in January 1968. Junior was found not guilty, and released after the trial. Solomon invited his family to a celebratory lunch. They drove around the small town looking for a nice restaurant. Sunshine told Solomon that he would be driving for days if he was looking for a four-star restaurant. They finally found a decent café, with a checkered floor, and shiny silver bar stools with a red seat. Complete with a fuzzy bearded busboy with a cigarette behind his ear. The jukebox was blasting country and western tunes that Solomon had never heard in his life.

There were plenty of seats available, but the waitress showed them to the section for colored people. It had grease stains, and torn seat covers. Solomon suggested they find a restaurant more suitable. Stanford laughed and told Solomon there was nothing more suitable in the delta of Mississippi. In the back, they noticed a young black man washing dishes for all of the people sitting in the colored section. Solomon could not believe his eyes. After a while he forgot about the blatant discrimination between the black and white patrons, and enjoyed the moment of winning his first case. They were so caught up in their celebration, they didn't notice the other black people leaving the restaurant. The waitress interrupted their little party by asking to pay for their check.

"Who's gon' pay for this meal?"

"I will," Solomon said.

"I'd like to congratulate my husband on his first of many victories as an attorney. Solomon Chambers, attorney at law. That sounds good, don't it?" Sunshine smiled.

"It sho' do, baby. Solomon Chambers, attorney at law," Orabell said, lifting her glass.

They stared at Stanford waiting for him to give his toast.

"Aw hell, Solomon Chambers, attorney at damn law," Stanford grunted.

"You act like you didn't want to toast your nephew, Unc," Solomon said.

"I wasn't actin'," Stanford said. "I don't!"

"That's OK, Unc. That's OK." Solomon laughed. "I would like to give a toast to my mother, my precious little girl, and my uncle for traveling all the way down here. And I would like to toast my wife for opening up the first twenty-four hour free clinic in Washington, D.C."

"Solomon, you don't have to recognize me every time someone is recognizing you. Enjoy your spotlight." Sunshine laughed.

"I just want the world to know just how proud I am of you."

"I'm proud of you, too, Sunshine baby," Orabell said.

"Me too, now can we finish this meal, and get outta here," Stanford snapped.

"I was so proud watchin' you stand up there in yo' starched white suit, and yo' starched white shirt. Usin' them big ol' saphistacated words. And you got Junior off, too," Orabell said.

"Although he was guilty as sin," Stanford added.

"Uncle Stanford, come on now. Junior was not guilty," Solomon said.

"The boy got caught wit' his ass hangin' halfway out the window of a gas station. How do you get stuck in a window when you robbin' somebody?" Stanford asked. "If he ain't guilty, nothing' else, he guilty of bein' stupid!"

"Hey, Mr Stanford, lay off my cousin. He's not stupid for getting stuck. He's stupid for going through the window when the front door was wide open," Sunshine laughed.

"You're laughing but what you consider to be stupid is the very evidence that got Junior off." Stanford smiled.

"How?" Sunshine asked.

"That's what I wanna know," Orabell asked. "How?"

"Mama, I'm thirsty," Michelle said to Orabell, before Solomon could answer.

Orabell reached for a glass of water and gave Michelle a swallow. Sunshine watched as her daughter was calling another woman her mother. She didn't blame Orabell, and she wasn't upset with her. But it didn't make her feel any better.

Solomon went on explaining his defense.

"Were you not paying attention at the trial?" Solomon asked. "By the front door being open it could not have been a breaking and entering because there was not a forcible entry through the window nor through any of the doors. The best they could do was simple loitering." Solomon smiled.

"That was a great strategy, Perry Mason!" Orabell shouted. "I know you ain't gon' brag on yo'self, so I'll do it for you."

"And I will, too," Sunshine added. "I am both proud and grateful that you came down here to help my family. My aunt and uncle can't thank you enough. You chose a state in the midst of racial turmoil to try your first solo case. And you did it for nothing. That takes a great attorney, and an even greater man. But for every risk, there's a reward. Yours is going to be a doozy," Sunshine said.

"I didn't do it for nothing, honey. It's not like I had opportunities knocking down my door in D.C. now," Solomon said.

"Look at him, Ma," Sunshine said. "I've watched this man grow from an arrogant, silly boy, into a respectful and responsible young man. You're a wonderful husband, father, son, and nephew. And you're well on your way to becoming a wonderful attorney."

"Oh yes he is," Orabell said, rocking Michelle to sleep.

"Would you two stop!" Solomon said.

"Yeah, would you two stop," Stanford said, slapping Solomon on the back.

Orabell changed the subject, as she thought the long trip back to Saginaw.

"I am dreadin' that ride back to Saginaw." Orabell sighed.

"Mama, you need to just come and live with us. We've been trying to take care of you for the last couple of years," Sunshine said.

"No, baby. Visits are just fine for me." Orabell smiled.

Sunshine looked as Orabell held her child, and her child held onto Orabell as if she were her mother. Sunshine wanted Orabell to come and live with them because she felt that Orabell was getting a little older and they could help take care of her. She was only fifty-three, but the years were taking hold of her youth. Sunshine also wanted Orabell to come live with them so that she could be around her daughter more often.

"I need to rip that boy away from my apron strang anyway," Orabell said.

"You ain't lyin', Orabell," Stanford said. "Up until that boy was fourteen, he used to..."

"Uncle Stanford!" Solomon interrupted.

"You wanna hear this, baby?" Stanford asked Sunshine.

"Of course," Sunshine answered.

"Orabell used to breast-feed this boy up until he was old enough to have a paper route. I had to tell her that if she let that boy suck on her titty any longer, she either gon' have to marry him, or just give him a cow. 'cause she was gettin' close to incest. Either way, she was goin' to jail." Stanford laughed.

"You spoiled him, too, buyin' him all those fancy clothes," Orabell said. "That's why the boy turned out so uppity."

"Ma, I am very grounded for a man of my age. I'm focused, I'm ambitious, I'm determined..."

"You're a stuck-up big brat!" Stanford interrupted.

"Why me?" Solomon laughed.

"'Cause we love ya, boy," Stanford said. "This boy, as spoiled as he is, got the hand of God on him. I don't even know if this boy even believe in God. I love him like he's my own son."

"Thank you, Unc."

"You my boy, and I'm proud of you. No matter what I might tell you when you piss me off, I am proud of you."

"Thanks Unc. That means a lot to me."

"Shut up," Stanford joked.

"Yeah, my baby is due for something special, and it's more than bein' a lawyer. I ain't worried though, 'cause he got two good women who will put their foots up his butt if he don't wanna act right," Orabell said.

"And an uncle with a size twelve," Stanford added.

"You know, I appreciate two beautiful women offering to place their feet up my posterior, and I don't want to leave out your size twelve, Unc. But all I am destined to be, is the best husband, father, son, and nephew I can. I'm not asking either one of you to be anything more than who you are. So please, I'm asking you, please accept me for who I am?"

"Unfortunately, son, you can't just be you," Stanford said.

"Solomon, I wouldn't care if you were a lawyer, or a streetsweeper. I love you, for you. But this is not at all about my love for you, baby. Like your uncle said, you have a certain something that none of us can explain, but it's obvious to all of us. We can feel it. Everyone around you can see this special thing. Everyone but you," Sunshine said.

"I'm sorry, I just don't feel anything special. I feel like a man. Nothing more, nothing less."

"You're right. You are only a man, but you're a man with a destiny. A destiny that only you can fulfill. But I'm lettin' go," Stanford said, throwing his hands in the air. "I'm off your back, and I'm leavin' you alone."

As they were talking, the waitress walked up and started to clear their table.

"Can you hold on a second, ma'am, I ain't quite finished?" Orabell said.

"You been sittin' here for over two hours yappin'; ya ain't through yet?" the waitress asked.

"Almost, ma'am." Orabell smiled to the waitress who was young enough to be her daughter.

"Mama." Solomon whispered, "Why are you addressing that young lady as ma'am? She's young enough to be your daughter; she should be saying that to you."

"Oh, don't worry about that none. That's the way of the South," Orabell said.

The waitress walked back to their table and asked them to leave. This time her approach was a little more aggressive.

"Look around. Can't y'all see the rest of ya bunch done left?" she asked. "Nigga hour is up. Ya stoppin' good-payin' white folks from comin' in. I did my civic duty; now get on up, pay ya bill, and go swing back in the tree you fell out of."

"Excuse me?" Solomon asked in disbelief.

"You heard me. Pay ya bill, and get ya monkey asses outta here."

"Ma'am, this kind of behavior is totally unacceptable. We will pay our bill when we are ready to leave. On second thought, can you please get your superior?" Solomon demanded.

"Get 'em, champ!" Stanford laughed.

"Don't worry 'bout it, baby. Let's just leave," Orabell said.

"No, Ma. She has no right to behave so belligerently. We haven't done anything, and we are not leaving until we have finished our meal," Solomon said.

The waiter heard the confrontation and walked over to the aid of the waitress.

"Lissen here, boy. We ain't gon' keep tellin' you to get ya fancy-talkin' coon ass outta here. Are you gon' leave, or am I gon' have to make you leave?" the waiter shouted.

"I don't think any of this is necessary, sir. As my husband said, when we are finished with our meal, we will leave your establishment," Sunshine said.

The waiter started to pick up the dishes, then screamed at Sunshine.

"You are finished. Now get the hell out!"

"I think you need to lower your voice when you to talk to my wife, mister!" Solomon shouted.

The waiter grabbed a knife and stuck it to Solomon's throat.

"You gon' leave, and you gon' leave now, or I'll cut you from ear to ear."

"Lord Jesus!" Orabell shouted. "Please let him go, mister!"

"Please, please, let him go!" Sunshine cried.

The waiter had a hard time trying to keep the knife to Solomon's throat. Solomon tossed the man to the side, but then, two other men jumped on his back. The table turned over, making a loud noise. The noise woke Michelle, and she cried hysterically from all of the loud noise.

Stanford stood behind the turned-over table, and laughed as Solomon was tossing the men around like paper. One of the men picked up the knife again and cornered Solomon against the wall. He jabbed at Solomon sticking the knife into the side of his shirt.

"Please don't hurt my baby!" Orabell screamed.

"Don't you beg this thug for nothin', Mama. I'd rather die than hear you beg this idiot for anything!" Solomon mumbled, as the knife's edge pressed against his neck.

"I guess the fun is over," Stanford said, reaching into his back pocket and pulling out a gun. "Now can't we handle this like civilized human beings?"

Stanford placed the nose of the gun to the back of the man's head.

"Now take that knife away from my nephew's neck, and we'll leave your restaurant. Here's a little something for ya troubles," Stanford said, dropping dollar bills on the table.

Stanford peeked out of the window, and he saw a couple of trucks pull up with a gang of young white boys. He hadn't been gone from Mississippi long enough to forget what that meant. He told Solomon to take the women back to Sunshine's family, while he kept the group of boys at bay.

"Take your mama, and your wife, to your in-laws and wait for me until I get there. I think I got a little business to handle with these good ol' boys," Stanford said, looking out of the window.

"I'm not leaving you here all by yourself. Are you crazy?" Solomon asked. "Sunshine, take Mama and Michelle over to your aunt's house."

"Stanford, put that gun up, and come on!" Orabell said, walking with Michelle in her arms.

"It's too late, Orabell!" Stanford shouted. "Solomon, don't you go back to that hotel. You go out the back do', and take them to your in-laws!"

"I'm not leaving here with out you, Uncle Stanford!" Solomon shouted back.

"Get the hell outta here, boy, before we all get killed. NOW!" Stanford screamed.

"OK! OK!" Solomon yelled reluctantly, "OK, but I'll be right back to get you, Unc!"

"I love y'all," Stanford whispered to them. "Now go!"

"I'll be right back, Unc!" Solomon said, pacing back and forth between Stanford and the back door.

"Leave, son!" Stanford screamed louder.

"Come on, Solomon!" Sunshine sighed.

Solomon crept past the rowdy crowd outside, and mingled with the black people standing around watching. He quickly dropped Sunshine, Orabell, and Michelle at her aunt's house. Junior, the boy he was defending in the trial, and a group of black boys loaded in a truck and followed Solomon back to town. Solomon pointed to the café and they zipped upon the curb in front of the store. Solomon leaped off of the truck before it stopped and ran inside.

He dropped to his knees, and screamed at the top of his lungs when he saw his uncle tied to a ceiling fan with a rope around his neck. Two bullethole marks were etched in the middle of his chest, and blood dripped profusely to the ground.

"Oh no!" Solomon cried. "Oh no, you old fool. I told you not to stay, didn't I?"

Solomon cut Stanford's body down, and held him in his arms. As Stanford's limp arms swayed to the side, Solomon kissed him over and over.

"I told you, didn't I?" Solomon cried. "Why, man, why would they do something like this to you? How can a man treat another man like this, Lord?"

Solomon wrapped his arms around Stanford, and pulled him closely to his chest. Stanford's blood-stained body soaked Solomon's shirt so badly, that if it wasn't for Stanford's limp body, it would be difficult to tell which man was actually the source of the blood. Solomon reached on the floor and picked up Stanford's hat. He tucked the hat under his armpits and clutched it tightly.

When the ambulance arrived, Solomon would not release his hold on his uncle's body. He made them wait, and he held him tightly, until he felt his uncle's soul had passed to glory

Chapter Fourteen

T hree months after Stanford was murdered, on April 4, 1968, Senator Robert Kennedy made the following astonishing announcement to the American people.

"Ladies and gentlemen, I'm only going to talk to you just for a minute or so this evening, because I have some very sad news for all of you. And I think uh, sad news, for all of our fellow citizens. And people who loved peace all over the world. And that is that Martin Luther King was shot and was killed tonight in Memphis, Tennessee.

"Martin Luther King, dedicated his life to love, and to justice, between fellow human beings. He died, in the cause of that effort. In this difficult day, in this difficult time for the United States, it's perhaps well to ask what kind of a nation we are, and what direction we want to move in. For those of you who are black, considering the evidence evidently is that, there were white people who were responsible. You can be filled with bitterness, and with hatred, and a desire for revenge. We can move in that direction as a country, in greater polarization. Black people amongst blacks, and white amongst whites, filled with hatred, toward one another. Or we can make an effort as Martin Luther King did, to understand, and to comprehend, and to replace that violence, that stain of bloodshed that has spread across our land, with an effort to understand, compassion, and love. For those of you who are black, and are attempted to fill with, to be filled with, hatred and mistrust of the injustice of such an act, against all white people, I would only say that I can also feel in my own heart the same kind of feeling. I had a member of my family killed, but he was killed by a white man. But we have to make an effort in the United States, we have to make an effort to understand, to get beyond, or go beyond these rather difficult times. My favorite poet was Aeschylus, and he once wrote, '...even in our sleep, pain that cannot forget falls drop by drop upon the heart.' Until in our own day in despair, against our will, comes wisdom, through the awful grace of God. What we need in the United States is not division. What we need in the United States is not hatred. What we need in the United States is not violence, and lawlessness; but is love, and wisdom, and compassion towards one another. And the feeling of justice towards those who still suffer within our country. Whether they be white, or whether they be black. So I ask you tonight to return home and say a prayer for the family of Martin Luther King; yeah, it's true. But more importantly to say a prayer for our own country, which all of us love. A prayer for understanding, and that compassion, that which I spoke. We can do well in this country; we will have difficult times. We've had difficult times in the past, and we will have difficult times in the future. It is not the end of violence, it is not the end of lawlessness, and it's not the end of disorder. But the vast majority of white people, and the vast majority of black people in this country want to improve the quality of our life. And want justice for all human beings that abide in our land. And want to dedicate ourselves to what the Greeks wrote so many years ago, to tame the savageness of man, and make gentle the life of this world. Let us dedicate ourselves to that. And say a prayer for our country, and for our people. Thank you very much."

★★★

Although Kennedy tried to alleviate the potential for racial violence, King's assassination set off a barrage of riots across the country. The most notorious were in Detroit and Watts, California. There was widespread devastating looting, and violence.

On the day Martin Luther King, Jr. was shot, Solomon was in Detroit visiting his Uncle William, en route to getting Orabell and taking her back to Washington, D.C. Orabell was going to stay with Sunshine while Solomon was in Mississippi. The trial for Stanford's murder was beginning, and Solomon was the primary witness. For Sunshine, she was most excited about Michelle coming to live with them permanently. After eight long years of medical school, Sunshine was receiving her M.D., and she could begin her full-time careers as daytime doctor, and nighttime mother.

In Detroit, Solomon and William sat in William's living room the day after King's murder and watched the scenes of the riots unfold on television. The more Solomon sat and watched the angry people on television, the more he felt that he should be out there doing something in protest. He didn't want to loot or destroy property, but he wanted to express his anger for the murder of his Uncle Stanford. After his frustration intensified to the point of no control, he jumped up, and grabbed his jacket. He headed for the door, but William realized his intention and made an effort to stop him. He stood in front of the door with a broom and told him that he was not going to let him out of the house.

"Uncle William, get out of my way, before you get yourself hurt," Solomon said.

"No, son. I'm not letting you out of this door. I've already lost your father, and your uncle to this stupid mess. You're not leaving this house."

"Uncle William, please, move out of my way!"

"What are you going to do, son?" William asked. "You think you're going to go out there and make those white folks listen to you about Stanford's murder?"

"I don't know, but I can't sit here and do nothing," Solomon said. "Move, Uncle William!"

William braced his old body against the door, and tightened his grip around the broom. Although he was an old man, he was still a big man.

"Well, what you going to do, Solomon?" William asked.

Solomon reached around William and clutched the doorknob in his hand. William frowned as it took every ounce of strength he had to keep his balance, and strike Solomon with the broom at the same time. He held the broom in the air to prepare for his second strike, but Solomon released his grip on the doorknob.

"What's the matter with you?" Solomon shouted.

"I told you, you're not leaving this house until these fools stop all this craziness."

"That kinda hurt, Uncle William," Solomon said, rubbing his head.

"Sit down, and I'll get you some ice for your head," William said. "As hard as it is, I'm surprised I didn't break my broom in half."

"I have never stood up for colored people," Solomon said. "Never!"

"So are you trying to make up for twenty-eight years of not caring by running out there in those streets with those hooligans?"

"Somehow, I can't help but feel that if I would do more, maybe it would make a difference."

"And that's how you should feel. But going down there while they are rioting is not the way to do it. Because you're not going down there out of justice, son. You're going down there out of guilt. If you go down there today, you'll regret it tomorrow, because your heart's not in the movement. That's pain talking, not commitment."

"But didn't this whole movement begin from pain?" Solomon asked.

"Yes, but it progressed with commitment. You're not committed to the movement of all black people. You just want to make a statement for yourself because your uncle was killed by bigoted white men," William said. "If you're going to walk out that door and fight with those young folks, go down there with your heart in the right place. Don't use their cause to fight your battle for you. When you could care less about them, and their cause."

"That's not the case, Uncle William."

"I'm afraid that is the case, Solomon. I've known you your whole life, and you could care less about being black, or the Civil Rights Movement."

"That's not true at all. You have me all wrong."

"Boy, who do you think you're talking to?" William said. "Name one time when you have said, or done, anything constructively for black people's equality in the country?"

"I think my actions speak for themselves."

"Well, what have you acted upon constructively for black people's equality?"

Solomon thought long and hard, but he could not think of one single solitary thing.

"Well, today is a good day to start!" Solomon shouted as he grabbed his jacket the second time and headed for the door.

"Boy!" William yelled. "Sit yo' ass down now!"

Solomon stopped in mid-stride and looked back at his uncle. He saw the concerned look in his face, and remembered the vulnerable feeling he had when he left Stanford in that café. He threw his jacket against the door and squeezed his fist tightly

"Uncle William, you don't know how it feels to see someone you love die at the hands of another, and you could have possibly stopped it," Solomon cried.

"I don't know?" William asked. "I let your father catch that train to Mississippi, and I never saw him again. What do you mean, I don't know, son?"

"But Uncle Stanford was standing right by my side; he saved my life. And when it was my turn to save his, I couldn't."

"I know how you feel, son, but there is nothing you can do. Except go out on those streets and get yourself hurt. Stay in here with me until things cool down, then go on and get your mother."

"You just don't understand, Uncle William." Solomon sighed.

"Do you think this is the first time black people haveever rioted?" William asked. "I'll never forget it, Sunday, June 20th, 1943. A riot broke out right here in Detroit that was much worse than what's going on out there on those streets right now. Black folks been tired of this shit for a long time, son. So don't tell me I don't understand the frustrations of being treated like an animal. Or having my brother murdered. Watching my wife and child die, because they didn't receive proper medical attention. Oh, I understand all right. I also understand that if I can help it, I won't see another one of my family members die that way. You've only had to deal with this world for twenty-eight years. I've had to deal with it for sixty-seven. So if I can take it, you can, too."

Solomon turned toward the television and watched some of the mobs on the screen run from the cameras as they looted the stores. Everybody rioting was not looting; there were others who stood before the camera and demanded justice for themselves, and the murder of Martin Luther King Jr.

Solomon looked at his Uncle William and wondered what his father would do in a situation like this. He knew his father would be right in the midst of things. That was enough to keep him planted in his seat. He didn't want to go out in the streets for the sake of freedom and be killed to say that he died in the name of justice. Solomon knew that agonizing lonely feeling in his heart of not having his father, and he didn't want Michelle to grow up resenting him for such selfishness.

William dozed in and out of sleep, but he kept one eye on Solomon at all times. Later on, Solomon drove to Saginaw to get his mother.

Orabell's youthful face seemed as if it had aged ten years in the three months since Stanford's murder. Her wily perception of life had diminished to a conversation of senseless babble. Solomon was deeply concerned, but he didn't want to badger Orabell on her mental health. She had always been prideful when it came to her mental strength. Michelle played in the back seat, and Orabell's frustration became apparent as she constantly yelled at the child for making too much noise. Solomon wanted to intervene, and ask his mother to have a little more patience. But how could he when she had raised the child from birth? He didn't know if her frustration was from Stanford's death, or the fact that after raising Michelle for four years, they were all of a sudden asking her to give her back. Particularly, when it was so soon after losing her brother. Orabell would be alone for the first time in her fifty-odd years on earth. Solomon thought that if it were him, he would certainly be cranky.

When they arrived at Solomon's house, Sunshine greeted them all by running to the car and hugging them. Sunshine wrapped her arms around Orabell and welcomed her into their home. That moment of affection from Sunshine was all that it took to bring her back to her usually witty, loving self. Michelle ran behind Sunshine, and pulled on her dress. Sunshine picked her up, and spun her around a few times and they danced their way into the house.

Orabell found Solomon and Sunshine's huge spacious home to be much more comfortable than the small one-room apartment they were living in when she had visited years earlier. She had her own room with a color television. She was used to seeing everything in black and white. Watching her favorite weekly shows, *Gunsmoke* and *Bonanza* in color, was a surprise she was not quite prepared to see. She enthusiastically called Solomon and Sunshine into her room to watch the shows with her.

Orabell would sit on their porch and watch the neighbors come and go. She would count the cars passing by based on their colors and models, then write it down. One day she decided to count the number of black people who passed. At the end of her count she had an astounding number of one. And that one was Sunshine. The only black family in the neighborhood was the Chambers, her family. Orabell sat with amazement, and concern.

A week after Orabell had settled in, Solomon packed his bags and headed for Mississippi. Sunshine and Orabell had great concern for him going back to the Delta as a witness against that group of white boys. Even after Stanford's murder, Solomon still didn't realize the common danger of being a black person in Mississippi. He tried to assure Orabell and Sunshine that he was protected by the law. His attempt at assurance was returned with criticism and doubt. Their only consolation came from the federal agents who guaranteed around-the-clock protection for Solomon until he returned from Mississippi.

Stanford nor Solomon were important enough for the federal agents to be involved in this small Mississippi murder, but the men involved were suspected members of the Klan. The President had declared on the Ku Klux Klan, and Stanford's murder captured the attention of federal agents who investigated the case. They subpoenaed Solomon as their star witness. They wanted Sunshine and Orabell to testify as well, but they figured they wouldn't hold up under the racial pressure.

Solomon was eager to testify to convict the men who killed Stanford, but he would be gone an extensive time and his business was just beginning to flourish. Fortunately for him, his boyhood friend Donovan O' Shaughnessy was also an attorney who had recently set up his own corporate law firm in the District of Columbia. Donovan started off doing civil and criminal cases, so he volunteered to take over Solomon's practice until he returned from the trial. It would keep him busy, and fresh, until his litigation trials began.

On the morning Solomon left for Mississippi, Orabell again tried to hand him Isaiah's necklace for good luck. Solomon moved his hand away from the necklace, and refused to take it. He asked her that if he believed in luck, then what good was it to pray to God? Orabell slipped the necklace back into her pocket, once again disappointed that her son was rejecting his father.

Solomon arrived in Mississippi safe and sound. He called home for the first three days of the trial. He limited his information about the trial on the telephone, and explained in more detail through letters. After the third day, the telephone calls stopped without warning. After the second week, the letters stopped and Orabell and Sunshine became frantic. They called Solomon's hotel room, but couldn't get an answer. They called the front desk several times, and each time they called they were told the same story: there was no way Solomon could have been staying in that hotel because coloreds were not allowed. They were certain that they were calling the correct hotel. The name and the number of the hotel were given to them by Solomon after he had checked in. The name and number of the hotel were correct, and it was because someone from that hotel had verified the information. And if they verified the information, then why were they saying that Solomon never checked in?

There was nothing much they could do to find his whereabouts. They couldn't call the local police; they were undoubtedly protecting the boys who killed Stanford. If something were to happen to Solomon the local authorities would probably see it as a blessing in disguise. They couldn't call the federal authorities because they had no direct contact information.

Sunshine called Donovan and explained the situation to him. Donovan's litigation battles had made him come in contact with some of the most influential people in the country. Some of those people turned into good friends, while some turned into ruthless enemies. However, friends or enemies, they both owed him favors—mostly for keeping their secrets confidential.

Donovan contacted the Federal Bureau of Investigation in Michigan, where he still had connections, and a chain of favors started to be returned from one branch to the next, searching for Solomon. He finally found a contact name for Solomon's case, and gave it to Sunshine. But before she could make the call, she received a call from them.

"I'm gon' miss my brother." Orabell sighed, as she looked at Stanford's hat in the center of the coffee table—clean and spotless as always.

"You're not the only one." Sunshine smiled.

"That was the second man in my life killed by hate. The third, if you include my daddy. My husban' used to always say the Lord ain't gon' put no more on you than you can stand. Well, he can't put no more on me, baby, 'cause I can't take no more. I keep liftin' my head, and sayin' everything is all right. But it ain't! I gotta big hole in my heart. My husban' dead, my brother dead, and now my only child done went back down there and I don't know if he's all right or not. If anything happen to my baby, I don't know if I could take it. I just don't know, I tell you."

"Don't worry, Ma. Solomon will be home soon."

"We ain't talked to him. We ain't heard from him in weeks. If somethin' done happened to my child," Orabell said, shaking her head, "I don't know what I'm gon' do."

"He's fine, Ma," Sunshine assured.

"How can you be so sure?"

"He has no choice. God is just getting started with that boy. We have to believe that he won't be taken away from us. We have to have faith that Solomon is coming home."

"I tried to tell him not to go down there messin' with them folks. I told him to leave well enough alone," Orabell said.

"I didn't want him to go down there either, Ma. But that boy was going no matter what we said. After Mr. Stanford was killed, Solomon stood like a tree in front of you. He wanted to be your means of support. At night, he would put his head on my lap and stare into the darkness. When he got that opportunity to do something for Mr. Stanford, there was nothing going to stop him. He felt responsible for his death, as if there was something he could have done against that mob. He's a big man, but not that big. Just like you, I tried my best to talk him out of it right up until he walked out of that door. I have to believe he's coming back home to me. The trial should be over any day now, and when I talk to that boy I am going to give him the tongue-lashing of his life." Sunshine laughed.

Orabell was about to speak when she was interrupted by the loud ringing of the telephone. Sunshine ignored it and waited for Orabell to respond.

"Get the phone first, child; we can finish talkin' when you get off."

Sunshine hurried to pick up the telephone before the caller hung up the line.

"Hello. Yes, this is Mrs. Chambers," Sunshine answered. "Who may I ask is calling? What office are you calling from again? Yes, I understand who you are, but why are you calling me about my husband when you are supposed to be protecting him?"

"Lord, no!" Orabell gasped. "Oh, Lord, not again!"

"I have not heard from my husband in two weeks! Where is he?" Sunshine shouted.

The caller tried to calm Sunshine by telling her that Solomon had not reported to his hotel room in two weeks, but he doesn't think anything had happened to him. Despite the caller's efforts, the two women became unraveled and screamed hysterically through the telephone.

"Look, you find my husband, and you find him now! You guaranteed his protection; if anything has happened to him, it's on your head!" Sunshine shouted. "Don't tell me to calm down. My husband is missing, you calm down! I don't care about your stupid case. I want to know that my husband is alive!"

Sunshine slammed the telephone while the caller was in mid-sentence. She covered her mouth, and tears ran from her eyes. She ran into Orabell's arms, and hugged her tightly.

"What they say, baby?" Orabell asked.

"They say they can't find him, Ma!" Sunshine wept. "What are we going to do?"

"I don't know, baby. I don't know," Orabell cried, rubbing Sunshine's back.

As Sunshine's face was snug and tight into Orabell's bosom, and the two women stood in the middle of the living room comforting one another, they didn't hear the continuous sound of the doorbell ringing.

"What's going on in here?" Solomon said, walking through the front door.

"Son!" Orabell shouted.

"Oh, baby, you're all right!" Sunshine said, running into Solomon's arms.

"I'm fine; what's going on?" Solomon asked.

"They just called and said they didn't know where you were! Ma and I were scared to death that something had happened to you." Sunshine smiled, wiping her tears.

"They couldn't find me because I left and didn't tell them. I was disgusted with that circus of a trial. I had to leave before I was on trial for murdering somebody. I personally provided enough evidence to lock those serpents up for the rest of their lives. The prosecutors questioned me thoroughly about every single occurrence that went on that day. Over and over, they drilled me. They even prepared me for the questions the defense might ask. But when they got me on the witness stand, they asked me general questions that the defense could shred to pieces. And that's exactly what they did. I tried to offer incriminating statements, but both the prosecuting and defense teams interjected and told me to stick with the line of questioning. They went strictly by the good ol' boys 'try 'em and let 'em go by supper' script. I told the prosecutors to go to hell. Then I walked out of that courtroom, and came straight home."

"Why didn't you call us, to let us know?" Sunshine asked.

"I couldn't, baby. After the first few days, they moved me to another hotel. I think my room was bugged. We were being followed everywhere we went. The agents felt I needed to be in a place where the local townsfolk could not find me. It was only three of them, and thousands of the locals. The odds weren't in our favor. They moved me in with a nice elderly colored family. I mean *black* family."

"Black?" Sunshine said. "What happened down there that you are not calling us colored anymore?"

"I got a chance to talk to that elderly family, and they enlightened me on a lot of black history that I wasn't aware existed. For example, using the term colored."

"And I am assuming that you didn't know that colored was an old oppressive term, and black was a term of empowerment?" Sunshine asked sarcastically.

"Shut up," Solomon joked back.

"For as long as you live, you bet' not ever do nothin' like this again in your life," Orabell said, hitting Solomon on his arm.

"All right, Ma," Solomon said. "How have you two been holding up?"

"We've been leaning on, and lying to each other for support," Sunshine said.

Michelle walked out of her bedroom rubbing her eyes, wiping the sleep's residue from her long nap. When she saw Solomon she ran and jumped in his lap. Solomon was surprised, he picked her up onto his shoulders and carried her throughout the house. Upstairs, then back downstairs. He sat in his favorite chair, and placed Michelle on his lap. She put her head on his chest and she listened to the sound of his breathing as he talked to Sunshine and Orabell.

"Ma, you raised me to be a God-fearing man, and I am. But Ma, why does God let men have the power to kill other men without punishment?" Solomon asked. "Uncle Stanford's life is gone, and there is nothing we can do to bring it back. Why does God let men rule over other men, and do nothing about it?"

"Who say they ain't gon' be punished for what they doin'?" Orabell asked. "They ain't gettin' away wit' nothing! Every last one of 'em gon' pay for what they doin'. God may not punish 'em the way you wont Him to, son, but He gon' get 'em!"

"But, Mama, when are black people going to be treated like people, and not like second-class citizens?" Solomon asked. "I'm mad! I'm frustrated! I don't understand, Ma. I just don't understand this. I've never robbed anybody. I've never laid a hand on anybody unless they touched me first. What have I done to be treated this way? Why can't I be treated with the same dignity as any white man who walks this earth?"

"Solomon, your mother can't answer those questions and you know it," Sunshine said.

"You just have to pray that everything will be all right," Orabell said.

"But, Mama, don't you get tired of praying sometimes? Don't you just want to see some things change?" Solomon asked. "Why should I have to pray that another man, who is no better than I am, treats me like a man?"

"Solomon, do you remember the last time you went to church with me in Saginaw before Stanford was killed?" Orabell asked.

"Yes."

"Do you remember a man coming up to us, and he asked you to represent him in court?" Orabell asked.

"Are you talking about that bum?" Solomon responded. "The man clearly couldn't afford representation. He was talking out of his head. I couldn't help the man, Ma."

"But you paid money to travel all the way to Mississippi to help Junior."

"But Junior's Sunshine's cousin."

"There's your answer, son. You helped Junior because he your wife cousin. You just as much at fault as everybody else. And that ain't God fault. Let me tell you somethin' about that man you called a bum. You wanna know how he knew who you was?" Orabell asked. "Me! I heard him talking in church about the problems he was havin' in his life. He said that no matter what kinda trouble come his way, his faith would not be shook. He told us how his wife had cancer, and they used all the money they had on her hospital bills. And just when they thought she was goin' to be all right, she died. He live in a shelter with five babies, and the govament is tryin' to take his kids away from him. Now that man ain't never hurt nobody that I know of. And he ain't never robbed nobody that I know of neither. And he only asked you for help because I was braggin' on my son. Now what make Junior betta than that man?"

"Not one thing!" Sunshine added.

"I'll be the first to say I may not know a lot about books, but I know plenty about God. Before you start blamin' Him for everything man do, you betta take a look in the mirror. Besides it ain't gon' do you no good to ask why God doin' this, or God ain't doin' that 'cause it ain't gon' change one thang!"

"Solomon, do you think you can help him?" Sunshine asked.

"That's been a while ago. I don't know but I'll try. Ma, you have to understand that I have to make a living. I have to retain clients who can afford to pay my fee. I have to put food on the table for us, too."

"Son, I wasn't tellin' you that for you to run and go help the man. I was tellin' you that so you can understand that it ain't God that's the problem; it's us!" Orabell said.

"OK, I understand, Ma. If you can find the man, I'll do what I can to help him."

"And son, don't worry about us. If God will feed the birds in the sky, the fishes in the sea, surely He will feed us."

"That question goes two different ways. If God will feed us, fish, and birds, why hasn't He fed your friend from church?" Solomon smiled.

"He tried. But the food was not ripe and was not good for the man to eat at that time. You was the food, son." Orabell smiled back.

"OK, Sister Mary," Solomon joked. "You got me. Just stop the revival. Ladies, I am completely exhausted. I think I am about to go take a nap."

Solomon laid Michelle in Sunshine's arms, then headed upstairs.

"You need one. You betta pray before you go to sleep, you heathen!" Sunshine yelled to Solomon as he walked up the stairs.

"Sunshine, baby, I wanna thank you for lettin' your old mother-in-law come stay with you for a while. Some wives would feel like the mother would try to take over, but you treat me good. And I really appreciate it," Orabell said.

"You appreciate me?" Sunshine asked. "You cared for my child in your home until I graduated from medical school. You never once asked me for anything in return. You always try to make me feel comfortable in my decision when even I know it was slightly selfish, and yet you say you appreciate me?"

"I didn't do anything a mother wouldn't do for her child. Just like you did what you did for your child. I know what it's like to be poor. To want to give your child what it need, but can't, 'cause you don't have no money. I know what that feels like, and it don't feel good. I know it hurt you to have to see somebody else raisin' your child. But that was so she won't have to wont for anything," Orabell said.

"Maybe some wives would feel threatened by their mother-in-law, especially when the husband is a big mama's boy like Solomon. But I stopped thinking of you as a mother-in-law a long time ago. Ever since we met, you have treated me like your own daughter. You have never tried to come in between Solomon and me, even when we've had our disagreements. Even when one of us tried to get you on our side, you stayed neutral. As much as you love that son of yours, if you can manage to keep your nose out of our business, that is saying a lot about how you feel for me as well. Now we will have those mother/daughter squabbles, that mothers and daughters have, but we will keep those squabbles between us. My house is your house, for as long you want. How 'bout we kick Solomon out of my bedroom tomorrow night, and you, me and Michelle have a slumber party." Sunshine smiled.

"I don't know what no slumba' party is, but if it's anything like spendin' the night, count me in." Orabell laughed.

"I know one place you and I will never have a squabble, Ma."

"Where's that, baby?"

"The kitchen. You want it, you can have it. The pots, the pans, the stove. It's all yours, take it!" Sunshine laughed.

"You young wives of the sixties. You act like cookin' is the plague."

"I try; I'm just no good at it. I can't cook to save my life."

"I'll see what I can do. By the time I get through with you, you'll be a go'met cook. Collards, turnips, sweet potatoes, Solomon won't know the diff'rence."

"I know when you cook, you can put your foot in some food, Ma. But if you can teach me to cook like that, it will be nothing less then a miracle from God." Sunshine laughed.

"You'll see, baby, you'll see."

"Ma, there's something else I want to ask you."

"Sure, baby, ask me anything."

She looked at Sunshine's face, and she knew she wanted to say something very important.

"What's the matter, baby?" Orabell asked.

"This is the hardest thing I've ever had to do in my life. When you go back to Saginaw, I want you to take Michelle back with you," Sunshine said, patting Michelle on the back.

"Why baby, what's wrong?"

"She's not going to stay with us, without you. She doesn't realize that we are her parents, and I don't think my heart could stand seeing her reject me. Not even if she's rejecting me, for you. I want my baby to run to me so badly, and call me Mama the way she runs to you and calls you Mama. But she doesn't."

"Give her time, baby, and she will."

"Ma, I look in her eyes, and it's not there. She doesn't need me. She doesn't cry for me, or yearn for me, like a child is supposed to yearn for its mother."

"Sit down, girl," Orabell said. "This child does not know you as her mother. So how can you expect for her to run to you just because you are ready to run to her? That ain't how it work. She is a baby, she don't know everything we goin' through. And she don't understand it the way we understand it. Give her time, she'll be fine."

"OK, Ma. I hope you're right." Sunshine smiled.

"Ya husban' must ain't told you. I ain't wrong about nothin' but the weather and the numbers. 'cause those the only two thangs that change every other minute. But if I live long enough I'll figure them out, too!"

"Oh, he told me. I'm just surprised to hear you admit it." Sunshine laughed.

A few weeks later, Solomon drove Orabell back to Saginaw, leaving Michelle and Sunshine to start their lives as mother and daughter. Solomon stayed a couple of days in Saginaw with Orabell. It hurt him to leave his mother all alone with no family. He imagined dreadful thoughts of her being consumed with loneliness, and whittling away into a state of irreversible depression. He stopped several times on his way back home, and called her to see how she was doing. She tried to assure him that he had nothing to worry about, and that if she had an emergency, William was only ninety miles away in Detroit. He told her that it wasn't too late for him to turn around and come back and get her. She laughed and made him continue on to be with his family.

One month later on June 5, 1968, in Los Angeles, after winning the California primary for the fall presidential election, Robert F. Kennedy was shot three times by a man named Sirhan Sirhan. The following day, on June 6, he died from the results of those gunshot wounds. His assassination brought to reality just how serious the oppositions for equality stood against the Civil Rights Movement. However, the undercurrent explanation for his death was that it had nothing at all to do with black or white, but the age old color of green. Some say both John and Bobby Kennedy's deaths were vendettas being settled by the syndicate operators they brought down during the JFK administration.

As the summer gave way to autumn, and autumn gave way to winter, the comfortable tie between parent and child diminished more and more. Michelle became increasingly unmanageable. She stayed up into the early mornings crying for her grandmother. She threw tantrums everywhere they went crying for her grandmother. When they called Orabell to let Michelle speak with her, she begged her to come and get her. She told Solomon and Sunshine she hated them for making her stay with them. Sunshine was devastated, the few words her child could speak to her were, "I hate you." When Christmas rolled around they went to visit Orabell as planned. She asked them not to come, to give Michelle time to become used to them. Solomon told her that they couldn't hide from her forever because the child loved her.

While visiting in Saginaw, the Christmas holidays were very enjoyable. Michelle laid on Solomon's lap, as always. She slept in the bed with Sunshine with no crying or tantrums. So, they figured that she had just missed her grandmother. On the day they were supposed to leave, they loaded their suitcases into the car, and said their goodbyes to Orabell. They left Michelle in the house while they were taking the suitcases outside because it was freezing cold. When they were ready to leave, they looked for her all over the house, but she was nowhere to be found. They called for her, but she would not answer. Solomon searched for her outside of the house, then he expanded his search to other houses in the area. They searched for over an hour but could not locate her. Sunshine finally called the police and asked for help.

The police showed up, and joined in the search. Sunshine explained that they were taking their suitcases to the car and when they went back inside to get Michelle, she was gone. The police took Sunshine, Orabell, and Solomon into three different rooms and asked them for their specific versions of what had occurred earlier in the day. Solomon and Sunshine went peacefully. Orabell thought they were being treated like criminals, and she expressed her opinion very clearly.

She would not cooperate with the police or answer any of their questions. They told her that she was bringing suspicion upon herself by not cooperating. That made her even more uncooperative. She screamed to them that instead of wasting time asking them questions, they could be looking for her child. She snatched away from the police officer, and went to her closet. She wrapped her scarf around her neck and started to walk out of the door. A police officer stopped her, and told her she had to stay in the house. That was all that she could stand; she exploded with anger, and told the policemen what she thought of them.

"Young man, I am a fifty-three-year-old woman. How dare you tell me I can't leave my own house?" Orabell said. "Now if you and your little friends wonta stand around here and impress ya self by makin' us look like some crooks, then help ya self. But you betta take yo' hands off my arm, and I mean right this minute!"

"Ma'am, I can't let you leave," the police officer said.

"I ain't askin' you to let me leave. I'm leavin' on my own. I'm goin' to get my baby, and by the time I get back, if y'all still here, you betta have my son and my daughter out of them rooms so they can take care of each other," Orabell snapped.

The police officer looked at another officer, and he shrugged his shoulders. She was not under arrest, and they had already asked her questions. They had no legal reason to keep her. Orabell left and she returned in just under an hour. When she returned she was exhausted, and could barely walk. As she got closer to the house, the police could see that she had a child in her arms. They ran to meet her, and took Michelle out of her arms. They helped Orabell into the house, and laid her on the bed. She was gasping for air, but she was in no physical danger.

"Mama, where was she?" Solomon asked, putting a blanket on Orabell's legs.

"Where is the place we always take her?" Orabell said.

"I don't know," Solomon asked. "Where?"

"Ojibway Island?" Sunshine asked.

"Yeah, baby. Ojibway Island," Orabell said.

"Excuse me, ma'am, are you the mother?" the officer asked. "We need to ask you a few more questions."

"Help me up, Solomon," Orabell said. "Sunshine, don't you move one foot!"

"Lie down, Ma," Solomon said.

Sunshine laid Michelle on the bed with Orabell and she went to talk to the police officer.

"Sunshine, I told you not to move; now you stay put!" Orabell said. "Solomon, help me up right now!"

Solomon helped Orabell to her feet and she limped her way into the living room.

"Leave my family alone, and get the hell out of my house right now!" Orabell screamed. "If you wahdn't spendin' all ya time tryin' to make it seem like we did somethin' wrong, you could have found the baby ya self."

The police officers gathered their things and walked out of Orabell's house. Orabell lay on the couch, and Solomon lay on the floor beside her while she rested. Sunshine and Michelle lay on the floor next to Solomon. Sunshine asked Michelle why she had run away and she told her that she didn't want to leave her mama. Sunshine smiled, and told her that she didn't have to worry; she wasn't going to leave her mother.

Michelle stayed with Orabell for the remainder of the Christmas holidays, and the upcoming years that followed. As she grew older she realized that Sunshine and Solomon were her parents, and she addressed them as such. Solomon played with her by picking her up, and walking with her on his shoulders until her legs were too long to fit over his shoulders. He would throw her over his lap, and tickle her until she screamed for Sunshine to make him stop. He fixed her cups of hot cocoa, and read her bedtime stories up until the point when she started to fix the cocoa, and read him bedtime stories. She continued to live with Orabell, but she loved her parents dearly, and enjoyed visiting them as much as she possibly could.

Michelle followed in her parents' footsteps and excelled in academics.

Like her father, she was placed in an accelerated program where she was advanced two grade levels. She was placed in a school for gifted students called Saint Mary's School for the Gifted. The intellectual competition was equal to Michelle's, but the competition didn't impede upon her personal academic accomplishments. She was one of a small number of blacks enrolled into the school. She would tell her father and mother that she wished there were more black students at the school. Solomon would encourage her by saying that if she accomplished all of her goals while she was there, that it might provide a way for other blacks to follow as he did at Saginaw Vista High.

Michelle admired Solomon, and could find no fault in him. Every word he said was filled with wisdom. Solomon was equally as proud of Michelle. He boasted of her awards and achievements to everyone he could. He and Sunshine would travel to all of her award ceremonies no matter how small the event. Michelle always bragged that she wanted to be a woman like her mother, and a lawyer like her father—a woman of elegance, and a professional of integrity. Sunshine would sarcastically say to her that if she wanted to be a professional of integrity, she should be a doctor, and not an attorney. But that was no deterrent; Michelle wanted to be just like her father, and she was following in his big footsteps.

CHAPTER FIFTEEN

Ninety-seventy-eight started off with one of the worst blizzards in a hundred years. It ripped through the northern portion of the United States from the Midwest to the Northeast, leaving behind catastrophic damages. Orabell and Michelle were trapped inside their home for three weeks, until Michelle could make her way out of the house, and walk to the store to get them more food. They kept their food outside on the porch to keep it refrigerated because they had no electricity. It took the city a month to recover from the power outage brought on by the fallen trees onto telephone and other cable wires. The city looked like a picture out of a nineteenth-century fairytale, with candles used as the primary source of light.

The telephone lines were the first to be restored. Once they were on, Solomon called to check on his mother and his daughter every morning and every evening to make sure they were all right. He had no idea that the blizzard was only a forecast of the personal suffering which awaited him for that year.

It looked as if his luck would change with the season. In the spring he bought a new Caprice Classic, black, sunroof top, and four-inch-thick whitewall tires. Complete with cruise control, automatic windows, and an eight-track tape player, he drove the car one time, and never drove it again. He was told that it was not in his best interest to drive such a flamboyant car around town now that he was a nationally known lawyer.

Solomon had become one of the highest-paid attorneys in America. In ten years, he went from creating his own firm working only small criminal and civil cases to owning a conglomerate of legal specialties.

After building his firm from ground level, he was able to hire young aggressive attorneys who helped him accumulate some of the biggest names in the Washington, D.C. area.

His success did not go unnoticed; he was awarded the Business Man of the Year award from 1974 to 1978. He received humanitarian awards consistently from 1972 to 1978. He was awarded three honorary degrees from 1975 to 1977. As his success mounted, so did Michelle's pride in her father. He did not disappoint her by continuing to pile up the awards.

On the evening he attended the award ceremony for Businessman of the Year for the fifth year in a row, Solomon received a call from Orabell that his Uncle William had died earlier in the day. He and Sunshine flew into Detroit Metro Airport the next day, and drove to Detroit. After the funeral they visited with Michelle and Orabell for a couple of days in Saginaw.

Michelle was fourteen and anxiously looking forward to visiting her parents in the summer. She had only a couple of months remaining until the first week of June when the school year would be completed. At fourteen, she was a sophomore in high school. She wanted to transfer out of Saint Mary's, and into her father's high school alma mater, Saginaw Vista High School. Over the years, it had become a predominantly black public school. Solomon forbade her to transfer, but Michelle persistently nagged Orabell to let her spend her junior and senior high school years as a normal student. She worked to enjoy the normal experiences high school students enjoy. Orabell and Sunshine tried to talk Solomon into letting Michelle transfer, but their pleas fell upon deaf ears. Solomon would not even consider it. As much as Michelle loved, and adored her father, she began to feel that he expected for her to be as successful in her life, as he was in his. The pressure associated with that feeling intimidated the teenager tremendously. For as successful as Solomon had been, through Michelle's admiration, the success was magnified even greater. She didn't want to disappoint her father by not living up to his expectations of her. As she grew older, she realized that she didn't want to commit herself to a lifetime of awards and ceremonies. She certainly wanted a successful career, but a humble lifestyle.

When Solomon and Sunshine returned to the District of Columbia, Solomon relaxed by watching the evening news while reading the newspaper. He was listening to the report of a local man and his family who were killed in a small airplane crash in Montana. He pulled the newspaper from his face, and stared at the television. He heard a familiar name, and it caught his attention. He heard that a Donovan O'Shaughnessy was killed while vacationing in the mountains of Montana. He was not certain if it was his friend Donovan because he had caught the tail of the story.

Donovan was now a state senator for Michigan. Solomon figured that if it was Donovan there would certainly be news coverage. He switched to different channels on the television but he was unable to find the story.

He called Donovan several times, but could not reach him. He told Sunshine when they went to bed that he had heard that a Donovan O'Shaughnessy was killed in an airplane crash, and he was concerned that he could not reach their friend Donovan at that late hour. Sunshine told him that it was a coincidence, and that he should try to get some sleep.

Later that night, he received the second tragic telephone call in as many weeks. This time it was from Donovan's office to tell him that it was indeed his friend who had been killed in the airplane crash.

Donovan, his wife, and his two younger children, along with the pilot were killed in the crash. His oldest daughter, Summer, who was fourteen, was attending boarding school and did not travel with the family on their vacation. Solomon had the unenviable task of informing Summer that her family was dead.

He wanted to tell her before she heard it from the media. He went to her in the late evening and woke her from her sleep. As expected, Summer received the news badly, and cried hysterically until morning. Solomon stayed by her until she was in a composed state of mind.

After the funeral and reading of the will, Solomon assumed control of the O'Shaughnessy's estate at the request of Donovan's will. One of Donovan's requests was that if he were to be survived by his wife, that Solomon reprieve the power of attorney from his wife. He had wanted Solomon to assist her in resolving all of their financial affairs. He also had another request, a personal request that if he and his wife were to be survived by their children, that Solomon and Sunshine assume legal guardianship.

Solomon discussed Donovan's request with Sunshine. They agreed Summer should stay with them until the school term was over, but she would be better off with one of her own family members afterwards.

After the school year was completed, Summer moved to Vermont with her mother's sister. She kept in contact with Sunshine and Solomon throughout the summer. When fall rolled around, and it was time for her to enroll in school, Solomon received a call from her aunt informing him that she had reconsidered guardianship of Summer, and he should move her back to home. Sunshine did not believe that it would be a good idea for them to bring Summer into their home when their own child was living with someone else. Solomon felt they had no choice, and he eventually convinced Sunshine to move Summer into their home permanently. He assumed full custody, and enrolled her into an elite all-girls private school for the fall term, pulling strings to bypass a mile-long waiting list.

While Summer was arriving, Michelle was departing from her summer vacation with her parents. Although she felt betrayed and unappreciated to see her father show so much attention to another person, she didn't express her pain and disappointment to her parents. She held it in and carried it back to Michigan with her. She pretended it didn't affect her, and told her parents she understood why Summer was living in their home. But what she didn't tell them was that she didn't understand why she was not

When Michelle returned to Michigan, she refused to go back to Saint Mary's. Orabell fussed and argued with her, but at sixty-three, she didn't have the energy to sustain her aggressive approach. Solomon called Michelle day after day to talk to her about returning to the school, but she would not speak to him. She told Sunshine that if she could not go to Saginaw Vista, she would not go to school at all.

By this time, school had begun and Michelle was not enrolled. Sunshine flew to Michigan to talk to Michelle and enroll her in school. After their mother/daughter conversation, Sunshine had convinced Michelle to go back to school, and Michelle had convinced Sunshine to enroll her into Saginaw Vista High School—a fair trade for both parties.

Being placed in the public school system cost Michelle her advanced grades and she returned to the ninth grade. Saginaw Vista had become the most populated and popular school in Saginaw County. It was the hub for an urban education.

Michelle's academic excellence did not stutter nor stumble. She kept up the perfect grade-point average, and participated in extracurricular activities as well.

At the end of the fall semester, Solomon sent for her to come to Washington, D.C., but she declined and stayed in Michigan with her grandmother. Solomon and Sunshine decided that if the mountain won't come to Mohammad, Mohammad must go to the mountain. So they went to Michigan for the holidays, taking Summer along with them.

Summer and Michelle had played with each other frequently while growing up, and were close friends, in Washington and Saginaw. Donovan would bring Summer to Saginaw to visit Mrs. O'Shaughnessy when she was still alive. During vacations, the girls would get together and have the times of their lives. Orabell would even keep Summer overnight on occasions. The color of their skin was never a topic because they had yet to experience the differences in the two. Growing up, they would get so excited when they found that the other was coming to town. This trip was quite different though; Michelle found no enthusiasm in Summer's arrival. She went as far as to ask Orabell if she could spend the Christmas holidays with a friend who lived in Bay City, Michigan, which was fifteen minutes north of Saginaw. Orabell scornfully rejected her offer, and told her that they were going to have a nice family-filled Christmas and she was going to behave herself.

When Solomon and Sunshine arrived with Summer it was snowing heavily. Their plane arrived on schedule at Bishop Airport in Flint, Michigan, which is only twenty-five miles south of Saginaw. After Solomon rented a car, he called Orabell and told her that they were on their way, and should be at her house in thirty minutes. Getting a flight that landed so close to

Saginaw would have been a welcoming convenience, if it had not been for the blizzard which arrived shortly before them. The snow was heavy, and the roads had not been shoveled. That turned the thirty-five minute ride into a three-and-a-half-hour journey. Their late arrival started to make Orabell and Michelle worry. Michelle regretted the way she had been acting towards her parents and stared out of the window, waiting to apologize. She couldn't wait to see them turn into the driveway so that she could. But minute after minute, then hour after hour, her hope was not realized.

After the third hour passed, Michelle went into the kitchen and fixed a hot pot of water for cocoa. She knew that when her father arrived, he would be cold and in need of some of her hot, soothing cocoa. Orabell told her not to worry, and that they would be there as soon as the roads were cleared. Michelle sat at the big picture window and stared outside, as so many others in her family had done before her. She was a little disturbed that she didn't know what kind of car they had rented. So every time she saw a pair of headlights, she followed them with her eyes until they passed by the driveway.

After three hours of waiting impatiently, she saw a car slow down, put on its blinkers, and turn into their driveway. She waited as long as she could, then she grabbed her coat and ran outside to greet them. She hugged her parents, then snatched Summer by the hand and dragged her into the house.

"You two could have at least grabbed one bag on your way in the house," Solomon yelled.

He and Sunshine filled their arms with suitcases and gifts and carried them into the house. Orabell helped them put away their things, and they got an opportunity to relax. Solomon yelled for Michelle to fix him a cup of hot cocoa. She told him that she had already prepared the water and the cup; he only needed to pour the water into the cup. Solomon made her pour the water into the cup for him, then bring it to him. When she did, he pulled her onto his lap and tickled her until she called for Sunshine to make him stop. Michelle, once again, was daddy's little girl.

On Christmas morning, they sat around the tree and swapped gifts. When it was time for Christmas dinner, Orabell, who normally delivered the dinner's prayer, asked Solomon to lead in the prayer. Solomon was slightly nervous, having never openly prayed in front of his family. He suggested that they should stay with tradition and let Orabell continue to lead the prayer. Orabell strongly stated that she wasn't doing it, and neither was any of the other women sitting at the table. Solomon asked everyone to bow their heads, and reluctantly began to pray.

"Our Father, who art in Heaven. I thank You for allowing us to commune together, on this glorious day of Your birth. I thank You for caring us safely from our home in Washington, to our home here in Michigan. Lord, I thank You for watching over my family, and protecting them when I can not. Lord, I want to thank You for my wife, my mother, my little girl, and also for the new addition to our family. As we eat our meal, filled with plenty of nourishment, we pray for those who are not as fortunate as we are, that they may find nourishment from Your love and compassion. In Jesus Christ's name, Amen."

One by one, they went around the table giving their Christmas thanks.

"I thank You for bringing my parents home safely, and I thank You for my grandmother. Oh, I almost forgot. I thank You for finally answering my prayers, and giving me a sister. Amen," Michelle joked.

"Lord, I thank You for bringin' my family home safe and sound. And I hope and pray You return them back to Washington, safe and sound. Amen," Orabell prayed.

"Although You took my family away, I know You had your reasons. Through all of my loneliness and pain, I have found peace and understanding with the loss of my family. And I have found compassion and joy from my new family. I thank You for Mr. And Mrs. Chambers, Mrs. Orabell, and my new sister, Michelle. Amen," Summer said.

"Amen!" Orabell added emphatically.

"Thank You for blessing us to be with our family at this time of the year. We give You all of the glory. I thank You for my family. Our health. And I pray that when we get up from this table, You let us rise and walk in your name. Amen," Sunshine prayed.

They raised their heads, and began to eat their Christmas dinner. After dinner, Michelle and Summer tried on each other's new clothes, and pretended they had dates. The hours passed like minutes, and before long it was time for them to go to bed. As they lay beside each other in the bed, Michelle confessed to Summer that she was jealous that she got to live with her parents, and not her.

"You know what, Summer?" Michelle asked.

"What?"

"I was really mad at you and my father when he told me you were going to live with them. I felt like you were going to take my place as his daughter."

"Why would you think a foolish thing like that, Michelle?"

"I don't know. I guess it's because I have never lived with them, and then they ask you to come live with them."

"Michelle, it's not like they came to my house and begged my parents to take me home with them. My parents were killed, or have you forgotten?"

"I know, and I'm sorry. But if you can go live with them, why can't I?"

"Well, have you asked them?"

"No," Michelle said. "If they love me, I shouldn't have to ask."

"You know they love you. Stop acting like a baby, Michelle. I've lost my entire family. I have to live with people who are not even white, and you're feeling sorry for yourself?"

"Wait a minute. What do you mean, you have to live with people who are not even white?" Michelle said, sitting up in the bed. "Those people are taking care of your white butt!"

"You know I didn't mean it like that, Michelle," Summer pleaded, also sitting up in the bed.

"Well, how did you mean it then?"

"I mean that I'm white, they're black, and we're different."

"Are you different when you're eating their food, or sleeping in their bed?"

Summer pulled one of the blankets off of the bed and lay on the floor.

"I don't need their money!" Summer shouted. "My father left me enough money that if I was old enough, I could live better than both of your parents put together!"

"Then where is it?" Michelle shouted back.

"Where's what?"

"Where's your so-called money?"

"Your father has control of my trust and my estate until I have graduated from college," Michelle snapped, rolling herself in the blanket, then tucking it tightly beneath her to prevent the draft from the floor from sneaking inside her blanket.

"You keep talking about what your father left you. If he left you so much, why do you have to live with my family, and not his?"

Orabell heard the girls shouting, and knocked on the door to see what the ruckus was all about.

"What are y'all doin' in there?" Orabell asked.

"Nothing!" they both shouted in unison.

"Sound like I hear some hens hacklin' in there! Y'all better bring that nothin' down a notch or two so ya mama and daddy can get some sleep."

"OK!" they both shouted in unison again.

They looked and at each other and chuckled as they both answered Orabell at the same time, saying the same words. Orabell walked off, and Michelle laughed again.

"Girl, you know you're not going to sleep on that floor, as cold as it is. Don't let your white pride have you turning purple up in here."

"Don't worry. I was only going to wait for you to fall asleep, then sneak back up here anyway," Summer said, climbing back into the bed. "Do you notice that your grandmother talks to me as if I am her very own grand-daughter?"

"You know what, Summer, my grandmother is nothing like us. She sees people as people. No matter what color you are, no matter how much money you have, it doesn't matter to Grandma. She loves everybody. And in her mind, you are her very own granddaughter."

"She is a sweet old lady. I feel comfortable around her," Summer said.

"Summer, you've been around her your whole life; why wouldn't you?" Michelle asked.

"I know, but she treats me the same way she treats you, like a grand-daughter."

"I told you that's just my grandma. She can't help herself."

"Promise me that no matter what happens, we won't ever argue like that again. You've been the best friend I've ever had. Now that we're sisters, I want you to still be my best friend, OK?" Summer asked.

"OK. You're my best friend, too."

The next morning they woke to Solomon blasting record after record of Motown music. Solomon was an avid Motown fan. Nothing else compared to the music he grew up listening to on the radio. He had gone to Detroit more times than he can count with his Uncle Stanford to watch their revues. He had a special fondness for Marvin Gaye and Stevie Wonder. This Christmas tape brought back teenage memories, and made him do something Michelle had never heard him do, and that was sing, and sing loudly. Michelle and Summer peeked through their bedroom door, and watched as this giant six-foot-nine man bounced around the living room as if he was a child. They laughed so hard, they fell through the door with Summer on top of Michelle. They looked up to catch Solomon with a brush in his hand, and his mouth wide open.

"Daddy, I love you." Michelle laughed. "But you can't sing a lick."

"Oh, I can't sing?" Solomon asked.

"I'm afraid not, sir," Summer joked.

"Oh, OK," Solomon said, then trapped the girls on the floor until they called for Sunshine to make him stop. Sunshine waited for a while, because she enjoyed seeing the three of them playing together, then she made Solomon leave the girls alone.

The Christmas holidays passed, and so did the years. Michelle accepted Summer living with her parents, and resumed visiting at every school vacation. She and Summer became as close, or perhaps even closer then most biological sisters.

In 1982, it was time for both girls to graduate, and it created a huge problem. Coincidentally, their graduations were to be on the same day. Solomon was perplexed on how they could attend both to make both girls happy. He and Sunshine contemplated many different scenarios, but they could not come up with a positive resolution.

"I suppose you'll have to go to one, and I go to the other," Solomon said.

"The only question is who will be going to which graduation?"

"I can answer that question for you right now. I'm going to my baby's graduation. I've waited for this moment all of her life, and I'm not going to miss it for the world."

"I don't want to miss it either," Solomon said.

"Then don't!"

"One of us has to be at Summer's graduation. She'd be crushed if neither one of us was there."

"Michelle will be crushed, if both of us are not there with her," Sunshine said.

"Look, when we accepted responsibility for Summer, we accepted all of the responsibilities of being a parent. And this is one of those responsibilities," Solomon said.

"I did accept responsibility to raise this child, but I never accepted responsibility to put anyone else's child before my own."

"OK, Sunshine, you go to Michelle's graduation, and I'll go to Summer's. But you know that Michelle will be much more forgiving to you, for not coming, than me for not coming."

"I'm not missing my baby's graduation, and that's all there is to it."

"OK, if that's the way it has to be."

"I'm sorry, Solomon, but that's the way it has to be."

And that's the way it went. Solomon attended Summer's graduation, and Sunshine flew to Michigan to attend Michelle's graduation.

On graduation day, Summer drove to her commencement ceremony with a group of her friends. She had her cap and gown in her hands, and they cruised the streets honking their horn. They waved at bystanders and held their caps and gowns in the air. When they arrived at the school, they found that they had enjoyed themselves a little too much. The rest of their Class of 1982 had already rehearsed and were getting dressed for the ceremony. Their participation in their graduation was then put on hold. The girls had to learn where they were supposed to be, and the other activities involved in the graduation ceremonies in a matter of minutes, so that they would not throw off the other students who had just rehearsed. The principal threatened to have them watch the ceremony from the audience. But they learned quickly, and he eventually decided to let them take their places with their class.

When Summer's name was called to receive her diploma, Solomon looked at Summer and thought of how much she's grown since her adoption. He felt blessed, and cursed, to have two stunningly beautiful daughters. He also felt his blood pressure rise when he thought of having to defend these two beautiful young ladies until two lucky young men married them away from him.

Solomon watched Summer as her thick, long, blond hair swayed back and forth. Her eyebrows matched the color of her hair. She had light green eyes, with brown olive skin. Her exotic skin was like her grandmother's, a native of Colombia. Her grandfather was white, a blond-haired, blue-eyed gentleman, while her grandmother was Colombian with shiny, black hair. She also had deep brown eyes and a curvaceous body. Her mother, however, had taken on her grandfather's physical attributes with blond hair, blue eyes, and pale white skin.

Summer had full lips and a thin nose. She was five feet eight inches—tall in comparison to most women. She was shapely, having straight shoulders, and her back curved inward at her waist, forming a perfect V-shape. Her bottom half was often compared to a black woman's. That comparison was having firm and protruding buttocks. Her long, muscular legs seemed to travel for a mile from her hips to the ground.

Summer's graduation commencement was combined with its all-boy brother school. They played the traditional commencement song. The students smiled, and kept walking, as they accepted their reward for twelve or thirteen years of hard work. The audience applauded each student in appreciation of hard work.

After the graduation, Summer and Solomon were invited to her boyfriend's house for dinner. Her boyfriend, Charles Webster, was a tall, thin, blond-haired, blue-eyed swimmer. Charles had told his parents that Summer was adopted after her parents were killed, but he didn't tell them that she was adopted by a black couple. Their first introduction was at the graduation, after the invitation had been offered. Summer held Solomon's hand as she led him to the Webster's family car for a formal introduction. Their mouths dropped as they saw this huge black man being introduced as her adopted father.

"Mr. and Mrs. Webster, this is my adopted father, Mr. Solomon Chambers," Summer said. "Dad, this is Mr. and Mrs. Webster."

"Good evening, pleasure to meet you," Solomon said, extending his hand.

"Yes, a pleasure it is," Mrs. Webster said, not extending hers in return.

"Good to meet you, Mr. Chambers," Mr. Webster said, shaking Solomon's hand.

"We certainly appreciate your invitation to dinner. I think that your son is a very mannerly young man," Solomon said.

"Well uh, Mr. Chambers," Mrs. Webster said. "I think it may be better if we postpone this dinner thing to a later date."

"Why?" Solomon asked. "Is there a problem?"

"No. The graduation, and all the excitement have made me completely exhausted is all." Mrs. Webster sighed.

"Oh, I think I understand," Solomon said.

Summer stood in shock as Mrs. Webster shunned Solomon. Her shock soon turned to anger. Although Summer was not biologically born a Chambers, she had developed the women's characteristics for being outspoken and confrontational.

"How dare you stand there and talk to him that way?" Summer yelled to Mrs. Chambers.

"Summer...," Charles said.

"Don't Summer me!" Summer interrupted. "Are you going to stand there and let your mother insult my father?"

"I don't know what you are talking about, young lady!" Mrs Webster said.

"You know exactly what I am talking about. You invited us to your house, and as soon as you find out he is black, you suddenly want to postpone the engagement. Well, my father and I would not dine with you if you were the last bigot on this earth!" Summer shouted.

"Oh, I'm glad I didn't let you into my home, and I'm not going to stand here and listen to any more of your garrulous nonsense," Mrs. Webster snapped back.

"I apologize for my daughter's outburst," Solomon said.

"You should. Perhaps you need to take her home and teach her some manners," Mrs. Webster added.

"Perhaps she's not the only one here who needs to be taken home and taught a few cordial manners," Solomon said.

"Summer, I'll call you later," Charles interrupted.

"No you won't!" Mrs. Webster said.

"I'm sure she'll survive." Solomon smiled.

"It was a pleasure to meet you, Mr. Chambers, and I apologize for my wife's behavior," Mr. Webster said, taking Solomon to the side for a private conversation. "My son really cares for Summer, and we old people need to keep our opinions to ourselves and let the children enjoy their last night of school."

"I have no problem with that, Mr. Webster," Solomon said. "I just don't want my daughter to be subjected to that ignorant racist mentality."

"I'll do my best with my wife." Mr. Webster smiled.

"I'm afraid doing your best is not good enough. Unless your best is making sure she never shuns my daughter again," Solomon said.

"Mr. Chambers, it wasn't your daughter she was shunning," Mr. Webster said.

Solomon realized that Mr. Webster was right. It had nothing at all to do with Summer. It was because he was black. Success often makes us forget the reality of the times in which we live. Solomon was no stranger to that delusion.

"I understand," Solomon said. "If Summer wants to go with your son, I will not prohibit her from doing so. But she is not permitted to go to your home under any circumstances, until your wife reconsiders her opinion on race relations."

"I understand, Mr. Chambers," Mr. Webster said. "You look like a golf man; if you ever want to play, let me know. I play at the most beautiful course in the District of Columbia. It's so private, President Reagan has to call for reservations."

"Now you're talking." Solomon laughed. "We may end up being family after all."

"What's your handicap?" Mr. Webster laughed.

"My skin." Solomon laughed. "My biggest handicap is just getting in the club."

Mr. Webster laughed loudly, then he and Solomon walked back to their families.

"Summer, if you want to go out with Charles later on, that's fine with me. But you're not going to stay out too late," Solomon said.

"That's OK, Dad," Summer said. "I've changed my mind."

"Come on, Summer, let's hang out with the other kids," Charles said.

"Son, if she doesn't want to go, she doesn't want to go." Mrs. Webster smiled.

"Would you be quiet, and let the children talk," Mr. Webster said.

"I'm still hanging out with the other kids, I just don't feel like hanging out with you anymore," Summer said. "Maybe, I'll see you around somewhere tonight."

"Maybe so." Charles sobbed.

"Well, it's been nice, but we must be going," Mrs. Webster said.

"Mr. Chambers, I'll be giving you a call, and we'll see what kind of swing you got." Mr. Webster smiled.

"Looking forward to it," Solomon said.

"Looking forward to what?" Mrs. Webster asked.

"Shut up and get in the car, Martha," Mr. Webster whispered.

Solomon and Summer went home and continued to take pictures. Summer left shortly after that to go out with a few of her friends.

★★★

In Saginaw, Orabell and Sunshine were sitting in the audience at the Saginaw Civic Center as the names for the Saginaw Vista High School Class of 1982 were being announced. Sunshine sat admiring how Michelle had grown into such a beautiful young lady. Michelle was dark brown, with dark eyebrows and long eyelashes. She had dark brown eyes and smooth unblemished dark brown skin—skin like her father and grandmother. She was very athletic, so her body was tight and muscular. She had long muscular legs with huge muscular thighs; and an extremely tiny waist, which magnified the proportion of her hips. Michelle was not as tall as Summer, but she was by no means a short woman. She was five feet six inches. Sunshine used to warn her that she would be envied by women, and hunted by men, for being blessed with such a dynamic figure.

At Michelle's graduation, the students, and the audience, were much more demonstrative in receiving their diplomas than those in Washington, D.C. They danced, and cheered, and waved back to the audience. There were signs with photographs of graduating students. The students with the most family and friends in the audience received the most cheers. It was nothing short of a pep rally. A tradition of celebration and jubilation.

After the graduation, Orabell and Sunshine took Michelle out for dinner. They took plenty of photographs, including the neighbors from Emily Street, Phelon Street, and Crapo Street, neighbors they had never seen before in their lives. Michelle didn't mind the intruders at all. They blocked off the street, and had a party for all of the graduates. Orabell and Sunshine sat on the porch and watched the young people dance. Two young men came up to the porch and asked Sunshine and Orabell to dance with them. They laughed at the boys, and told them their dancing days were way behind them. Michelle encouraged the boys to keep bugging them until they got them to dance. Their persistence paid off, and the two women walked embarrassedly to the street to dance with the young boys. Michelle laughed and laughed when she saw her mother and grandmother dancing in the middle of the streets. She also felt sadness because her father was not there to dance with her. She took plenty of photographs of her mother and grandmother as they danced, to embarrass them later. They ate, and danced well into the night. Slowly the cars and people began to leave until there was nobody left but those cleaning up the garbage. Orabell yelled out to Michelle that her father was on the telephone to congratulate her. She dropped the garbage bag she was holding and ran in the house.

"Hi, Daddy," Michelle said.

"Hi, Angel, congratulations!"

"Thank you, Daddy. I wish you were here."

"Don't worry, baby, that's why I called. Summer and I will be there tomorrow evening to celebrate with you, and we can all come back together."

"For real, Daddy?" Michelle screamed.

"Yes, Angel," Solomon said. "You know that I wanted to be at your graduation more than anything, but if we both would have come to your graduation, no one would have been here for Summer. Do you understand?"

"Yes, Daddy. But you'll be here tomorrow, won't you?" Michelle asked.

"First thing."

"Wanna speak to Mom?" Michelle asked.

"Yeah, put her on the phone."

Michelle called Sunshine to the telephone.

"Hello," Sunshine said. "How was Summer's graduation?"

"It was nice, although my heart was aching to be with Michelle, too."

"Boy, stop that. If you had come here, you would feel even worse about Summer having none of her family there to support her, so shut up, and get up here."

"Tell Ma I'll see her tomorrow," Solomon said. "We got tickets all the way into Saginaw this time. You can pick us up tomorrow at noon at Tri-City Airport. You know how to get there?"

"I went to college here. I know my way around. Besides, Saginaw is not so big a person can get lost." Michelle laughed.

"Like Greenwood, Mississippi is a metropolis!" Solomon joked.

"Just make sure you're at that airport tomorrow at noon."

"Do you know how many times I've been back and forth from D.C. to Saginaw?" Solomon asked. "I need to get me a house there, because I'm there almost as much as I'm here."

"Amen to that." Sunshine laughed.

"Bye, woman!" Solomon laughed. "I love you."

"Goodbye, and I love you, too."

The next day Solomon and Summer arrived in Saginaw at the airport at their scheduled time. Michelle and Sunshine were waiting impatiently at their gate. Summer and Michelle swapped graduation gifts, and Solomon wrapped his arms around Michelle and walked her to the car. Orabell had planned a barbecue goodbye picnic with some of Michelle's friends. Michelle was going to spend the summer with her parents, then leave from there going to college. She would be attending the University of Michigan in the fall, so she would still be near her grandmother. The barbecue was an opportunity for all of her friends to say goodbye to her. She had male and female friends at her party. Most of them had no idea who Summer was, or what she was doing at the party.

"Hey, Michelle, who is that white girl?" Michelle's friend Brian asked.

"That's my sister," Michelle answered.

"That ain't your sister; that girl is white."

"That is my sister, boy. She's adopted, and don't mess with her. She's not used to being around all of you crazy black folks, so be nice." Michelle laughed.

"Damn!" Brian said. "She is fine as hell, Michelle. Hook me up!"

"I told you, leave my sister alone. She doesn't want to be bothered with any of you tired knuckleheads, so leave her alone."

"You don't know that. I just wanna be her friend." Brian smiled. "You know what I'm talkin' 'bout."

"Brian, if you hurt her feelings, I am going to kick your butt!" Michelle said. "Don't you still go with Ida, anyway?"

"Hell, naw! We broke up."

"Go 'head, but you better not say anything stupid to her Brian. I'm serious."

"I won't, I won't." Brian smiled. "I promise."

Brian went over to Summer who was sitting alone, and started talking to her. Michelle kept her eye on them until she saw Summer's smile, then she turned her attention to the other guests at her party. They were having a great time until Brian's girlfriend Ida showed up with a gang of girls. She stood between Brian and Summer and started yelling at them both. Orabell noticed them through the kitchen window, and started on her way outside to break up the fight before anything serious happened. Sunshine stopped her and told her to let the girls handle it. Solomon was on Orabell's couch in his normal position—asleep. Orabell and Sunshine watched through the window as Summer was confronted by the girl.

"Brian, I know you're not over here with this white chick!" Ida said.

"Girl, go 'head! I don't go with you no more!" Brian shouted.

"Look, I'm not trying to start any trouble. I am just here for my sister's party," Summer said.

"Who yo' sister?" Ida said, looking around.

"I'm her sister!" Michelle shouted.

"I know this white bitch ain't yo' sister! But whoever she is, you better tell her to keep her ass away from boyfriend, before she get her ass whooped!"

Orabell grabbed a broom and headed outside. Sunshine stopped her, and convinced her to let Michelle and Summer handle the girl.

"I don't appreciate that little fast girl comin' in my yard cussin' like she ain't got no home trainin' like that," Orabell said.

"I know, Ma, but the girls can handle that little witch; watch and see."

Michelle stepped in between Ida and Summer, and took over the argument. Orabell and Sunshine gave each other high-five.

"If there's any butt going to whooped, it's going to be yours!" Michelle snapped. "Don't you come in my grandmother's yard, with your ghetto butt, cussin' like you ain't got no sense!"

"Well, you better tell that white bitch to stay away from my boyfriend then!"

"If you see a bitch, slap her!" Summer said.

Orabell heard Summer using foul language and enough was enough. She grabbed her broom again and headed outside. This time Sunshine didn't stop her. Instead she grabbed a mop, and followed her outside.

"I don't know who you are, but you and your little friends need to get out of my yard, right now!" Orabell shouted.

"That's OK, Grandma. She can get some of this, if she wants some!" Michelle said.

"Some of what?" Sunshine asked. "You and Summer need to be quiet."

"But they came over here in our yard starting a fight," Summer said.

"All of y'all be quiet!" Orabell said. "Now get outta my yard before I call the police on every last one of ya!"

"You need to tell yo' grandkids to shut up if they can't back it up," Ida said.

"Let me tell you somethin', you little smart-mouth heffa'. You ain't even a hundred pounds soakin' wet. What do you think you gon' do with them big ol' girls?" Orabell said, pointing at Summer and Michelle. "If you keep on talkin' I'm gon' let 'em whoop on yo' ass up and down these streets! Now get out my yard!"

"Y'all get out her yard!" Brian said.

"I better not see you out nowhere, Michelle. You and yo' white sister!" Ida said.

"You know where I hang out; you can see me anytime you want!" Michelle screamed at her.

Ida and her gang of girls turned and walked away. Both sides continued to yell at the other.

"Brian, I told you not to start trouble with my sister, didn't I?" Michelle asked.

"I don't go with that girl no more, Michelle. She just crazy!" Brian pleaded.

"Leave Brian alone, he can't control that little trouble maker," Sunshine said.

"What were you going to do with that broom, Grandmother?" Summer laughed.

"I was going to whoop some butt, or sweep up you and your sister," Orabell joked.

"We could have taken on all of those girls, Grandma," Michelle said.

"I heard you out here cussin', Summer. I bet not ever hear nothin' like that come outta yo' mouth again, you hear me?" Orabell said.

"Yes, Ma'am." Summer sighed.

"When y'all get through cleanin' up out here, Summer, you gon' wash all them dishes by yo' self. That oughtta give you somethin' cuss about," Orabell said.

"I told you she wasn't just a sweet old lady," Michelle whispered to Summer.

"Be quiet, because you're still going to help me," Summer whispered back so that Orabell couldn't hear her.

They continued to have fun the remainder of the day. Solomon eventually woke up, and got his dance with Michelle and Summer.

They went back to Washington the following week, and traveled together as a family for most of the summer.

The years began to zoom by, and as time changed, so did the Chambers family. When it was time for the girls to start their collegiate careers, the entire family went with Michelle to the University of Michigan in Ann Arbor. Michelle majored in journalism with a minor curriculum in literature. The following week the family flew to Stanford, California, and Summer enrolled at Stanford University. Summer double majored in pre-law and criminal justice.

Michelle dropped her minor curriculum and graduated with honors in 1986 from the University of Michigan. Summer completed her pre-law studies in 1986 and criminal justice studies in 1987. Summer went from Stanford, California in the summer to Cambridge, Massachusetts in the fall as a law student at Harvard University

Solomon and Sunshine tried to convince Michelle to continue on to graduate school, but she chose to intern at a television station in Chicago. Michelle soared up the corporate ladder and in four years, she was an anchorwoman in the third largest city in America.

Michelle married a college professor from Northwestern University in 1993. Michelle and her husband, Stephen Clayborne, moved to the suburb of Glenwood, Illinois. They had a daughter that they named Bria in September of 1994. Summer was the maid of honor at Michelle's wedding, and later of course, Michelle would be maid of honor at Summer's wedding. Sunshine cried throughout the wedding ceremony. She and Solomon liked Stephen, and they were happy that Michelle was marrying him. Unfortunately, Solomon did not attend the wedding. He was in South America as an ambassador on behalf of the United States. Michelle was terribly disappointed but she understood how important her father's mission was to America.

Summer graduated from law school in 1990, and after three attempts, she successfully passed the bar in 1993. She was hired on at Solomon's law firm, where he left her in the hands of the firm. He wanted her to develop her own legal personality with no influence from his status as Senior Partner. His expectations were met, and surpassed, as she made a name for being one of the best litigating lawyers on the East Coast. She also made a name with a young junior partner named Robert Salisbury.

Summer married Robert in 1995, and moved back to California. They lived in the Los Angeles area, where he was born and raised. Solomon, Michelle, and Sunshine flew to Los Angeles to attend Summer's wedding. Michelle was maid of honor, and Solomon gave her away. She had her first child, Donovan, in 1997, and her second child, Solomon, in 1999. They visited Washington, D.C. and Saginaw as often as they could. When they went to Michigan, Orabell spoiled Summer and her boys. Over the years, Summer had fallen in love with the old woman, and she couldn't imagine not having her as a grandmother. Robert was amazed to see the old black woman love and treat his white children as if they had come straight from her womb. He, too, fell in love with Orabell.

★★★

The Christmas holidays were always spent at Orabell's in Saginaw. And now that Solomon and Sunshine were nearly sixty years old, their visits were limited to one a year, and that was at Christmas. Michelle visited Orabell regularly, and Orabell would often stay with her extensively in Chicago. Outside of the Christmas holidays, Summer took two weeks vacation every summer, to spend one week in Washington and the other in Saginaw. Her husband, Robert, had a brother who lived in Virginia, so when she traveled to Saginaw with the children, he would stay in Virginia with his family. Michelle and her daughter, Bria, would always schedule their vacation to Saginaw to coincide with Summer's week. They would enjoy themselves spending time with Orabell, listening to her repeat stories she had told for over thirty years.

Michelle and Stephen began to grow apart after their careers took them in different directions. This eventually led to a bitter divorce in 2002. Summer represented her in court, and represented her well. Michelle ended up with primary custody of Bria, and a healthy monthly child support settlement. She was awarded most of their assets attained while they were married, and kept all of the assets in her possession prior to their marriage.

Michelle used her experience with her divorce to write a best-selling novel, *The Nature of a Woman*. She went on to write three consecutive best sellers that catapulted her literary career into international notoriety. As her career skyrocketed, her family saw less and less of her. In age, Michelle was middle, but in life she was only beginning.

She moved to Paris in the spring of 2004 to write a book on the romances of French women. She left her child with her grandmother until she returned the following year. Solomon did not approve of her stay in France, mostly due to the reminiscing guilt it brought back to him for not raising his own child. After the completion of her book, she returned to the States to receive rave reviews on her new best seller.

Christmas of 2005 was the traditional Chambers holiday celebration. They all met in Saginaw with their families. With all of the new additions to the family, they had to bring another long table to accommodate the children. Time had proven to be an unkindly adversary to the once youthful Solomon and Sunshine. They were almost seventy years old, and instead of playing with the children, now they sat in the living room with Orabell and watched television. Summer and Michelle had become the core of the holiday festivities.

After dinner, Michelle announced that she would be going back to Paris for the summer to promote her book. Solomon let it be known that he did not approve of her spending so much time overseas, so far away from her family. Michelle was angered by Solomon's statement; she found it hypocritical. She tried to control her emotions, but forty years of pent-up frustration exploded, and it erupted with a bang.

"Daddy, why do you have such a big problem with me going to Paris?" Michelle asked. "I will only be gone for a short time, and when I return, I can spend all of my time with my family."

"Baby, all that I am saying is that I don't want you to make the same mistake I made."

"And what mistake is that, Daddy?"

"Michelle, don't start!" Summer said.

"I'm not starting anything," Michelle responded. "I just wanna know what Daddy means when he says he doesn't want me to repeat his mistake."

"Michelle, all that I'm saying is that you need to spend as much time with your child as you can," Solomon said. "You never know, you may regret it one day."

"Do you regret it, Daddy?" Michelle asked.

Solomon bowed his head, and looked away.

"Do you, Daddy?" Michelle repeated. "Do you regret that Grandma raised me, and not you?"

"That's enough, Michelle; shut your mouth!" Sunshine said.

"Girl, you ought to be shame of yourself," Orabell said.

"That's OK. Let her say what she has to say, and get it over with," Solomon whispered.

"What's the matter, Daddy; your hypocrisy eating at your morality?" Michelle asked.

"No, child, you just don't understand."

"Well, make me understand then, Daddy!" Michelle yelled.

"What do you want me to say, Michelle?"

"If I have to tell you, there's nothing for you to say," Michelle said. "Bria, get your coat."

Bria pulled her coat from out of the closet, and slowly slipped it over her shoulders. She looked at Sunshine in confusion.

"Michelle, stop overreacting," Summer said. "Bria, sit down, sweetheart."

Bria started to pull her coat off again, when Michelle screamed at her.

"Bria, put your coat on right this minute!"

"Michelle what is wrong with you?" Summer asked.

"You really don't know do you, Summer?" Michelle asked.

"No, I don't," Summer answered.

Michelle gathered her belongings, then hugged Orabell and Sunshine goodbye.

"I'm sorry to ruin your holiday, but it's time for us to go," Michelle said. "Bria, tell everyone goodbye."

Bria walked around the room and hugged everyone. After she hugged Solomon and turned to walk away, he reached for her again and pulled her in his arms.

"I love you, little girl. Don't ever forget that, OK?" Solomon said.

"I love you too, Granddad." Bria smiled.

"Let's go, Bri," Michelle said.

Summer walked Michelle to her car, and held her tightly.

"I don't know what's the matter, but talk to me," Summer said. "I can't stand seeing you like this. What can I do?"

"I love you Summer, more than I can say," Michelle said. "But this time, you can't fix it."

"You know I love you, don't you?" Summer asked, pulling Michelle's hair away from her face.

"And I love you, too." Michelle smiled. "You're the only sister I have."

"Just like Daddy is the only daddy you have," Summer said. "Talk to him."

"I've been trying to talk to him for forty-one years," Michelle said. "It's his turn now."

"Maybe he doesn't know what to say, Michelle."

"That's too bad, because at this point, neither do I," Michelle said. "Go back in the house and warm up; it's freezing out here."

"Be careful on that highway," Summer said.

"I will, and call me when you get back to Los Angeles."

Summer stood in the street and watched Michelle drive off before she turned and walked back into the house.

CHAPTER SIXTEEN

An act is a product, such as a statute, decree, or enactment, resulting from a decision by a legislative or judicial body. In the spring of 2005, a shocking announcement was made to the citizens of the United States of America, that the Affirmative Action Act was a violation of the Constitution. The United States Supreme Court voted to abolish the Affirmative Action Act as it existed, and issue to the state the authority to affirm their state Constitutions to recapture the true premise of the Constitution that all men are created equal. To enforce the belief that one race, or color, of people should not be given preference over the other.

The revised Affirmative Action Act would establish equality for the disenfranchised, and no longer the underprivileged black man. Most of the state's Constitutions were outdated and didn't reflect the progressive changes that had occurred in the previous seventy-five years for minorities. The response to its effect from black people went without a declaration of dispute, because most black people were unaware that the change had even occurred. Only the educators and political leaders took notice. And even they held back their tongues, and their honest opinions from the nation.

White educators and political leaders, however, produced nationwide debates on the repercussions of ruling Affirmative Action unconstitutional. Some said that it would be catastrophic to the social structure the Civil Rights Movement had sacrificially worked so hard to establish. Others believed it would enable all Americans to survive on their merits as individuals, disallowing the opportunity for race to give an advantage against a person with equal credentials.

The monumental blow for Affirmative Action came on March 27, 2001 when U.S. District Court Judge Bernard A. Friedman declared the University of Michigan law school admissions to be unconstitutional. The judge proclaimed the school was in violation of Title VI of the 1964 Civil Rights Act. He admitted the long and tragic history of race discrimination in this country, but the school's justification for using race to assemble a racially diverse student population was not a compelling state interest. This case became the centerpiece of legal battles regarding Affirmative Action across the country. The case was Gutter vs. Bollinger, case# 97-CV-75928-DT. Barbara Gutter vs. Lee Bollinger, Jeffery Lehman, Dennis Shields, Regents of the University of Michigan, and the University of Michigan Law School. Barbara Gutter, a white woman, was rejected by the University of Michigan Law School in June, 1997. She claimed that the University of Michigan Law School used preferential admissions policies for minorities. Her suit stated the school discriminated against her on the basis of her race.

On December 22, 2000, the court heard oral argument in the case of Gutter vs. Lee Bollinger. Over a period of fifteen days in January and February 2001, the court conducted a bench trial. In this Opinion, the court shall move on the motion and make findings of fact and conclusions of law. After the evidence was presented from both sides, Judge Bernard Friedman concluded and ordered the following:

IT IS ORDERED that plaintiff's request for declaratory relief is granted. The court finds and declares the University of Michigan Law School's use of race in its admissions decisions violates the Equal Protection Clause of the Fourteenth Amendment and Title VI of the Civil Rights Act of 1964.

IT IS FURTHER ORDERED that plaintiff's request for injunctive relief is granted. The University of Michigan Law School is hereby enjoined from using applicant's race as a factor in its admissions decisions.

IT IS FURTHER ORDERED that the parties' various motions for summary judgment are denied, except that the motion of the individual defendants for summary judgments on grounds of qualified immunity is granted.

IT IS FURTHER ORDERED that the clerk schedule the damages phase of the trial.

Dated: March 27, 2001

Detroit, Michigan.

Another case which brought Affirmative Action to the forefront of America was Jennifer Gratz and Patrick Hamacher vs. Lee Bolinger and the University of Michigan. Supreme Court# 02-0516. Jennifer Gratz, a white woman, applied to the University of Michigan in 1995. Her grade-point average was 3.8, and her ACT score was 25. Patrick Hamacher, a white man, applied for admission in 1997. His grade-point average was 3.0, and his ACT score was 28. They were both denied admission, and in October of 1997, sued the University of Michigan for reverse discrimination.

The University of Michigan had a policy that was partial to students from three disenfranchised minority groups: Hispanics, African-Americans, and Native Americans. In 1995, every minority student who applied to the University of Michigan with comparable ACT scores and grade-point averages of Gratz and Hamacher was accepted. In contrast, only 32 percent of white students with similar scores and averages were allowed.

The case was argued on April 1, 2003, and the decision was handed down on June 23, 2003. In a six-to-three vote, the United States Supreme Court found the University of Michigan's undergraduate point system unconstitutional and not suitable for the Affirmative Action program. However, it upheld the Law School's admissions policies.

These cases were paramount to the destruction of Affirmative Action. They began nationwide debates and as the debates grew, the definition of constitutional and unconstitutional varied from argument to argument. It was altered to best fit the debater's point of view. The insanity of winning the arguments of civil liberties became much more important than the integrity for which the Constitution existed.

It was agreed that black people were progressing in certain areas, but not significantly enough to show that Affirmative Action was the influential cause of the progress. On the other hand, there were white people protesting that Affirmative Action was the direct influential cause of them not progressing on the corporate and academic levels. Their point was heard, and measures were taken to rectify the thirty-year discrimination white people claim to have suffered. The supporters of Affirmative Action debated that even if white people had suffered from discrimination in the past thirty years, it was only a mild comparison to the four-hundred years that black people of America had endured.

Inevitably, the Affirmative Action Act became the first brick to be knocked from the once impregnable wall of civil rights, but soon after, they all came crumbling down.

The repercussions of ruling the Affirmative Action Act unconstitutional would not be realized until the year 2007, when the Voting Rights Act was also ruled unconstitutional. The Voting Rights Act provided protection for all Americans to vote regardless of race or color. It was the assumption of many that the United States government felt that time and circumstances had progressed to the point that Americans were truly equal.

The unconstitutional rulings of the Voting Rights and Affirmative Action Acts were politically motivated. The lawmakers needed to ensure the white American voters that they would no longer be subjected to discriminatory social, political, and economic laws. In order to fulfill their commitment to white voters, the American government resorted to drastic measures. They used tactical and manipulative constitutional methods. Methods which proved to be most effective. Congress voted to pass down the jurisdiction of voting rights to each state. One by one, the states began to vote the Voting Rights Act unconstitutional. But while all fifty states, excluding Hawaii and Alaska, were voting the Voting Rights Act unconstitutional, not one state amended the voting rights to protect the disenfranchised voters.

Redistricting of geographical regions from 2005 to 2006 led to disproportionate large numbers of white political candidates winning and taking over their respective districts. As the newly voted white political leaders took their place in office, state by state, the voting laws began to change.

Surprisingly, the most crucial voting law did not originate in the historically racist South, but on the progressive West Coast, in the state of California. The California State Constitution, Article II, Section 4, read that the legislature shall prohibit improper practices that affect elections and shall provide for the disqualification of electors while mentally incompetent or imprisoned or on parole for the conviction of a felony. The California State Legislature used this article of their constitution to revoke the voting rights of Blacks and Hispanic men and women who were imprisoned. The next deterrent for the high minority crime rate for the California Legislature was to revoke the voting privileges of the inmate's family. This law was challenged initially by African-Americans, but then the protests waned. The California success saw neighboring states follow their lead. Soon states in the Midwest and on the East Coast found ways to amend their state laws to comply with the new California laws.

Though it wasn't until the laws were passed that the common man realized what was happening in America, it brought forth a cry of freedom that no one was prepared to defend. Despite a lifetime of witnessing discrimination and racism, even from a defensive peripheral perspective, blacks did not see their own freedom being taken away until it was gone. In hindsight, they were not the only ones blinded to the results of the Voting Rights Act. For if the American Legislatures could have foreseen the devastation which was to follow, they surely would not have ruled in that favor. But unfortunately, God did not bless them with the luxury of foresight. And now the United States stood on the brink of a civil war that could possibly destroy its very existence.

By 2007, African-Americans were totally without the privilege of voting. It didn't matter if you were a doctor, lawyer, or a multimillion-dollar professional athlete, no black person was excluded. The financial status of African-Americans was of no consequence. The few African-Americans privileged to vote were federal government and military employees, and they were allowed to vote only in the District of Columbia. The message was sent loud and clear. If you were not a part of the government, you had no privilege to vote! And no matter how much money blacks possessed, they could not buy a vote.

African-Americans began to assemble and protest the new voting laws. Eventually, some people became impatient with their leaders and representatives. African-Americans blamed their political leaders more so than the white politicians who had manipulated them out of their right to vote. They believed that while their political leaders were holding their offices, they should have done something to prevent them from losing their right to vote. If it was nothing more than to warn them that the impossible would soon be possible.

With no solid leadership, different groups formed to combat the new American laws. They fought with protests, and they fought with violence. Riots became rampant, as neighborhoods were burned to the ground. There were millions of arrests, and thousands of deaths during the summer of 2007. The police and National Guard began to lose control in major cities like Chicago, Philadelphia, and Los Angeles. A high percentage of their manpower was minority. Regaining control of these cities became an impossible feat. From the view of the law, it was difficult to determine who was on their side, and who was not.

Throughout the years of 2006 and 2007, attorney Henry Lee moved to the forefront for leadership of the African-American protest for reinstating their right to vote. He was a young, bright attorney who couldn't hold his tongue, even while he was asleep. He journeyed to all forty-eight continental states and petitioned their Constitutions. A journey which began long before the rest of the nation, blacks or whites, were aware of the new voting laws. When most people signed his petitions, they had no idea what they were signing. Henry's charisma convinced them that if they didn't sign it, one day they would surely regret it. He later used the petitions to charge each state with violating the civil rights of their African-American constituents. His case was thrown out of court until a Mississippi State Supreme Court judge by the name of John Hankins Jr. agreed, and fought for his case to be heard. In the case of Lee versus the state of Mississippi evidence was presented to show that the state had violated the civil rights of its African-American constituents. The ruling, however, did not make the change swift. The pattern followed in Georgia and Tennessee.

Henry knew that he had to get the case to the U. S. Supreme Court, but before he could do that, he would first have to get one of the states to amend its voting laws. Henry realized that although he had the determination to win his judgment, he did not have the experience. He and his partner, Jonathan Navarro, an Italian kid with a yen for overreacting, combed the country to find the attorney who would be able to try the case. Their first choice was Solomon Chambers. Solomon had made quite an impression on them when he lectured a class to them in law school. They attended Harvard Law, and they were well aware that Solomon's daughter was an alum. The young attorneys sent Solomon letters, but their letters were not met with responses. They eventually gave up on Solomon, and sought the next best suitable attorney. His name was Julius Greenbach. He was Jewish and nationally known for winning civil rights cases. As they began to research similar civil rights cases, Mr. Greenbach focused on the attention from the media. Henry believed that Mr. Greenbach's motives were not about equality, but notoriety. He addressed his belief with Mr. Greenbach and their differences of opinion caused Mr. Greenbach to leave the case.

Henry and Jonathan spoke with several other prestigious attorneys about leading the case, but none of them was the attorney to head their team. Henry decided to try a longshot. He tracked down Summer's contact information, and called her. He asked her to set up a meeting between himself and Solomon. Summer advised him that her father would not be interested in trying the case. Henry kept at her until she finally agreed. He asked her to be present at the meeting to assist him in convincing Solomon. He did not want to make any mistakes by saying the wrong thing, and if Summer was present she could tip him about when he was going in that direction. For even without the privilege of voting, Solomon Chambers was respected and revered by many. Summer reluctantly agreed to attend the meeting, but she warned him that he was wasting his time.

When Summer made the call to Solomon for the meeting, she didn't ask him, because she knew she would get a definite no. She used the only resource she had to even have a small chance at getting Solomon to listen to the young attorneys; that resource was Sunshine. She called Sunshine and asked her to set up the meeting. Sunshine told her that she was going about it the wrong way. If she wanted Solomon at the meeting she had to make sure he didn't know it was a meeting. Sunshine planned for Henry and Jonathan to come by their house spontaneously while Summer was there for the Thanksgiving holiday. Everybody planned their schedules accordingly, and the scheme was in motion.

In his old age, Solomon had not deviated from his belief to live, and let live. Justice had taken away his privilege to vote, and yet he was content to live life within the laws of justice. He frowned upon the violence and rioting African-Americans were exhibiting. He disassociated himself from the entire voting situation. Life was simple for him and Sunshine, and he didn't want anything to change. Sunshine, on the other hand, protested, attended rallies, and wrote letters to Congress, the president, and anybody involved with the government. But she knew her husband, and doing acts such as those simply was not him. So she respected his right to be content with the situation. Solomon, on the other hand, knew his wife, and being content with any situation where she was not being treated fairly meant aggression and action. And he respected her right to fight. The two mixed and matched perfectly.

The Friday following Thanksgiving Day, and the family gathered at Solomon and Sunshine's for dinner. Everyone but Michelle. She and Solomon still had not spoken, or seen the other since Christmas of 2005.

There was a knock at the Chambers' door. The knock disturbed Solomon's sleep, which made him very irritated.

"What's all that commotion?" Solomon yelled, opening the door.

"Mr. Solomon Chambers?" Jonathan asked.

"Yes, yes I am," Solomon answered.

"Good evening, sir. My name is Jonathan Navarro."

"And my name is Henry Lee," Henry said, shaking Solomon's hand. "And it is a pleasure to finally make your acquaintance, sir."

"We're sorry to disturb you, Mr. Chambers, but we are here on behalf of the Unified Minority Voters Coalition. May we come in and speak with you for a minute?" Jonathan asked.

"I don't think it would be a good idea for you to speak today, son. How about another day?"

"Mr. Chambers, it is imperative that we speak to you today, sir," Jonathan insisted.

"Let the boys in," Sunshine said, entering from the kitchen. "It probably won't take long."

"It won't take long at all, ma'am," Henry said, peeking around Solomon's big frame. "Can we have just a few minutes of your time, sir?"

"Oh, I suppose so, but please, make it quick," Solomon said. "I'm a little exhausted."

"Oh we will, sir." Henry smiled.

"Come on in," Solomon said. "Now you're here on behalf of who?"

"The Unified Minority Voters Coalition, sir," Henry answered.

"You all are not some kind of gang, are you?" Solomon asked, looking over his glasses.

"Of course not, sir." Jonathan laughed.

"Mr. Chambers, we need to speak with you about the current crisis we are facing in our country. We are representing fifteen million minorities who are charging the United States government with violating their constitutional rights. I will get straight to the point. We are here because we need a lead counsel for this case. We need someone who has the prestige to be heard, and the experience to litigate this case. Mr. Chambers, we need you," Jonathan said.

"How can I represent your case?" Solomon asked. "What can I do?"

"Mr. Chambers, we have searched all over this country for an attorney to represent this case to the Supreme Court. We understand that this is not the proper protocol of the U.S. judicial system. But this is an extraordinary case, and it deems extraordinary tactics. My colleague and I simply do not have the experience to present this case." Henry sighed. "Mr. Chambers, have you looked in the streets lately?"

"What do you mean, son?" Solomon asked.

"I mean that there are blacks killing whites, and whites killing blacks with no concern for the value of human life. Something has to be done."

"Mr. Chambers, African-Americans have every right to exist in this country as equal human beings. And we will be the voice to demand that equality!" Jonathan exclaimed, speaking so fast Solomon could barely understand him.

"Calm down, son. I can barely understand what you're saying! But as far as your case is concerned, I don't think I'm the man who can help you," Solomon admitted. "But I will try to give you a little advice though. You'd better get yourself a Plan B, just in case your first plan fails. Have you considered your options?"

"There are no options, Mr. Chambers," Henry said.

"Oooooh, wrong answer, son. What do you plan to do after you get all of these black folks to believe that it's your way, or no way?" Solomon asked.

"It's not my way, it's our way. And it has to be our way, or no way. I don't know about you, Mr. Chambers, but I am willing to die for my freedom," Henry said as he clutched his briefcase.

"Oh you are?" Solomon asked. "Are you also willing to jeopardize the lives of the people you claim to represent?"

"Every voice has a right to choose his own destiny. And judging by the long list of names that have joined with us, the people have spoken. I'm not making anyone do anything they don't want to do, sir. Whatever our destiny will be, it will be."

"Son, if you go to the Supreme Court with no option, you are placing these people's lives with no option. Remember, the government controls the army, the weapons, and the ability to wipe black people from the face of the earth."

"With all due respect, sir, what options do they have now?" Jonathan asked.

"They have the right to live." Solomon sighed.

"But under what circumstances?" Jonathan whined.

"Under any circumstance. Living is always better than dying."

"You know, sir, that type of thinking is why our voices are falling upon deaf ears now. If they believe we will not defend ourselves, what threat do we bring to them?" Henry asked.

Solomon sat down and crossed his legs, then continued with his conversation.

"Martin Luther King once said, it's no longer the choice between violence and nonviolence in this world; it's nonviolence or nonexistence. And that holds true for us living in this day. It worked for us in our era then, and it will work for us today," Solomon said proudly. "What do you think Martin Luther King would say about leading our people into this racial war?"

"First of all, did it really work, Mr. Chambers?" Henry asked. "Or maybe that's our problem. Maybe black people have lived on the backs of the social victories of the people from the fifties and sixties for so long, we have grown too weak to fight for ourselves. We have lived off of the chants and cries of the past for far too long. We've elevated people like Dr. King, and Rosa Parks into mythological beings. When I try talking to the survivors of the Civil Rights Movement, all that I hear is their arrogant perspectives of history because they lived through it, and I didn't. Those people, the people from your era, had a responsibility to me, and my generation to keep that movement active. But you didn't; instead you hold it over our heads because we were fortunate enough to live afterwards.

"I wonder how the civil rights survivors would feel if there were slavery survivors telling them that their civil rights struggle was nothing compared to being a slave. Perhaps my generation is different, because we are tired of being treated this way. And whenever we try to fight racism in our day, in our era, the first question that's asked is, what would Dr. King say?

"I live with the fear of knowing my life can be taken any day just because of the color of my skin. I walk the streets with a bull's eye on my chest, defending those who can not defend themselves! I will give my life right this minute if it meant that all people in this country would be treated as they should, and that's like a human being! So I say to you, Mr. Chambers, what right do you, or anyone else have to ask me what would Dr. King say about what I am doing?

"As much as I adore and revere Martin Luther King, I don't give a damn what he thinks about what I am doing. When I close my eyes at night, and open them in the morning, he is not who I am asking for forgiveness; it is God. And if I offend you by referring to him as just a man that I admire, and not my God, let me apologize to you now, and I will pray for you later."

"What made these people extraordinary is their resolve for nonviolence. Their cry was for freedom. But yours, son, yours is of vengeance!" Solomon cried.

"No, sir, my cry is of justice!" Henry said. "Because I was born free."

"We must keep our composure, for to lose it, could mean we lose our existence," Solomon shouted.

"Mr. Chambers, that's what we said when they ruled affirmative action unconstitutional. That's what we said when they ruled the Voting Rights Act unconstitutional. When are we going to stop being afraid to die, so that maybe, just maybe our children will finally get a chance to live?" Henry shouted back.

"They chipped away at the principle of affirmative action to the point that I almost believed that it was unfair to white people," Jonathan said.

"The barometer of equality for all people can not, and should not, be measured by the oppressor, but by the oppressed. In our case, Mr. Chambers, we have allowed the oppressor to determine what equality should be for us. Somehow they were convinced that by actually utilizing the affirmative action program, black people became privileged, and not equal. And we both know that's a load of crap, don't we?" Henry said.

"Henry is right. African-Americans became so complacent with their opposition to the constant changing of affirmative action, that complacency has brought us to the crisis we are facing now," Jonathan said excitedly.

"Calm down, son," Solomon said to Jonathan. "You better get this boy some barbiturates, and keep him far away from the caffeine. I'm still a little confused on this complacency theory."

"Allowing state government to permit colleges, and businesses the option of affirmative action set the foundation for its dismissal. Which later led to the dismissal of the Voting Rights Act, which leads us to today. I suppose their hypothesis was that there was no need to pacify black people any longer because we had attained the equality of white people. But the inefficiency of their hypothesis was that there was no alternative to the elimination of opportunities for those oppressed minorities whose only chance for equality depended upon the affirmative action program," Henry said.

"To add to what Henry is saying, once African-Americans started to accept the laws being softened for the offenders of affirmative action, you were unwittingly submitting to the end of freedom. The wheels were set in motion, and it has steamrolled ever since. The Voting Rights Act was not unconstitutional by its laws, but by man's perception. Our government believed that our humanity had equaled our laws, but as you can see, Mr. Chambers, our government was wrong," Jonathan said.

"You young men have good points. I can't argue with you there. But still, I am not the man for the job." Solomon sighed.

"Mr. Chambers, if you can't try this case, no one can," Henry said solemnly.

"I wish there was something I could do. But even if my heart was willing, I don't think this old body could endure a case like this. It will take a lot of energy, energy that I no longer have. If I thought I could win this case, I would accept it in a heartbeat, but I can not."

"Sir, we're not asking you to guarantee us a victory. We only ask that you fight, and show us how to fight. We can be your arms, and your legs," Jonathan pleaded. "Please."

Solomon shook his head with sadness. He could not jeopardize the lives of so many people.

"I'm sorry, son. But I can't place the burden of a nation on these old shoulders."

"I'm sorry, too, Mr. Chambers," Henry said, standing to leave. "You spoke of Dr. King, and his words. You must have forgotten some of the last words he spoke that night in Memphis, Tennessee. I believe he used the Good Samaritan parable. He said that when the priest and the Levite saw the man lying on the ground, they asked the question of, what will happen to them if they stop to help the man? But eventually the Samaritan came by, and in those days Samaritans were lowlife people that everybody despised. But when that Samaritan came by and saw the man, he did not ask the question of what would happen to him. He asked exactly what Martin Luther King asked himself the night before he was killed, and the question you should be asking yourself here tonight, Mr. Chambers. And that question is not, what will happen to you if you stop to help these people?

The question is, what will happen to these people if you do not stop and help them?"

Solomon stood before Henry and looked him in his eyes, and he saw passion, determination, and also desperation. He saw all of the conviction he never had as a young man toward defending, and upholding his own race. He realized the young man before him was not a radical, misguided martyr that would bring further shame to black people. But rather a well-informed leader, willing to give his life to make life better for others. Solomon felt a sense of shame that a man less than half his age was willing to give his life for the sake of humanity. He thought that if these young men could risk their lives for equality, he could surely do something.

"All right, son, I'll do it," Solomon said. "But before I do, we need to discuss some of the parameters of our strategy for this case. The first is that we don't present ourselves as a hostile legal team trying to demand equality by any means. The second is that we don't try to condemn an entire race for the actions of a few. I will not take part in a campaign for anti-white activities. These two demands are not up for discussion, nor debate. There is no compromise, do you two understand?"

"If we are not charging white people, then who exactly do we charge?" Henry asked.

"You charge those who did it," Solomon stated. "The United States government, and the United States government alone! It is not within our best interest to alienate our allies. Our allies will be white people, and will we need them. We can stomp, scream, and march all we want. But white people put us here, and they are the only ones who can take us out of it. And we need to humble ourselves to them."

"Haven't we been humble enough?" Henry asked.

"We're not humbling to them as cowards, son. But in appreciation. Appreciating the fact that they do not have to do anything to help us, but they choose to do so anyway. When you're dealing with racism there is always a risk of violence and hatred. Justice and equality will take a back seat to survival of the fittest. Right or wrong give way to black and white, and the significance of the cause loses its merit. I have seen racism up close.

My family has been murdered by its evil. But to combat hate with hate, will only bring forth more hate, and everyone dies. If it becomes a black versus white war, who do you think will win?" Solomon asked.

"It's already a black and white war. Figuratively, and literally," Jonathan said.

"If that's the case, young man, whose side are you on?" Solomon smiled.

Jonathan looked at Henry, and Henry looked at Jonathan. Neither could come up with an answer. Listening to Solomon speak made the two men understand the brilliance in which so many others had admired for years.

"We will represent this case to the Supreme Court, and all that we can do is hope that there are enough white people out there with the compassion of Jonathan here," Solomon said.

Solomon walked the two men to the door. Henry peeked around Solomon again, and saw Summer and Sunshine give them the thumbs-up in approval.

After Henry and Jonathan left, Sunshine made Solomon a cup of hot tea and listened as he informed them of the two strangers' visit. He would have preferred a hot cup of cocoa, but he had given it up years earlier for health reasons. They listened, and never gave a hint that he had been snookered.

The Argument began in March of 2008. With Solomon at the helm, Henry and Jonathan occupied themselves researching the Supreme Court civil rights cases. Nights became days, and days became nights. They worked around the clock, and the stress took its toll on Solomon. He collapsed in his study one afternoon, and Sunshine discovered him a short time later. Henry asked him to relax until it was time for the Supreme Court hearing. Solomon didn't think he would have the strength to complete the trial, not to mention the numerous death threats he had received, but he had involved himself too much to turn back.

They began their opening statements with case after case of U.S. Supreme Court civil rights trials: *Hirabayashi v. United States* (the World War II Japanese curfew); *Brown v. Board of Education I & II* (segregated schools); Irene *Morgan v. Virginia* (a woman arrested, tried, and convicted for not giving up her seat on a bus, prior to Rosa Parks); *Shelly v. Kramer* (racially restricted housing); and *Loving v. Virginia* (interracial marriage).

Then they proceeded into the Affirmative Action and Voting Rights cases. *Nixon I & II* (Texas election voting cases); *Regents of the University of California v. Bakke* (affirmative action); and finally, *Gratz vs. The University of Michigan* (affirmative action academic enrollment discrimination to a white student).

He specifically used the 1978 case of the *Regents of the University of California (at Davis) v Bakke*. Bakke was a white man, who like Gratz, Hamacher, and Gutter sued on the basis of reversed discrimination. He claimed that the School of Medicine at the University of California at Davis, which was designed to assure the admission of a specified number of students from certain minority groups, violated his civil rights by denying him admission. Even though his credentials academically surpassed some of the minority students who were accepted. The Supreme Court of California held the admissions program unlawful, enjoined the petitioner from considering the race of any applicant, and ordered Bakke's admission. This was the first case to challenge affirmative action.

As the trial proceeded in the weeks to come, Henry broke down the various issues with the Supreme Court ruling of the Voting Rights Act. On one occasion he went on to explain a myth that was spread around in the late 1990s about black people losing their rights to vote. The scare began when a story suggested that the Voting Rights Act of 1965 was not a law, but just as it proclaimed, an act! The story also suggested that the Voting Rights Act was never passed into law. And in 1982, then President Ronald Reagan amended the Voting Rights Act for another twenty-five years. Black peoples' right to vote would supposedly expire in the year 2007, if Congress and the approval of thirty-eight states did not extend it for another twenty-five years. He read a version of the story which was circulated through email to the Supreme Court and everyone listened in total silence.

The subject matter read, "VOTE OR LOSE IN 2007", "WE HAVE A LONG WAY TO GO!" And also, "BLACKS CAN LOSE VOTING RIGHTS IN 2007" with an attached message encouraging the addressee to forward the information to as many people as possible. He went on to read the following message:

"And I quote, 'I am wondering if anyone out here knows what the significance of the year 2007 is to black people? Did you know that the right to vote will expire in the year 2007? Seriously! The Voters Rights Act signed in 1965 by Lyndon B. Johnson was just an ACT. It was not made a LAW!!!! In 1982 Ronald Reagan amended the Voters Rights Act for only another twenty-five years. Which means that in the year 2007 we could lose the right to vote! Does anyone realize that blacks/African-Americans are the only group of people who require PERMISSION under the United States Constitution to vote? In the year 2007 Congress will once again convene to decide whether or not blacks should retain the right to vote (crazy, but true). In order for this to be passed, 38 states will have to approve an extension. In my opinion and many others, this is ludicrous! Not only should the extension be approved, but also the Act must be made a law. Our right to vote should no longer be up for discussion, review and/or evaluation. We must contact our congresspersons, senators, alderpersons, etc., to put a stop to this! We have come too far to let the government make such a huge step backward. As bonafide citizens of the United States, we can not drop the ball on this one! So please, let us push forward to continue building the momentum towards gaining equality. I urge all of you that are able, to contact those in government that have your vote and will be voting on this issue.' End quote," Henry stated.

He went on to admit that although this story was a hoax, the events of the day had proven that it wasn't far from predicting the outcome for the year 2007. He went on to explain that according to United States Department of Justice, the 15th Amendment to the Constitution and the Voting Rights Act of 1965 guarantee that no person can be prohibited from voting because of race or color. Lawmakers in 1982 did, however, add revisions to the Voting Rights Act to extend through the year of 2007. Items to include: circumstances of bans on poll taxes. Another was allowing the government to register voters if the local registrars of the voters refused to do it themselves. Also, the monitoring of elections where they might be a situation where all voters were not being permitted to vote.

He explained that both acts were laws of Congress, and that there were no limitations to the extent of their existence. And that in the original

Constitution, thirty-eight states were required to vote and pass the decision for voting rights. But this did not apply to the Voting Rights Act of 1965. And the 15th Amendment once again protects everyone from discriminatory race and color in reference to voting. However, he also explained that by there being no limitations to the extent of the existence of the Voting Rights Act, and the 15th Amendment, they could last forever, or as recent events had proven, be whittled away with time.

One afternoon, as the trial neared its end, Solomon received an emergency telephone call and had to leave the courtroom. He was greeted by three detectives who rushed him into a waiting car to drive him home.

As the detectives led Solomon into his home, he was wondering what could have happened to cause him to leave during the middle of a U.S. Supreme Court session. Once he saw Sunshine standing in the doorway, he breathed a deep sigh of relief.

CHAPTER SEVENTEEN

The detectives walked Solomon into his living room, and helped him into his chair. They knew they had been moving pretty fast, and they wanted him to catch his breath. Sunshine sat on the couch across from him and asked him if he was feeling all right. He answered that he was feeling fine, then in his old cranky way, demanded to know what could be so important to call him away from the U.S. Supreme Court.

Sunshine held his hand, and told him that Orabell was sick and not expected to make it through the night. Solomon was unaware that she had been taken to the hospital, or that she was severely sick. Orabell made Michelle promise not to tell him because she did not want to raise his blood pressure. Michelle felt that if she contacted her mother instead of her father she would not be breaking her promise. She didn't feel comfortable talking to her father anyway, so that situation worked itself out.

Sunshine had already packed Solomon's bag, so as soon as she told him about Orabell, they were off to the airport.

Michelle had already notified Summer, and she was on her way to Michigan to be with Orabell. Summer arrived at the hospital a few hours after Michelle had called Sunshine. She was in Minnesota attending a conference when her office contacted her and told her that her grandmother was near death. She cancelled her trip, and went to Michigan immediately.

Michelle had admitted Orabell into the hospital three days earlier. She and her daughter, Bria, had rushed to Saginaw after not being able to reach

Orabell by telephone. Michelle made the five-hour drive from Chicago in three and change. She arrived to find Orabell lying on the floor unable to move. Her eyes were glassy and her speech was incoherent.

Orabell had suffered a mild stroke, but most of the damage occurred due to the fact that the stroke had gone untreated. Her blood was clotted so badly, and her heart was so weak, that by the time medical help arrived all that they could was make her last days comfortable.

Orabell drifted in and out of consciousness. She was not aware that she was so ill. She made Michelle promise not to tell Solomon until she was out of the hospital. The doctors broke the news to Michelle that her grandmother would never leave the hospital alive. Her heart was barely beating, and her lungs were breathing with the assistance of an oxygen machine. Summer arrived and walked in, and saw Michelle and Bria asleep, lying in the bed beside Orabell. She tapped Michelle on her feet, and woke her up.

"Wake up, sleepy head," Summer whispered.

"Hey, girl, when did you get here?" Michelle yawned.

"Just now," Summer answered. "How's Grandma?"

"Let's go outside and talk."

Michelle followed Summer into the hallway and told her the news.

"She's not going to make it, Summer," Michelle said, staring into the room.

"Is that what the doctors said?"

"She's only alive now because they have her on those damn machines."

"Is she conscious?" Summer asked.

"In and out." Michelle sighed. "Mostly out."

"How are you holding up, Michelle?"

"I really don't know. I felt like I had to keep things in order until Daddy got here, and then I can cry all I want."

"Oh Michelle, you don't have to hold anything down until Dad gets here," Summer said, hugging Michelle and rubbing her back.

"Why don't you take Bria home and you two get cleaned up. I'll stay here and hold down the fort." Summer smiled.

"Yeah, a good fresh shower will do both of us some good."

"Get on out of here, girl. If anything changes I'll give you a call, OK?"

"OK."

Michelle took Bria to Orabell's to get her cleaned up and get her some hot food. While she was gone, it was Summer's turn to lie in the bed with Orabell. She kicked her shoes off and stretched her legs alongside the short, feeble old woman. As she closed her eyes, and prepared herself for sleep, she heard the faint whisper of Orabell's voice calling out to her.

"Summer, baby, what you doin' here?" Orabell sighed.

"I just came to check on you, young lady. How are you feeling?" Summer cried, holding back her tears.

"I thought I was doin' fine, but if you here I must not be doin' as good as I think."

"Oh, you're doing fine, Grandma," Summer said.

"Naw. Not this time. I feel tired, but that's it."

"I told you you're fine."

"Baby, can you do your Grandmama a favor?"

"Sure, Grandma, anything."

"Can you take me home?"

"Grandma, you are in no condition to be moving anywhere."

"Please, baby," Orabell cried. "Don't let me die in here."

Summer wiped away the tears falling from the sides of Orabell's eyes.

"OK, Grandma," Summer cried along with her. "If that's what you want."

Summer called Michelle and told her that Orabell wanted to go home. The first couple of times she called Michelle she reached her voicemail, until finally Bria answered the telephone.

"Hello," Bria said.

"Hey, Bri, this is your Aunt Summer. Is your mother around?"

"Yes, she's in the shower."

"Can you tell her to come to the phone; it's an emergency."

"OK," Bria said. "Mo-mmy! Aunt Summer says hurry up and come to the telephone!"

Michelle rushed to Bria, and snatched the telephone out of her hands.

"What's the matter?" Michelle shouted into the telephone.

"Grandma wants us to bust her out of this joint!" Summer laughed.

"Are you crazy? She's too sick to move."

"Well, I can use your help, but I don't need it," Summer said.

"Girl, you can't move Grandma!"

"Watch me."

"OK, you stubborn thing. Here I come," Michelle snapped. "You and Grandma are the two most stubborn women I have ever met in my life!"

"Don't forget you, and your mother." Summer laughed.

"Fruitcake!" Michelle yelled.

"I love you, too!"

Michelle went back to the hospital, then she and Summer had Orabell released from the hospital. They were warned that if they took her home, she would probably die within a few hours without oxygen. They told the doctor they understood the risks, but Orabell wanted to go home, and home was where she was going.

An ambulance drove Orabell back to her house, and set up a temporary oxygen tank. She lay in her own bed unconscious, yet peaceful. Summer and Michelle played cards at her feet to keep their minds occupied. They would periodically check on Orabell to see if she was breathing. She looked as if she was taking one of her regular naps.

A few hours later, Sunshine called and told them they were in Flint, and on their way to the hospital. Summer told them that they had brought Orabell home at her request. Twenty-five minutes later, Solomon sped into the driveway and as fast as his old bow legs could carry him, he ran into the house.

"Where's Mama?" Solomon asked.

Michelle walked outside and sat on the porch.

"She's in her bedroom, Dad," Summer answered.

Solomon walked into Orabell's room and saw the oxygen mask clinging to her face. He called out to her but she did not answer. He grabbed her hand, and shook it, but she didn't respond. He knelt beside her bed, and buried his in her chest. Sunshine walked in, and saw Solomon weeping over his mother, then turned around and walked back out. She quietly closed the door, and asked her daughters not to disturb until he came out.

Shortly after midnight, Solomon walked out and covered each of his women. All of them were piled in the living room asleep. As he placed a blanket on Michelle, he stared at her for an instant, then kissed her on her forehead.

"I love you so much, little girl," Solomon said, rubbing her cheek.

After he made sure everyone was nice and warm, he went back into his mother's room and laid his old, long body against the hard, cold floor. Sunshine woke as Solomon was going back into his mother's room. She wrapped her blanket in her arms and followed her husband into Orabell's bedroom.

"I'll come in here with you, but I'm not gettin' on that floor," Sunshine said, folding herself into a small chair.

"I'm still down here, because I can't get up." Solomon laughed, rolling over on his back.

"I wish I could help you up, but there's nothing I can do with your big ol' butt."

"Do you think Ma is going to wake up?" Solomon asked.

"I don't know, baby," Sunshine answered. "But look at her over there sleeping so peacefully."

"Looks like she will wake up at any time, doesn't it?"

"Sure does, baby."

"Well, let's try to get some sleep. Who knows what tomorrow is going to bring."

"Go to sleep, baby, and let the good Lord worry about Ma."

"Good night, sweetheart," Solomon spoke.

"Good night."

It didn't take them long before they were both asleep. Summer and Michelle routinely checked in on their grandmother to see if her condition had improved or worsened. Every time they checked, they found that there had been no change. She was still lying in the same position they had placed her in when they had brought her home from the hospital.

Around four-thirty in the morning, Sunshine heard moaning coming from Orabell, and she kicked Solomon until he was awake. When he realized what was going on, he raised up quickly, and nearly popped every bone in his body.

"Mama! Mama!" Solomon said, patting Orabell's hand.

"Solomon, is that you, son?"

"Yes, Mama, it's me!"

"I didn't think you was gon' make it, son, but here you is."

"Yes, I'm here, Ma."

"Is Sunshine here, too?" Orabell sighed

Sunshine raised herself from the chair and slowly made her way over to Orabell.

"I'm here, Ma."

"Oh, baby." Orabell smiled. "My Sunshine is here, too."

"Yeah, Ma, I'm here."

"I love you, baby."

"I love you too, Ma."

"Solomon?" Orabell cried out.

"I'm right here, Ma."

"I know, son."

"You know what, Ma?"

"I know God's plan for you."

"OK, Mama. Get you some rest."

"Listen to me, son," Orabell whispered, gasping for air. "I done came as far as I could wit' you. It's time fa me to get some rest. Yo' time has come, Solomon, and my time, my time is done. You don't need me no more. It's time fo' you to face yo' destiny. Yo' whole life was made for this case, son. This is what folks been tellin' you all the time."

"No, Mama, you'll be fine; just get you a little rest, and you'll be fine."

Sunshine covered her face with her hands and cried. Solomon reached and sat Orabell up in a desperate attempt to keep her from falling back to sleep.

"Now what y'all cryin' fo?" Orabell said. "Take care of my boy, Sunshine; take care o' my boy. Take care o' my boy."

"Mama! Mama, don't you leave me!" Solomon shouted.

Solomon's shouting woke Michelle and Summer and they ran into

Orabell's room. They walked in and saw Solomon and Sunshine crying over Orabell.

"What's going on?" Michelle asked.

Neither Sunshine nor Solomon answered.

"Mama, you can't leave me, Mama!" Solomon cried.

"Son, I don't feel no mo' pain." Orabell sighed. "Let me rest, please, just let me..."

"Mama, you're not going anywhere!" Solomon cried, rocking his mother in his arms. "Just hold on, Mama; everything will be all right."

"Our Time Has Come, Solomon!" Orabell whispered. "Our Time Has Come! Our Time...Has Come!"

At the ripe old age of 93, Orabell Moore Chambers, closed her eyes, and rested forever. Closing the last chapter of the Chambers' migration from Mississippi to Michigan. Isaiah, Stanford, William and now Orabell had all perished to time. The fulfillment of Alexander Chambers' prophecy solely relied on the shoulders of a sixty-eight-year-old man who didn't care whether he was black, white, or yellow, so long as he was successful.

"Mama?" Solomon cried. "Mama!"

Solomon kept raising Orabell's head for a response, and each time her head dropped back into her bosom. After seeing her father cry this way, Michelle could not help but release her emotions. She lay across her grandmother's legs and wept uncontrollably.

"She's gone, Solomon," Sunshine cried.

"No! No! No!" Solomon shouted. "Mama, wake up! Wake up, Mama! Please, wake up!"

Michelle raised from Orabell's legs and lay across her chest.

"Mama, I love you so much! Don't leave me, Mama! Please! Please! Please!" Michelle cried.

Summer managed to pull Michelle away from Orabell's body, and walk her into the living room. They sat on the couch and cried in each other's arms.

Sunshine sat beside Orabell and tried to break Solomon's grip on her body, but she could not.

"She's gone, baby, let her rest," Sunshine pleaded.

"No baby, she's gonna wake up!" Solomon cried.

"She's gone, baby. She's gone," Sunshine whispered, wrapping her arms around him as he finally released his grip on his mother.

"I'm going to miss you, Mama." Solomon sighed. "I'm going to miss you."

"We all are, baby; we all are."

Three days later, Orabell was laid to rest in Forest Lawn Cemetery. She split the value of her property in Mississippi between the immediate four remaining family members: Solomon, Sunshine, Michelle, and Summer. She divided her personal assets in Michigan between Michelle and Summer evenly, including her modest bank account, her house, and everything within its walls. Summer was overwhelmed by Orabell's generosity. She knew that Orabell loved her dearly, but she could not understand that even with the kindest heart, a person could be as generous in death as they were in life.

The family made it through Orabell's death and tried to move forward. Incredibly, throughout the painful ordeal, Solomon and Michelle did not utter one word, or offer one sign of condolence to the other.

Throughout the trial the media coverage increased on a daily basis. They went as far as to transmit the case live on the internet for those online. Everyone was aware of every word said in the courtroom. As the case approached its conclusion, the country paused in its widespread violence and chaotic behavior and to focus on the decision of the Supreme Court.

Solomon tried his best to stay out of the spotlight. Henry did most of the talking, both in and out of court. Solomon was content with advising the team on how they should present the case, and not getting too involved.

During the trial, Henry and Solomon developed a father and son relationship. Henry moved out of the hotel room and moved in with Solomon and Sunshine. On the days when Solomon was ailing, Henry would be at his side until he was feeling better. The Sunday before the closing statements, Henry joined Solomon and Sunshine at an afternoon church sermon. When they were leaving, people greeted them, and praised them for standing up against the government. As they approached the street corner, Henry noticed a vehicle with dark tinted windows slow down and head towards them. He cautiously watched as the front passenger window rolled down.

He stopped, and held his arms in front of Sunshine and Solomon to stop them as well.

"Mr. Chambers," Henry said.

"Yes, son."

"Mr. Chambers, get back in the church, hurry!"

"What's the matter, Henry?" Sunshine asked.

"Mrs. Chambers, get down! Get down!" Henry screamed.

Tat! Tat! Tat! Tat! Tat! Tat! The bullets scattered within the crowd. The car sped off spinning its wheels, and screeching down the road.

On the ground, Henry lay on top of Solomon and Sunshine trying to shield them as best he could. A few feet away a child lay on the ground in agonizing pain from a gunshot wound to the leg. Her mother screamed hysterically for someone to call an ambulance. A man ripped off his shirt and wrapped it around the girl's leg until the ambulance arrived.

Henry rolled off of Solomon and Sunshine, and they slowly stood to their feet. Solomon looked around and witnessed the chaotic situation he had caused. He knew those bullets were meant for him. He held Sunshine's elbow to keep her stable. She was visibly shaken from the ordeal. Henry was still lying on the ground staring in disbelief. Solomon reached down to give him a hand, and offer support. But he didn't move, he continued to stare with his eyes and mouth wide open.

"Son, are you all right?" Solomon asked.

"I don't think so, sir," Henry muttered.

"Henry!" Sunshine said, as she kneeled beside him. She sat him up, and blood quickly turned his nicely pressed white shirt into a dark red rag. "Oh my God!" Sunshine shouted as she dropped Henry's body back to the ground.

"Lord no, not again! Not again!" Solomon cried. "No, not this time."

Solomon struggled to lift Henry, but he managed to carry him to his car. Sunshine and others followed behind him. Sunshine jumped in the back seat with Henry and placed his head in her lap, and talked to him all the way to the hospital. Solomon sped to the hospital's emergency ward and carried Henry into a room himself. It wasn't until the nurse inquired of Henry's injuries that Solomon realized he was short of breath. He couldn't stand up erect, and he couldn't speak a word. They gave him an oxygen tank to stabilize his breathing. Sunshine paced back and forth between the two rooms to make sure both men were doing all right. Once the hospital officials were made aware that Solomon Chambers and Henry Lee were patients, they immediately alerted security and isolated them from the general public. After Solomon regained his breath, he demanded to be taken to Henry. They put him in a wheelchair and carried him to Henry. As they stopped in the hallway, Sunshine was watching through the window as they poked and filled Henry's youthful body with cords and wires. He slipped into unconsciousness, and the doctors were not very optimistic that he would ever awake. After they stabilized his condition Sunshine and Solomon sat at his bedside and talked to him.

"Look at him, barely old enough to know what life is all about," Sunshine cried.

"He's going to wake up, Sunshine. I know he is," Solomon said.

"Let's pray to God he does."

"You know, Ol' Lady, when I look at Henry lying on this bed, I don't feel sadness. What I feel inside is envy. It may be selfish of me, but this young man has done everything he ever wanted to do. If he died right now, God can only be proud of him. And here I am an old man who hides behind his career to shield a lifetime of cowardly behavior."

"Stop that foolish talk, Solomon. There's not a lot of sixty-eight-year-old men who could have withstood what you've been through the last year with this trial."

Solomon didn't respond. He just stared at Henry as he lay on the bed motionless.

"I talked to Michelle today; she told me to tell you hello," Sunshine said.

"Umph," Solomon grunted.

"It's time for you to call her, Ol' Man."

"After all this time, I don't even know what to say."

"You can start off by saying you love her."

"Michelle knows I love her, Ol' Lady."

"How do you know that, unless you ask, or unless you tell her?"

"I miss her so much, it hurts."

"Then stop the hurt from hurting, and call your child."

"Looks like I'll have to give the closing statement now. Do you think she will come if I ask?"

"You never know unless you ask."

As Solomon was about to respond, Jonathan burst through the door, and ran to Henry's side. He sat on the side of the bed and held his hand. Lying in the bed was his friend who protected him from grade school throughout college. He helped him through law school, and also got him a job in his law firm once he passed the bar. Jonathan was beside himself with grief. He felt vulnerable seeing Henry unconscious, and not being able to help him. Sunshine rubbed his back as he cried convulsively. Watching Jonathan's grief strengthened Solomon's resolve to complete the closing statement.

"What are we going to do now?" Jonathan asked.

"What do you mean what are we going to do?" Solomon asked. "We are going to make the Supreme Court understand that even if they shoot us, or beat us, they will not defeat us! Because they don't have enough bullets, and they don't have enough bats to keep us from coming at them."

"I'm ready. I'm ready right now!" Jonathan cried.

"Our time is coming, son, our time is coming," Solomon said.

The next morning Henry regained consciousness. Although he could understand what was being said to him, he could not speak in response. He was informed that he had been shot in his back and it had shattered his spine. He would be a quadriplegic for the remainder of his life.

He tried desperately to communicate with his nurse, but he was not strong enough to convey what he was thinking. His question was answered when Solomon walked through the door. He wanted to know if Solomon had survived the gunshots. When he saw Solomon's face, a tear ran down the side of his face. He knew that as long as Solomon was alive, so was the chance for equality. He blinked his eyes rapidly to let Solomon know he was happy to see him.

They developed a system of communication for Henry to convey his thoughts. He would blink his eyes as many as times as the letter was numbered in the alphabet. For example, the letter "a" was one blink. And the letter "l" was twelve blinks. It was a slow method, but it was effective. As they communicated with each other, Henry told Solomon he had no ill feelings toward anyone, including the shooters, who had been captured. Henry told Solomon that he put his life on the line knowing that it may be taken at any moment. But if his life was lost as a result of others being saved, he'd have to consider his life a blessing and accept death humbly.

Henry would spend the next ten months in the hospital rehabilitating. During his rehabilitation, he would leave the hospital once, to travel to Saginaw to see Solomon. He learned to speak again, but as the doctors diagnosed, he never walked another day in his life.

When Summer watched the evening news, she couldn't believe her eyes when she saw that Henry and Solomon had been shot. She tracked Sunshine down, and Sunshine cleared up the media's mistake. She told her that Henry was severely injured but Solomon was fine. Sunshine explained that she should probably come to support her father during his closing arguments because he would need all the help he could get.

Shortly thereafter, Michelle called Summer and asked if she had heard that their father had been shot. Summer was furious that Michelle called her first instead of calling their father personally.

"Michelle, this has got to stop," she said. It was time for the nonsense to cease.

"I don't know what you mean, Summer."

"You know exactly what I mean. Your father could have been killed yesterday, and you're still holding some stupid grudge."

"I don't know what you're talking about."

"Hold on a second, Michelle. I have a call on the other line." Summer switched lines and called Sunshine. She waited for her to pick up before she switched back over to Michelle's line.

"Hello," Sunshine answered.

"Mother, this is Summer. I have your daughter on the line and she wants to know how Daddy is doing. What do you think I should tell her?"

"You tell her that if she can be so prideful as to not call her father when someone tried to kill him, she doesn't need to know how he's doing."

"Ma, it has nothing to do with pride. If Daddy wanted to talk to me, he would call me sometimes. But I never receive a telephone call, do I?"

"I don't believe you. You're a forty-four-year-old woman, and you're still acting like a four-year-old brat. Now you listen to me, and you listen to me good. Your father needs you, and you better hop yourself on a plane and come to him. And quit with this nonsense!"

"Mama, I…"

"Don't Mama me!" Sunshine interrupted. "Get yo' ass on a plane and get down here as fast as you can!"

"I'll try, Mama." Michelle sighed. "I am in Michigan gathering some of Grandma's things."

"No, you won't try; you are going to do it! I am not your father, so don't even try to run that guilt trip on me because I got over the guilt a long time ago. If you hadn't been so stubborn growing up, you could have come to live with us at any time, so if you want to blame somebody, blame yourself."

The line became silent until Summer sarcastically said, "Thanks, Mommy."

"No problem, sweetie. See you in a day or two," Sunshine said. "Bye, Michelle."

"Bye, Ma." Michelle sobbed.

Sunshine hung up the telephone, and Michelle and Summer resumed their conversation.

"Why did you call her, Summer?" Michelle snapped.

"Because if you're going to act like a child, your mother needs to treat you like a child."

"I'm getting ready to go. Bye!"

"See you in Washington." Summer laughed.

"Bitch!" Michelle snarled.

"I love you, too, dear." Summer laughed again, then hung up the telephone.

CHAPTER EIGHTEEN

The next couple of days were hectic for all of the Chambers family, but finally, the eve of the trial had arrived. Solomon's house was smothered with local and federal agents. He received permission to enter the courtroom, to have private time for his case. But he really needed the time for meditation, and prayer. He sat in the courtroom, tired and exhausted.

Summer was scheduled to arrive in Washington, D.C. early the next morning in time to make the closing statements, but avoid the media harassment. She said it would be best if she did not bring the children, because she didn't want them to be subjected to a barrage of questions the media might ask.

Michelle was sitting in her grandmother's living room, going over a lot of their family's memorabilia. She had pulled a trunk from the basement, and inside was a dusty little box with her grandfather's name on it. Inside she discovered a stack of his old speeches. She sat on the floor, and placed them between her legs. The paper had turned brown, but they were in pretty good condition. As she read she became entranced with Isaiah's foresight of life. She felt that he was way ahead of his time.

She began to wonder why her father never spoke of her grandfather, and it made her think of her relationship with Solomon. She ran across a book titled, *The Chambers Family Bible, Our Time Has Come.* She sat and read most of it, then thought to herself, *here it is in the year of our Lord 2008, and my father has yet to add his generation's verse to the family's Bible. He is a* sixty-eight-year-old man and his opportunity to pass the Bible to me with his verse inscribed is rapidly decreasing.

My father does not believe in the prophecy as my grandfather, and great-grand-father. He believes in today, and making the most of it. He wants his legacy to be remembered for what he has done as a scholar, and professional, and not as a martyr, or activist. He does not believe in the struggle for the advancement of black people. He believes that every man should make his own way through education regardless of the circumstances. He believes that success is colorblind; all that it sees is determination and hard work. Any circumstance can be overcome by determination and hard work. I adamantly disagree with my father. I believe that success, first of all, is a relative word. I think that one can dream of success, but when one arrives at the reality, he has lost so much of himself that the passion for success has turned into a mere achievement.

My father has a lifetime of achievements; certificates, honorary degrees, memorials, foundations. If you can think of any outstanding award that is bestowed upon a human being, my father has one somewhere with his name on it.

He is one of the most famous attorneys in the United States. His name alone is said to have settled cases without ever going into litigation. This man, is my father.

A man of strong character, and resiliency. He has suffered as all men have suffered. But through all of his sufferings, he emerges a stronger and more determined man than he was before his crisis. A trailblazer in the field of law for African-Americans who follow in his footsteps. A title he publicly denounces. He is called a paramount of an attorney not just for African-Americans, but all Americans. When asked of his contributions to law, he humbly refers to Thurgood Marshall and says, "Without his contributions, there would be no place for my own." This is my father.

At this hour, my father is doing what he has done his entire life. Searching for the perfect solution to his current problem. This time the issue he faces is greater than any other he has faced in his life. For the issue is not about losing or winning a case. It is not about the prestige of his name, or his crafty courtroom tactics. It is not about awards, certificates, or foundations. It is about an issue he has eluded, and escaped for sixty-eight years. It is time for my father to relinquish his past, and embrace his future. The time has come for my father to face his ultimate nemesis, himself.

Michelle's thoughts were interrupted by the ringing of the telephone. "Hello," Michelle said.

SPRING, WASHINGTON, D.C., 2008

An old man sat in a courtroom talking to Solomon Chambers about his significance to black people in America. He had come all the way from Mississippi after being released from prison for serving a sixty-eight-year prison term.

"I came to tell you about a man. But befo' I tell you 'bout anybody else, do you know who you are?" the old man asked. "I ain't talkin' 'bout you bein' no lawyer. Do you know who you is inside? If not, you need to think. Think, son! Before I go any furtha."

"Of course I know who I am. I am Solomon Chambers," Solomon answered.

"Naw, son, let me tell you who you is. In the sprang of 19 and 40. I was at the railroad depot in Derma County, Mississippi. Ya see we used to all time hang out there helping white folks load and unload they bags. One e'ning, there was a colored man sittin' on the train; white folks pulled him off for no reason. I remember how they threw a sack over his head, and drug him to the back. Most of the colored folks ran, but I stayed. I hid underneath a bush, so they couldn't see me. I saw 'em; I saw 'em beat that man, and they beat that man. They beat that man with sticks, and bats. They stabbed him with knives. Poured gasoline and hot boiling tar all over his body, and set him to fire. They drug his body by a rope all the way to the front of the depot and hung him up to a pole for all us colored folks to see." The old man sat down and used his thumb to wipe his tears away.

"And all while they tortured that man, he never hollud one time. Not one time. Imagine if somebody had done all those thangs to you, son. The man never once screamed. I'm sorry, yes he did. When he was lyin' on that ground, I looked at him. I looked at him dead in his eyes, and I could feel his pain, even when he couldn't. He somehow moved his hand at me, and I knew he was telling me to get outta there. So I ran, and when I ran somebody heard me, 'cause I heard somebody come runnin' toward me. But the man let out a scream so that they would know that he wasn't dead. And he could take a little more from them. When he screamed, the footsteps stopped, and turned around and went back toward him. But he screamed not 'cause they was hurtin' him, but to save my life.

"I got away from 'em, and I told my mama and daddy what I saw. They told me they was going to have to get me out of town. Quick! But they wasn't quick enough. Later that night, they bust opened our do'. My daddy got up and tried to fight him off, but it was too many and they beat him wit' a shotgun. They beat my mama up, and locked her in the closet. Then they tied a rope around my neck and drugged me to a tree. They put one end around a branch, and the other around my throat. They kep' on askin' me to give 'em the name of the people they saw. I kep' telling' I didn't see nothin' but they keep pullin' that rope harder. It got so tight around my neck, I passed out. When I woke up, I was in another county, locked up forever. Ain't seen nor heard from my mama and daddy since that day."

"I'm sorry, sir," Solomon said.

"What ya feel sorry for me fa?" the old man shouted. "I didn't come here for no pity. I came here to tell you about freedom. It ain't nothin' you gon' find in yo' lawyer books. You see, Solomon, you can't teach freedom, and you can't learn freedom. You either free, or you ain't! Can't nobody make you free; you got to make yo'self free. 'cause as long as you live, somebody, somewhere, gon' have tell you what to do. Freedom don't mean you run around actin' uncivilized; it mean you do what is in your heart, and in yo' mind, and you be willin' to face whatever it is you have to face to stand by yo' belief. If it's yo' job, yo' woman, whatever it is, freedom is believin' what you think is right, and then livin' yo' life as you believe. When you step befo' them judges tomorra, don't you think fo' a second that if they give colored folks back the right to vote, or they don't, that they can give you freedom, or not. You already free, 'cause you know you right, and it ain't nothin' they can do 'bout it. Just like the man at that railroad depot; it wasn't nothin' they could do to take that man freedom from him. They beat him, they stabbed him, they burned him, and then they hung him, and when he died, he died the same he lived, with pride and dignity!"

"You have been a blessed source of inspiration. Thank you, and may God be with you," Solomon said, as the old man stood up and turned to walk away. "Excuse me, sir, whatever happened to the men who killed the stranger?"

"Nothin' that I know of. And that man, that man was no stranger. That man was yo' daddy," the old man said walking away.

"Excuse me?" Solomon asked startled.

"I said that man was no stranger; that man was yo' daddy," the old man repeated.

"I'm afraid you're mistaken. My father was Isaiah Chambers, and he was shot and killed in Mississippi," Solomon said.

"Yo' daddy was, and is, Isaiah Chambers, and he was not shot and killed. He was beaten, burned, and hung, and I know because I saw with my own two eyes! Is that what you thought all these years, that yo' daddy was shot?" the old man shouted.

"My mother told me that he was shot and killed on his way back from visiting Mississippi. Your story is very interesting, but the man of whom you are speaking could not possibly be my father," Solomon said.

"Boy, listen to me; that was yo' daddy I saw killt that night. And if he could take a death like that for freedom, sho'lly you can stand befo' a court. I know it may seem scary. Even for an old pro like yourself. Hell, we all scared! I was scared just to walk out my prison gate. 'cause this world done changed since I was outside. When they locked me up, it wasn't no planes flyin' over my head like this here. Wasn't no televisions, or no phones you can carry around in your pockets. This is like outer space to me. But you know what, Solomon, I'm free. Oh, yes I am! I am free. And if I woulda died on my way up here to see you, I woulda died a free man. 'cause I'm doin' what I know I'm s'pose to be doing, and that make me free. We all got a cross to bear, Solomon, and I just carried mine all the way from Calhoun City, Mississippi to Washington, D.C. Now it's up to you to pick it up and carry it to freedom. Your time has come, son; our time has come," the old man said, then quietly walked out of the courtroom.

Solomon watched as the old man slowly took one step at a time, leaning on his cane, until he disappeared.

On the drive home, Solomon stopped by the supermarket to pick up some fruit and vegetables for dinner. He was two hours late so he figured he would have to cook for himself. He passed a gallery of fast-food restaurants, and drooled over the greasy aroma of fried food lingering into his car. He was exhausted and he knew that his wife was not going to cook for him at that late hour. He considered stopping by one of the restaurants; it had been nearly thirty years since he had eaten a piece of meat. Although the thought entered his mind, he knew that being a vegetarian was much more important than any temptation.

Solomon reached in his console, and using his touch remote, he dialed his mother's house.

"Hello," Michelle answered.

"Hello, Michelle, it's your father," Solomon spoke.

"How did you know I was at Grandma's?"

"Word travels quick. Aren't you coming? I thought you would have been here by now."

"I'm not sure if I'm going to be able to make it, Daddy. I'm reading a very good book and I have to finish it," Michelle replied.

"What do you mean, you have to wait to finish a book?" Solomon stuttered. "Are you telling me that book is more important than I am?"

"Honestly, Daddy, I didn't think you cared if I came or not."

"What?" Solomon laughed. "You are still my daughter, aren't you?"

"Am I?" Michelle answered back. "I thought that maybe you would rather be with your other daughter, the white one, on the eve of your big day."

"Baby, what are you talking about?" Solomon sighed.

"I am talking about Summer. All of my life, you have put me second to her, Daddy. All of my life! You raised her in your household, and you left me in Michigan," Michelle cried.

"I did not leave you, baby; you wanted to stay in Saginaw. You didn't want to come with us. You could have come to live with us at any time," Solomon pleaded.

"If you wanted me to come, you would have made me come; you're the parent, not me! You left the decision up to me, as a matter of convenience for your conscience."

"I don't understand, sweetheart. Why do you harbor so much animosity towards me, but not your mother?" Solomon asked.

"Because my mother never wanted your precious little white girl to come live with you in the first place. It was you who took her from her family in Vermont so that you could have your precious white daughter! It was you who adopted her! It was you who personally signed her birthday cards, while Mama forged your name on all of mine!" Michelle shouted.

"Honey, please, lower your voice," Solomon said.

"Let me ask you something, Daddy. Was it my dark skin that made you want to give me away? Do I remind you too much of yourself?"

"Michelle, I am your father, and I demand that you lower your voice!"

"You can't demand anything from me, Mr. Chambers. Perhaps you have me confused with your other daughter," Michelle ranted, then slammed the phone in Solomon's ear.

"Michelle! Michelle!" Solomon spoke into the phone.

He called her back, over and over again, but she would not answer. Finally, he gave up and left her a message.

"Michelle, I know you're there. I just wanted you to know that I am an old man, and I have made many mistakes in my life. Unfortunately, I can not go back in time and change them. However, I would run my car into a brick wall right now, just to hear you say you love me. Yes, I love Summer, but you are my daughter. You are my legacy. You are a Chambers. I think about you, and I wonder how you can feel so much hostility for your own father. I know how honey, because I have felt that same hostility toward my own father. I found out tonight..."

The answering service concluded its message time, then hung up. Solomon hit redial and Michelle's answering service picked up again.

"Michelle, it's me again. As I was saying, I found out tonight that my father was not shot and killed. He was beaten, stabbed, and burned at a train depot. Sixty-eight years baby, sixty-eight years I've held a grudge against my father because he wasn't there for me. I can't tell you how I feel right now for being so ridiculously selfish. But I will give you a bit of advice: don't waste the rest of your life resenting me, baby, because, some-how, someway, it will come back to haunt you someday. Well, that's all I have to say, honey. I'll talk to you whenever you can call me back. I love you," Solomon said.

"Daddy?" Michelle said, as she quickly picked up the telephone. "I love you, too."

"I know you do, sweetie. I know you do."

They paused waiting for the other one to speak.

"Bye-bye, Daddy," Michelle whispered.

"Bye, Angel," Solomon whispered back, holding the phone, wanting to ask her to come one more time.

On the other end Michelle held the phone, wanting to hear him ask her once more. As she reached to hang up the telephone, she heard her father's voice say, "Michelle."

She put the telephone back up to her ear and spoke, "Yes, Daddy."

"Baby, if you can, please, please, be there tomorrow." Solomon sighed.

"I'll try my best, Daddy," ichelle answered back.

"OK then, I hope to see you tomorrow."

"Hopefully."

"Bye," Solomon said. holding the telephone tightly.

"Bye, Daddy," Michelle said for the last time, then hung up the phone. She picked up an book full of old papers. She threw her coat over her arms, clutched her airline ticket bound for Washington, and walked out of Orabell's house.

Solomon pulled into his driveway, and used his remote to open the old familiar first garage door, which was also the closest to the house. Policemen surrounded his house twenty-four hours a day to protect his family. They cleared him to park his car and they stood beside his door until he was out. He stepped out of his car, but instead of going into the house he walked down to his third garage, passing his new edition of the Mercedes-Benz that he drove to church on Sundays, and peeked in at his 1978 Caprice Classic. The police watched as he stared at his black, sunroof-top automobile with four-inch whitewalls and an eight-track player with an unknown eight track still inside. Solomon had not driven the car since he had first bought it. He thought the car was too flashy at the time, and inappropriate for an attorney.

"How are you doing, old friend?" Solomon said, rubbing the hood. "One day soon, I'm going to take you for a spin. You're tired of sitting up in here this garage, aren't you?"

He walked back into the house and Sunshine was sitting at the kitchen table waiting on him. Solomon walked into the house with his bag of fruit and vegetables clutched tight to his chest.

"Hey, Ol' Lady," Solomon said to his wife. "Thought you'd be sleep."

"You know I can't sleep with you having to go to court in the morning. I wish you would lie down and get you some sleep. You're going to bee so exhausted tomorrow, you won't be able to appear in front of the Supreme Court," Sunshine said.

"Oh no, like my mama used to say, it's all over but the shouting and the moaning." Solomon laughed. "I'm ready for anything they may throw at me."

"You need to get you some rest, Solomon," Sunshine stated again, taking the sack out of his hands. "Go upstairs and take those clothes off while I fix you a plate right quick."

Solomon sat down and sighed heavily to catch his breath. Sunshine fixed him a plate of food, and he slowly took his time to eat. They talked as he ate his meal, and he told her about his conversations with the old man, and their daughter. He was very upset about hearing the news that his father was murdered so tragically. Then to hear his daughter accuse him of neglecting her all of her life was unbearable. Sunshine did what she normally did when Solomon got down on himself. She fixed him a cup of cocoa, his only snack-food allowance. As he sipped his cocoa, Sunshine placed her head on his shoulders, and closed her eyes. They fell asleep in each other's arms, until Solomon woke up several hours later. Sunshine woke up and began to rub Solomon's hands. While she was rubbing his hands, Solomon glanced down, and he noticed the wrinkles in both of their arthritic hands. He took his hand, removed her silver hair from over her face and stared into her eyes.

"We're getting old. But when I look at your face, Ol' Lady, through my eyes, all that I see is that same smart-aleck, pretty little girl I met fifty years ago. I can't tell you the amount of times I have had to lean on you. You have been the strongest fixture in my life," Solomon said.

"Even stronger than Ms. Orabell?" Sunshine joked.

"Ask me no secrets, I'll tell you no lies." Solomon smiled.

"That's what I thought." Sunshine laughed.

"Well, that's my mama!" Solomon muttered.

"We need to get you in the bed so you can be fresh for tomorrow, Ol' Man."

"I'm not worried about that case anymore. It's in God's hands now, honey. No matter what happens in that courtroom tomorrow, I'll be coming back home to you. And I know that then, everything will be just fine." Solomon sighed.

"You'll be fine, Ol' Man. Go on down there to that courtroom and let all of those bigwigs know where you're from. Now let me hear it, baby, where you from?" Sunshine joked.

"I'm from Saginaw, Michigan! And these folks are about to find out what it's like to rile up a native of Sagnasty!" Solomon shouted. "Whoo! That hurts; I don't need to get all excited like that wit out taking my Geritol first, honey. Rub my elbow for me."

"You raise your voice, and your elbow hurts?" Sunshine asked, rubbing Solomon's elbow.

"Actually, when I raise my voice, everything hurts!" Solomon answered.

There was a loud knock at the door, Solomon jumped, and told Sunshine to go in the closet. She grabbed Solomon by the back of his robe, and stood behind him. Although he had grown old, Sunshine realized that her husband was still a big, and powerful, man. Solomon yelled at the person beyond the other side of the door to reveal themselves.

"Who is it?" Solomon yelled.

"It's your daughter, Daddy," Michelle shouted. "These goons won't let me in."

Solomon ran to the door and snatched it open.

"Let her in! Let her in!" Solomon shouted. "Baby, how did you get here so fast?"

"I was on my way to the airport when you called, Ol' Man." Michelle smiled.

Sunshine hugged Michelle and took her luggage out of her hands.

"Damn police! If you had been somebody trying to get us, we'd be dead!" Solomon grunted.

"Ready for your big day tomorrow, Ol' Man?" Michelle asked.

"I am now that you're here," Solomon said, closing his eyes, and giving her a long kiss on her forehead. "I am now."

"It took you long enough. I nearly passed out myself sitting up here trying to keep this boring old man awake. Well, there he is. I'm going to bed. I'll see you in the morning, baby," Sunshine said, kissing Michelle on her cheek.

Michelle poured hot water into a cup and made her favorite drink, which happened to be the same as her father's: cocoa. She pulled a chair close to her father, as she did as a child and sat down beside him.

"Good night, Mom," Michelle spoke.

"Oh, I get it. This was a set-up." Solomon laughed.

"Yup!" Michelle laughed, patting him on the hand.

Sunshine climbed the stairs to their bedroom and fell asleep.

"I can't begin to tell you how happy I am to see you, Michelle." Solomon smiled.

"It has been a long time, Daddy, too long," Michelle replied.

"Before you go any further, Summer is going to be in court tomorrow. I want you to be nice to her, OK?" Solomon asked.

"I have always been nice to Summer, Daddy; she is my sister. I was only mean to you." Michelle laughed. "Actually I look forward to seeing her."

"Now that's my daughter talking?" Solomon said, squeezing her nose.

"Yes, it is, and leave my nose alone." Michelle laughed, tapping her father's hand away from her nose.

"Well, you wanted me alone to tell me something, so come on, let's hear it."

"Daddy, let me hear the statement you have prepared for court tomorrow," Michelle said.

"OK," Solomon said.

He went into his study and returned with his notes. He laid them in front of Michelle, and she reached into her pocket and pulled out her reading glasses.

"You're a little young for those, aren't you, kiddo?" Solomon joked, pulling on Michelle's eyeglasses.

"Go get yours, while you're sitting here cracking jokes, Ol' Man," Michelle answered.

Solomon went back to his study, then he returned with his reading glasses. He sat down next to Michelle, and watched her as she read over his statement. He looked at her hair, and her neck, and thought of how much she resembled her mother when she was a younger woman. He could also see the gray streaks taking form. He looked at her, and an image of his young impressionable daughter appeared in front of him. He had not shared a moment like this with Michelle since she was a child. But then, it was Michelle, watching him going over her homework. Michelle read quietly for about thirty minutes as Solomon secretly dozed in and out of sleep, often dropping his chin to his chest. She pulled her glasses from her eyes, waking her father, and stacked his notes neatly on top of each other.

"Well, what do you think?" Solomon asked.

"Are you serious, Daddy?" Michelle said sarcastically.

"What?" Solomon asked back.

"Is this what you're going to present to the Supreme Court of the United States of America?" Michelle said, shaking her head, and thumbing through the stack of papers.

"What's wrong with it, honey?" Solomon asked, finally waking up, then sitting up straight.

"It has no passion, Daddy," Michelle replied. "Your words are articulately written, and eloquently spoken. But Daddy, you are talking about a race of people who have lost their right to vote, not a corporate criminal who misappropriated funds. Great words mean nothing if they are not supported with great passion. Ask yourself, Daddy, how do you feel about presenting this case to the Supreme Court, and not being privileged to vote? How does it feel to know that you are not considered an equal in the country where you have lived, and loved your entire life? How does it make you feel, Daddy? Angry? Sad? Frustrated? What?" Michelle urged.

"I don't know, baby! I just don't have the strength to get sad, frustrated, or angry anymore. I just want to go into that courtroom tomorrow and tell the truth. The truth that's in my heart, and leave the rest up to God," Solomon said.

"That's not enough, Daddy! You're going to have to help the Lord, help you. I know you're tired, but you still have one more race left in you, Ol' Man."

"I've never been as proud of anything as I am of you right now, darling," Solomon said.

"Daddy, you have been honored in almost every state in America for something. In your many accomplishments, I know there has to be something that sticks out in your mind as the proudest day of your life," Michelle said.

"You're absolutely correct. On June 27th, 1964, at 6:26 p.m., when you were born." Solomon smiled.

"Daddy, I want you to take a look at something I brought along with me. It may help you with your statement tomorrow." Michelle went into her briefcase, and pulled out an old book.

"What do you have there?" Solomon said, looking over his glasses.

Michelle handed the book to Solomon, and he glanced over it. He read the title, which was handwritten, and it said, "The Chambers Bible, Our Time Has Come." He sat back and read through it, page by page. Inside were the notes written by his father, Isaiah. They told of his experiences in Mississippi, and how he had to leave after Stanford killed Dr. West. It also told of how he, William and John Hankins were all bastard sons of Dr. West. He told of the experiences of traveling, and the many encounters with death he faced, all because he was trying to stand up for what he believed was right.

Michelle stood up and put on a fresh pot of water to make some more cocoa. She wanted to give her father time to finally realize who his father, and grandfather, truly were, just as she had done earlier in the day.

She found the book going through her grandmother's old chest. She never even knew it existed until then. She started off reading it because she thought it was her grandmother's diary. But once she realized what it was, she couldn't put it down. As she read, she compared her grandfather to her own father, and the differences between the two men. She knew that the night before her father's biggest legal day in his career, he would be in the courtroom trying to strategically scrutinize his own weaknesses to prepare himself for his opponent's attack. That made her think of how dedicated he was to his career, and not his family. It made her think of how much she resented him for raising another man's child in Washington, D.C, while she lived in Saginaw with her grandmother. And when her father had called earlier that evening she was in the middle of confronting her feelings for him, just as he was in the midst of confronting his feelings for his father. She released resentment pinned up for thirty years in one telephone call, then she was ready to love him, and be his child.

Now she was ready to make up for the past few years of loneliness of missing her father. She fixed her father another hot cup of cocoa, and sat it in front of him. He continued to read the book until it was completed. He slowly closed it, and pulled his glasses down from his eyes.

"I suppose this is the book you were reading when I called you tonight," Solomon asked.

"Yes it is, Daddy," Michelle answered.

"I thought this old thing was lost forever. My mother tried to give me this book when I was a young man, but I avoided it. I didn't want to get caught up in all that Mississippi family roots mess. I resented my father. I thought he was a martyr, who selfishly sacrificed himself to gain prestige with his name, leaving Mama all by herself to raise me. Over the last year, I have learned that I was a fool the first sixty-seven years of my life. Because I've been wrong. Terribly wrong! I am extremely proud to have that man as my father.

"My father, I am told, was a small man in stature, but his character made him stand like a giant. Your Uncle Stanford was one of the most egotistical, proud men I have ever met. But even he had nothing but praise and respect for him. As I sit here and read this book, I see how much my father revered his own father. He adored him. He found him dead, and dragged his body all the way home, I wonder if I would have had the same courage if I was in his position. My grandfather set a precedence of self respect for our family that I have ignored and denied for sixty-eight years. I should be shamed to call myself a Chambers baby." Solomon sighed, looking away.

"No, Daddy, you should be proud. For you, Alexander and Isaiah Chambers are men for whom you should always stand proud to carry their names. For me, Alexander, Isaiah, and Solomon Chambers, are men for whom I stand proud to carry their names. And no matter what you have, or have not done in your life, Daddy, tomorrow will be the day when your life will be defined. That's why you have to go in that courtroom with my great-grandfather, and my grandfather's prophecy in your heart; your time has come." Michelle smiled. "Our time has come!"

Michelle reached into her briefcase and handed Solomon some of Isaiah's old speeches.

"This is what you need, Daddy. Grandfather may not be here, but he didn't leave you alone. Take these and use them," Michelle suggested.

Solomon stood, and placed their empty cups in the sink. He told Michelle to go to bed while he tied up some loose strings.

"Night, night, Daddy." Michelle yawned.

"Good night, baby."

FINAL CHAPTER

Solomon picked up his father's speeches, and began to read them all—one by one, page by page. After he finished, he then picked up a pen, and he began to prepare the speech of his life, using the words that once crossed his father's lips.

It was nearly daylight when he completed his speech, but he didn't feel tired. He was anxious, and impatient to tell the Supreme Court just how embarrassed America should be for having revoked the civil liberties one is entitled from birth. Through his father's words, he discovered that self-pride, and self-awareness should be a source of strength, and not a detriment to character. Solomon walked upstairs and looked in on his wife and daughter. He looked out of the window and saw the first sign of sunrise. For the first time in his sixty-eight years on earth, he was going to sit and watch the sun come up. He thought to himself that this was another example of just how impractically he had lived his life. For sixty-eight years, he never found it important enough to see how the day begins.

He opened the blinds to his patio to catch every moment of the exchange of night to day. He fixed a fresh pot of coffee. Sunshine had prohibited Solomon from coffee drinking unless it was caffeine free, and no sugar. But Solomon made regular coffee, and added three spoonfuls of sugar. He took the steaming cup of coffee onto his patio and sat down. The morning was still cool and damp from last night's chill. The new morning brought with it blue skies, and no clouds.

He heard the steps of someone coming from behind him, but he didn't bother to turn around to find out. Sunshine had fixed her a cup of coffee and joined her husband on the patio. The aroma of the fresh-smelling coffee also woke Michelle, and she joined them on the patio sipping on her steaming cup. The sun was almost completely up by then, and Solomon sat in amazement. He thought of all the small wonders he may have overlooked in his life, because his eyes were always focused on the big picture.

Sunshine could tell that her husband was somewhere other than their patio, so she went into the kitchen to fix breakfast. Michelle stopped her and told her to rest on the patio with Solomon while she prepared breakfast for them. Sunshine relaxed, but she didn't utter a word.

When the sun had completely risen, Solomon greeted his wife and daughter good morning with a silent kiss to each of them. He went up to his attic, and dug through a small box of his childhood archives. And at the bottom of the box he found exactly what he was looking for, an old dictionary, and an old Bible. He took his hand and wiped off the dust, then he took them downstairs and placed them beside the notes he had written the night before.

He went back upstairs, took a shower, and got dressed for the day. When he walked back downstairs Sunshine and Michelle stopped what they were doing, surprised to see him fully dressed. After all, he wasn't due to be in court until 2 p.m., and it was only a quarter of 6 a.m. He gathered his materials and prepared to leave. Solomon placed his briefcase on the breakfast table, and took out everything in it. He replaced it with his old Bible, old dictionary, and the notes he had written from his father's speeches.

"Where are you going, Ol' Man?" Sunshine asked.

"I'm on my way to court, Ol' Lady," Solomon answered.

"You have eight hours. What are you going to do all that time?" Sunshine asked.

"I don't know, probably think a little, sleep a little, and pray a lot."

"Do you want me to get dressed and come with you, Daddy?" Michelle offered.

"I would love nothing more. But stay here and wait for Summer, and your mother. They'll need you a lot more than I will."

He started to walk out the door, and Sunshine stopped him.

"Ol' Man, you're forgetting all of your documents. Here, put them in your briefcase," Sunshine said urgently, handing them to Solomon.

"I won't be needing them today, sweetheart. I have all the notes I need right here," he said, pointing at his briefcase, "and right here," he added, pointing at his heart.

Michelle smiled as Solomon winked his eye at her. Mother and daughter watched as the giant man seemed to stand taller that morning than he ever had; even before his old age made his body bend back towards the ground.

He grabbed his keys and walked out to his garage. He was assigned extra security that day in anticipation to the reaction of the Supreme Court ruling. Extra security included a chauffeured automobile, front and rear caravan escorts, and bodyguards leading in and out of locations.

Solomon, however, walked past the entire entourage. He walked past his long Cadillac in the first garage. He walked past his Mercedes in the second garage, then he walked into his third garage with his Caprice Classic. He had no remote, so he had to use his keys to open the car door. By that time, his entourage of security was dead on his tracks. Solomon locked each door as he passed through, and it bought him a little time to get in his car without his shadows. Door by door, they burst through until they reached the garage with the Caprice Classic. By that time Solomon was raising the garage door to the driveway. As he backed out, the police were trying desperately to get him to stop, but he ignored them as if they weren't even there. He backed out of his driveway, and headed down the street. The policemen raced to their cars in pursuit. The paparazzi formed their line closely behind the police. Solomon drove slowly down the street, he looked in his mirror, and he could see the crowd form their line behind him. He smiled and shook his head, and kept driving. He looked down at the eight-track player, and saw the tape sticking out. He pushed it in, and Stevie Wonder's melodic voice echoed through the car.

The lyrics of Stevie Wonder's tune, "Pasttime Paradise," seemed most appropriate for the day. He passed a donut shop, and he considered stopping for a second. When he stopped at a red light, he said to himself, "What the hell?"

The old man made a screeching U-turn in the middle of the street. He hunched his shoulders, as he heard the screeching sound of all the cars behind him having to make that same emergency U-turn. He checked his mirror to see if everybody was intact, and upon his glance everyone had filed back into a safe single line.

He ordered a half-dozen glazed donuts, and a half-dozen jelly-filled. One of the policemen tried to reason with him to get in the chauffeured automobile. Solomon kindly told him that he was fine as he was, and gave the man a donut. As he approached the Supreme Court building, he pulled over and let the commanding security officer enter the car on his passenger side.

"Mr. Chambers, with all due respect, sir, you are compromising my job and your life, with your lack of respect for these threats against you. Please let my men escort you into the building. Please," the officer pleaded.

"No problem, son," Solomon agreed. "This is good music right here, son; I grew up on it. Motown! Detroit, Michigan!"

The police officer stared at the side of Solomon as if he had lost his mind. Solomon entered the secured area, and drove towards the security entrance. They showed their IDs to the officer at the gate. Their cars were inspected along with the other cars in their caravan. The media people were turned around, and told to use the media entrance.

Because it was so early in the morning, the grounds were not yet covered with spectators. There were only a few scattered people sitting on the grass. The rest were technical people setting up for telecasting. Solomon looked out at them and to his surprise he saw the old man sitting alone on a stack of bricks. He asked one of the policemen to bring over the old man. The policeman led the old man to him, and Solomon gave him his seat in the chauffeured vehicle. He gave the old man his remaining donuts, and sent him on his way. He told the police officer to make sure the old man got a security badge, and as a special favor, get him a close seat in the courtroom.

At first, the police officer warned Solomon that it may not be in his best interest to bring the old tattered man into court. Solomon told him that thinking that way was the reason why they were in court in the first place.

He told the man that he should have known better than to judge a man based upon how he looks, after all he was a black man, too. The police officer reluctantly agreed, and when they arrived inside the building he escorted the old man as far his jurisdiction allowed. Then he requested a favor from a friend inside the courtroom to get the man a seat close behind Solomon.

Solomon entered the courtroom and watched, as little by little, it filled with people. His legal team arrived shortly after 10 a.m., and they prepped one another on questions they thought the media would ask. Jonathan went over each item they were to address. Their legal research team was giving interviews on their opinions on how the ruling would go. Solomon sat quietly and observed everyone's behavior. He wondered if he had been so enraptured with the publicity of the trial that he had forgotten that if they left the courtroom the way they entered, a nation of black people would be susceptible to the rebirth of slavery. A nation of black people, forty million or more, including themselves.

Solomon breathed a sigh of relief when he saw Sunshine, Michelle and Summer enter the courtroom. Michelle was in the middle, with Summer's hand clasped in hers. It made him extra proud to see his daughter standing as the new matriarch of the family. He knew that his family, and his family's name, were in good hands.

As he sat there, the assortment of speakers, and historical evidence were presented. Solomon absorbed the moment of just being Solomon Chambers, the man. For in a matter of moments he would be Solomon Chambers, the attorney. A man with the weight of a nation on his shoulders.

When Solomon stood up to begin his statement, Summer's palm became nervously sweaty. Michelle felt the perspiration, and gripped Summer's hand tighter. Summer looked at her to apologize for being so nervous, but without looking in her direction, Michelle gave her a smile to assure her that everything was all right. Summer took her thumb, and rubbed along Michelle's hand as a measure of affection. Michelle acknowledged her by doing the same thing to her.

Michelle was nervous herself. For she had never seen her father at his job, in court. She didn't know what to expect. She didn't know if his age would bring him embarrassment by making him forget his notes, or maybe his old body just couldn't stand for as long as it should. She looked at her father, an old man. An old man who once walked with her on his shoulders. A man who towered over most men wherever he stood. She looked at his old body gingerly standing to talk to face the entire world, and she wanted to save him from himself. She thought that maybe he was right; he was too old a man, to be in such a young man's position. But once he was standing completely on his feet, his back and neck straightened out, and his chest raised three inches higher, and four inches outward. He smiled at her, and she reverted back to her childhood, and that big, young, strong handsome man she knew as her father once again stood before her.

"Good afternoon. I am both honored and privileged to serve as counsel before our most high and distinguished court. I hope that my colleagues and I have provided beyond a shadow of a doubt, that this nation, though the greatest nation on this earth, has committed an act of atrocity against her own children. I have asked myself over and over, how would I perform on this important day. I asked myself, how would I articulate the legal linguistic terms I have so meticulously rehearsed in my mind, just for this day.

"I am told that this should be the most glorious day in my life. This day is supposed to put an exclamation point on an already illustrious career. I am supposed to be the example of the perfect American dream. For I was born a poor black child in the ghetto, and now I stand before you trying the most crucial, and significant trial in the history of this country. Yes, this is the perfect American dream."

Solomon rested against the guard rail separating the pews from the judges, and glanced back at the people sitting in the courtroom, and continued his argument.

"But this day will pass me for glory, because glory is not mine. Nor is it yours!" Solomon said, pointing at the people in the court. Then he turned back to the judges and pointed his finger at them one by one. "Nor is it yours!"

Solomon touched his heart and spoke, "This moment of glory will be remembered as freedom."

He stared at the ceiling for what seemed like an eternity. Michelle adjusted herself in her seat, and prayed that her father would hurry and begin talking before everyone thought of him as an old absentminded fool.

"As you can see, I am an old man. My bones are old. My, my skin has grown so long that it falls from these old bones. Throughout my life, I've always believed that this black skin was a hindrance to my success. I drove myself so hard. I really mean that. I drove myself so hard to prove to myself, that this black skin would not stop me from being anything I wanted to be. I believed that I had to work that hard, because I was manacled by this skin.

"You know what I did? I even went as far as to tell myself that I was beyond my skin. I thought my intelligence made me beyond the average black man! I believed that my intelligence made me beyond my skin. It made me a man, and not a color. This is what I believed!

"I said the right words. I lived the right way. I even let my mother raise my child, while I raised another man's child. Don't get me wrong, I love both of my girls. I think of Summer as my own, but that's no excuse for letting Mama raise mine. I did this, because I had to become a lawyer; anything other than that would've mean that maybe I was nothing more than just another black man!

"So guess what? I did become a lawyer, and to be honest, I deserve to be standing here in front of you to present this case. But there is one factor that distorts this picture of the American dream. And that factor is this, when a man is beyond his skin, he is beyond himself. Because there is no distinction between the two. And would you believe that for as many times that I have tried to hide, or deny, or disown this skin, it continues to stick by my side. It has become apparent that it was not my skin who manacled my lifestyle; it was my lifestyle which manacled my skin," Solomon said, tugging on the skin hanging from his arms.

Solomon reached inside of his shirt and pulled out a necklace.

"You see this?" Solomon asked, holding up the necklace. "This may be nothing but a worthless piece of old rope, but to me it's the cost of freedom. My mother gave this to me when I was a child. She told me that my father left me this necklace to always remember him. I never understood that out of all the things he could have left me, why would he leave me this old cheap rope. Well, I found out last night.

"About a hundred years ago, my grandfather went out into the woods to hunt for his family's Christmas dinner. And he never came back. He never came back because a group of white men caught him, and they hung him. My father found his lifeless body hanging from a tree, and him and his friend, John, a white boy, dragged my grandfather's body home and buried him. In appreciation for John's willingness to help my father, he gave John all that he had to offer, which was a necklace he made out of rope, this rope," Solomon said holding the necklace up in the air again.

"After my father was killed, John sent the necklace back to my mother, and she gave it to me. I refused to wear it, until today." Solomon paused, when he looked in the crowd and saw Michelle crying. Then he continued.

"My father, and his father, were killed because they believed that all men should live as free and equal men. My father was murdered! Beaten! Stabbed! Burned, and hung. All because he wanted to be treated like a man, and not like an animal. My young, strong associate, Henry Lee was shot trying to protect me and my wife from an assassin's bullet. He was paralyzed, and the doctors say the young man will never have use of any of his limbs below his neck. These men that I speak of, are men of valor. These are men of honor. Men who would give their lives because they believe that they would rather be dead, than to live like a slave.

"Some people believe that the cost of freedom is death, but I strongly disagree. I say the loss of freedom is death. For the cost of freedom is but to be born, no matter the skin that's worn upon the child. For the child least born will one day rise above the sun, to shine the brightest one. We, ladies and gentlemen, as a people, we, are that child.

"Black people's cost of freedom has been paid way too much, and our refund is long overdue. And today, yes, yes, yes! Today, before us, freedom will bask in the glory of herself. And today, before God, freedom will bow and humble herself.

"I say to you that I have researched every item, every article, and every amendment of our Constitution in search of some order to bind all men of color to the same liberties of life as white men.

"I dissected monumental civil rights cases to reference on behalf of my case, and I could not find that one hard piece of evidence to bind all men as one equal man.

"This is what Mama would call book sense, versus good sense. Because I did not realize, like many of you listening, I didn't realize the content of the Constitution. Because I had not studied it for its true meaning. I knew the words by mind, but I did not know them by heart. I had rehearsed in my mind that they meant equality and justice, and when I looked at those words I could see nothing else."

Pointing to the people sitting in the court, Solomon asked, "Do you know your Constitution? Do you know your rights? If not, then what rights do you have?

"All of these years I thought I knew, but I didn't until our government voted for me, and black people like me, and when I say like me, I mean rich, poor, light, dark, big, small, short, and tall, all of us! I didn't know until our government voted that we should not have the right to vote. I asked myself, how could this happen?" Solomon said, raising his hands in the air.

"The answer is simple. This happened because of the University of California versus Bakke in 1978. Gutter versus the University of Michigan in 2001, and Gratz and Hamarech versus the University of Michigan in 2003.

"I suppose we can't totally blame our government. In 1995 the Supreme Court ruled that a federal program requiring preference based on race is unconstitutional unless the preference was designed to make up for specific instances of past discrimination. Thus, creating the loophole America had been searching for, for thirty-five years to rid itself of affirmative action. So, in 1996 the state of California approved Proposition 209, which banned the use of racial or gender preferences in public hiring, contracting, and education. This was the beginning of the end for affirmative action, and we as African-Americans did nothing to stop it. You would think that when the Voting Rights Act was being challenged we wouldn't casually leave it up to Congress to decide for us. Well we did, and he we are.

"But being in this precarious position has forced me to take another look at the Constitution. And when I did it told quite a different story. It told me that it's over four-hundred years old. And since its creation, the planet has changed its form, but we still live by the same Constitution. That doesn't sound logical for a nation who was then the infant nation of this world, but has now grown to be the world leader. Especially when black people are major contributors to its success, with our minds, and with our backs. If everything else has changed to accommodate the changing of time, why hasn't our Constitution?

"Sure we have amendments made to reflect the changing of times. But writing amendments is like treating the symptoms, but not treating the disease. And we know that if you do not cure disease, it becomes a recurring ailment, and that is what blacks face today in America. We are the victims of an age-old disease that has come back to destroy us. It seems for black people, we have reached our pinnacle as Americans, and now we are regressing down the other side."

Solomon stood still and stared at the judges in an exaggerated moment of silence. Once again, Michelle was worried that he had forgotten his argument. He paused for so long this time, other people in the courtroom started to look with concern.

Then, all of a sudden, Solomon began to recite the preamble to the Constitution.

"We the people, of the United States of America, in order to form a more perfect union, must establish justice, insure domestic tranquility, provide for the common defense, promote the general welfare, and secure the blessings of liberty to ourselves and posterity. We the people do ordain and establish this Constitution for the United States of America."

Solomon paused again, but only for a moment. He clutched the rails with his mighty hands, and spoke loudly and clearly, these following words:

"In 1818, the 14th amendment, section 1, declares that all persons born, or naturalized in the United States, and subject to the jurisdiction there of, are citizens of the United States, and of the state wherein they reside. No state should make or enforce any law which shall abridge the privileges or immunities of citizens of the United States, nor shall any state deprive any person of life, liberty, or property without due process of law, nor to deny any person within its jurisdiction equal protection of the laws.

"In 1870, the 15th amendment, section 1, declares the right of citizens of the United States to vote shall not be denied, or abridged by the United States or by any other state on the account of race, color, or the previous condition of servitude.

"In 1920, the 19th amendment, section 1, declares the right of citizens of the United States to vote shall not be denied, or abridged by the United States or by any other state on the account of sex; we call this period in our history, suffrage!

"In 1964, the 24th amendment, section 1, declares the rights of citizens of the United States to vote in any primary or other election for president, or vice-president, for electors for president, or vice-president, or for senator or representative in Congress shall not be denied, or abridged by the United States, or any state by reason of failure to pay any poll tax, or other tax.

"And finally, in 1971, the 26th amendment, declares the rights of citizens of the United States, who are 18 years or older to vote shall not be denied or abridged by the United States, or by any state on the account of age."

Solomon cleared his throat and continued his argument.

"I have examined every word in this grand document of order, even to the point where I thought my mind was lost. But nowhere in the Constitution does it refer specifically to black people, and our right to vote. It doesn't refer specifically to Negroes, coloreds, blacks, African-Americans, or whatever term, in whatever time you wish to choose. Nowhere! How then can I make the case that we are protected by the Constitution specifically, if we are not mentioned, specifically?"

Solomon paused and stared around the room before he continued.

"In 1965, Lyndon Baines Johnson signed into law the Voting Rights Act. Ironically, President Johnson signed the act in the same room that Abraham Lincoln used to sign a bill freeing the slaves who had been pressed into service of the Confederacy. One century later, and our presidents are still signing documents to make us equal.

"How can we be the world leader in the free society, when we so irresponsibly revoke the very first rule of democracy? Which is to vote for the representative of your choice who best speaks for you.

"That's freedom! That's democracy!

"The year 2007 will always be remembered as the year America started to wilt. And she will not be resuscitated until she has acknowledged, and addressed this atrocity as an indignity not just to African-Americans, but all people who claim to be a part of any free society.

"I recall September 11th, 2001, when our nation was attacked by terrorists. We were truly a nation united. We stood as one people, Black! White! Latino! And Asian. We were a nation of one!

"I have always been a pacifist, but I would have taken a weapon and stood on the frontline with any man willing to protect this country. Seven years later, look at us now. We're fighting and killing each other in the streets. Rioting and looting as if we've lost our minds. Perhaps we stood as one nation seven years ago because we all had a common foe to hate outside of the normality of hating races different from our own.

"My whole life I have praised our Constitution as if it was the Holy Bible. I ask you, if our Constitution stands for all Americans, why was there a need for President Johnson to sign the Voting Rights Act?

"And if this Constitution does not stand for all Americans, we need to stop pretending, and get ourselves another Constitution.

"For what I am saying today, some of our white brothers and sisters may say that I am singing an old song but with a new tune. They are probably asking to themselves, why am I accusing our founding fathers of racism?

"Well I ask you, if I have been victimized, and I'm not talking about being called a nigger, as I have been called many times in my life! No, words can't hurt me! I'm talking about some of the most vicious crimes known to man. Murder! Rape! And slavery!

"I ask you again, if I have been victimized in this manner, and then I am placed in front of the judge as a witness for these crimes which were committed against me, do I withhold the truth in fear that I may offend my perpetrator?

"Do I not testify that I have been a victim of slavery from the 1600s to the slavery of today?

"Do I not testify that my wife, my sister, my daughter, my mother and my grandmother were raped?

"Do I not testify that my brother, my son, my father, and my grandfather were murdered?

"Do I not testify to the truth of these crimes?

"Why of course, I do. I would not be a man, if I didn't. I would stand before that judge and I would tell him the truth just as it happened, and let my perpetrator deal with my testimony however he wishes.

"Today is the day for reparation for black people, and minorities alike! Today is the day that we get to stand before the judge, and plead our case!

"Today we get to stand before the highest judge of them all, and that judge does not sit behind a bench; he sits above it. And that judge is the Almighty God. Today we let him lay down the verdict, and the sentencing. For vengeance is mine, sayeth the Lord!

"This is paper!" Solomon said, holding up the Constitution. "And no matter how much we worship this document, it's only paper. What makes this work is humanity.

"To know that you have an obligation to treat a man like a man!

"To unite in equality with all men, in times of peace, as well as in times of war!

"To know that it is wrong for one man to have liberty over his brother!

"To know that your skin only makes you human, but it is your soul which makes you humane. Sometimes, even though we are humans, we behave as if we are animals who lack that humanity." Solomon looked at the judges and saw no compassion or understanding in their eyes. The reaction of the Supreme Court judges infuriated him, and he lost all concern for courtroom procedure or etiquette.

"If you can not empathize with what I am saying, then you are worth no more than the paper this Constitution was written on." Solomon balled the Constitution in his hands and threw it toward the judges. The judges slammed their gavels and threatened to place Solomon in contempt of court.

"If you do not want to live with me as an equal man, that is perfectly fine with me! But don't you dare hide behind your laws and your enforcers to oppress and discriminate against me to the point where I do not even have the common means to survive. You face me, free man to free man!

"If there is to be one more life lost to this unmitigated system of injustice, then let it be mine, by your hands! Let the men who make the laws, be the one who break the laws! And do not hide behind the cloth of the American flag to hide your hypocrisy, because that is my blanket of survival. Let the blood be on your hands, and let the guilt be on your conscience!"

Solomon banged his gigantic fists on the table and shouted to the top of his lungs.

"I will not leave this courtroom today, until you have silenced your voice of bigotry! Your bigotry! Your, your, your prejudice! And realize that no longer is the time when white men pick their charitable minority group of the season for their political agenda. Whether it's gay season! White woman season! Black man or black woman season! Your options have expired!" Solomon shouted.

"Mr. Chambers," a judge spoke into a microphone. "This behavior will not be tolerated in this court today. You have been warned, and now you are in contempt of this courtroom, and you will be removed from this courtroom until you have composed yourself. Once you have composed yourself, and you are in respect of this courtroom, you will be allowed to return."

The judge motioned for the removal of Solomon, and two security guards stood on either side of him and gestured for him to leave. Solomon did not resist them but as he walked backwards out of the courtroom, he continued his speech.

"No longer is the time when black women, and black men, live our lives by your judgment, and your laws! No longer is the time when we pray on our knees to be delivered from big brother's oppressive tactics. God answered our prayers a long time ago!" Solomon lowered his voice and sobbed as he was departing from the courtroom. "When? When people? When will the time arrive when America will see, a time when all are equal, a time when all are free? Today people, finally, our time has come. Our Time Has Come! Our Time Has Come!"

The two officers escorted Solomon out of the courtroom, and into an office. They stood outside the door while Solomon remained inside until the end of the session.

After Solomon left the courtroom, Michelle jumped to her feet and left the courtroom to find him. She was proud of her father for taking a stance in the courtroom, and she wanted to tell him. Because of the high level of security she was not able to locate Solomon until after the session.

Sunshine and Summer eventually left the courtroom to find Michelle. They found her in the hall in front of the courtroom door. The hall was filled with the news media. They were smothered by reporters, cameras, and microphones in their faces. Their security managed to squeeze them out of the building and into a waiting car. They sped off and made it home where the media was waiting for them there. They were escorted safely into their home, where they would wait for Solomon to arrive.

Sunshine knew that no matter what the Supreme Court ruled, America was facing a new day, a better day.

Back in the courtroom, Jonathan tried to maintain his composure once he saw them remove Solomon. He knew he would have to rest their case. As the judges fought to regain order in the courtroom, Jonathan's emotions overwhelmed him. He thought about Henry, and what he would do in this situation. He thought that Henry would probably try to help regain control of the court so that they wouldn't lose any more credibility with the bench. He knew that his legal hero Solomon Chambers would also probably do the same thing as Henry. But Jonathan also knew that he was not Henry, and he was not Solomon by a long shot, nor did he possess their litigation savvy. What he did know was that he was an attorney who had fought for equality because he believed that everyone should be treated as an equal man or woman.

When the bench asked him to conclude the case, he thought about Henry lying in the hospital paralyzed for the rest of his life. He thought about the sixty-eight-year-old man being restrained by officers, and he stood with tears in his eyes and softly spoke, "We conclude our argument by saying, finally... our time has come!"

As the world paused to hear the decision of the Supreme Court, Solomon Chambers sat in a small meeting room, and listened to the decision, alone:

"It is our conclusion that in the case of The Unified Minority Voters Coalition vs. The United States Government, the Supreme Court finds that the act of state government to withhold voting privileges from any person or persons, is unconstitutional.

"The 14th amendment, section 1, declares that all persons born, or naturalized in the United States, and subject to the jurisdiction there of, are citizens of the United States, and of the state wherein the reside. No state should make or enforce any law which shall abridge the privileges or immunities of citizens of the United States, nor shall any state deprive any person of life, liberty, or property without due process of law, nor to deny any person within its jurisdiction equal protection of the laws.

"The 15th amendment, section 1, declares the right of citizens of the United States to vote shall not be denied, or abridged by the United States or by any other state on the account of race, color, or the previous condition of servitude...it is granted to The Unified Minority Voters Coalition, that on this day, all rights and privileges be restored, and ordered to its representatives, and to all those which are alike."

FALL, SAGINAW MICHIGAN, 2008

Three months later, on Solomon's return to Saginaw, people gathered along the sides of the streets to welcome back their hometown hero. They chased the procession of cars, and kissed the car as Solomon passed by. They threw flowers along the path as he came their way.

The trail ran from Genesee Street, making a right onto Remington Street. From Remington Street, making a left onto Washington Street. Then the short ride on Washington Street until they reached their destination.

Slowly the procession made a left, and the never-ending stream of cars lined the driveway until they were pushed out of the gate. People climbed the fence to catch a glimpse of the great Solomon Chambers.

The media had been waiting for his arrival for hours. When his car came to a halt, cameras snapped constantly in anticipation of the opening of his car door. But instead, Sunshine, Michelle and Summer stepped out of the long limousine, along with their children. As usual, they had to wait for Solomon.

Next, Jonathan stepped out of a van, and he lowered Henry to the ground on the van's elevator. This was the first trip Henry had made since he was shot earlier in the year. He had not completed his rehabilitation, but he had to come to honor the man who fought and defeated the United States government.

Jonathan and Henry stood alongside the Chambers family, and they waited for Solomon. When Solomon took his place in front of the group they followed him along the meandering road. It seemed as if the entire nation was following behind them.

There were senators, governors, and Supreme Court justices. There were teachers, barbers, and cab drivers, all standing to say goodbye.

And as they lowered the long, leather, black casket into the grave, the world said its final goodbye to Solomon Chambers, Attorney at Law. Ashes to ashes; he left home a young man, afraid of the world. But he returned an old man with the world in his hands; And dust to dust.

As the dirt began to fill his grave, with her daughter Bria holding the Chambers' Bible, Michelle stood at the head of her father's grave and spoke to the world:

"Every family has a story. A chronology of time, where names and people in the history of that family serve a vessel from the past to the present. This is the story of my family. This is the story about the prophecy of a man named Alexander Chambers. Told through the hearts and souls of his children. A story that tells of three generations to fulfill one prophecy. The first generation was given the prophecy, the second generation interpreted the prophecy, and the third generation fulfilled the prophecy. I am the fourth generation of the Chambers legacy, and though my father Solomon Chambers would fulfill the prophecy, I am blessed with revealing the prophecy to you.

"My great-grandfather, Alexander Chambers, was born in a place called Derma County, Mississippi, in 1855. He was an only child, and a slave. He was college educated, and not accepted very well by white people because of it. He and my great-grandmother, Annie Mae, met when they were children growing up on the West Plantation in Derma County, Mississippi. After the Emancipation Proclamation, slavery was abolished, and Negro people were freed. My great-grandparents continued to work on the West Plantation. They eventually married and had one child, a son they would name Isaiah, my grandfather. He met and wedded my grandmother, Orabell, whom I loved with all of my heart. My grandfather moved to Saginaw, Michigan after being chased out of Mississippi. He became an activist for human rights. He lived his life believing that all men should be treated as equal. My grandfather's life was cut short when he was murdered on a trip back to Mississippi. He never got the opportunity to see his child, my father, Solomon Chambers, who was born months later.

"My father was a complex man. He had an overbearing presence, standing like a giant. But inside, beat the heart of a child. From a child to the day he died, I saw him lose his temper twice. Once when I was four years old, he fought a group of men to save his family. The other time was when I was forty-four, and he had to fight to save his nation. A fight, I'm sure, even God was proud to see him battle.

"This quiet giant possessed a spirit that people could feel whenever they were in his presence. My mother, my grandmother, we all knew that my father was destined for greatness. But the more we tried to convince him, the more he denied it. I couldn't understand at the time how a man could be so modest. But now I do.

"If you ever get the opportunity to talk to the sun, ask him why he can not see just how bright his light is? I'm sure he we tell you that his light shines from the inside out, and it is meant to shine upon the world, and not himself. This was my father. The light my father shined upon the world was shined from the inside out. And I guess that it would make it a little difficult. My father's light can never be doused by time, for I will carry his torch for the remainder of my days, and my child, and my sister's children will pass on his light to their children.

"My great-grandfather created a book to chronicle our family's history. He said it would be our family Bible. He wrote the title of our family Bible, *Our Time Has Come!* 'Our Time Has Come' is his prophecy that his family will one day overcome the manacles of slavery, and rise to the pinnacle of humanity. He started the Chambers' Bible with the first verse. Each generation was to incorporate his, or her, new verse to pass on to the next generation to come. And these are the words of our family Bible:

"Our Time Has Come"
Alexander and Annie Mae Chambers-1902

The dawning of a new millennium, sing songs of freedom, Our Time Has
Come. Our God send signs it's time for unity, this is our destiny,
Our Time Has Come.
Isaiah and Orabell Chambers-1939

Today begins the day thought never be, when we rise, in unity, One God, One Love. Our voices be the sound of victory, when we, stand proud and sing, Our Time Has Come!
Solomon and Sunshine Chambers-2008

The cost of freedom is but to be borne, no matter the skin that's worn, upon the child. For the child least born will rise above the sun, to shine the brightest one, we are that child! Our Time Has Come, for freedom, everyone! Our Time Has Come! We'll see the sun, for Our Time Has Come!

ABOUT THE AUTHOR

Born in Saginaw, Michigan, the seventeenth of eighteen children to Henry and Orabell Stephens, Sylvester was influenced creatively by his older siblings. They introduced him to music and art which were of their era as if it was contemporary. Reading and writing at the age of three, Sylvester's literary skills begAn to develop far before his interest. Eventually, his interest caught up to his skills and thus created the author of *Our Time Has Come*.

Saginaw was an industrial automotive town where the makings of a successful life was a high school diploma and a job working in one of the local automotive plants. After graduating from Saginaw High School, Sylvester migrated to Mississippi to attend Jackson State University. Going to the South from the North provided a culture shock and a lesson in history of the inexpiable past of racism and bigotry.

The experiences of college helped develop the writing style that has transitioned Sylvester into a playwright and author.

Sylvester has also written plays such as *Our Time Has Come*, *The Nature of a Woman*, *Max*, *The Office Girls*, *My Little Secret*, and *The War of the Gods*.

Please look forward to Sylvester's next novel, *The Office Girls*.

The Office Girls

I knew the day I was born with an umbilical cord wrapped tightly around my throat, my mother crying, and the doctor screaming, my life was going to be nothing but pure hell. I was the only black child in the nursery—not only that; I was the only male child as well. What were the odds? Even then, the white female babies in the nurseries looked at me like, "Niggah, I heard you had a rough time gettin' here." They, like myself, didn't know that times would be even rougher once I got here.

My childhood was one of confusion and misunderstanding. Meaning, I was always confused why people could never understand me. I was very bright for my age; I understood situations that were beyond my years. I had superior book sense without ever having to read a book. I was a social misfit, because I didn't fit in with the intellectual kids, and I certainly didn't fit in with the cool kids. I did, however, manage to indulge myself into mischievous behavior to hang out with the bad kids. But then after a while I would be too afraid of getting in trouble, and I wouldn't fit in with them either.

Loneliness is said to feed the prowess of the imagination. I can be a witness to that. I was a small scraggly kid and nobody paid much attention to me so after spending so much time with myself, I started to create my own friends. I'm not just talking about imaginary friends when you're six or seven; I was married and divorced twice before I let my imaginary friend Bernice return back to the world of the subliminal.

As a youth, I was extremely shy to approach girls. I created Bernice to be my confidante and adviser to girls. She convinced me to marry my first wife, and we divorced within one year of our marriage after dating for seven years. Then she suggested that I marry my second wife. We never had one single argument until six months into our marriage. After the argument, we were divorced within six weeks. At least I got my two beautiful girls, Brimone and Alexiah, out of my two ugly marriages. Shortly after my second divorce, I told Bernice to kiss my ass, and just like that, she was gone.

I must say that as painful as it was to be divorced, twice I may add, the lessons of love began my path to becoming a successful author. For it is said, an artist does not know his best work, until his heart has known pain. I can truly say, I know my best work, and I know it well.

I studied law while attending a small college in Cambridge, Massachusetts. However, I'm sure you knew that with my childhood, the inevitable path of my career choice would be writing. Physically, my small fragile frame had exploded into a strapping muscular man. A once tenor voice had become a deep baritone. I tried out for football, and made the team easily. As a matter of fact, I would have started at tight end, but after making the team I didn't want to commit to the practices. I just wanted to show up and play on Saturdays. As my sports career dwindled, my love career accelerated at high speed. Women were plentiful. I was six feet tall, with dark brown, smooth skin. A shaven head with dark eyelashes and a goatee. I had a size forty-two chest, with a thirty-two-inch waistline. It was once stated that if we ever had a problem landing a 747 at the airport, my shoulders were always an option. To add to my charm, I could write a poem about anything at any time. I guess most people would call this being a bit ostentatious, but I disputed that claim. In my case, it was merely an observation of one's self.

After college, I was offered a three-book deal with a major publishing company. I accepted, and I masterfully wrote creative, artistic books. Books that all Americans should have appreciated. Unfortunately for me, and my career, the books barely made it out of the printer's bindery before they were being shipped right back. Out of three books in three years, I think that my mother bought one, but I know for certain my father didn't. He wouldn't even read my mother's.

I felt that I had written some of the best fictional writings of modern time. They were political books based on American could-bes and should-bes.

The public didn't respond favorably to politically fictional books that didn't scandalize a political figure, so my literary career went down the tube quickly. I started to write entertainment news articles for a local newspaper about ten years ago to make ends meet, using the pseudonym, Cyrus. I now have my own weekly column in addition to the article and I make pretty good bread. Oh, bread means money.

One day I ran across an article that read, "Black Women: The New Civil Rights Movement!" I read the article and couldn't believe what I was reading.

The article was telling how black men had been left behind in the movement of political, economic and social progression. It stated that black women no longer need black men to raise a family. The article explained that women in corporate America could be just as competitive and productive as men, without the stress and agitation.

It gave the staggering statistics of black men in jail, in comparison to those in college. The difference of those jailed outnumbered those in college by twice the number. I was furious after I read the article. I thought to myself, *am I the only person angry by this bullshit?* I decided at that moment to do my part to set the record straight on the truth of black men. How, I had not a clue. But I was going to do something!

I contacted the lady who wrote the article, a Mrs. Jaline Dandy, and found that her column was her night job, but she was actually a manager of the claims department at Upskon Corporation. To my surprise, she was a divorced white woman who had been married to a black man. She had since remarried to a white man. I tried to get her to rewrite the article and not paint such a negative picture of black men. We had a few shared words of our differences of opinions, but she wouldn't change a word. I figured if she wouldn't rewrite the article, I would write an article myself defending black men. That's exactly what I did. I blasted the columnist for exploiting the plight of black men. However, I didn't mean to insult women in the process. I received more emails and telephone calls in one day than I had ever received in my entire literary career. Women of all races began to email me, calling me such names as misogynist, sexist, chauvinist, and racist. Luckily, they never found out my true name was Michael B. Forrester.

To make a long story short, after so many complaints for my politically incorrect statement, I was fired from writing my article. This sparked me to expose women in all of their glory. I knew that given the same circumstances, women would behave the same way as men, and I set out to prove it. But before I did that, I had to find a job.

I bought a Sunday newspaper and halfheartedly browsed through it. Mostly to prove to myself that I was at least making an attempt to find a job. I looked back and forth, and back and forth. What could a young washed-up author do besides write bad books? But as luck would have it, I saw an advertisement that took up half of the page, as if God didn't want me to miss it. It read, "Upskon Hiring! Claims Dept. Please fax to Jaline Dandy." I fell on my knees and shouted, "Thank you, Lord!" I wanted sweet revenge for the article and losing my job, but this seemed too good to be true.

I typed up a fake resume and faxed it over immediately. I wanted it to be the first thing this Jaline picked up from the fax machine. I must say, my resume was quite impressive. After I faxed it, I patiently waited for the confirmation. When it finally came through, I put the newspaper down and turned on the television. I had earned a day of relaxation after all that, and I treated myself to an afternoon of ESPN. As I lay there, I told myself that although it was a long shot that they would even respond to my resume, if I were hired at Upskon, I would expose every woman I could for the sake of manhood. That pleasurable thought brought me a pleasurable nap.

Two days later I received a call from Upskon asking me to come in for an interview. I jumped up and down like a big kid in a candy store. I called them back and confirmed an interview day and time. I will never forget my interview. That day started the beginning of my new life. My new life with the office girls of Upskon.

***

"Good afternoon Mr. Forrester, I'm Mrs. Dandy."

"Good afternoon, Mrs. Dandy."

"This interview should only take a few minutes."

"That's fine."

"Well, you're a Harvard man, huh?"

"Yes, yes I am."

"Why would a Harvard man want to work in a small claims department?"

"Harvard men have to eat, too."

"I like that."

"Thanks."

"Well, Mr. Forrester, we can start you off with an entry-level position. And I must say that with your credentials, you are well overqualified. But like you say, you have to eat, too."

"I sure do."

"Can you start on Monday?"

"No problem."

"Ok, we'll see you Monday."

"That's it? I got the job?"

"If you want it, you do."

"Sure I do."

"Oh, Mr. Forrester. I think it's only fair that I tell you that you are the first man to work in this department in five years so don't be surprised if you get a little more attention than everyone else."

"I'm sure I'll get no more attention than anyone else, Mrs. Dandy."

"Take my word for it, Mr. Forrester; you'll get more attention."

I wasn't sure but I almost got the feeling Mrs. Dandy was flirting with me, so I played along.

"If you say so."

"All right, our business here is done. Tazzy, your supervisor, will meet you on Monday and show you around. That's it. Guess I'll see you on Monday then."

"First thing."

As I shook Mrs. Dandy's hand, I couldn't leave the office until I'd said something about the article she had written. After all, that bitch got me fired!

"Oh, Mrs. Dandy, don't you write a column or something like that?"

"Yes, I do. How do you know?"

"I think I may have read one of your columns. You do great work."

"Thank you, Mr. Forrester. I'm flattered."

"You're welcome, and I'll see you on Monday."

I walked out of Mrs. Dandy's office and I could see aisle after aisle of women. I knew that in order for me to fulfill my mission I would have to deny the dream of every red-blooded straight American male. And that was to be the only man on an island filled with women. This may not have been an island, but it was the next best thing.

I showed up for work on Monday bright and early as promised. I didn't have a badge so I had to wait until Tazzy showed up. She was the first person to show up, and we greeted each other very cordially. Tazzy was a very petite young lady, cute, who looked as if she was straight out of high school. She was just short of five feet tall and a hundred pounds soaking wet. She showed me to my desk and informed me that a lady named Cynthia would be training me. She then showed me to the break room and told me to relax until Cynthia came to get me. I sat there and one by one the office girls started to arrive for work.

"Hey, how you doing?"

"I'm fine. How are you?"

"I'm Virginia. It is a pleasure to meet you."

"It's a pleasure to meet you, too."

"And your name is?"

"Oh, excuse my manners. My name is Michael Forrester," I said, standing to shake her hand.

Virginia shook my hand with the grace of an angel, and the elegance of a queen. There was something extraordinary about this ordinary lady. She was middle-aged, maybe early- to mid-fifties. Her hair was white, but her face looked young. She was thin with caramel-brown skin. As she left the break room I couldn't help but stare. For a minute, I thought I was attracted to her. And then I realized, I was. Not physically, but spiritually.

Susan, a white girl, came in the break room next and fixed herself a cup of coffee.

"Hey, are you the new guy?"

I started to say, *'What does it look like, fool?'* But instead, I courteously replied, "Yes, I'm the new guy."

"My name is Susan, and I'm the assistant supervisor here in the office. If there's anything you need, just let me know."

"Thanks. I'll be sure to let you know."

"Not a problem," Susan said, walking out of the door.

I sat there twiddling my thumbs for a while when Darsha, Valerie, Lisa and Amy walked in, in full gossip. When they saw me sitting at the table they all stopped talking and looked at me.

"Do you work here?" Valerie asked.

"Yes. Today is my first day."

"I'm Amy. Hi."

"Hi, Amy," I spoke.

Amy was a very attractive lightskinned woman with a 36-24-36 figure. She had long hair that was pinned up. Her eyes were gray, and very welcoming. It was all I could do to keep from asking her to marry me on the spot.

"Hi, my name is Valerie."

"Hi, Valerie, I'm Michael."

Valerie was tall—very tall. She was attractive herself. She was quite aggressive. I felt that outside of the workplace she probably had men on every block.

"Hey, what's up? I'm Darsha."

"Hey, Darsha. I'm Michael."

Darsha was a nineteen- or twenty-year-old hip-hop cultured girl who made me wonder what kind of business would hire such a young, inexperienced person.

"I'm last but definitely not least; I'm Lisa. How are you?"

"I'm fine, Lisa. I'm Michael."

"Who's training you?" Lisa asked.

"I think Tazzy said it was someone named Cynthia."

"OK. We better get on here and before the clock strikes eight," Lisa said. They cleared the break room and then Wanda and Pam walked in.

"Hey, man, you the new dude?" Wanda said, without even looking at me.

Wanda was tough-looking, with a tough voice. She had big eyes, a very deep voice, and a presence which demanded respect or she'd kick your ass. She was about five feet six inches tall, a little husky, with a delightfully friendly smile. I could tell by her introduction she would be quite a character.

"Yes, I'm the new dude."

"I'm Wanda. And that's Pam."

"Wanda, I don't need you to introduce me," Pam said. "I'm Pam; how are you?"

"I'm just fine. Good to meet you."

Pam was an attractive woman with an athlletic build. Her hair was cut perfectly to match the sculpture of her face.

Pam and Wanda walked out together, and I sat there playing with the salt and pepper shakers until Cynthia finally came to get me.

"Michael?" Cynthia asked as she peeked her head through the door.

Cynthia was short and pretty in a homely type of way. She wore a long skirt that had to be handed down by her grandmother's grandmother. She wore big glasses that she looked over instead of through. But I had a feeling that she was pretty nice.

"Yup. That's me."

"Let's go, man. You got a date with a computer."

I stood up and followed Cynthia all the way back to my desk. Passing everyone else in the office. As I got close to my desk, I saw Amy's beautiful face. Her desk was facing directly in front of mine. I had a picture-perfect view from the time I came in the door, until I clocked out to go home. Maybe my life of unfortunate mishaps was making a turn for the better. I told myself that no matter how attracted I was to any of the women in the office, I would maintain my objective and exploit them at any rate. There was also a vacant desk on my right. I found out my other neighbor was out sick.

Cynthia trained me for the entire week. On Wednesday she gave me a list of telephone numbers for all the women in the office. Strangely, the list consisted of both work and personal contact numbers. She told me that because they were all women, they would often call during the winter hours to make sure every one of them made it to their cars safely. Upskon was a huge building that employed over a thousand people. Parking was almost as difficult as driving through rush hour. The security was a joke; they always seemed to show up after someone was robbed, stabbed, or raped. All had happened in the parking lot of Upskon.

I kept to myself the first week. If I was going to develop any friendships, they would have to be the ones to make the first move. After working with

Cynthia for a week, I felt comfortable with her. I figured she and I would be OK as friends.

***

Over the weekend I did what I did every other weekend. Picked up my girls, went to the movies, rented movies. I had not had a social life since my second marriage. I found my children to be therapeutic. They looked to me for so much. The fact that they needed me kept me hanging on to my dignity.

My oldest daughter was ten, from my first marriage. And my youngest daughter was four, from my second marriage. Their mothers made no attempt to make sure they kept in contact, so I made arrangements to have them both on the same weekends and major holidays. They got along like most sisters: fighting one moment, and hugging the next.

Our weekend was going just as any other weekend, when Brimone called me into the bathroom.

"Daddy!" Brimone shouted. "There's something wrong with me!"

I leaped from the sunken hole in my couch, created by the countless hours of watching television in one spot, and ran into the bathroom.

"Are you OK, Brimone?"

Brimone looked at me still sitting on the toilet, and started to cry.

"Daddy, there's something wrong with me."

"What's the matter, baby?"

"Look!" Brimone said, raising tissue from her backside.

"What's that, baby?" I said, backing up.

"I don't know, Daddy, I don't know!"

"Oh shit!"

I scared Brimone when I shouted and she started to stand up and come to me.

"No, baby! Sit back down; everything is going to be fine. Just sit back down."

"Daddy, I'm scared."

"There's nothing to be scared of, baby. Don't move! Daddy will be right back, OK?"

"OK, Daddy."

"I'll be right back, OK?

"OK, Daddy."

"Don't move, baby. Please don't move, OK?

"I won't move, Daddy."

I ran into my bedroom and leaped over my bed to get to the telephone. I called Brimone's mother but I could only reach her voicemail. I left a panicky message and then called Alexiah's mother. She, too, was unavailable. I remembered that I had some of the office girls' telephone numbers and I called the first name on the list.

"Hello."

"Hello, Cynthia?"

"Yes, this is, Cynthia."

"Cynthia, I hate to disturb you, but I have a problem and I need to speak with someone. Got a minute?"

"Sure, what's up?"

"Well, well," I stuttered trying to tell her my dilemma without making a fool out of myself. "Well, Cynthia, I have a ten-year-old daughter, and she's with me for the weekend, and I think she just started her menstrual cycle."

"She what?" Cynthia laughed.

"I think she just started her period and I'm about to faint in here."

Lee, Darrien
All That and a Bag of Chips
0-9711953-0-7
Been There, Done That
1-59309-001-3
What Goes Around Comes Around
1-59309-024-2

Luckett, Jonathan
Jasminium 1-59309-007-2
How Ya Livin' 1-59309-025-0

McKinney, Tina Brooks
All That Drama (December 2004)
1-59309-033-1

Quartay, Nane
Feenin 0-9711953-7-4
The Badness (May 2005)
1-59309-037-4

Rivers, V. Anthony
Daughter by Spirit 0-9674601-4-X
Everybody Got Issues 1-59309-003-X
Sistergirls.com 1-59309-004-8

Roberts, J. Deotis
Roots of a Black Future: Family and Church 0-9674601-6-6
Christian Beliefs 0-9674601-5-8

Stephens, Sylvester
Our Time Has Come 1-59309-026-9

Turley II, Harold L.
Love's Game 1-59309-029-3
(November 2004)

Valentine, Michelle
Nyagra's Falls 0-9711953-4-X

White, A.J.
Ballad of a Ghetto Poet
1-59309-009-9

White, Franklin
Money for Good 1-59309-012-9
Potentially Yours 1-59309-027-7

Zane (Editor)
Breaking the Cycle 1-59309-021-8
(November 2004)